FINAL DELIVERY

A NOVEL

Will Dempsey

High Flight Books, Atlanta

This is a work of fiction. Names, characters, places, and incidents either are the product of the author's imagination or are used fictitiously, and any resemblance to actual persons, living or dead, business establishments, events, or locales is entirely coincidental.

Copyright © 2009 Will Dempsey
Cover design by Sean Calderbank

All rights reserved.
No part of this book may be reproduced, scanned, or distributed in any printed or electronic form without permission. Please do not participate in or encourage piracy of copyrighted materials in violation of the author's rights. Purchase only authorized editions.
For information address:
High Flight Books
3390 Campbell Road SE
Smyrna, GA 30080

Please contact the author at: willdempsey71@gmail.com or on www.facebook.com

ISBN: 144-1-461-1566

Printed in the United States of America

For my mom and dad who gave me unconditional love and a foundation for my faith, and Nancy for your sacrifice in giving me the gift of life, and in memory of Keith Lewis who inspired my return to the Church of my childhood, among other things.

"Social justice cannot be attained by violence. Violence kills what it intends to create."

-Pope John Paul II

"I've found the source of all of my anger. Anger comes from being *right*. I have never been angry when I also wasn't right. I have been right when I wasn't angry but never angry when I wasn't right."

-Scott Lee

"How's that knowledge of good and evil working out for you?"

-Anonymous

High Flight

Oh, I have slipped the surly bonds of earth
And danced the skies on laughter-silvered wings,
Sunward I've climbed, and joined the tumbling mirth
Of sun-split clouds-and done a hundred things
You have never dreamed of-wheeled and soared and swung
High in the sunlit silence. Hov'ring there
I've chased the shouting wind along and flung
My eager craft through footless halls of air.
Up, up the long delirious, burning blue,
I've topped the windswept heights with easy grace
Where never lark, or ever eagle flew.
And, while silent lifting mind I've trod
The high untresspassed sanctity of space,
Put out my hand and touched the face of God.

Pilot Officer John Gillespie Magee, Jr., RCAF
September 3rd, 1941

Foreword

To me, there is no other single invention of mankind that has been used to simultaneously bring the world closer together and utterly tear it apart than the airplane. In so far as creating new frontiers in aerospace technology, no other country in the world has the collective capability of creating more advanced aircraft than the United States of America. Since before I could walk, I have always been fascinated by aircraft and those that fly them. My parents tell me that by the age of one, I would point up at every airplane that crossed the skies above me and shriek with delight. I still do a somewhat subdued version of that today.

I have the pleasure of living in an aviation Mecca. Two miles north of my home in Smyrna, Georgia sits Dobbins Air Reserve Base and Lockheed Aeronautics Company where thousands of professionals craft and test the most advanced fighter jet in the history of mankind: the Lockheed F-22 Raptor and many other flying pieces of art. Ten miles north of me, there is a general aviation airfield that houses hundreds of examples of my idea of fine art. One of the busiest international airports on the planet sits twenty miles to the south of me and there isn't a day that passes where I don't see dozens of the beautiful pressurized steel tubes lifting off from there as they begin to streak across the sky. Throughout my life, I've never been able to hear an airplane overhead and not look up. I am compelled beyond any reasonable explanation. There has never been anything more captivating and beautiful to me than the lines and surfaces of highly-complex machines made of aluminum, steel, titanium, and a thousand other components that allow man to slip the bonds of earth and get ever so slightly closer to heaven. As anyone can tell, I clearly rank in the top one percent of aviation enthusiasts. I've had an interesting path in life and have, by either fate or by circumstance, met a very large number of the people our society considers heroes. I enjoy the buzz of meeting luminaries but if you want to see me transfixed, listening to someone, put a fighter pilot or astronaut in front of me. I'll listen to their stories until you have to pour hot coffee down my throat to keep my head from hitting the table. Those are the real larger-than-life personalities to me. Writing this book has given me the chance to get some extremely detailed experiences and knowledge from my true heroes: men and women who advance throttles and accelerate down runways, streaking upward, traveling at speeds unattainable to the earth-bound and toward infinity.

My love of airplanes was just one element that inspired me to write this story but there was another reason. While working on this, I was more than once moved to tears while writing some chapters, reliving certain experiences of the recent past. I have discovered that it is almost impossible to cry and type at the same time. There is not a soul in this country, and multitudes throughout the rest of the world, that didn't suffer a tremendous loss on that horrific Tuesday morning of September 11th, 2001. More than three thousand beautiful, unrepeatable lives ceased to exist between 8:47 a.m. and 10:06 a.m. Additional victims included tens of thousands of immediate family members of those who perished in New York, Washington, and Pennsylvania. Others have since lost family members who went out into the world to combat those addicted to hatred that visited such devastation on America that morning. Others had their illusion of unquestionable safety and security within our borders shattered forever, instilling a sense of fear unparalleled by any other single act in our country's history. Many others suffered, and continue to suffer, tremendous financial repercussions. Notably, the airlines that helped bring the world closer together over nearly nine decades of commercial flight are now currently suffering a seemingly never-ending series of financial catastrophes. To date, there have been over four thousand servicemen and women that have made the ultimate sacrifice to eliminate the resources and safe-havens of those spiritually lost souls that seek to do such hateful damage to the United States and our allies. Finally, there are always innocent victims of war. The numbers of non-combatant dead as a result of the two major combat operations are incalculable but the number is nothing short of awful. I offer no specific solution or theory on that other than to say that war sucks.

I know my personal loss from that awful day was totally insignificant relative to the sacrifices others have endured. It would be ludicrous to think anything else. Still, one of the main motivations for me while writing this book was the temporary theft of my ability to see aircraft as beautiful anymore. I watched as deranged men used the most *beautiful* thing I've ever seen to do the *ugliest* thing I've ever seen.

I realized early on in the writing of this, that it would touch some extremely sensitive areas for some people. Please hear me clearly when I say that, although this story has primarily Catholic characters, I don't believe any faith group in the world is less than any other, in any way. I have *no* opinion as to how anybody chooses to celebrate their relationship with God, Allah, Yahweh, or however they might refer to Him. The principles I used to heal from my own awful spiritual injury are consistently professed by every theology I've ever explored. This story could have had scenes written at temples, mosques, or any sort of Christian church in the world. I just wrote it from the perspective of what I know.

Everything in this story is purely fiction or used in a fictionalized manner but I attempted to link real aspects of aviation history in a feasible way, giving the reader insight into an area that fascinates many but is experienced by a relative few. For me, the two-year journey of crafting this story gave me a gift beyond just writing a book. I personally experienced a healing of my relatively minor, yet very painful wound. Today, I can once again look up and see the magnificence of things streaking through the air that have airfoils, ailerons, flaps, rudders, cockpits, and canopies. My illness of the spirit, which was a result of hatred toward those that attacked my country, has been largely healed as a result of doing the unthinkable: praying for those who perpetrated such a spiritually-eviscerating assault on every American and, to a large degree, the rest of the world. I don't know when the day will come that the Light will remove the darkness from this world and until then, there will always be the need for professionals willing to go into harm's way. I often joke with military or intelligence community friends of mine that if we ever start living by the rules (the first ones), they would have to seek employment elsewhere and they all agree. Every true warrior wishes for peace.

One of my great mentors told me that nothing can withstand love. I eventually believed him when he said, "God is Love and when you give Love, you give God and He is the highest Gift." My mission isn't to hate "them" but pray that the Light will reach those living in the dark and I *know* from personal experience that the dark cannot exist in the Light. Whether or not the people we perceive as our enemies ever feel the closeness of Him as a result of prayer isn't my business but I get to feel the closeness of Him as a result of praying for the most isolated and rage-filled of His children. I don't have to love what some people do, but I do have to love them despite their hatred. Even though I am enamored with aircraft, I believe it impossible for mankind can create a vehicle more perfect than His Love to bring us closer to heaven.

1

Photo by Will Dempsey

Final Delivery / Will Dempsey

2

Dahlgren Chapel of the Sacred Heart
Georgetown University
Washington, D.C.
12:42 P.M. Eastern Time
Saturday, July 4th, 1950

Prologue

It was stiflingly hot in the chapel and nearly impossible to hear Monsignor Byrd clearly from thirty rows back. Even though they were parish members of St. Patrick Catholic Church in Alexandria, Virginia, each Fourth of July, Tom and Clara Walsh would, as a family tradition, pack their energetic child, Christopher, and a picnic basket into the family Buick and drive into Washington to attend the noon Mass at the Dahlgren Chapel of the Sacred Heart.

The chapel, located on the campus of Tom's alma mater, Georgetown University, was a place very special to him. Tom always insisted, as a former naval aviator and combat veteran, that he and his family celebrate the birthday of the United States in the capital. The Independence Day itinerary for the Walsh family was always breakfast at the restaurant within the department store Tom worked at, Mass at Dahlgren Chapel, and then a leisurely day strolling through the Capitol Mall, capped off with the most intense firework display found anywhere in the country. Tom and Clara had kept the custom faithfully for each of the ten years of their marriage, with the exception of the years 1942 through 1945 when Tom was at war in the South Pacific. During those years,

3

Clara spent quiet holidays at home or with nearby friends in Alexandria with little Christopher, who had been born exactly five months after Tom had gone to war. Those were the hardest years for Clara because, despite his enthusiastic tone in his letters, Clara knew that the idyllic picture of the South Pacific her husband painted belied the fact that there was a deadly war raging. She knew her beloved husband was regularly in harm's way. Growing up the daughter of a distinguished naval officer, Clara had more insight into the true nature of war than most women. During those years apart from the love of her life, she often cried herself to sleep with deep longing and fear for her husband. Twelve thousand miles away, Tom was known to the men in his squadron as Lieutenant JG Thomas Walsh, USN. On an almost daily basis, Lieutenant Walsh piloted an Avenger TBM torpedo bomber over some of the most hostile skies in the Pacific.

When one of the deacons approached the pulpit, Tom and Clara stood to hear the Gospel reading. Instantly noticing that Christopher hadn't joined them, Clara snapped her fingers lightly in front of Christopher's eyes to signify for him to immediately get on his feet as well. With a moment of childish protest, he hesitated just long enough to elicit a withering glare from his mother. With that, he begrudgingly stood between his parents. With a sigh of satisfaction, Clara reached behind Christopher's back and took Tom's hand in hers. She only had to make the lightest contact with her fingertips on his hand for him to automatically intertwine his fingers with hers. She loved that about him. Momentarily reflecting on how lonely and painful the war years had been, and how grateful she was that Tom, unlike a lot of men, had returned home, Clara said a small prayer of thanks, smiled, and squeezed his hand.

Feeling her expression of affection, Tom felt a peace that he had come to value so much more after his experiences during the war. Tom looked across the top of Christopher's head back at her, smiled, and squeezed her hand back. In his left hand, within his pocket, Tom felt the little rosary he carried off to war. The two things he always took into the cockpit had been a picture of Clara and the rosary given to him by his father, Tom Sr. The

4

rosary was a treasured family heirloom that was obtained at the Vatican when Tom's father visited the Holy See as a young man on his honeymoon with Tom's mother. While there, they young couple had their marriage blessed by Pope Pius X in a special newlywed audience. After the blessing, the couple received a rosary—the one that was handed down to Tom from his father on his and Clara's wedding day—directly from the hand of the Holy Father in the receiving line. Just as Tom was about to walk up to the altar, Tom's father handed it him and said, "The family that prays together stays together."

Clara momentarily gazed into Tom's sapphire blue eyes, liking how distinguished he looked with his still youthful face and salt-and-pepper hair. The little lines around his eyes gave him an experienced, yet mischievous appearance. A wave of admiration for her loving husband welled up inside her and as he turned to meet her eyes, she winked at him. He loved it when she did that. In response, the smile he flashed back expressed the glow he felt inside. There had been some years after Tom's return from the war when he hadn't smiled much. She was so happy to see that, over the past year, he seemed to have really come out of the dark moods that were not uncommon after his return. He finally resumed being the charming, kind man with the heartwarming smile she had fallen in love with a decade earlier. Tom looked down at his boy sitting between them. It appeared the child was growing up at an increasing rate.

Tom momentarily reflected back on their morning and grinned.

"Honey, we've got to get a move on if we don't want to be late," Tom called up the stairs to his wife, two hours earlier, right after Christopher nearly knocked a valuable family heirloom vase from a credenza when he careened through the room 'flying' his little toy airplane through the air with the accompanying sound effect.

"Be right down, sweetheart," she called from upstairs, while she put the finishing touch of lip liner on. Glancing at her son the reflection of the vanity, Clara smiled as she appreciated how adorable her son looked in his church suit that her husband just brought home the prior Friday.

"Now, Christopher, why don't you go ahead and put your plane away because we are leaving in five minutes," said Clara as the boy, totally oblivious to anything other than the imaginary aerial battle he was waging in his head, joyously flew his toy plane around the room while simulating the attendant plane engine and machine-gun noises.

"Christopher!"

At his mother's second interruption, Christopher stopped in mid-dive and pleaded, "Aw, Mom, can't I *please, please, please* take it with? You let me take it to Aunt Jill's house."

Choosing to take the path of least resistance, and knowing they were running behind to get to church, Clara made a decision she suspected she would regret.

"I'll let you take it, but you better be on your very best behavior. No playing during Mass."

"I won't, Mommy…I promise."

Tom's Walsh's father, Tom Walsh Sr., had been a salesman for a pearl importation and jewelry firm in New York City before the Great Depression, having come to the United States from Dublin at the turn of the century. Though Tom Jr. never lived in a state even remotely resembling luxury, Tom Sr. had been a phenomenal salesman and sustained the Walsh family's comfortable middle-class lifestyle in their Glen Cove, Long Island home. Growing up an exceptional student and spectacular athlete, having won the New York State High School Batting Champion title three years in a row, Tom moved to Washington D.C. at the age of seventeen with a full athletic and academic scholarship to Georgetown University. After graduation from Georgetown, and prior to his Navy service, Tom followed in his father's footsteps as a salesman for a small jewelry store in Annapolis, Maryland. It was a frigid February in 1937 when Tom met Clara for the first time.

"We're looking for something nice for my daughter here. It's her birthday," the tall, slender U.S. Navy captain declared that morning. Standing next to the officer was the most strikingly beautiful girl Tom had ever seen, peering into his cases.

"I believe I've got something commensurate with her own beauty, sir," he blurted out to Captain John King, a history teacher at the United States Naval Academy two blocks away at the end of Maryland Avenue. The remark elicited a raised eyebrow from the captain but upon hearing those words, first Clara's eyes, then her entire head rose from the case, noticing Tom's smile for the first time. She smiled back him and gave him a look he immediately knew he would remember the rest of his life.

"Well aren't you the clever wordsmith, Mr....?"

"Walsh, ma'am. Tom Walsh."

"I'll remember that, Tom Walsh," she said with a gleam in her eye.

Somehow Tom knew instantly, within the very depths of his soul, that he had met the woman he wanted to spend the rest of his life with. He felt like his very soul was set aglow by the woman standing on the other side of the jewelry counter. Although he had socially called on a handful of women to that point in his life, there had never been a feeling remotely close to the utter awe Tom felt upon meeting Clara King. That night, he made a journal entry: "February 7th, 1939...I met the right girl."

The emerald ring Clara selected that day was slightly larger than her finger and required reducing the size of the shank to fit her petite, size-four finger. Tom was thrilled to have a perfect opportunity to call on her at the King residence within the row of Naval Academy faculty residences. The next day, when the alteration was completed, Tom walked toward the gate to the Academy clutching the bag with Clara's ring like it was the Holy Grail. With an act of courage that he, upon being admitted by the sentries at the guardhouse onto the campus didn't initially believe himself capable of, Tom respectfully asked Clara if he might have her permission to call on her socially as he handed her the little gift bag containing her emerald ring. Tom would never forget the sensation of the universe standing absolutely motionless during the three seconds Clara stood looking at him, appearing to consider his request. Her answer was, "Yes," the instant he asked but a dignified lady never seemed too eager according to her etiquette teacher. When she finally smiled and said, "I believe I would enjoy that," his heart resumed beating. After quickly winning the heart of Clara and slowly winning the approval of the quite discerning Captain King, Thomas Walsh and Clara King were joined in holy matrimony fourteen months later in the Naval Academy Chapel.

A year into the marriage, as sales began to hit a serious slump in the jewelry store, Captain King had buttonholed Tom at a party being held in honor of the new incoming Academy commandant, Admiral Sullivan. Although Captain King's current billet was teaching naval history at the Academy, he was a seasoned and brilliant star of the naval intelligence community and a member of a working group that assessed incoming intelligence that only a handful of people were granted access to. While analyzing the military actions and intent of the Japanese in China and Korea, and the rumblings of war being heard from the Germans, Captain King knew it was only a matter of time. He had seen very similar geopolitical scenarios throughout the world while a young ensign over twenty years earlier and knew war for the United States was almost a certainty.

Standing in the study of the Admiral when it was just the two of them, Captain King said, "Tom, you are a smart, hardworking kid. I wouldn't have let you get within a hundred miles of Clara if you hadn't been."

Tom tried to figure out what Captain King was getting at and felt uneasy by the tone of concern he detected in the captain's words. His discomfort increased as Captain King continued, "I know things aren't going so well at the jewelry shop. Everyone says we won't get into it but I'm telling you war is coming and our military is going to need the very best men our country has to offer. Have you ever considered military service?"

Stifling the pang of resentment toward Clara for laundering their family financial situation, Tom took a moment to carefully consider his answer.

"You know, sir, I think certain people are just born for serving their country the way you do. I'm sure things will look up at the store soon. It's just a slow patch."

8

After putting off Captain King's decreasingly subtle suggestions over the next few months that the Navy would offer him and his daughter a multitude of benefits and stability, Tom was urgently shaken awake on a December by Clara. She practically dragged him down the stairs to the radio in the living room where the radio announcer was reading news reports of an unprecedented tragedy a half a world away on a tropical island paradise. The newspaper's photos and radio reports of dozens of burning and sinking American ships shocked the world. The president was just finishing up his radio address as Tom abruptly stood and declared, "Honey, I've got to go see about something. I'll be back in an hour." Twenty minutes later, sitting in the study of Captain King's residence, Tom asked, "What are my chances of getting into flight training?"

Upon Tom's return from the war, the jewelry store where he first met his bride had closed. While Tom was off flying dangerous missions against the Japanese in the Pacific, Ken and Esther Wasserman, who were much like a second set of parents to Tom, closed Wasserman's Jewelry when business dwindled to almost nothing Having had enough of service to God *and* country, Tom separated from the Navy and went back to the world of retail. With a wife and child to support, and with no more checks from the Navy forthcoming, Tom's amiable personality, prior experience in jewelry, and an impressive war record helped him land a management position at a prestigious department store down in the District. Tom was the very first manager of the newly opened Precious Jewelry boutique that the upscale department store Neiman Marcus had just unveiled in downtown Washington. The department manager position in the jewelry boutique was a mixed blessing for Tom. The position paid well but the excruciatingly tedious process of completing the semi-annual inventory had just ended two days earlier. Twice each year, Tom and his staff spent three weeks preparing, counting, and re-counting thousands of small pieces of jewelry with even smaller item numbers on the price tags. Tom was desperate for a peaceful weekend.

In church with his family on that hot July day, the conversation in the admiral's study between Tom and Captain King seemed a

9

hundred years and a million miles away as Tom looked down at his boy and then over to the love of his life. The smell of incense reached Tom's nose. He always liked the pungent and spicy smell of incense used during Mass. At that moment, however, his enjoyment of the olfactory notes was interrupted by a series of recurring, annoying, and low-volume noises. Suddenly becoming fully conscious of the subdued airplane noises Christopher was making next to him, Tom looked down and then up at his wife. Over the next five seconds, Tom watched as Clara's face wore a series of increasingly displeased expressions that she shot at Christopher sitting between them. Instantly, Tom began to feel the probability of a calm day dropping sharply.

    Every bulletin handed to churchgoers entering the quaint building was fluttering back and forth, employed as a makeshift fan. There were apologetic signs declaring a technical problem with the air conditioning system on the bulletin board that the ushers pointing to as they entered a half hour earlier. Tom knew Clara disliked excessive heat as a general rule and the eighty-five degree heat inside the chapel wasn't going to be any help to her demeanor if Christopher didn't immediately knock off the misbehavior. The increasingly frustrated expressions on her face didn't bode well for either his ability to focus on the service or his prospect for a well-deserved morning of peace. Up to that point, Tom had really been enjoying the homily being given by Monsignor Byrd. The pastor possessed a communicative style that combined a true passion for his faith with a manner of speaking that reminded Tom of some of his favorite professors at Georgetown. The beloved priest was known for incorporating fascinating elements of Catholic history into whatever the topic of his homily was. Unfortunately, Tom was acutely aware that hew was tired, unable to focus on what Monsignor Byrd was saying, and most importantly, that his decision not to veto Clara's letting the boy take his toy airplane inside the church had been a big mistake. Still trying to listen to Monsignor Byrd, Tom could see from her expressions that Clara was about to, as one of his former fellow squadron pilots from Alabama used to say, "Lose her religion."

    With one more simulated radial engine noise from his son,

10

Tom's tolerance of the behavior reached an end.

"If you don't knock that off right this instant, young man, there will be no fireworks for you today!" whispered Tom fiercely to his eight-year-old son. Looking up at his parents, Christopher saw his father's expression left no invitation for debate, not that debate was ever tolerated, particularly during Mass. Other parishioners attending Mass that morning had given increasingly frequent glances at the child who was making intermittent airplane noises.

That's the last time I let him bring any toys to Mass, thought Tom.

Until his father's admonishment, Christopher was completely oblivious to the world around him. Snapped out of an imaginary scene in his mind that involved clouds and twenty thousand feet of altitude, Christopher looked up at his annoyed parents with a well-practiced expression of innocence and immediately sat upright and pretended to listen to Monsignor Byrd who, in truth, Christopher was neither inclined to, nor capable of hearing at all.

For the next five minutes, Christopher performed a passable impression of an exemplary young Catholic child until the heat and boredom got the best of his lack of impulse control. Again taking his replica airplane in his hand, Christopher attempted another carrier landing on the wooden pew bench.

The little die-cast metal and rubber toy was Christopher's favorite possession since the prior Christmas when he found it under the tree. The handcrafted toy had been expensive for a child's gift but with Tom's employee discount, however, Tom and Clara agreed that it was to be their son's main gift for the Christmas of 1949. Seven months later, Christopher rarely went anywhere without the blue and white plane. Pretending the pew was the pitching deck of his father's aircraft carrier, Christopher's imaginary carrier landing would have been unnoticed as he kept the soundtrack of an airplane engine within his mind but there was a serious complication during his approach. So engrossed in his play, Christopher didn't even notice when everyone in the church began to sit after they had recited the Nicene Creed. Clara inadvertently and painfully sat down on the vertical stabilizer of the foot-long metal plane, instantly emitting a shriek that she unsuccessfully tried to stifle. So shocked by his mother's yelp, Christopher recoiled from her, instinctively knowing he was in serious trouble. In an effort to put some distance between he and his mother, Christopher scooted closer to his father and, in doing so, accidentally knocked the plane to the marble floor. The hollow, metal plane made a highly audible crashing noise that prompted nearly everyone in attendance to turn his or her head toward the Walsh family.

Tom loved his son as much as any father was capable of but, with this cacophony of metallic clatter, he reached his absolute limit of tolerance. Precociousness was something he had grown accustomed to from their intelligent and enthusiastic child but public embarrassment was another thing altogether. Grabbing Christopher by his forearm, Tom dragged the boy out of the pew. As he was propelled by the force of his father's arm, Christopher had the presence of mind to execute a remarkable grab for the toy plane from the floor as he flew by it.

With the bearing and cadence to his walk identical to that he had used as a naval officer moving across the deck of his aircraft carrier, Tom strode with purpose toward the rear of the church and Christopher stumbled as he attempted to keep pace. Heading out the rear doors, through the narthex of the church, and ignoring the contemptuous glances of fellow churchgoers, Tom finally stopped, released Christopher's arm, did an immediate about-face and looked down at his boy when they stood alone on the steps outside.

"It was an accident, Daddy!"

"I believe you, but it was your *last* accident today. I don't know *why* we agreed to let you take that thing with you. This is God's house and not a play house."

He extended his hand and Christopher hesitated for a moment. The glare from Tom's eyes sent the perfectly clear message to hand the plane over. With the reluctance of a man in the desert would relinquish his last cup of water, Christopher handed the plane to his father.

"So, no plane for the rest of the week and if you so much as make a peep for the rest of Mass, we're skipping the fireworks and heading straight home."

12

Christopher' head told him, *keep quiet,* but from his mouth Christopher heard the words, "Awww, Daddy!" escape.

"That's *it* mister! If I hear one more noise from you until we leave here, you will never, ever see this plane again. I'm sure some less fortunate child at the orphanage downtown would love a fine gift like this!"

Christopher almost yelped a *"No!"* but he miraculously realized that *"No!"* would be the one word and his plane would be gone forever. He had never seen his daddy not do what he said he would. Christopher choked the word back with supreme effort. Tom could see the word forming on his son's lips and said, "You keep telling me you want to be a pilot when you grow up. Do you think you get to pick and choose which rules to follow according to what you feel like when they teach you to fly a plane? If you can't follow my direct orders when it comes to something as simple as behaving in God's house, you aren't pilot material. Guys I knew that had a hard time following orders in flight training either got dropped from training, got themselves killed, or even worse, got other people killed. So are you ready to head back in and not make so much as a peep for the rest of Mass?"

"Yes, Daddy."

"And while you are sitting there, I want you to tell God you are sorry for being disrespectful to Him and immediately after Mass, you will apologize for your lack of consideration for your mother. Understood?"

"Yes, sir."

With a curt nod, Tom took Christopher by the hand and began leading him back into the church. As a lone tear rolled down his cheek, Christopher looked around at the adults glancing at him and angrily wondered, *Why do they make me come here?* He decided, right then, that when he was a daddy, he'd never, ever make his kids come to church.

The Lee family, John, Eileen, and Jack, sat in the pews of St. Catherine Labouré in the Chicago suburb of Glenview, Illinois as Father Buckley celebrated the noon Mass. When it was time for

13

Holy Communion, two-year-old Jack Lee walked with a big smile in front his mother in the procession to the altar. Looking down at the child, Father Buckley smiled and gave a blessing on the forehead to the boy with the wide, expectant eyes staring up from knee-height. Both John and Eileen noticed that Mass seemed to have a remarkably calming effect on their little dynamo, as opposed to many other children at Jack's age in Mass who seemed to view the service as the perfect place to act like rambunctious two-year-olds.

"Are there going to be more planes than the airport?" asked Jack from the back seat of the family Packard as John drove them down the expressway into the Chicago Loop.

"Just you wait and see," said Eileen. John broke his attention away from driving for an instant and stole a glance at his wife. Eileen winked and smiled back.

The calming effect Mass always seemed to manifest in the child had been completely counteracted when, upon arriving downtown, their son had watched, spellbound, as a Lockheed P-38 Lightning screamed overhead in a low altitude fly-by while John had parked their car down at Lincoln Park. The two turbocharged Allison V-1710 engines of the world's most powerful fighter/attack aircraft send sound waves that shook the windows and quickened the pulse of the child.

"Are there more, Daddy? Are there more planes?" screamed Jack as the P-38 flew out over the coastline of the lake.

John scooped up Jack and placed him atop his shoulders. "You becha' kiddo. More planes than you can shake a stick at!"

"Thank you, Daddy! Thank you, Mommy! This is the best day ever!" shrieked Jack.

John and Eileen strolled through the crowds, making their way toward the shoreline of Lake Michigan where tens of thousands of people stood along the beaches, watching the various barnstorming acts and military planes. Collective 'ooohs' and 'aaahs' emanated from the crowds as the different aircraft passed overhead and performed various aerobatic maneuvers. The airshow was a spectacle that was not so much attended but witnessed. It was the most highly-anticipated event of the first annual Chicago Summerfest. Anyone along the three miles of

14

Lake Shore Drive simply had to look up to attend.

Atop his father's shoulders, Jack covered his ears, and screamed with glee as a flight of six U.S. Navy Grumman Hellcats rumbled overhead at five hundred feet. Their powerful radial engines combined to make a deafening roar but Jack wasn't frightened of the noise. To the contrary, it excited the boy into a state of unbridled joy. As the roar subsided, Eileen returned, handing her husband a sauerkraut and mustard-laden Polish sausage from one of the multitude of food vendors that had set up shop along Lake Shore Drive. John broke off a piece of the sausage and handed up to his boy. He and Eileen split the remainder and began enjoying the traditional Chicago food item. Just then, the sensation of something wet made its way from the top of John's head to his right ear. Without looking, he knew what the wet sensation on his skin was. Eileen, looking at her wide-eyed boy, broke into a giggling fit. Jack's eyes were still glued on the six airplanes flying in a tight formation, his mouth agape. The boy simply pointed at the flight formation as if he had totally lost his ability to annunciate words from the excitement.

The sauerkraut had almost made its way to John's collar before Eileen stopped its progress with a napkin.

"Jack, sweetie, eat your sausage," said Eileen, attempting to be stern but giggling nonetheless.

Grinning, John joined his wife in her laughter. He should have known better than to hand his child the sausage while there were airplanes aloft.

"Can we go watch the planes?" Jack often begged his father when he would arrive home from his office on Fridays. When Jack was fifteen months old, Eileen had brought Jack along as she dropped John at O'Hare airport to fly to New York on business. A rising star with a successful advertising firm, John had been sent to New York to present a concept for an advertising campaign to an important client. Since that first excursion to O'Hare, Jack delighted in being taken to the airport to watch planes take off and land. That day had been the beginning of a lifelong love affair with airplanes for Jack.

As John turned the key on the ignition and Eileen settled into their car for the drive back to their house in the suburbs, Jack

15

asked, "Daddy, do you think any of those planes can fly high enough to reach heaven?"

John looked over at Eileen, smiling broadly. Looking back over his shoulder at his boy, he simply answered, "You'll just have to find out for yourself, kiddo."

"I *will*, Daddy."

That evening, at dusk, The Lees walked from their house on Prairie Lawn Road with numerous neighborhood families toward the Glenview Golf Club a mile away, carrying a picnic basket with their fried chicken dinner. Every year, the club was the location of the biggest fireworks display in the Chicago suburbs. The staccato popping of exploding strings of lady fingers and whistling of rockets resounded from all directions as they walked, each holding one of Jack's little hands.

"Hey Beth, Neil, how are you guys?" asked John as he realized his favorite neighbors, the Freemans, who lived three houses down from his and Eileen's house, were walking a few yards behind.

"Hey, John, never better a day in our lives. Thanks for asking. So, have you ever taken this little guy to the fireworks show before?" replied Neil as Beth knelt down and tussled Jack's hair.

"Nope. We thought he was a little too young last year but the little poppers going off all over the place don't seem to bother him too much," said John.

"Do you know why we have all these fun things today?" asked Neil as he reached down and lifted up Jack, much to the boy's delight.

"Its happy birthday America day," answered Jack after shrieking with excitement from being lifted above Neil's head.

Neil set Jack down as the adults laughed at the adorable manner in which Jack had phrased his answer.

"What did you like doing the best today?" prompted Eileen although she thought she knew the answer.

To her surprise, her son answered, "The angel planes, Mommy."

John and Eileen looked at each other with bemused expressions and then at their friends who were equally struck by the wonderfully innocent and beautiful way the child perceived the world.

Eileen asked, "Don't you mean *air*planes, sweetie?"

"No, Mommy. They look like angels that people can ride."

"Out of the mouths of babes," said Neil.

"That is one special child," said Beth.

"Though I fly through the valley of death, I shall fear no evil. For I am at 80,000 feet and climbing."

-Sign over entrance to SR-71 operations area at Kadena Airbase, Japan

Part One:

Slipping the Bonds

The 1960s

Photo by Will Dempsey

19

Travis Air Force Base
San Jose, California
Bachelor Officer Quarters
0630 Hours
Monday, May 2nd, 1969

Chapter One

The rumble of the jet overhead wasn't what woke Captain Chris Walsh. The twenty-six-year-old Air Force pilot possessed an almost infallible internal clock that roused him just before the alarm went off each morning. Rubbing sleep from his eyes, Walsh yawned before reaching over and silencing the alarm clock on the nightstand with a practiced smack.

Many people regarded the intrusion into their dream worlds by the jarring sound of an alarm clock as a nasty assault on their place of refuge from the real world. To Walsh, the sound was like a loud mouthed, though well-meaning friend, signaling to him the beginning of another day of doing what he loved more than anything in life: flying.

Walsh stood, stretched, and padded across his college dormitory-style room to the bathroom where he started the shower running. As he waited for hot water in the shower, which wasn't always a given depending on how many other pilots were staying in the Bachelor Officer Quarters, he lathered and shaved at the sink, making himself presentable and respectable-looking. It was the look of an officer.

Being pilot-in-command of a three hundred thousand pound,

20

multi-engine cargo jet designated the Lockheed C-141 Starlifter meant a lot more than just being able to fly the plane. Good stick-and-rudder pilots were pretty common; men that could effectively lead aircrews in any situation were not.

Walsh had total confidence in his ability to drive an airplane so, although his personal grooming standards were always well within regulation, his adherence to the regulations about the uniform-specifically those relating to flight suits-wasn't always a look that would be found on a recruiting poster. There were some guys that could shave by their reflection in their boots. Were Walsh to attempt that, he'd be dead by his own hand.

The Lockheed C-141A Starlifter was the main cargo aircraft employed by the United States Air Force and the first jet aircraft in the world specifically designed to haul cargo. The manufacturer, Lockeed Aeronautics, was fond of giving their aircraft astronomy-inspired names, hence the 'Starlifter'. In 1969, Lockheed was rolling out twenty of the planes a month from their Marietta, Georgia production facility and the Air Force was putting them in the air as quickly as they could get their hands on them. The war in Southeast Asia demanded an ever-increasing flow of soldiers, supplies and ordinance. Whenever the Pentagon ordered soldiers or supplies from point A to point B, the call always went to the Military Airlift Command of the United States Air Force. Walsh had equally mastered the complexity of flying multi-engine jets and the intricacies of instilling confidence and respect in the aircrews he flew with. A crew that trusted and respected each other saved lives during crises on countless occasions.

That morning, Walsh had the electric vibe pulsing through him that he always experienced when he knew he was about to go flying but in addition to his excitement was an additional sense of anticipation. Having just been upgraded to instructor pilot, or 'IP' in military-speak the previous day, Walsh had been elated when the squadron commander, Colonel Larry Schauer, informed him that he would be flying a line-check ride with a new guy fresh from the basic C-141 training at Tinker Airbase in Oklahoma. That day, which happened to fall on his birthday, Walsh was getting his very own second lieutenant to tutor in the fine art of

21

leading an aircrew.

Just after the soap and just before the shampoo, a thought of Charlotte came. It was just as Walsh was reviewing all the things he would go over that day with his first official student when the unwelcome memory of Charlotte popped into his mind. Shaking his head and trying to refocus on his responsibilities as an instructor and push the painful thoughts away, Walsh began to anticipate important performance points he would need to cover that evening while debriefing Lieutenant Jack Lee in Hawaii. The preparation exercise in his mind worked for a few moments until the words of his last conversation with her, eight weeks earlier, forced their way into his consciousness with all the subtlety of a thousand-pound bomb.

"It's not you, it's me. I….just don't love you anymore. I didn't mean to fall for Steve. It just sort of happened," Charlotte half-sobbed and half-mumbled that evening.

"Well, I guess I'll just make a note to myself that whenever a woman I'm dating starts telling me about the really nice guy in the office who makes her laugh, it's clearly code for 'it's over.' Thank you ever so much for that valuable lesson."

"You just don't understand."

"Well the one thing I do understand is that I'm just one more in a long line of men that distract you long enough until you find another. I didn't see it until now but I guess I was just too into you to see what was in front of me the entire time."

"This is *exactly* why we would never work out."

"Yeah, well, don't spend too much time worrying about me. I'll collect my things and go. Oh, give my regards to Steve. You couldn't have happened to a more deserving guy. Just make sure to do him the courtesy of explaining that your love has an expiration date," said Walsh with a tone dripping with barely-suppressed anger.

"You jerk! Get out!"

Not the way he wanted to have a last conversation with Charlotte but then again, he hadn't been expecting a last conversation with her when he walked into the door of her apartment that night.

For a few minutes, Walsh let the warm water of the shower run

22

over him, thinking about all of his plans with Charlotte that had unexpectedly shattered with her admission of her being involved with the new, young attorney at her father's firm. Trying to determine exactly where he might have made a misstep occupied his thoughts for the next five minutes. Finally coming to terms with the fact that the post-mortem on the relationship was totally fruitless, Walsh turned off the water and stepped from the shower. As he wrapped the plain, Air Force issue towel around his midsection, the sound of a jet climbing into the cool morning sky above his building reminded Walsh that there were infinitely more important things to attend to.

When, three years earlier, then Second Lieutenant Walsh arrived at Travis a bright-eyed new Starlifter pilot, newly graduated from the training school at Tinker Air Force Base in Oklahoma, he was mentored by a wise, highly-experienced instructor pilot named Captain Dave Crawford. The senior pilot passed on many important lessons to Captain Walsh as he made his way through the processes of qualifying as a co-pilot, then aircraft commander and finally as an instructor pilot. In Walsh's estimation, the most important lesson he had absorbed from Captain Crawford was the two word definition of leadership: *Follow Me*.

As he walked past the mirror, Walsh paused and looked at his reflection. His sea-blue eyes had been inherited from his father, Tom, and had been an asset in making the acquaintance of his past girlfriends although he never understood what girls were talking about when complimenting them. To his silent dismay, he could see some grey hairs beginning to appear amongst the closely-cropped dark brown. Not a lot, but more than he thought was fair for the age of twenty-six. Captain Walsh stood just short of six feet tall with an athletic frame. His midsection showed just a hint of softness, courtesy of a less-than-ideal diet and a habit of trying the local beers on every continent and island he flew into. Even so, Walsh could still easily run six miles in under an hour and do fifty pushups in a row without even straining. Those personal benchmarks were all he needed to feel adequate about his fitness level. After toweling off in the bathroom, Walsh slipped on his nylon flight suit–a garment unquestionably

23

designed for functionality rather than fashion.

After pulling the zipper up on the ubiquitous olive-green suit, and zipping his lackluster boots, Walsh was ready for the first day of passing his considerable knowledge and experience in flying the Starlifter to his first student. From his nightstand, Walsh grabbed his dog-eared copy of Hemmingway's *The Old Man and the Sea,* and stuffed it into his helmet bag where his checklists, oxygen mask, and favorite headset already resided. Starlifter pilots didn't actually wear helmets while flying but the bag was a perfect size to be useful as a compact piece of luggage. As he packed the last of his personal effects he would take on the ten-day mission, Walsh glanced over to the nightstand at the last physical reminder of his five-month relationship with Charlotte. After an unpleasant fight three months earlier, Charlotte had given him a Bible as, what she claimed to be, a token of reconciliation. Something about the nature of the gift seemed more like a subtle indictment of his character, yet he somehow wasn't able to part with it. There had been times he considered leaving it at the base chapel but somehow he never got around to it. Looking at the only reminder that remained from his involvement with her, he had an odd inspiration to stick it in his helmet bag and look through it sometime during the upcoming mission. He went to the table, hefted the book in his right hand, and judged the extra weight more than he cared to tote just then.

I'll get around to reading some of this when I get back, he thought.

Pulling his door closed, Walsh mentally geared up for the command persona he would need to display to his crew, sharply turned on his heel, and walked from his room down a corridor with a highly-polished white tiled floor toward the front of the building. From the door, Walsh saw his student, Lieutenant Jack Lee, was waiting with his gear at his feet on the sidewalk. Waiting with the lieutenant was Major John Hightower who Walsh had flown dozens of missions with. The major was the navigator for the mission and would sit at a station along the port wall of the cockpit, directly behind the pilot, constantly monitoring the two navigation computers and completing an impressive quantity of paperwork regarding everything from meteorological data to the plane's exact location. During flight, Hightower occasionally used a periscopic sextant to shoot a three-star position and plot their position using the stars in the exact same manner Christopher Columbus had done so five centuries earlier.

Glancing at his watch, with his hand on the door handle, Walsh noted the time was 0659:52 hours. Eight seconds later, as his watch flipped to precisely 0700:00 hours, he pushed on the door and walked outside. A stiff breeze blew from the north, being funneled down the Suisun Valley and across the airbase. *Suisun*, from the Patwin Indian tribe word meaning 'Land of the West Wind', was often an apt description of the conditions in the valley. Travis Air Force Base was a great place for pilots to become experienced with crosswind landings.

As Walsh approached the pair of officers standing at the curb, Lieutenant Lee turned toward him at the sound of the door opening. Looking at his watch, Lee noted the time was precisely 0700 hours.

The captain really likes to be timely, thought Lee.

"Morning, Captain Walsh. Looks like a great day to fly," said Lee.

With a quick salute to the major that was reciprocated, Walsh turned toward his eager-eyed student, and said, "Roger that, Lieutenant. It's always a great day to fly." Just then, the blue crew transport bus turned onto the street, stopping moments later at the curb with its doors directly in front of three officers. Through the windows of the small bus, Captain Walsh saw his enlisted crew in olive-drab flight suits: three tech sergeants and one single master sergeant.

"Time to meet the crew, huh, Captain?" remarked Lee.

"Yeah, Lieutenant, and when we get to base ops before departure, we'll have a crew briefing and formally introduce you. That will be your first important lesson, Lieutenant. I'm going to show you the difference between commanding a flight crew and leading one."

Lee felt confident that he had a thorough knowledge of the material that was to be covered as prescribed by the Crew Briefing Guide. He was well-versed in cargoes, normal and emergency procedures, weather penetration procedures, and a multitude of other information 'the book' provided.

The difference between commanding and leading? This should be interesting, he thought.

The three officers boarded the bus which was really not much more than a panel truck fitted with seats.

"Morning, Airman," said Major Hightower to the bus driver.

"Morning sirs," replied the young airman with a nod as they began to pull away from the curb.

Walsh and Lee took seats across from each other in the front row which had intentionally been left empty by the enlisted men. The major took a seat directly behind them and immediately began looking over the sports scores in his newspaper.

Walsh turned around to the enlisted men who would make up his flight crew and said, "Morning, gentlemen." Almost in unison, the two tech sergeants and single master sergeant replied, "Morning, Captain." Master Sergeant Steve Turner, a dark-haired man with an equally dark mustache sat closest to the three officers. Sergeant Turner held the highest rank of non-commissioned officer and would have command over the two other tech sergeants. Sergeant Turner was the engineer assigned for the mission, meaning he would sit at an instrument panel just aft of the cockpit and directly across from Major Hightower at the navigator's station. Sergeant John Curtin was an experienced loadmaster or, in Air Force parlance, a 'strap stretcher', and was responsible for ensuring the cargo was loaded and secured correctly aboard the aircraft. Joining Sergeant Curtin in that responsibility was Sergeant Dave Sloan who was newly assigned to the 96th Airlift Squadron and just out of training at Tinker. Both Captain Walsh and Major Hightower had flown with Sergeant Turner numerous times and he would be the crew's official NCOIC, or Non-Commissioned Officer-In-Charge. Leaning over to Walsh, Sergeant Turner said, "Captain, I'll introduce him formally at the briefing but this is Sergeant Sloan. He's just in from training at Tinker for a loadmaster's slot and Sergeant Curtin will be administering a line training ride for him on this mission."

Walsh turned to the seat across and behind him and shook the

26

hand of the smiling, brown-eyed, baby-faced kid.

"Welcome aboard, Sergeant. If you listen to everything Sergeant Curtin has to teach you, you'll do just fine," said Walsh good-naturedly.

The bus proceeded across the base, stopping at the parking lot of the 96th Squadron building and all aboard filed off the bus with their bags and made their way into the building. Five minutes later, after the three officers downed some coffee from a machine in the flight planning room, Walsh, Lee, and Hightower approached the three sergeants waiting outside the briefing room. Walsh leaned over to Lee and whispered, "Pay close attention, Lieutenant."

The six men went into the briefing room together and then the three officers turned to face the three sergeants. Sergeant Turner called the other three men to attention. Turner, Sloan and Curtin immediately braced to attention.

"At ease," said Walsh and began the briefing he always delivered to crews new to him: "My name is Walsh and I'm pilot-in-command. This is Major Hightower, our navigator, and to his right is Lieutenant Lee who will be sitting in the left seat up at the flight deck as I evaluate his performance during certain legs of this mission. Lieutenant Lee is my student so if we encounter any problems, let there be no mistaking the fact that *I* am in command of our plane. There are only a couple of things you need to know: I expect you to show up on time, looking sharp, and ready to go to work. We'll be all business from now until we get to the top of the climb. Once the level-off checklist is completed we play liar's dice, deal the cards, tell some stories, or get some sleep, I don't care. What I do care about is having somebody alert and awake on the engineer's panel and somebody alert and awake on the front row at all times. From the descent checklist until we close the flight plan, we'll be all business again. On crew rest, whatever you do suits me fine. You know the rule; twelve hours from bottle to throttle so I don't want anybody showing up at the jet who isn't up for the game. If you get in trouble on crew rest, try to reach me and I'll save your tail if I can. It's my job to move this mission. I expect us to have a lot of fun. This is a great airplane and I think we are really going to enjoy ourselves. That's about it gentlemen. Any questions?"

The sergeants stood relaxed but ready. Walsh had a manner of speaking that, while maintaining a model of military professionalism when necessary, seemed to radiate a genuine good nature.

Walsh turned to exit the room but immediately halted, did a sharp about-face to look directly into the eyes of the three enlisted members of his new crew, smirked slightly, and added, "Oh, I almost forgot to tell you the single most important thing: Do *not* urinate on the seat in *my* crew latrine. If, at any time, I find one single, tiny, yellow droplet on, or around, my latrine, you gentlemen *will* live in abject misery for the balance of our time together. Are there any questions?" Walsh turned to Master Sergeant Turner and said, "Sergeant Turner, the other officers are going to join me down the hall for an officer's briefing and you may take this time to brief your men."

Major Hightower and Lieutenant Lee filed out of the room behind Walsh. Lee turned and asked, "May I ask two questions, Sir?"

"Fire away, Lieutenant."

Well, sir, I've never actually heard specific instructions about the use of the crew latrine. Were you…serious about that? Secondly, sir, I think you covered the basics. What would Turner be briefing the other men about?"

Walsh stopped, turned to Lee and said, "First, Lieutenant, I just gave the men orders about how to take a leak and did you hear anybody questioning me? That's establishing command authority. Secondly, for all I care, Turner might be briefing them about the girl he went out with last night. The point is that I just made the tech sergeants *his* men. If they have a problem, they'll go to *him* first, not me. That's establishing chain-of-command." Lee, so new to the Military Airlift Command, was a fast learner. He immediately saw the brilliance in his instructor pilot's briefing and the lack of foresight in his questions. He uttered a quick and respectful, "Understood, sir."

The three officers and three sergeants walked from the base operations building a hundred yards out to the jet they were assigned to. The early morning sun glinted off the cockpit glass

28

of the nine giant Starlifters on the flight line. Forty feet above them, the tail number 60192 was the only visible difference between their assigned jet and the other eight aircraft on the ramp. After everyone placed their various bags on the tarmac just outside the forward crew door on the side of the jet, Major Hightower climbed up into the jet first and continued up to the flight deck. Just inside the crew door was a small galley where coffee and other portable food items could be warmed on the hot plates during flight. Beyond that, within the cavernous cargo area, sat nine pallets upon which all of the cargo would be secured for flight The inside of the jet was filled with the metallic mixture of smells that if a pilot were placed into blindfolded, he'd still know it was an aircraft. The telltale odor that would always give it away would be the, oily, petrochemical smell of jet propellant-grade four, commonly referred to as JP4. Up in the crew loft, just aft of the flight deck, Hightower stood adjacent to the two bunk mattresses affixed to the wall,

Following Major Hightower up into the jet, Walsh ascended the folding stairs into the cargo hold, taking a position just below the stairs to the crew loft. Just short of the galley, Lee took up a similar position. Sergeant Sloan, the newly-trained loadmaster, already checked the cargo they would be flying five hours to Hickam Air Force Base in Hawaii. Presenting the completed cargo and balance forms to Walsh for his signature, Sergeant Sloan said, "Its fifty thousand pounds of high-explosive tank rounds today, sir. There will be no smoking in the cargo area."

"Roger that, Sergeant."

The group walked back toward the base operations building so Walsh could file the flight plan and other miscellaneous paperwork the Air Force required before any of their multi-million dollar jets could even start their engines.

"Gentlemen, go ahead and grab a bite to eat if you want, but meet back here in precisely fifteen minutes ready for departure," said Walsh as the three enlisted men filed past him into the base operations building.

While Walsh went to finish the administrative tasks of filing paperwork prior to flight, Lee and Hightower continued down to the end of the hall and walked into the fifteen-by-fifteen foot

29

room that contained shelves full of maps, charts, terminal letdown procedures, and several large tables. The two men sat down and the major spread out the necessary paperwork.

"Lieutenant, I'm sure you know that unlike the fighter jockeys, we just don't pull up to the pump and say, 'Fill her up.' We compute our fuel load because it costs fuel to haul extra fuel. So why don't you impress me and quote to me what you learned about fuel loads from your time at Tinker?"

Without missing a beat, Lieutenant Lee began, "Major, our fuel load should be the gas necessary to start engines, taxi, take off, climb to our requested altitude, cruise at our planned mach number in the forecast wind which, if the weather guesser is right today, is a fifteen knot headwind, descend at destination, shoot an approach, go missed approach, shoot another approach, go missed approach, climb to the minimum safe altitude and proceed to our alternate, descend again, shoot another approach, go missed approach, shoot another approach, and land."

The major smiled and said, "I thought you looked like a nice boy who pays attention." Lee grinned at the complimentary remark. Continuing, the navigator said, "Captain Walsh told me your file says you are a gifted stick and rudder man. Now if we can just teach you everything else under the sun, you'll fit in just fine."

Lee's slight grin erupted into a full smile.

Major Hightower added, "I'm sure you know our maximum landing fuel load under normal conditions is eighty thousand pounds; any more in the tanks than that and we risk overstressing the wings if we have a firm landing. We always try to land with exactly eighty thousand pounds of fuel whenever we go into Viet Nam. That keeps us on the ground for as little time as absolutely necessary. Understood?"

For a moment, Lee considered that statement. He had always accepted that someday he may be flying into hot combat zones. When the major briefed him on how to be on the ground for as little time as possible, the possibility became much more real to him. It wouldn't be described as anything close to a panic, but his stomach muscles definitely tightened a degree. Nodding his understanding, Lee observed while the major completed the pre-

30

flight paperwork. Ten minutes later, everyone was at their appointed spots throughout the aircraft as the extensive checklists were performed.

Walsh began making his way down the takeoff checklist by calling out, "APU." Lee checked out his starboard window. He noticed the olive-drab colored auxiliary power unit, which was nothing more than a cart-mounted V-12 engine with large hose attached, used for pumping air and turning the large blades of the engine fans until they were ready to fully start the engines, had been rolled clear of the jet. His response, "Clear," was the first in dozens of such exchanges until the list was completed.

One of the most basic but critically-important lessons Walsh had absorbed in training was that as aircraft had become more complex over the prior sixty years of flight, certain knobs, switches, and levers had to be set absolutely right, every time. Mistakes in configuring machines with thousands of moving parts could, and did, kill people.

As the number one and two engines started, the familiar sound and vibration of the jet coming to life gave Lee a small rush of adrenaline cascading down his spine, as it always did. Moments later, when the number three and four engines came online, the feeling intensified.

Looking out the cockpit window, Walsh saw the crew chief for his plane, Sergeant Peterson, standing on the tarmac exactly where he should be, wearing ear protection. Holding his fists up with the thumbs pointed toward each other, he gave the signal to remove the chocks securing the wheels in place by quickly rotating his fists outward. Sergeant Peterson acknowledged the signal by repeating the motion with his own fists and quickly disappeared underneath the aircraft to pull the chocks away from the wheels, freeing the plane to taxi. Dashing back into view of the cockpit, Sergeant Peterson gave the signal that the chocks were free by displaying fists with his thumbs pointed outward.

Walsh checked the RPM indicator of the number one and number two engines as they began to spin up perfectly.

Sitting in the left seat, Lee keyed his microphone and transmitted: "Travis Ground Control, MAC 60192, taxi."

In his headphones, the tower responded, "192, taxi runway

three-six right. Winds light and variable. Altimeter 2998, hold short."

Keying the microphone once again, Lee responded with a quick, "998, roger."

As Walsh was setting the flaps for takeoff, Lee advanced the throttles slightly and the big jet began to roll toward the taxiway. Continuing to drive the airplane along the taxiway to the cross-taxi section leading to runway three-six right, both pilot and co-pilot scanned the tarmac for any potential problems in their path. As the last pre-departure tasks were completed, Lee's anticipation mounted. For most pilots, takeoff was never quite as exciting as the first time, but for the young lieutenant, the sensation had never diminished.

As the jet reached runway three-six right, both pilots heard in their headsets, "MAC 60192 is cleared to Hickam as filed to climb and maintain flight level three-three-zero. Maintain runway heading to five thousand feet then left turn on course. Contact tower on 122.5"

As Lee took the runway, the tower broadcast: "MAC 192, you are cleared for takeoff. Contact Departure Control on frequency 122.75."

"Roger."

With that, Lee advanced the throttles and a combined eighty thousand pounds of thrust erupted from the four engines. The jet began to rocket down the runway. The feel of the acceleration from brake release was one of the greatest parts of flying for Lee. He absolutely lived for the feeling of being pushed into his seat. The joy was always the same as he sat in a plane that was breaking its earthly bonds. Any pilot in the world knew the feeling.

Twenty seconds later, as the plane reached one hundred and thirty-five knots, Walsh called out, "Rotate." Lee applied some backpressure to the yoke and the jet vaulted into the central California sky. The sense of the Earth falling away was a treasured experience for both men sitting at the controls. Captain Walsh always had the sense of control of his life while in the cockpit as he lifted off. Lieutenant Lee always felt the experience was nothing short of communing with God.

O'Neill's Pub
46 Great Victoria Street
Belfast, Ireland
10:42 P.M. GMT
Monday, May 2nd, 1969

Chapter Two

Keely Kennedy stood behind the hundred-and-twenty-year-old bar and wiped it down while waiting for the head on Patrick Rafferty's Guinness beer to settle.

"I'd give you the world if you'd marry me today, dear Keely," said the fifty-eight-year-old with thinning grey hair, and bad teeth. Patrick was as much a fixture at O'Neill's as the collection of taps in the center of the bar. Wearing a threadbare tweed jacket, Patrick tipped his tam-o-shanter when Keely set the dark beverage in front of him, taking care to avoid knocking into his ashtray. She considered Patrick one of her more amusing regulars. The proposal from Patrick had become as regular as clockwork. Patrick fell in love with the dark-haired, dark-eyed bartender each night he drank at O'Neill's Pub, which, by definition, made it a nightly custom. It was always some silver-tongued wordsmithing from Patrick and she could see how the weathered-looking man must have been quite impressive to the ladies in his time.

"Kind of hard to afford the world on a postman's salary, isn't it mate?" jibed Michael O'Shaunessey, who had been sitting with his brother, Padraig, at the table directly behind Patrick's barstool and had overheard the proposal. Keely's highly developed sense for trouble put her immediately on alert. She absolutely loathed the jeering tone of the powerfully-built twenty-four-year-old Michael. Patrick Rafferty was a harmless drunk. The O'Shaunessey brothers were something more insidious altogether. She had known the two boys since her primary school days. Michael had always had an obvious crush on Keely, but her father, Liam, told her a long time ago to steer clear of the entire O'Shaunessey family. He expanded on why but he didn't need to. Keely respected her father and when he told Keely anything, she listened. Over the years, she had watched the brothers grow into violent thugs that commanded more fear than respect in the neighborhood. It was rumored they were part of the Provisional Irish Republican Army but nobody ever discussed such things openly.

At the unwarranted insult, Patrick took a healthy swallow of his beer, turned on his ancient leather-covered stool with a smile and said, "Ah, my boys, I've discovered there's no price to be placed on the most valuable things in life. Sitting in the company of God's greatest creation, who pours me fine glasses of ambrosia, is worth far more than all the money in the world."

"I'm impressed, old man. I'd have thought you drank away all your clever words at that rate."

Keely had heard enough.

"Better to have drunk them away than to never have possessed an adequate command of the language in the first place. That's' it, for you two this evening; I've no patience for that sort of rudeness in my bar. You'll be doing your drinking elsewhere tonight Michael O'Shaunessey. Both you and your brother. I'll thank you both to finish your drinks like gentlemen and excuse yourself!"

"Is that a fact?" he shot back. His tone was laden with the assumed invincibility of muscular men in their twenties.

"My boy, it is a fact. I'll not have you questioning my favorite bartender," said Kevin O'Neill, the owner who had silently came up from behind the O'Shaunessey brothers as they sat at their table. As Kevin had emerged from the storeroom to fetch another keg of beer, he sensed the rising tensions by watching the expressions of the young O'Shaunessey boy and Keely, the daughter he had never had. Towering over the boys, holding the

34

full keg of beer in one hand, Kevin was a jaw-dropping six-foot seven inches tall and nearly two hundred and ninety pounds. His biceps were larger in diameter than the thighs of the two young men he stood over. Although in his late fifties and with a girth that had been enhanced by plenty of beverages, everyone with functioning brain matter knew tangling with big Kevin was extraordinarily stupid and dangerous.

Swallowing his pride with great effort, but knowing that the discussion was concluded, without any room for argument, Michael looked at his brother Padraig, winked, polished off the last of his beer, and stood.

"Well then, we'll be wishing you all a fine night," said Michael with a tone that bordered on snide, but not quite.

"Nothing personal, mind you. Come back tomorrow and I'll buy you both a beer," said Kevin as he firmly clasped Michael's shoulder.

"No offense taken," said Michael as he pulled his shoulder out of Kevin's impressive grip and nodded to Padraig. The two stood and made their way to the door through the tables.

"Well that was a bit unpleasant. Calls for a drink," said Patrick Rafferty.

"You've got one right in front of you, Patrick."

"Well isn't that just perfectly convenient."

Keely kindly but firmly chased the last drunk out of the bar twenty minutes earlier. After counting the till and doing the final chores of the evening, Keely inserted the old brass key into the lock, securing O'Neill's Pub for the next nine hours until it would reopen at eleven that morning. Fortunately, she wasn't expected to be back behind the bar until seven the following evening. Kevin's son, Steven O'Neill, handled the day business, freeing his evenings for the pursuit of beverage-enhanced entertainment and acquainting himself with as many of the young ladies of Belfast as possible. There had been a brief two weeks, back when Keely had started working at the bar, where Steven had made several valiant attempts to charm her but she quickly made it clear that any romance between them just wasn't in the cards. She considered Steven a nice enough lad, but not nearly as mature as

35

she would require from any serious suitor. Since that time, six years earlier, their relationship had developed into a brother-sisterly friendship. She often provided him with insights into the female mind in regard to romantic involvement—which was helpful as Stephen was perpetually involved.

Steven's little forest green 1961 Morris came to a halt at the curb just as the bolt engaged.

"Can I offer you a ride, miss?"

She turned and asked, "What happened with your date with Siobhan tonight?"

With a shrug, he replied, "Guess it wasn't meant to be."

"But you've been telling me all week she was the one, haven't you?"

"If it's all the same, I'd rather not talk about it. So would you like a lift or not?"

As he said it, a pair of British Army jeeps pulled onto Great Victoria Street. Keely could hear Steven mutter a profane word as he watched the jeeps approach in his mirror. Not wanting to attract the attention of the soldiers, Keely walked to the passenger door and got in. Even so, the lead jeep sped up to the side of the little car, came to a stop, and a soldier, clearly a few years younger than Keely, shined a flashlight into the car.

"What's your business being out this time of night?" demanded the baby-faced soldier while another soldier in the passenger seat glared along with him.

"I'm the bartender here at O'Neill's. I've just closed up. The owner's son here is giving me a lift home."

The soldier looked down at them and, after a moment of silent scrutiny, intended to be a display of authority, said, "Carry on, then."

As the two British Army vehicles slowly passed by, Steven muttered, "Why thank you ever so much for your permission, Governor," with a tone of bitter contempt.

Five minutes later, Steven turned onto McNulty Street, continuing his commentary on the rapidly increasing tension and episodes of violence between the British Army and local citizenry that had been escalating in frequency and bloodshed.

"Those maggots have no right to be telling us anything.

36

Maybe someday they'll get the point." As he continued to rail about the British troops and government's meddling in the affairs of the people of Northern Ireland, Keely chose to keep quiet. He just let him rant. Her fears that Steven was associating with the Provisional Irish Republican Army had grown over the past weeks with his increasingly angry tirades. He vented his anger in almost every conversation. He was possessed of a seeming unwillingness to talk about anything else. There had been a time when they had talked about everything under the sun, especially the lasses. Over the past few months, it seemed like everything out of Steven's mouth sounded startlingly close to official I.R.A. dogma.

Steven took a right onto Northumberland Street. Just as Keely was about to try to calm her friend, she was surprised to see the O'Shaunessey brothers walk directly across the street, fifty yards ahead of their car, into their apartment building. Seeing them wasn't unlikely but what struck her as odd was that each brother was carrying an empty beer keg. She knew the kegs were empty because of the ease with which each brother carried his with one hand. The only man she knew that could carry a full one in that manner was big Kevin. It seemed odd to her that the O'Shaunessey boys were bringing empty aluminum beer kegs *into* their apartment building. It was even more noteworthy that they would be doing so at nearly three a.m.

Strange boys, those ones, she thought. Once past the O'Shaunessey brothers, she turned her head forward and said, "I wonder what the O'Shaunessey brothers are doing this time of night with empty beer kegs?"

"What are you talking about?" asked Steven although she knew he had to have seen them. They had crossed the street directly ahead of them ten seconds earlier.

"Michael and Padraig...they just walked right in front of us. You know, the two guys carrying the beer kegs?"

"I didn't see anybody carrying beer kegs."

Her heart sunk as she began to open her mouth.

"Are you sure you want to throw in with that lot?" asked Keely with a temerity to her tone never present in the years she had known Steven.

37

"Are you sure you want to be asking?" was his reply.

Two wordless blocks later, Steven pulled to a stop in front of the Kennedy family house.

"Thanks for the lift," she said to Steven as she closed the passenger-side door.

"See you tomorrow," was all he said before pulling from the curb and speeding off into the night. She watched him drive off with a sense of longing for less fearful times. Retrieving her keys from her bag, Keely felt a wave of exhaustion run through her. Bone-weary, as her mother, Siobhan, would put it.

Twenty minutes later, as Keely brushed her hair, she glanced over at the airline ticket on the dresser. The conversation she had with her parents two months earlier seemed unreal as she ran the brush through her raven hair, until she glanced back at the ticket.

"Sweetheart, I really don't like what's happening around us and I don't know when things will get better. I mean it's really becoming dangerous. People are just disappearing and I know some of the people involved do their drinking at O'Neill's. It would be so easy to get caught up in all this mess. Won't you please do this for your dear old dad?"

"But America is on the other side of the world. I like it just fine, right here. Besides, I don't even have a visa."

Liam had sighed and reached into a drawer, extracting the visa he had applied for in her name. Seeing it, Keely knew her father was not simply asking her to leave Belfast.

"Damon and Erin say they would love to have you stay with them. Their boys could use a good influence like you. Please, Love. I really want you as far from this mess as you can be until things get better."

Two weeks after that conversation, with a heavy heart, Keely had gone to Kevin and given her notice. Tears had formed in Kevin's eyes when she gave him the news but after a moment, he told her that it really was for the best and that she could have her old job back whenever she returned from across the pond.

As she pulled the brush the last few passes through her hair, staring into her dresser mirror, Keely reflected on the talk with her long-time employer and friend a month ago. A pang of sorrow erupted from her heart as she realized she had only two more weeks at O'Neill's Pub. A minute later, as she brushed her teeth and prepared for bed, Keely tried to quell the sadness with optimistic thoughts about what might lay ahead. Her favorite uncle Damon and his family lived in the United States and had offered her a chance to come and stay with them and help out with their children. They lived in a place that sounded pretty, called Riverside—a western suburb of the city of Chicago. Praying the night prayers she always said just before bed, Keely tried to give her fear of leaving Ireland over to God. Her mother was a deeply spiritual woman and had passed her love of the comfort of prayer on to Keely since she was a little girl. It was as essential to her peace of mind as the air she breathed. Although she was ambivalent about moving seven thousand miles away from home, she knew her dad only wanted what was best for her. Besides, she thought, she could come back when all the ugliness ended.

    It couldn't drag on too much longer.

39

Cockpit of C-141, Call Sign: MAC 60192
250 Nautical Miles Northeast of Hawaii
Altitude: Flight Level Three-Three-Zero
1355 Hours Local Time
Monday, May 2nd, 1969

Chapter Three

Captain Walsh paid close attention to Lieutenant Lee's inputs on the controls as his student proceeded through the beginning stages of the descent checklist. Lee completed his final radio call to the over-water section of the FAA and switched over to the local VHF frequency that all aircraft used to communicate with Honolulu Control.

"Honolulu Center, Honolulu Center, MAC 60192 is with you at flight level three-three-zero."

Across the VHF, the voice of FAA Senior Air Controller Johnny Ho replied, "Roger MAC 60192, this is Honolulu Center."

The man sitting at the Honolulu Center console, who had answered the hail from the inbound Air Force jet, was a thirty-five-year-old native Hawaiian named Johnny Ho. He was a man extremely proud of his Hawaiian heritage. Johnny's mother was able to trace the family blood lines back to King Kamayamaya. Johnny loved everything about his pacific island paradise with the single exception of the Japanese tourists who had been traveling in increasing numbers to the island over the past ten years. Although a principled man in many areas of his life, Johnny still held on to the dark resentment toward the Japanese for their

40

bombing of his homeland. Johnny remembered in vivid detail when he was seven years old and the planes with strange red spots painted on them screamed across the skies, the sounds of the bombs detonating like thunder. His father had been a civilian clerk at the Army airfield. Some Army officers came to the house four days after the attack and Johnny could still remember his mother's shrieks and cries at the news that his father was dead.

Johnny sat at his duty station within what he and the other controllers referred to as the "mole hole." The room was darkened to improve the visibility of the radar screens. The only sound was the low humming of the air conditioning unit. He had just started his shift, having taken over for his colleague, Carl Dishneau. Looking over the screen, Johnny noted the traffic was fairly light then with only nine blips on his radar. One of those blips was the inbound Air Force Starlifter that had just checked in. Another radar contact was a Japan Air Lines Boeing 747 that should be check in any moment.

Japan Air Lines Flight 311, inbound to Honolulu International Airport the same time MAC 60192 was preparing for final approach to Hickam Air Force Base, was piloted by a blonde-haired, blue-eyed former surfer from California named Captain Tim Gross. Sitting to his right in the co-pilot seat was an accomplished, skilled aviator named Yoshi Okamura. Although it would appear that nothing remarkable was occurring in the flight deck, that day a very significant milestone in aviation was occurring. It was the first time since the end of World War Two that a Japanese man had sat in the front row of an aircraft in flight. Yoshi wasn't the captain yet, but things were looking up. The driving ambition in Yoshi's life was to one day sit in the left seat as the captain of a jetliner. It had been an amazingly difficult path to take just to get to the co-pilot seat. Due to a provision of surrender agreed to at the end of World War II, absolutely no Japanese were permitted to train as pilots of any sort for a minimum of twenty years. In 1965, when the moratorium

41

expired, hundreds of Japanese men had eagerly lined up to be accepted to pilot training. Yoshi Okamura had been one of the first ones hired by the airline and had easily ascended through the training and qualifications. He had finished in the top five percent in his class and had been honored to be assigned to the largest, most advanced aircraft in the JAL fleet: the gargantuan Boeing 747, commonly and appropriately referred to as a "Jumbo." Until that day, all of his time in the flight deck was spent as the engineer or second officer.

Never overtly complaining about the still lingering prejudice against his people throughout the pilot ranks of the airline, Yoshi silently abhorred the terms of the surrender of a war he had nothing to do with. With supreme discipline, Yoshi had never vocalized his distaste for the ability of the United States and the allied powers dictating what either he or his country was or was not permitted to do. Yoshi had been a child during the war and always hated the penalties imposed on his generation for the mistakes of the previous one. Above all of the difficulties Yoshi endured, the most infuriating was the condescending tone he almost always received from most airline captains. Captain Gross, however, was a welcome variation from that theme and always a model of professionalism and courtesy. Yoshi was quietly elated whenever he saw on the flight schedule that he would be flying with Captain Gross. Others however, almost without exception, treated Yoshi more like an indentured servant than the talented, hard-working aviator he was. Yoshi always conducted himself in a dignified manner toward pilots that possessed a bigoted view of him, but with supreme effort. A deeply spiritual man, he prayed at the Meiji Shrine often for the ability to overcome his hardships when at home in Tokyo.

The Japan Air Lines aircraft, with two hundred and three passengers aboard, was just passing into the range of the radio signal used by Honolulu Control. Yoshi switched to the Honolulu Control frequency, looked over at Captain Gross, and instantly knew his captain was cognizant of the magnitude of the moment as he beamed with pride at his long-time colleague from the pilot's seat. Yoshi keyed his microphone, and proudly transmitted his first official approach call to a control center in his

42

career.

"Hono-ru-ru cen-tah, hono-ru-ru cen-tah, Japan Air *tree-one-one* is with you at *fright reber tree-tree-zeh-roh."*

In the control room, Johnny's eyes went wide. Ho had never, during his entire career, even dreamt of hearing a Japanese voice on the radio. In a half-second his shock subsided and, unfortunately for Yoshi, Johnny's resentment toward all Japanese overrode his sensibilities. Knowing there would be a serious reprimand for what was on the tip of his tongue, but quickly calculating that he was too senior to face any real consequences, Johnny keyed his microphone and responded, "Roger Japan Air *Tree*-One-One, this is *Hon-o-RU-RU cen-tah.*"

In the cockpit of MAC 60192, Walsh, Hightower, and Turner roared with laughter with one exception. Lee looked around at the others in the cockpit. In moments, the three other crewmembers were nearly in tears. Lee wanted to say something to admonish the others but knew it would not be taken well from the newest guy on the crew. Still, he was not impressed at the laughter from seemingly professional aviators, especially at the expense of a fellow pilot. It wasn't that Lee lacked the ability to enjoy a good joke, but the values instilled in him by his parents had shaped his character such that he intensely disapproved of jokes at other people's expense. The situation deteriorated further when pilots in almost all of the other seven aircraft within radio range momentarily keyed their microphones to share their laughter. The guffaws and howling transmitted over the normally ultra-professional frequency increased when Yoshi lost his temper and furiously broadcast, "You know I can't say *Hon-o-ru-ru!"*

The laughter finally subsided and Lee was given clearance to descend to four thousand feet for his approach to Hickam.

Over the interphone, Walsh broadcast, "Sergeant Sloan, uniform-of-the-day, please."

From Sloan's station down in the cargo area, he responded, "Clean-dirties, sir."

Curtin also checked in, "Roger, clean-dirties."

Lee looked over at Walsh with a look of pure confusion. As he began to key his microphone to ask, Walsh said, "Sergeant

43

Sloan has been assigned the important responsibility, among his other duties as loadmaster, also the uniform-of-the-day NCO."

Sergeant Turner sitting at the engineer's panel and grinning, chimed in over the interphone, "Sir, as this information isn't in any manual, I'm not violating any rules of check rides to brief you on that particular responsibility. "Cleans" are flight suits that have been washed since they were last worn. "Clean-dirties" have only been worn once and "dirty-dirties" have been worn twice. "Goatskins" are anything after that. Seeing as how the United States Air Force has graciously issued us only three flight suits, and the captain doesn't plan to factor any time to do laundry on this mission, we'll all smell the same on each leg if we're wearing the same uniform."

Lee simply shook his head and smiled. Having time to do laundry was something he hadn't given any thought to until then. Pushing his right earphone off and leaning across the throttles toward Walsh so he could privately ask a question, Lee gestured to his instructor pilot sitting next to him to do the same. Walsh quickly lifted his left headphone. Over the sound of the engine noise, Lee asked, "Sir, do you mean to say that a junior tech sergeant is able to tell not only other sergeants that outrank him but also a lieutenant, captain and a major to wear dirty flight suits?"

Walsh smiled, returned his interphone headset to its original position and transmitted, "Co-pilot, navigator."

Major Hightower, responded, "Navigator, co-pilot."

"Did you copy the uniform-of-the-day, sir?"

"Roger that. Clean-dirties."

Just before turning on final approach to Hickam, Lee reflected on the communication between the tower and the JAL flight moments earlier. Knowing what he was about to ask might not go over well, Lee still felt compelled to ask, "You think the guy in that JAL bird is going to make a big deal about the radio chatter and everyone laughing at him?"

Keeping his eyes on instruments for a moment longer, Walsh then glanced over at his protégé.

"You know, I have to admit the laughter was pretty unprofessional and kind of inappropriate. I can't say I've ever

44

heard anything like that myself."

That was all that was said about the incident while in flight, but Walsh's conscience was unsettled by what Lee said. Had it been his communications to a tower that had been treated like that, he would have personally paid a visit to the tower after landing. *Yeah, it was inappropriate,* he though.

Due to a strong crosswind, the landing was particularly firm at Hickam. As Lee engaged the thrust reversers to slow the jet, Sergeant Turner quipped, "We've apparently *arrived*."

If the sergeant had been any less senior in rank and had not had such a familiar working relationship with the captain, he would have never uttered a veiled insult, even at a junior officer. Air Force jargon referred to particularly rough touch-downs as 'arrivals' as opposed to 'landings'.

Once the bags had been transferred to the bus and the officers had closed the flight plan at Hickam's Base Operations, Walsh turned to his student and said, "Lieutenant, we have two choices here. We can debrief formally here or we can grab a shower and meet at the main bar for a beer and debrief informally. I'd personally opt for plan B because I've got some things I'd like to go over with you about the first leg."

"Eighteen-thirty good for you, Captain?" asked Lee.

"Roger that."

Walsh freshened up with hot shower and changed into some jeans and one of the two Hawaiian shirts he packed, Arriving at the main bar on base twenty minutes later, Walsh walked in and surveyed the place. There was an unusually high concentration of attractive women in uniform in the place but it made sense that the pretty ones would find a way to get stationed in paradise. Across the room, Walsh smiled when he saw Lee, beer in hand, standing and chatting with undoubtedly the most exceptionally attractive female captain in the room; possibly on the island. Captain Jennifer Moret worked in the office of the commanding general. Noting that several other officers had looks of sheer envy on their faces as she talked to the young lieutenant, Walsh thought with a measure of crew pride, *I've got a real Don Juan on my bird*. He wondered how difficult it would be to pry his student away from the woman and get down to the business of reviewing Lee's performance during the first leg of their mission.

Much to his shock, there was no difficulty whatsoever.

"Captain, how are you this evening?" asked Lee, with a more enthusiastic tone than Walsh ever expected, given the company Lee was in.

"Just fine, Lieutenant."

"Are you ready to go over your notes, sir?"

Glancing at the beautiful, raven-haired officer glaring at him, Walsh could tell from her expression that she was barely tolerating the interruption. Looking back at Lee, he couldn't imagine why, but it looked like the lieutenant was actually relieved to see him. Had the situation been reversed, Walsh wasn't certain he'd even acknowledge Lee, let alone break off a conversation with the most desirable woman in the room.

"We can postpone the debriefing until later if you'd care to, Lieutenant. I wouldn't want to interrupt…"

"No, sir, I'm quite alright with doing things on your schedule."

The instructor pilot watched in total amazement as his student turned to the woman and said, "Ma'am, if you'll excuse me, I have some business to attend to with my IP here."

Her look of incredulity gave clear indication that she wasn't going to take the brush-off well. First, looking at Walsh with an expression of contempt and then back to the young lieutenant she had had plans for later, Captain Jennifer Moret said, with a totally icy tone, "Suit yourself." Turning on her heel, she muttered, "Gentlemen," and strode back to the bar under the watchful eyes of every man in the room.

After taking a seat at the nearest table, and feeling the eyes of numerous men in the room on them, Walsh had to ask.

"Lieutenant, please tell me that I'm not flying with someone possessing mental deficiencies. That woman was apparently the reigning Ms. Louisiana before she joined the Air Force."

Looking at his instructor squarely in the eye, Lee said, "She came on a bit strongly, sir. Honestly, she just wasn't my type."

"Yeah, well the way she was looking at you, it was pretty clear you were *her* type. I mean what would the harm be in having a pretty spectacular night with a woman of that caliber? It's the military. This is Hawaii. One night doesn't mean you have to marry the girl!"

Lieutenant Lee just shrugged his shoulders and smiled. Walsh knew the lieutenant possessed some obvious gifts that would attract women. Why his student had decided to pass up an undoubtedly sure thing was beyond his capacity to understand. The thought did occur, however, that Lee's shoot-down of the former beauty queen would be the stuff of legend among his crew. The almost inconceivable incident would definitely be something to talk about in the cockpit on the next flight. After ordering a beer from a waiter, Walsh flipped open his notepad. Over the next hour, the two men talked over areas where Lee had done well at the controls and areas where he could use improvement. The areas where he had done well far exceeded those that needed work but Jack still had much to learn.

Once the debriefing was completed, and after some limited talk about college football, both men stood and began to make their way to the door. As they passed the bar, Captain Moret was engaged in conversation with a confident-looking lieutenant colonel. It was easy to see the former beauty queen look away from her current admirer and directly at Lee. With a raise of her eyebrows and shrug of her shoulders, she sent the wordless message to the young lieutenant that he had been given his chance.

Amazingly, Lee didn't even acknowledge her.

Outside, Walsh stopped and said, "Hey Lieutenant, what's the deal? Are you insane or just insanely picky?"

Turning around to face his instructor, Lee replied, "I wasn't raised to hop in the sack whenever the opportunity presented itself. Yeah, she was beautiful but it's just not me, sir."

Walsh heard something in his student he truly admired on a deep level: real conviction.

"It was actually a good thing you showed up when you did, sir."

"Why's that, Lieutenant?"

"Because she was quite convincing and I never said I was perfect."

**Travis Air Force Base
David Grant Medical Center
San Jose, California
1732 hours
Monday, May 2nd, 1969**

Chapter Four

M ajor (Dr.) Erika Jensen walked from the airbase medical center toward her red Corvette Stingray in the physicians' lot. As she inserted her key in the door, she became aware of two pilots standing by another car, looking her way very approvingly. The sports car was one of the few extravagances in her life and, had her father not bought it for her as gift for completing medical school, she would have never purchased the powerful vehicle for herself, yet she enjoyed it thoroughly. Slipping into the seat, she started the car and enjoyed the feeling of its rumbling engine, the throaty sound turning the heads of several airmen and officers walking to their own cars in the lot. Smiling, she pulled from her spot and drove past the two gawking captains without as much as a nod. She remembered one of them having made a fairly juvenile, drunken pass at her one night at the officer's club a few months back.

"So, gorgeous, can I get you a drink?" the junior officer had asked, oblivious to the fact that a fresh martini had sat directly in front of her.

"Gee, Captain, I'm flattered but I already have one," she

politely replied.

"Well, why not have another one with me? I'll make sure you'll enjoy it."

She smiled slightly while trying to formulate just the right thing to say to the overly-confident, boorish offer spoken with an abundance of alcohol on his breath.

"Aw…come on, Major, I'm not a typical hot shot pilot. I'm a… goood guy...I can tell you like me already."

With a smile that would melt glaciers, Major Jensen responded, "If your approaches on the runways are as good as the one you're failing miserably at right now, I'm surprised you're not dead yet. Do your career a favor, slick. An about-face and double-time to anywhere than here will be your flight status' saving grace.

"But…"

"Captain, as your flight surgeon, I'd like to draw your attention to the fact that excessive drinking is just the sort of thing that can, and will, clip the wings of a strapping young gent as yourself. Is there anything else you require of me, *Captain?"*

She rolled her eyes as she relived that unfortunate exchange between her and one of the two pilots as she drove past. Being hit on was a common experience with her looks but she wished that every man that tried to make her acquaintance didn't act like a predictable child.

Erika stood five feet, ten inches tall, with high cheekbones, piercing blue eyes, and a statuesque figure that had turned heads since the summer she turned thirteen. Those attributes could have guaranteed a career in the glamour world of modeling but Erika had always been enamored with a higher purpose. The idea of helping people called to her soul more than runways and vapid conversations in a world of self-love. Erika was blessed with a genius I.Q. that she had applied to graduate top of her medical school class. The one man she admired most in her life was her father, Dr. Erik Jensen, the chief of cardiovascular surgery at Northwestern Medical Center in Chicago where she had grown up. Erika's proudest moment ever was the one where she took the Hippocratic Oath and received her degree from medical school as her father and mother beamed with pride from the crowd.

49

Throughout her life, Erika had many notable accomplishments but that one stood out in her mind as her favorite.

Erika's introduction to the idea of a military career had come during her emergency medicine rotation at Northwestern Medical Center, when an old friend of her father's came for dinner one night. Sitting in the formal dining room within their home in the North Shore suburb of Glenview, Colonel Peter Jacques had come to dinner at the invitation of her father while in town for a medical conference. The colonel had been a classmate of Dr. Jensen's back in their days at Harvard Medical School and was currently commanding officer of the First Aerospace Medical Squadron at Langley Air Force Base in Virginia.

Erika's father had run into his old classmate when he had given a presentation on a new medical device he was working on patenting at a conference in Washington D.C. After having dinner and a few drinks, reliving some of their wilder experiences at university, Colonel Jacques had promised to come for dinner if ever in Chicago. The colonel had made good on the promise and that dinner would alter the course of Erika's life forever.

"Colonel, how do you like being a military doctor?" asked Erika as she passed the mashed potatoes to the man with bushy eyebrows crowning eyes that radiated exceptional intelligence."

With an accent that immediately identified him as being from *Bas-tan,* the colonel smiled and said, "You know, I'm glad you asked. It's really exciting medicine. You are responsible for the health and well being of the best aviators in the world and you make a contribution to your country at the same time."

With hands raised in protest, Erika's father said, "Easy now, Peter. I don't need my baby girl being swept away from Northwestern into the arms of Uncle Sam!"

"Pardon me, Daddy, but are you referring to this twenty-six-year-old baby girl who was top of her class and can stabilize a gunshot wound blindfolded?" she had retorted with an impish smile.

Sighing, her father had come to grips with the idea that his little girl was an adult, but he reacted in the manner all fathers always did when coming to terms with that fact.

"You'll always be my little girl, princess."

A few weeks later, at their customary Sunday family dinner, Erika had broached the subject of possibly serving in the military. After lengthy discussion and debate over the pros and cons of such a career move, Erika made an appointment with the Air Force recruiter. Three weeks later, Erika was indoctrinated into the United States Air Force and after completing basic training, was immediately sent for an advanced seven-week aerospace medicine program at Brooks Air Force Base.

Erika's first duty station had been Travis Air Force Base where she had been for almost two years tending to all manner of infirmary that airmen suffered. The ailments ran the gamut from emergency traumas to ingrown toenails. Some of the airmen returned from overseas missions with complaints of an embarrassing nature and she always inwardly groaned when they would fumble and stumble over the words to describe exactly how they came to have the clap. One of the things that had really begun to concern her, however, was the incidences of acute alcoholism and drug usage that she was seeing in startling numbers. What was more frustrating for her was her total inability to reach those patients. The substance abusers had a fairly predictable pattern. They would show up in her emergency room a few times for detoxification treatment after being ordered by their commanding officer or being arrested by the Security Police. Shortly after, the tough cases would completely disappear when they did something to get themselves discharged, jailed, or, in three sad cases the past year, take their own life.

"People always try to find ways to dull the pain in war," Colonel Stevens, the commander of the 60th Aerospace Squadron had told her when she had voiced her concern in a staff officer meeting that afternoon. She had read him the report of the charge nurse on duty that attended a young airman that overdosed on pills and liquor the prior shift. The boy currently lay in a coma.

"It's just so frustrating. Is there anything we can do to really help these people?"

"Honestly, Dr. Jensen, in my experience the answer is next to nothing. I don't see a lot of druggies and alkies take to medical treatment. I can't really say why. All we can really focus on is whether or not they are able to do their jobs without jeopardizing themselves or the people around them. Sometimes there have been some lucky ones that take to the A.A. stuff, but I've given up trying to cure them. I don't have the time, the patience, or the resources to do it. With that one particular affliction alone, it is our sole responsibility to gauge whether these airmen and officers are medically fit to serve."

She hated hearing that but somehow knew her commanding officer and mentor was right.

Driving out of the main entrance to Travis and onto Airbase Parkway, the sun glinted off of the ring on her right hand and it brought a smile to her face. Erika always wore the gold ring with the family crest that her father had handcrafted for her sixteenth birthday. The elder Dr. Jensen was quite a renaissance man, being an accomplished violinist as well as a bench jeweler. With the hands of a surgeon, he was very skilled in creating, in his little workshop down in the basement, pieces of jewelry for the two women in his life. He had discovered jewelry making in an undergraduate elective college course and, with superior hand-eye coordination and patience, had become an artisan skilled enough to make work for the finest jewelers in the world had he been so inclined. Dr. Jensen's position at Northwestern University Hospital demanded a majority of his time but he still found a few hours here and there to craft little expressions of love for his girls.

Glancing at the ring, Erika admired its intricate lattice-work patterning on the shank and the delicate embellishments that had been created by fusing tiny gold wire to its surfaces in amazingly rich patterns. Both her and her mother's jewelry boxes housed several beautiful pieces he had created over the years. Dr. Jensen liked to say that if he didn't have the patience and hand-eye coordination to make a few shiny trinkets for his girls, he had no business opening up the chests of his patients and trying to piece together their delicate heart muscles, veins, and arteries. Over the past three years, he had been working diligently on a tiny, flexible, tubular device he invented in his workshop that would, theoretically, be able to structurally stabilize damaged veins and arteries. She made a mental note to ask him how the FDA approval process was grinding along when she called him on

52

Sunday. She always called her dad on Sundays.

After two miles on Airbase Parkway, Erika took a right onto North Texas Street and a half mile later pulled into her condominium complex. In ten short minutes, she changed out of her uniform into some light cotton slacks and a colorful paisley top. Just as she was putting the finishing touches on her look, her doorbell rang.

"Hey Erika, you look amazing!" said Captain Wendy Riley who was in charge of the emergency nursing staff at the medical center and had been the first person Erika had developed a friendship with when she had come to Travis.

"Thanks! That dress is so cute and you look awesome too. I'll be ready in just a second so just make your self comfortable."

Wendy was an intense woman with straight, dark hair, intelligent eyes, athletic figure from her five-mile daily runs, and pixie-like attractive looks. Despite her aesthetic attractiveness, any man who attempted to approach her was met with a response that ranged from smug superiority to unbridled hostility. Unapproachable was the look she cultivated, with a wardrobe of primarily black items in her civilian dress choices. Wendy was a walking example of hell having no such fury as a woman scorned.

"So did you go take a look at that A1C that the SPs brought in at 0500 hours?" asked Erika as she came down the stairs from her bedroom, referring to the comatose kid lying in intensive care. Thank God some of his buddies living in the same building had called the SPs when they did.

"You mean the kid that smelled like he pumped whisky through his veins? Yeah, Dr. Dresner worked on him when he first came in. A belly full of booze is just stupidity but that kid had a bottle of pills for a chaser. That was no accident," responded Wendy.

"Yeah, well, according to statements from his buddies, he had been drinking like that since yesterday afternoon. If he pulls out of the coma, he'll probably live but you're right; his report is being written up as a suicide attempt. We stabilized him but he was darn close. That kid got lucky his buddies called the SPs when they did. Another twenty minutes and I'm sure we would be burying him," exclaimed Erika.

53

"Did anybody on your shift find out why he was on a mission to check out like that?" asked Wendy

"According to the SPs, his buddies said his girlfriend sent him *the* letter."

"Oh, that's just ridiculous," said Wendy with a tone of disgust. "The kid's going to get discharged and have a lousy service record as a result of this stunt. I mean if these boys don't get the letter, they didn't have a girlfriend when they joined. I just don't understand how someone could get to such a dark place from a breakup. Nobody is worth that "

"Never truer words said, sister. It's taken you some time but *you* are getting back on the horse again. You could be sitting in your apartment trying to drink yourself to death. Now if we can just get you to lower the phaser shields a bit," said Erika with a smile, trying to bring a bit of lightness back to their conversation. Erika knew Wendy immensely enjoyed the new science fiction television show, Star Trek, which was quickly becoming a cultural phenomenon. Borrowing from its vernacular was an attempt to win a smile from her.

It worked.

With a grin that Erika was happy to see, Wendy said, "Well, when he-who-shall-remain-unnamed sent me that letter telling me he had fallen for that hussy at the bank, I probably could have used a few belts of whatever that kid was drinking but somehow I knew that wouldn't do any good."

"You're right. It wouldn't. So let's go and have a bit of fun tonight."

"Agreed. How about that new place on Maxwell? I heard they have a decent band and saw there is an outdoor patio when I drove by."

"You got it. Let me grab my bag. Just promise me one thing?"

"What's that?"

"No phaser shields. Just Wendy being the Wendy I know."

"I promise, sister."

**Hickam Air Force Base
Operations Building
Oahu Island, Hawaii
1422 Hours Local Time
Wednesday, May 4th, 1969**

Chapter Five

Captain Walsh returned to the fight planning room after submitting all the flight plan paperwork to the duty officer. Enduring four hours of what aviators referred to as ramp time, meaning sitting around waiting for something on their aircraft to be repaired, had left him in a testy mood.

"Is it possible that the tire could have waited?" asked Lee.

"If Sergeant Turner said it was badly out of limits, it needed changing. Your enlisted guys are riding on the same jet you are and they don't hate ramp time any less. So if your guys ever tell you there's some issue that makes your bird a no-go, you *always* listen to them, understood?"

"Yes, sir," replied Lee, wishing he'd never asked and making a mental note about advice from his enlisted flight crew.

Just then, Sergeant Sloan walked into the room and said, "Sirs, the maintenance guys say the jet will be ready in fifteen minutes. We've already drilled the bags aboard."

"Thanks, Sergeant. That's the best news I've heard all day," replied Major Hightower.

Walsh caught his navigator's eye for a fraction of a second, winked, and with a false tone of relief added, "Roger that, nav. I was hoping to get into Wake City by no later than 21:00 hours at the latest. You know how wide open that place gets."

Hightower, immediately catching on to what Walsh meant, played along perfectly and added, "Oh, yeah. I really hope that blonde Pan Am stewardess from last time is laying over. That would be just perfect."

Sergeant Sloan looked at both officers with a perplexed look. Not wanting to overstep his boundaries while addressing senior officers, he hesitated for another moment and then said, "I'm sorry, sirs, but I thought Wake Island was just a rock in the middle of the ocean west of everything and east of nothing."

Walsh looked at Lee for an instant and, winking so the sergeant couldn't see, turned to the young enlisted man and answered, "Negative, Sergeant. Wake City is the Las Vegas of the Pacific but we try to keep that under our hats so the brass don't break up a good thing. We'll give you a good look on our approach. That is if we ever get out of here."

The young sergeant from Georgia searched the three officers' faces for any sign of deception. Seeing none, a big smile grew. The idea of exploring yet another wild spot while traveling across the globe on Uncle Sam's dime brought a wave of excitement to the young airman.

"Just you wait, Sergeant. We'll show you a time on Wake Island you'll be telling your grandchildren about," said Walsh.

Major Hightower, reaching over and firmly clasping the impressionable sergeant's shoulder added, "We'll hit the ground running, close our flight plan, and get to our quarters at warp speed to clean up. Oh, before I forget, Sergeant, I'd suggest wearing your class-A dress shirt and necktie. For some reason, the stewardesses like guys in ties."

"Are you guys for real?" asked the wide-eyed boy of twenty-four who wore an expression most similar to that worn by children on Christmas morning.

"Yeah, Sergeant, and don't worry if you don't hit a home run with the stews. We'll show you a few of the wilder places to get entertainment you just don't find stateside. Even if you don't partake of that particular type of fun, it's a blast to watch!"

Sergeant Sloan looked like he had just won the lottery.

If it were true, none of that sounded the least bit appealing to Lee but he sensed that things didn't add up. As he did during the incident with the Japanese Air Lines pilot, he opted to keep his tongue.

"I'm definitely going to try to get some shuteye on the leg to Wake. I'm not all that tired but I want to be ready for this!" exclaimed Sloan as he turned to leave. With that, the young airman left the flight planning room with a mile-wide grin across his face.

Barely suppressing his own laughter, Major Hightower peeked around the door jamb. As soon as he was certain the sergeant was out of earshot, he turned back to Walsh and Lee and began to howl. "You really set the hook hard, Captain. That kid ate it up like candy!"

Between choking fits of laughter, he managed to say, "Yeah….He'll be mad as the devil….but it will….be worth it to…..see the look on his face!"

Lee's suspicion was confirmed. "There really is no Wake City, is there?"

"Tell him, nav!"

Hightower glanced around the door jamb one more time to insure the sergeant wasn't within earshot and said, "Wake City is a time-honored custom we old-timers victimize all the new guys with."

"I gathered."

Walsh pulled a map of their destination from the collection of maps on the shelves and laid it out for Lee's inspection. With the tip of a pencil, Walsh pointed out the airfield and another feature on the island.

"As you can see, the island is shaped like a boomerang. Right here, on this end, the island is covered by a huge antenna array. The antennas have an impressive collection of lights illuminating them at night and when the sun goes down, that end of the island looks like the Las Vegas Strip from the air."

"Yeah, we'll call the sergeant up to the jump seat on approach and really get him salivating right before landing," added Major Hightower as he began to regain the ability to talk coherently.

With intermittent barks of laughter, Walsh continued.

"Truthfully, Lieutenant, the action on Wake Island is slightly less than zero. No airlines ever stay on Wake. Logic dictates no stewardesses either. There is, however, a little saloon known as Drifters Reef that is shared by both officers and enlisted men. Sergeants Turner and Curtin are old pros at this gag. They know the drill. When they get to their quarters, they'll hog the latrine to ensure Sloan is the last one to clean up and make himself beautiful for the stews in his perfect class-A uniform. He'll be in uniform alright, but out-of-uniform for Wake Island, right, nav?"

"Precisely. The uniform-of-the-day on Wake is always tee-shirt, shorts, and flip-flops. The last thing Sloan will see as he heads for the shower will be the other two sergeants ironing their dress shirts and ties. Once Sloan hits the shower, Turner and Curtin will jump into the appropriate evening attire and zip over to the Reef. When they hit the door, they'll tell everyone that they have a new guy heading for Wake City. Once Sloan hits the Reef in his spiffy dress shirt, his facial expression will make all the effort involved with this admittedly juvenile prank worthwhile." Major Hightower, having already judged that Lee seemed to be wound a bit tightly, watched him for his reaction. After the shoot-down of the former beauty queen at the O-club the night before, the navigator had begun to have more than just a passing concern about the newest member of the crew.

The corners of Lee's mouth began to upturn and in moments, he was laughing almost as uproariously as the other two officers had been moments earlier.

"Yeah, don't feel so bad for the kid, Lieutenant. He'll drink for free the entire night."

"A fair tradeoff, Captain!"

Walsh and Hightower gave each other a high-five, laughing again. It wasn't that the joke had gotten any funnier but their concerns about the new lieutenant being a total stick-in-the-mud had been alleviated.

On the crew transportation bus, Sergeant Sloan was regaled by fictitious story after story from Sergeants Turner and Curtin about wild nights they never had in a den of debauchery that didn't exist. The three officers put on an Oscar award-winning performance, feigning offense to the locker-room talk they were hearing. Lee even added, "Sergeants Turner and Curtin, I will *not* hear one more word about your amoral conduct. You gentlemen are not exhibiting an ounce of leadership for Sergeant Sloan whom you are entrusted to train on this mission."

Attaboy, Lieutenant, thought Walsh.

After arriving at the aircraft, Walsh and Lee did a walk-around check of the plane, and satisfied, climbed aboard and up the ladder into the flight deck. Squeezing past Hightower at the navigator station and Turner at the engineer's panel, the two officers strapped themselves into their seats. Good pilots got into their seats but great ones strapped a plane to their backsides. Walsh was of the latter variety and, based on his student's performance on the mission up to that point, he was of the opinion that Lee had the potential to achieve greatness.

The flight from Hickam to Wake Island was just under eight hours. Crossing the International Date Line halfway to their destination put MAC 60192 on final approach at 2015 hours, local time on May 5th.

Walsh depressed the curved interphone radio button on his yoke and broadcast, "Pilot, loadmaster."

An excited voice responded, "Loadmaster, pilot"

"Please come forward to the jump seat for a moment."

"Roger that!"

In half the normal time than would be expected for the sergeant to make his way from the cargo hold to the cockpit, Sergeant Sloan appeared with a wide grin on his face.

"See it out there, on the northern tip of the island?" asked Walsh as he pointed to the glowing mass of radio equipment several miles off.

"Sure do, Captain! That's Wake City, huh?"

"Roger that, Sergeant. I just wanted to let you get a bird's-eye view."

With saucer-wide eyes, the sergeant looked at the glowing lights and several vignettes of what might await him flashed across his mind. Seeing the excitement on the sergeant's face, Walsh was certain that if not for the confined space, the boy would be jumping up and down.

"Go ahead and prepare for landing Sergeant. We just wanted to give you a sneak-preview," said Sergeant Turner from the engineer's panel.

"Yes, sir!" replied Sergeant Sloan as he scrambled back down to his position to prepare for landing.

"Alright, Lieutenant, look fifteen hundred yards down the runway to gauge your altitude. You can't really feel it by looking over the nose," said Walsh to coach his student. The lieutenant's landing at Hickam had been acceptable but slightly firm. Following the captain's advice, Lee made his best landing yet and smoothly engaged the thrust reversers.

Lieutenant Lee taxied the giant aircraft into its assigned parking spot. After turning the jet over to the ground crew, the men hopped aboard the transport and rode the short distance to their quarters. Sergeant Sloan, grinning ear to ear, led the three enlisted men off the bus when it stopped in front of the enlisted quarters. Following behind, Sergeants Turner and Curtin gave discreet thumbs-ups to the three officers.

Thirty minutes later, Major Hightower and Lieutenant Lee emerged from their quarters. Walsh wore a loud, primarily red silk Hawaiian shirt, Bermuda shorts, and the requisite flip-flops. Lee, not having packed anything as colorful simply wore a Notre Dame Athletics tee-shirt in substitute. Waiting for them outside was Major Hightower wearing his own yellow silk Hawaiian shirt featuring a collection of multi-colored parrots. The three officers walked across the road to the unimpressive building all seasoned aviators familiar with Wake Island called 'The Reef'.

"We'll have to see my tailor and augment your wardrobe for the next trip through here, Lieutenant."

Lee, looking at the attire of the other two officers, actually felt underdressed in his grey tee-shirt with block stenciled letters on it. Enjoying the unspoken message of acceptance in that statement, he just smiled and answered, "Roger that, Captain."

The Drifter's Reef was a single-story, single-room building built for a drinking, gambling, and, most importantly, story-telling. The last emergency someone had in a plane was the number one most popular topic. Women were a close second. As in any contest of testosterone-fueled storytelling between men in bars, one-upsmanship always was the main pastime. The interior of The Reef was seventy-five feet square. Along one wall, the bar ran the entire length of the building. The opposing wall was floor-to-ceiling windows and during daytime, offered a soothing view of the Pacific Ocean. Twenty small wooden tables were spaced throughout the place where numerous officers and airmen enjoyed glasses of beer, hamburgers, and enthusiastically lied while playing a popular game known as 'liar's dice'. Three regulation pool tables, constantly surrounded by players, sat along the back wall furthest from the entrance. As the three officers entered through the screen door at the front, they took in the cacophony of cracking pool balls, loud conversation, tinkling ice, rolling dice, and flying cards. The place smelled like every bar in the world, with beer and cigarette smoke being the primary olfactory notes. All three men headed for the bar, paid for their beers, and headed directly toward the nearest table. As soon as they sat down, Major Hightower saw somebody he knew and excused himself.

"So, Jack, what do you think of the hottest little spot in the Pacific?"

Being addressed by his given name by his instructor pilot surprised the lieutenant.

"Uh, well, Captain, I…"

"Hold on a second there, Jack. Look around you. Do you see any uniforms here?"

"No, sir…uh, I mean, um, no…Chris."

"Perfect. Everybody's the same in here. It's kind of a rare treat to let your hair down, so feel free. Obviously, when we go back to work, it's a different story, but in here I'm Chris and you're Jack."

Just then, Hightower returned to the table with an excited look.

"Hey guys. The dude I was just talking to is a major named Collin Stoops and he's the tower officer here at Wake. We served together at *Bien Tuy* Airbase on my last tour. He's got a little fishing boat and says he might take us out on the lagoon for some fishing. What do you say?"

Before either man could answer, Sergeants Turner and Curtin entered the bar. In his bellowing voice, Sergeant Turner got the

61

attention of everyone inside by announcing, "Gentlemen, I apologize for the interruption but it is my duty to inform you all that we have a young sergeant on his first line training ride who is heading across the island tonight for Wake City! He'll be along momentarily!"

The announcement was met with a wave of laughter and applause. When the laughter died down, Walsh turned back to the major and said, "I'd love to drop a few lines in the water. Guys always tell me there are some pretty big fish out there."

Five minutes later, Sergeant Sloan, dressed impeccably in his Class-A uniform shirt and tie, opened the creaky screen door to The Reef. Immediately, his face screwed up into a look of confusion. His arrival was met with a roar of applause. The young sergeant's fair complexion immediately flushed with embarrassment but he quickly regained his composure and made his way through the tables of laughing, applauding men to where the three officers on his flight crew sat.

"Sirs, I'm gonna' take a wild stab in the dark and guess there is no Wake City, huh?

"No, but there darn well should be!"

Seeing the sergeant's face fall, Walsh let him off the hook.

"Don't worry, Sergeant. I actually took the time to shine my shoes when they pulled that gag on me. Why don't you go change into attire a little more befitting for this little slice of paradise, and come on back. The downside to the Wake City gag is everybody gets a laugh, upside is beers are on us."

That news seemed to cheer the young man up. The sheepish look on his face was quickly replaced with a grin as he stood and headed for the door.

"Be right back, sirs."

"We'll save a few stews for ya', kiddo," jibed the major. Lee and Walsh had a quick laugh at that.

Biting his tongue, Sergeant Sloan nodded and his eyes narrowed as he thought, *Don't hurt yourself trying to keep up with us youngsters, Grandpa.*

"Go easy on the kid, nav. You owe him a beer," said Lee.

With that, Sloan exited the Drifter's Reef to go change into the requisite shorts and tee shirt, being offered high fives from all within arm's length as he made his way to the door.

Turning toward Lee, Hightower said, "So, Jack, what's this about you shooting down the aide to General Blanton back at Hickam? I heard about it from just about every guy I knew at the base. Apparently some hot young buck on my flight crew sent the former Miss Louisiana down in flames?"

"Well, John, truthfully she just wasn't my type. Besides, I could tell by the way she talked to me that she really had only one thing in mind."

"Yeah…so, no beauty queen, huh? So, sport, *do* you have a type?"

"Hey now, don't get too far ahead of yourself, John," said Walsh, heading off a potentially violence-inciting remark. "This young stud here was the star wide receiver for Notre Dame. I'm surprised you didn't recognize him with as much as you lose to your bookie."

Suddenly put on the spot, Lee asked, "How did you know that, sir?"

"Jack, my boy, you don't think we read personnel files around here? If that wasn't enough, you don't think that shirt is a bit of a giveaway?"

With a sudden recognition, the major exclaimed, "Well, I'll be darned! You're *that* Jack Lee! Leading receiver for Notre Dame in what, 64' and 65'?"

"Something like that," answered Lee, wishing it hadn't been brought up.

"So with a couple of NCAA records under your belt, weren't there any offers from the pro teams, Mr. humility?" asked Major Hightower.

Looking at both men from whom he wanted to win acceptance, Lee answered, "Yeah, there were a couple of offers but it wasn't my passion in life. Ever since I was a little boy in Chicago and my dad took me to an airshow out at Lake Michigan, I just knew I would be a pilot. I mean how many good years does a guy get in the pro football game? And when you're through, you're almost always pretty much a cripple. Nope, I just knew I wanted to fly."

"Yeah but I mean think of the women who would be throwing themselves at you if you were a pro jock." said the major.

Even as his long-time colleague said it, Walsh knew the major's remark hadn't gone over well. He was beginning to get some insight into the kid he was assigned to teach. The kid just had principles and lived by them.

Lieutenant Lee looked directly at the major and said, "Well John, the truth is that when I look at airplanes I see artwork. Some people like paintings, others architecture and other people like sculptures. I think the greatest piece of artwork ever created by man was the airplane. Oh, and just to set the record straight, and since we're on informal terms here, I'll be candid, John. Item one: I never compromised on my values even in college and I had more of what you'd apparently call 'opportunities' than both of you, put together, *ever* will. Item two: if you care to question me for it, or perhaps suggest things that are just plain stupid about it, I'd be happy to answer any questions directly, outside, with no rank involved. Any questions, *Major*?"

Hightower, realizing he had seriously offended the powerfully-built young lieutenant fifteen years his junior, smiled, held his hands open in a gesture of non-aggression, and apologized.

"Hey, I meant nothing by it, Jack. Really. Sorry if I ticked you off. I've just never seen anyone who could resist the charms of a woman like that."

Lee stared at Major Hightower for a moment longer but then a smile began to break across his lips. "Well…it wasn't easy."

Walsh and Hightower laughed and raised their beers. Lee clanked his Budweiser can against theirs, smiled and added, "I'm just holding out for a better offer."

Just then, Sergeant Sloan reappeared at the door in a yellow Hawaiian shirt, shorts, and flip flops. All three officers at the table smiled and gave him thumbs up at the wardrobe change. Calling across to the bartender, Hightower said, "Hey, Martin, could you give this kid a beer on my tab?"

"You got it."

Sloan retrieved the cold beer from the bar and walked over to the table. Pulling an empty chair from an adjoining table for the sergeant, Walsh said, "Welcome to Wake City, Sergeant."

**Wake Island Airbase
Island Dock
1155 Hours Local Time
Friday, May 6th, 1969**

Chapter Six

Sergeant Turner was anxiously waiting for Captain Walsh on the dock as he, Major Hightower, and their fishing guide, Major Stoops, puttered up toward the dock. All three men aboard the boat had the mixture of smells about them that always resulted from fishing: sunscreen, tobacco from cigars, and the oily smell of fish. In the cooler were two impressive grouper that would make several mouthwatering meals on the grill that evening. Unfortunately for Walsh and Hightower, there would be no grouper sandwiches for them, despite their two hours of work involved in landing the fish. Until pulling alongside the dock, Walsh was under the impression that he had three hours to clean up, catch a bite to eat, file their flight plan to Clark Airbase, and meet the aircraft they would be taking on its next leg.

    The Air Force Military Airlift Command operated under the premise that aircrews needed rest but airplanes didn't. In an effort to keep supplies, personnel, and wounded in the constant motion that the combat action in Viet Nam required, the Air Force had developed a system known as 'staging'. An aircrew on a fourteen day mission traversing the globe with stops in eight different airbases would almost always crew at least that many different aircraft. As the little boat came alongside the dock, Sergeant Turner caught the rope.

"What's up, Turner?" asked Walsh, sensing his sergeant's presence was indicative of something gone wrong. He was right. As Turner helped tie up the boat, he said, "Sir, somebody apparently didn't do the math right. The command post called and our inbound bird is due at 1300 instead of 1430. The duty officer is really having a fit over it and wants to talk with you ASAP."

Climbing onto the dock, Walsh sighed and asked, "Does everybody know yet?"

"Yes, sir. I've got my men ready to go whenever you are. Lieutenant Lee is aware as well. Strange thing though."

Walsh hopped up to the dock. Reaching down to help pull the cooler of fish from the boat, he turned his head toward the sergeant and asked, "What do you mean 'strange thing', Sergeant?"

"Well, sir, when I called his quarters, he wasn't there so I took a walk over to tell him personally. He wasn't there either so I started asking around. Another officer said he had seen the lieutenant heading over toward the beach a few minutes earlier. When I finally caught up with the lieutenant, he was sitting on the beach with a Bible and one of those things with the beads and the cross all the nuns carry."

"A rosary."

"Yeah, a rosary, I guess. Hold it a second sir, how do you know that? I ain't never seen you so much as look in the direction of a chapel."

"Well, Sergeant, Sister Sean Morley, the principal at Saint Patrick's and I used to be on a first-name basis. She'd call me, 'Chris, you again?' and I'd call her, 'Yes, Sister Sean'."

"Ha! I never figured you for one of those Catholic schoolboys."

"Truthfully, neither did I."

Laughing and shaking his head, Sergeant Turner turned and headed back to the enlisted men's quarters to make sure his men were ready to meet the inbound aircraft for the next leg. Walsh considered what the sergeant had told him about Lee. Although, he had never seen a real-life example of someone living in a manner the priests and nuns used to encourage-who wasn't actually a priest or a nun-Walsh was beginning to believe that his young protégé pilot might just be the real deal. It explained the incident with the alluring beauty queen back in Hawaii. Captain Walsh's own Catholic upbringing had urged living by principles he saw the young lieutenant actually adhering to. It was impressive that the kid didn't compromise when, in the military, men were expected, and often encouraged, to act like drunken fraternity boys. The more Walsh thought about it, the more he respected Lee.

The sound of Major Hightower and his old friend Major Stoops dropping the cooler full of fish into the bed of an old Ford pickup truck snapped Walsh out of his thoughts. Walsh strolled up to the bed of the truck just as Hightower said, "Hey Stoops, me and Walsh here can't thank you enough for taking us out on there today. It was great to catch up with you!"

"Heck of a lot more fun that sitting through inbound mortar rounds at *Binh Tuy* airbase, huh nav?" said Stoops.

"Darn right," answered Major Hightower.

During the course of the morning fishing, all of them traded stories about their experiences in-country. There was a special bond between guys who had experienced lethal threats to their lives and had lived to tell about it. Watching the two men say their goodbyes, Walsh understood the feeling perfectly. He'd seen his fair share of combat.

Prior to coming into the transport community, Walsh had piloted a year's worth of missions in the cockpit of heavily-armed AC-119 gunship. The reliable cargo aircraft had been fitted with four SUU-11A mini-guns protruding from the side of the aircraft and was referred to by the call sign 'Shadow'. While loitering over an area, the slow-flying gunship could rain down a combined twenty-four thousand 7.62 millimeter rounds per minute, killing every living thing within a football field sized area within three seconds. Walsh had seen more than his fair share of action.

"Any time you guys come through my little patch of paradise, we'll try to snag some fish, alright?" said Major Stoops.

The major drove both officers back to their quarters and it took a twenty minute shower and multiple scrubbings with the cheap, military-issue soap until Walsh was satisfied that the fish smell had been successfully removed. An odor like that would be a special sort of unpleasantness in the confined, sealed cockpit of a jet for five hours. Ten minutes later, the entire crew assembled on the veranda of the Drifter's Reef wearing 'dirty dirties' as had been dictated by Sergeant Sloan the night before. The humidity in the Philippines was so high that time of year that if the air held any more moisture, people were liable to drown walking down the street. The crew was certain to break a sweat over the next day and Viet Nam would be even worse. There was no need to wear any crisp, new flight suits. Thirty minutes later the crew bus collected the entire crew and delivered them to an empty parking slot on the tarmac.

MAC 40592 came to a stop in front of Walsh's assembled crew and shut her engines down. The crew door came open and the folding steps came down from the jet. The crew began removing their baggage as the aircraft commander from that flight walked straight up to Walsh.
"The bird flies like a dream and all the systems are perfect."
"Glad to hear it."
"Say, buddy," asked the pilot whose name on the flight suit identified him as Captain Giffin, "I'm kind of in a real bind here and was wondering if you could do a favor for me."
"What sort of favor?"
The fellow aircraft commander looked around to see if any of his crew was looking. Seeing they were busy offloading their personal effects from the jet, he reached into his A-3 bag and retrieved a plush teddy bear that had been tied to a box of chocolates and an envelope with the name 'Sarah' handwritten on it.
"Look, this is a big favor but you're my only hope. There's an orphanage I go to visit about fifteen klicks from Clark whenever I'm at the base. There is a little girl there who I sort of unofficially adopted. I was supposed to see her last trip through and got alerted to take an Air Evac mission and never made it to see her."
"So how can I help you out there?"
"I was going to go this time but command forwarded a

message that my wife went into labor and I'm taking an emergency leave to go be with her. I tried calling the orphanage to explain to Sarah but the priest that runs the place said she cried for a whole day when I couldn't make it last trip through. If you'd be willing to go out to the orphanage, give her the gifts, and explain to her what's going on, I'll make it worth your while."

Walsh looked at the box and the stuffed bear lashed to it with red ribbon. It wasn't anything he relished doing in the slightest.

"Hey, man, I'd love to help you out there but on the last two times through here, my aircraft has been converted to a positioning Air Evac just like yours was. If we get alerted to convert again, you know I won't be spending crew rest there long enough to help you out."

With a look of desperation, Giffin grabbed Walsh's wrist, slapped a hundred dollar bill into his palm, and pleaded, "Look, I'm on the next bird heading back to Hickam and then on to Dover. I've got a two-day journey ahead of me and you are the last crew headed for Clark before I go. If you can't deliver it, could you just try to find someone you'd trust to do it and to explain to Sarah? What do you say there?"

Walsh looked at the hundred dollar bill and then the collection of items. He shook his head, quickly stuffed the chocolates and bear in his own A-3 bag, sighed and asked, "She's really that special, huh?"

"You have no idea," answered Giffin as he handed Walsh a hand-drawn map with the address of the orphanage and directions to it. By the looks of it, he estimated the trip would require a thirty-minute drive off the base.

"Alright, Captain. I'll make sure your little girl gets this, one way or another."

With that, Giffin shook Walsh's hand and headed toward the base operations building to wait for the jet he'd be flying back to the U.S. with. Walsh watched the fellow pilot sprint off to catch up with his crew. He wondered if Giffin actually intended to adopt the girl or just provide her some temporary happiness. It was an awkward position to be in, having to explain the situation to a little girl in an orphanage about a pilot he barely knew. Still, a Ben Franklin was a lot of money.

69

Lieutenant Lee, having watched the handoff of the tokens of affection and the cash, walked up to Walsh and asked, "What was that all about, sir?"

"Well, Lieutenant, I've got a special delivery for a little lady outside of Clark when we get there. Actually, it wouldn't be a bad idea for you to come with me on your first trip through the Philippines. You can help me spend the c-note the good Captain Giffin gave me for postage."

"If you don't mind me asking, sir, why can't the guy just mail it to her?"

"Well, see, Giffin is in a bit of a bind. At our next destination, there is a young lady really upset with him and his wife just went into labor back in Virginia..," began Walsh.

"Hold it just a second, Captain! Let me see if I understand this correctly. Are you telling me that we are helping a guy stay in the good graces with his mistress while his wife is giving birth to their child?"

Walsh laughed, realizing that it did sound pretty scandalous without knowing the rest of the facts. Holding up his hand, Walsh smiled and began to explain. In a few moments, a wide smile broke across the Lee's face.

"Wow, that's fantastic! My family used to volunteer at a home for children in Chicago and sponsor orphan kids for Christmas when I grew up. I'd be thrilled to help accomplish that mission, Captain."

Ten minutes later, MAC 40592 lifted off the island and turned due west toward the Philippines and beyond, Viet Nam. Three hours into the flight, Walsh decided it was time to teach his student an important lesson. The sun was positioned perfectly on the horizon to cast a blinding glow into the cockpit, making it impossible for either Walsh or Lee to see the instrument panel, and impossible to fly safely. Reaching into his pilot's briefcase, Walsh retrieved a chart and began to tape it to the cockpit window in front of the right seat where he sat as co-pilot.

"Uh, sir, please correct me if I'm wrong but isn't it a direct violation of regulations to obscure the view of the cockpit for any reason?" asked Lee.

"Lieutenant, who is flying the plane right now?"

"We're on autopilot, sir."

Keying his microphone, Walsh said, "Gentlemen, this is simulated. I say again, simulated. We have just simulated the loss of the autopilot. Engineer, co-pilot."

Sergeant Turner depressed the foot button, activating his interphone microphone and responded, "Co-pilot, engineer."

"Open the circuit breaker and cut autopilot, engineer."

"Roger that."

A moment later, with no more excitement to his voice than if he were announcing coffee was ready, Turner broadcast, "The autopilot main circuit breaker is now open, sir."

Lee was instantly shocked at the situation. They were now in a three-hundred thousand pound jet, six miles above the ocean, traveling at five hundred miles per hour, and nobody was really flying the plane.

Seeing Lee's immediate attempts to shield his eyes and discern what the instruments were indicating about their altitude, heading, and airspeed, Walsh asked, "Lieutenant Lee, what is your exact altitude and airspeed?"

"I can't really read them, sir. I know we were at flight level three-five-zero and dead-on heading when we leveled off. Right now, I honestly can't tell you." In the ten seconds that Lee attempted to process the situation and try to read the instruments, the plane had lost one hundred feet of altitude and began a slow roll to the right."

"Pilot from co-pilot, we're in almost ten degrees right bank and we've lost nearly two hundred feet altitude. Do you want me to notify Manila Control that we intend to change our flight plan?"

Expecting Lee to become somewhat panicky at the test, Walsh was amazed as he watched his student suddenly relax and take a deep breath. Most guys he'd ever seen faced with simulated emergencies speeded up their movements and frantically searched for the solution. A guy that knew to take a breath and think clearly had the makings of a great pilot.

Lee depressed the microphone button on his yoke and said, "Negative on contacting Manila Control. I know it's against regulations to have that chart affixed to your window but since I cannot do anything to keep the aircraft in level flight and on course, it occurred to me that my co-pilot has full view of flight and engine instruments. Co-pilot, your aircraft."

Inside, Walsh beamed with pride. It was the right decision. The kid had real potential.

"Co-pilot to engineer, close the circuit breaker on the autopilot."

From the engineer's panel, the metallic 'click' sound of the circuit breaker being closed could be heard.

"Roger co-pilot, the circuit breaker is now closed."

Walsh applied light backpressure to his yoke to initiate a shallow climb back to their assigned altitude and correct their roll. As soon as the aircraft was back in its original heading at the assigned altitude, he keyed his microphone again.

"Crew from co-pilot, the simulated autopilot failure is now terminated."

Looking over at Lee who was sitting with his hands in his lap, wearing a concerned look on his face, Walsh smiled and gave him a thumbs up to indicate he had handled the simulation well. On the exterior, Lee just nodded and kept the cool, detached appearance of the confident aviator he tried to affect. Inside, he felt pure happiness. He knew he had done well and really began to feel a part of the team.

**Immaculate Heart Children's Home
Ten miles northwest of Manila
Luzon Island, Philippines
1930 Hours Local Time
Saturday, May 7th, 1969**

Chapter Seven

Sitting in the taxi just outside the main gate of Clark Airbase, Captain Walsh lamented his decision made back on Wake Island. He was positive that agreeing to the favor had been a lapse in judgment and poor idea, especially after a harrowing experience of losing an engine at a thousand feet on final approach. The turbofan blades had totally shredded several birds in a flock, knocking the engine out and starting an engine fire. It was an energy-sapping experience bringing the jet safely down with only a few seconds until touchdown. By the time he finished writing the report on the engine damage, Walsh was in no mood to go anywhere but to the officer's club. If it weren't for Lee showing up at the bar between Walsh's first and second beer, reminding him of his promise to Captain Giffin, Walsh was of the mind to simply mail the package and hundred bucks back to Giffin with a note of apology.

When Walsh and Lee hopped into the cab just outside the base, and the cab driver looked over their directions, Walsh again almost gave in to his reluctance and nearly scrubbed the entire mission.

"Twenty-five dollars," said the driver.

"Twenty-five dollars to take us there and back?"

"Oh, you want to go round trip? No that would be fifty."

"Forget this, Lieutenant. Let's go," said Walsh as he reached for the door handle.

"Relax, Captain. I've got it," said Lee as he pulled the cash from his wallet.

Despite the challenges to completing the task, once there he didn't regret coming for a second. When he and Lee walked out of the officer's club earlier that evening, Walsh was taken aback when Lee had asked what they were going to bring the other forty-two kids at the orphanage. The possibility that bringing some treats to one child could make the others jealous hadn't occurred to Walsh until Lee asked that question. He had asked how Lee had known how many kids were at the place and was told that his student had called Father Jalandoni to find out.

The young airman behind the checkout counter at the Base Exchange possessed enough tact to avoid making any wise cracks to the two officers purchasing almost a hundred dollars worth of various toys and chocolate bars. On the trip to the orphanage, Walsh believed that he had allowed himself to be talked into wasting a perfectly good hundred dollars. That thought had been completely obliterated by the reaction the kids had to the unexpected treats.

The little girl stared up at Walsh and Lee with beautiful, brown eyes brimming with tears. She cradled the little teddy bear in the same fashion a new mother would an infant, stroking its fur and intermittently kissing the top of the doll's head.

"So you see, Sarah, Captain Giffin really wanted to come and visit you but because an emergency came up, he couldn't, but he made sure to send us to see you. You are that important to him."

"Nothing bad happened to him? He's really coming back?" asked the little girl. A wave of emotion unexpectedly shot through Walsh at the little girl's words. He didn't know the circumstances that had brought little Sarah to become a resident of the orphanage but immediately grasped the reason for the little girl's concern without any explanation necessary. It had taken some convincing to assure little Sarah that Captain Giffin was, indeed, perfectly fine and attending to family business. As the adorable little girl had asked, "Are you sure? Are you really sure?" through her diminishing sobs, some faces Walsh had known that hadn't come back popped into his mind's eye. He knew the pain of someone being snatched out of his life instantly and without any forewarning. With considerable effort to maintain his composure, Walsh answered, "Yes, Sarah, I promise. Nothing bad happened to him."

"What do you say to the nice men, Sarah?" asked Father Jalandoni, the Philippine Catholic priest who ran the orphanage.

Without saying a word, the beautiful little five-year-old girl ran up to Walsh and threw her arms around him. The other forty-two children in the room, bouncing off the wall from sugar intoxication, played with the toys and ate the little chocolate bars Walsh and Lee had distributed after eating dinner as honored guests with the children. Looking around the room at the immense joy their small gifts had given the children, a sense of happiness that Walsh hadn't experienced since childhood washed over him. As Walsh and Lee finally exited the sleeping dormitory, escorted by Father Jalandoni, Walsh's eyes began to well up with tears. He quickly tried to brush them off on the sleeve of his flight suit.

"The children were made so happy by your visit. Sarah was thinking that her friend forgot about her. To children in an orphanage, the worst thing they fear is somebody abandoning them or losing someone again."

Walsh heard Lee begin to answer the kindly priest. He could tell by the slight cracking of Lee's usually confident timbre to his speech that he was also emotionally moved by the children. Embarrassed to let the lieutenant or priest see how it had affected him, Walsh turned back toward the lieutenant and priest only after he was satisfied he had covertly wiped away his tears. To his amazement, he saw the priest smiling as his student pilot, totally unashamed, smiled back with big tears streaming down his face.

"I'll promise I'll try to come back whenever I'm at the airbase," said Lee.

"Have a safe trip back to the base and God bless you both for your kindness" answered Father Jalandoni.

"He already has, Father," said Lee.

Walking back to the cab parked out front, Lee playfully slugged Walsh in the arm and said, "Now what could you buy for a hundred bucks that would be worth more than seeing how happy you made those kids?"

"Point taken and duly noted, Lieutenant. But drinks are on you tonight, sport."

"With pleasure, sir."

Walsh and Lee sat enjoying cold beers at the Officer's Club. They were alerted for an 1800 hour departure for Da Nang airfield in Viet Nam and Walsh didn't want to give it much thought that night. Walsh hated only one thing more than flying into Viet Nam and that was flying into Viet Nam at night. He avoided dwelling on very rational fears of flying a large, unarmed, slow-moving target over hostile airspace. Instead, Walsh chose to bask in the emotional high from their visit to the orphanage.

"You know, Lieutenant, I was thinking about something the entire ride back from the orphanage."

"How you were originally going to spend your hundred bucks?"

"No, but you aren't far off. I mean think about what we do for a living. We sit in jets that the government pays nine million dollars apiece for, moving cargo all over the world. If a general says he wants three hundred cases of .50 caliber ammo flown across the world in twenty-four hours, we're the guys that make it happen."

"Yeah, I follow you, sir."

"And if a guy in a time crunch wants to make sure a little girl gets a special package the next day, he's apparently willing to pay a hundred bucks for it, right?"

"Yeah, apparently so."

"So I was just thinking that there's got to be a lot of civilians that want things flown as expeditiously as the military does but instead of paying me twelve hundred dollars a month plus two hundred for flight and combat pay, I bet the private sector would pay more."

"It always seems to, but I'm not in this for the money, sir."

"From you, I'll actually take that at face value, Lieutenant. I've only known you a few days but I've been paying attention. You probably could be throwing the pigskin around on television right now if you'd wanted to, for more money than I'll ever see in my lifetime. When you say you do this for the flying, I believe you. Truthfully, I do to. But I'm just getting a little worn out flying things around to help wage war or the casualties or corpses that result from it."

"I hear you, Sir. So you don't see yourself staying in until retirement?"

"I used to, but something inside of me says that there is more to life than being Uncle Sam's airborne mailman. Don't get me wrong, Lieutenant. I believe in what we are doing over here but I've just been around long enough to see things I'd rather forget."

"Well, sir. I've learned that if you are meant to do something in life, God just seems to make the pieces fall into place for it to happen."

Chris looked into his student's eyes. There was an almost visible light in them. Normally, whenever anybody brought up the word 'God', he tended to become disinterested and immediately dismissive of the topic. Oddly, in that moment, his natural inclination to bristle at the use of that word was absent. There was something about the way Lee conducted himself that impressed the hell out of Walsh, regardless of whether the boy was a bit touched for Jesus.

Looking at his watch, Walsh finished his beer and then gave the non-verbal signal of twirling his index finger around, in the same signal that meant 'starting engine', that it was time to wrap the evening up. Looking over at his protégé, he said, "So our little adventure tonight is classified. This is just between us, right, Lieutenant?"

Smiling, Lee replied, "My mother always said, 'Do good things and don't get caught,' sir."

At 1700 hours, the following afternoon, the entire crew met at the Airlift Command Post an hour prior to departure. As always, every crewmember, regardless of rank, assisted with the baggage drill. The jet they were assigned to fly on the next leg was a specific jet Walsh had flown in on several times. The tail number, he noted, was 60177, which provided him a slight measure of comfort. He absolutely hated flying into Viet Nam. Their destination, Da Nang, occupied the number one spot on his roll-call of hated airfields. The airbase at Da Nang was so prone to attack that many loathsomely called it 'Rocket City'. No aviator relished the idea of flying over hostile territory in a huge target the enemy knew was either delivering vital supplies or removing wounded. Sitting at the controls of a jet he was familiar with didn't eliminate Walsh's abhorrence of flying over Viet Nam but it was a small comfort.

    Aircraft manufacturers would claim that any two jets they manufactured were completely identical but any pilot who flew them would give a completely different assessment. Like people, airplanes seemed to have varying personalities. Some were highly reliable and had relatively low incidents of malfunction. Others were so prone to systems failures that they were referred to as 'hangar queens'. Tail number 60177 was a jet Walsh regarded as dependable.

    Inside the flight planning room, Major Hightower continued to assess Lee's familiarity with the details of mission planning while Walsh did a walk-around of their jet. Sergeant Sloan emerged from the cargo hold and informed him that there was again a load of high-explosive cannon rounds secured to the nine pallets in the back.

    "The loadmaster has turned on the no-smoking sign for the entirety of this flight, sirs," quipped the young sergeant. Walsh saw through the brave façade of humor Sergeant Sloan was putting up. Mixed in with the jet fuel fumes, he picked up the smell of fear. For both Sergeant Sloan and Lieutenant Lee, this was their first flight into a combat area and both had been around long enough to hear some stories from other men who had been there. Everyone was dressed in the "dirty-dirties" that Sloan had dictated the night before, the masculine smell of sweat increasing as the day warmed. At precisely 1800 hours, Walsh assumed pilot duties in the left seat and Lee took his place as co-pilot in the right. Lee finished flipping the last of the switches while Walsh advanced the throttles. Lee let his hand ride along his set of engine throttles as Walsh advanced his set. One of Lee's shortcomings was his tendency to advance his throttles too quickly so feeling the pace which Walsh advanced them was helpful. Noticing Lee's effort to learn, Walsh was pleased that the kid was a good student who paid attention. More than that, there were qualities about the young man he admired on a personal level. Although Da Nang was one of the most hated places Walsh ever had flown into, he was happy to be at the controls for the young lieutenant's introduction to a live combat zone. If an emergency occurred, Walsh's experience might just save their lives.

Fifteen minutes into the flight to Da Nang, a transmission from the Manila Air Traffic Center reached the radio on the fight deck.

"MAC 60177, this is Manila Center."

Walsh responded, "Roger Manila, this is 177."

"177, we have a request for you to make contact with ACP on UHF."

"Roger Manila, WILCO."

Walsh had a suspicion why they were being asked to contact the regional Airlift Command Post. Keying his interphone button, Walsh broadcast to the entire crew, "I'm going to contact the Clark Airlift Command Post on U-1 if any of you boys care to listen. Lieutenant Lee, please continue to monitor Manila Center on V-1."

"Roger that."

Adjusting the radio frequency to contact the command post over the long-range ultra-high frequency radio, Walsh broadcast, "Clark ACP, this is MAC 60177."

"Roger 177, Clark ACP. We thought you'd want to know your destination remains Da Nang but you are now a positioning Air Evac. Your next destination will most likely be Japan."

"Roger Clark, 177 out."

Everyone aboard heard the response. The collective energy of the crew and the feel of the atmosphere inside the half-million pound pressurized steel tube streaking through the air at thirty-three thousand feet instantly changed with that radio transmission. Everyone on the crew, with the exception of Lee and Sloan, had flown an Air Evac mission before. Within a few short hours, the aircraft Walsh was commanding would no longer be just an airborne delivery truck but an airborne hospital complete with a rudimentary operating room, ferrying badly wounded soldiers out of harm's way. Walsh believed in all of military aviation that an Air Evac mission was the noblest of services he could provide as a pilot. As he prepared himself mentally for what he knew would be an emotionally-charged situation, his mind wandered into the place he kept memories about two childhood friends who had both ended up flying out of Viet Nam on Starlifters.

    Walsh's best friend all through grade school, Tyler Dumars, had joined the Army within months of his joining the Air Force. His best friend from college, Earl Franks, had joined the Marines a year later. Tyler had eventually gone into the Army Special Forces, first through Ranger School at Ft. Benning, Georgia and then selected for the new and secretive Green Berets at Ft. Bragg, North Carolina. Earl had been a tank commander serving in the First Marine Division throughout his Marine career. Throughout the war, the three had kept in contact and playfully traded disparaging jibes at each others' respective armed services. Chris even met up with Earl for a night on the town once while both men had been on twenty-four hour leave in Tokyo.

    Within a span of three months, both of Walsh's close friends had been horribly wounded in combat. Tyler survived a bullet through the spleen from a firefight and had made it to the hospital in Japan on an Air Evac aircraft. Four months later, Tyler was back in-country again, working with the fearsome mountain people called the *Hmong*, training them to fight against the Viet Cong.

    Captain Earl Franks, USMC, died mid-flight on an aircraft Walsh, in a tragic and extremely painful coincidence, happened to be flying. A rocket propelled grenade had impacted Captain Franks' tank while his crew was working on repairing a thrown tread. Two other Marines on Earl's crew died instantly. Earl had taken a huge piece of shrapnel in the chest and had bravely fought to survive for almost twenty hours by the time he was brought aboard Walsh's plane. While airborne on that flight, Walsh had gone aft to the cargo area that had been transformed into an operating theatre to check on his friend. Walsh had been stunned to see his friend being brought aboard back in Da Nang. It felt like all the air had been sucked out of him as he came off the ladder from the crew loft just in time to see the surgeon pulling the sheets over Earl's bloody, lifeless body

The memory of Earl and other lost friends brought a wave of emotion and sense of loss that made Walsh shudder, remembering that moment of that particular Air Evac mission. Ever since his first experience on an Air Evac mission, ferrying wounded, scared soldiers out of harm's way was the one mission he loved doing but absolutely hated having to.

Staring out his window to clear his mind, Walsh keyed his interphone microphone when he felt he had regained his ability to talk.

"Pilot to crew, check in on interphone," was the phrase to inform everyone aboard, in no uncertain terms, that he wanted everyone to be clear about his next orders. Up to that point, during the prior five days of the mission, the tone of Walsh's voice had been professional but relaxed. As he called for an interphone check-in, he did so in a very different voice. Major Hightower, who had flown with Walsh on several other occasions, knew from experience that the intensity of the mission had just ratcheted up several notches.

As soon as the last check-in over the interphone from the aft cargo area was acknowledged by Sergeant Sloan, Walsh began.

"Gentlemen, as you all heard from Clark, we have now been tasked as an Air Evacuation mission out of Da Nang. That requires Sergeant Sloan to offload nine pallets of ordinance and immediately reconfigure his cargo area as a flying hospital. I'm sure everyone aboard knows the amount of work required to pull that off smoothly and we will accomplish it with the highest level of efficiency we are humanly capable of. Every minute we waste on the ground emptying the jet or making her ready for the wounded might just be the difference between life and death for the boys we will be taking aboard. I expect everyone to give one hundred and ten percent to make the reconfiguration happen."

Every station checked in with a "Roger" or "Roger that, sir."

"Nav, can you dot all our 'I's and cross all the 'T's on all of our paperwork for the leg to Tokyo before touchdown?"

"I'm halfway done already."

"Sergeant Turner, how much fuel will we have in the tanks at touch down in Da Nang?"

"Just over eighty-seven thousand pounds, give or take a few hundred pounds, sir."

"Nav, I need you to calculate whether we can make it to Tokyo at three-five-zero with our current fuel load. If not, give me an altitude to climb to so that we will make it. We will *not* be wasting any time fueling this bird in Viet Nam."

Lee sat in the right seat thinking back to the training he had received regarding hospital ship missions. He knew he was a competent pilot but the intensity in Walsh's voice as he took command of the aircraft created more than a twinge of nervousness. As he silently reviewed in his mind everything that needed to be done to convert the aircraft into a flying hospital, he concluded the list of tasks with the prayer familiar to all pilots: *God, please don't let me screw up.*

Over the interphone, the voice of Sergeant Sloan came across from his position down in the cargo area.

"Co-pilot, load."

"Go ahead, load."

"Sir, based on new information not available upon departure from Clark, I am officially changing the uniform of the day. Today's uniform of the day is now clean flight suit with all zippers and snaps in perfect compliance with regulation. In addition, fully-shined boots will be worn by all. Loadmaster out."

An expression of pride in the young sergeant bloomed across Walsh's face in the form of a huge grin. Lee looked over at Walsh and also smiled. Turning to Sergeant Turner sitting at the engineer's panel, they shared a 'thumbs up'. Young Sergeant Sloan had just demonstrated exceptional leadership and in every crew member's opinion, the kid just had just earned an A+ in the professionalism department.

Lee unfastened himself from his seat and headed aft to change. Sergeant Turner retrieved an infrequently-used tin of black shoe polish and began working some of it into his highly sub-regulation boots.

"Can I get some of that, Sergeant?" asked Major Hightower who had just returned to his station from slipping into a new flight suit.

"Sure Major, I'll pass it around to everyone just as soon as my boots stop soaking it in. I think the last time I used this stuff was on another Air Evac six months ago and the ol' boots seem to be thirstier for polish than Dean Martin is for scotch."

"I'm next," said Lee who had just returned from slipping into his own fresh flight suit in the cargo hold. After bringing his boots to a shine that would past muster in basic training, Lee returned to his seat.

"Lieutenant, your airplane," said Walsh as soon as Lee was back in the right seat.

"Roger that."

Heading aft, Walsh came across Sergeant Sloan putting the final touches on his own uniform in the cargo hold.

"I'm darn proud of your thinking of changing the uniform, Sergeant. You've got a hard job ahead of you and everyone aboard knows to do exactly what you say to get the cargo offloaded and reconfigure the hold."

"Thank you, sir. I won't let you down," he replied with more confidence in his voice than resided in his heart.

After Walsh's flight suit was zipped, snapped, and a model of Air Force regulations, he climbed back up to the crew loft and headed forward past the engineer and navigator stations to the front row again. Passing Sergeant Turner, he felt a hand come to rest on his shoulder.

"Excuse me, Captain. I'm not sure exactly where you came from but our bird's aircraft commander is a guy named Walsh. I'm going to have to ask you to return to your seat."

"Funny, Sergeant. So can I get a bit of that polish?"

With a grin, Turner handed it over but not before declaring, "By the looks of your footwear, sir, might I respectfully recommend consulting Air Force Regulation Manual U-1165 for explicit directions on how to use this footwear upkeep equipment?"

Just then, the aircraft hit a bit of turbulence, jostling the airplane slightly as Walsh resumed his place in the left seat.

"My airplane," said Walsh as he resumed control of the jet. Keying his microphone again, he transmitted, "Pilot, Nav, do you have the required altitude for us to reach Tokyo on our current fuel load?"

"Roger, Pilot, flight level three-five-zero or above will get us to Tokyo and hopefully out of this choppy air."

Walsh pulled back on the yoke to begin a climb to thirty-five thousand feet to extend the fuel efficiency of the four engines and get the aircraft out of the turbulence. Coming forward with a thermos of warm coffee, Sergeant Sloan happily noted the cessation of the aircraft's bumping and jarring as they gained altitude.

"Anybody in the front row care for a cup of jo?" asked the sergeant.

"You bet, Sergeant. Now that we are out of the chop and there won't be whitecaps in my coffee," said Lee.

**Cockpit of C-141A Call Sign: MAC 60177
Thirty miles East of Da Nang Airfield
1945 Hours Local Time
Sunday, May 8th, 1969**

Chapter Eight

As Captain Walsh and Lieutenant Lee piloted MAC 60177 together in the flight deck, they crossed over the coastline of Viet Nam, leaving the waters of the South China Sea behind them. What had been a mild sense of apprehension grew into full-blown fear in Lee's chest. While attending to the duties of co-pilot, Lee silently prayed. Although Walsh had flown the approach many times, he too was in a state of hyper-alertness. Looking off to the starboard side of the aircraft, ten miles inland, both pilots saw a string of sun-brilliant white and red fireballs erupt from the jungle canopy.

"Fast-movers unloading willy-pete on an enemy position," said Walsh

Describing the ordinance dropped from the attack aircraft as 'willy-pete' seemed almost comical to Lee. The innocuous-sounding name described a weapon that sent shards of white-hot phosphorus out in all directions faster than a bullet. Upon contact with human skin, the burning metal would stick and continue to burn unless deprived of all oxygen by covering with petroleum jelly. It was part of a class of weapons the military referred to as 'anti-personnel'. Although he would never say it aloud, Jack thought such weapons were more aptly described as 'anti-human'.

Lee thoroughly believed in winning the war but often had a difficult time reconciling his absolute faith in God and how God's children were continually inventing increasingly brutal ways of removing each other from the planet.

Out the starboard cockpit window, five miles to the south of the site of the airstrike, both pilots could see a brilliant white flare floating through the air. A moment later, a second flare popped and began illuminating the night like an artificial sun before the first disappeared into the trees. It was the odd time near dusk when it was dark on the ground but still daylight at altitude. MAC 60177 was passing through fifteen thousand feet on its approach descent. Being too far away to actually see the aircraft, both pilots knew it was a gunship ahead when a stream of tracer rounds materialized from a point in the sky, diagonally screaming into the ground and throwing up small explosions at the impact area. The three-thousand-round-per-minute rate of fire from the side-mounted mini-guns on the gunship gave the tracer-bullets the appearance of a pinkish-red death ray rather than individual rounds being fired.

"That's not too far from the airfield, Lieutenant. It appears Charlie is busy tonight," said Walsh.

"Super, sir."

Over the radio, both pilots could hear Da Nang Approach Control was busy. There were often dozens of aircraft aloft near the demilitarized zone. Checking in when the frequency was clear, Walsh broadcast, "Da Nang Approach, MAC 60177 out of fifteen for four"

Walsh received an immediate response in a harried tone, "Roger 177. I have you on radar contact twenty-six miles east of the field. You are cleared for an ILS to runway one-seven left. Winds are light and variable; temp is eighty-four degrees, altimeter 2996. Call level at four."

"177 roger."

There was an elegance and beauty to the efficient manner of aviator communication that Walsh loved. It had been boiled down to the most essential information and was like a secret language between lovers. No earth-bound people ever understood it. It was just for pilots. Although always hating to fly into Da

Nang, he still loved everything about being a pilot.

The sun had truly set beyond the horizon and the plane was flying in darkness as they descended through ten thousand feet. The lights of the airfield were visible ten miles off to the left and looked like a band of daylight surrounded by a universe of darkness.

Walsh radioed Approach Control.

"177 is level at four. Field in sight."

"Roger 177, you are cleared to land. Contact Da Nang Tower."

Switching over frequencies from the regional approach control to the tower at the airfield, Walsh keyed his microphone and broadcast, "Da Nang Tower, MAC 60177, final approach."

The response from the tower sent a wave of apprehension through every crewmember's body.

"177, Da Nang Tower, you are cleared to land. Be advised we are now on yellow alert. We expect to go red fairly soon." That grim transmission meant that the tower expected the airfield to be under attack any moment by rockets or mortars. It was a common experience at Da Nang.

"Roger, Da Nang."

Four minutes later, the entire crew let out a collective exhale. The touchdown was exceptionally smooth with Walsh at the controls. Again, Lee let his hands gently ride along the controls to feel exactly how his instructor pilot had manipulated them to achieve such a textbook landing. Walsh engaged the thrust reversers and applied the brakes with a level of expertise that impressed and inspired Lee. Walsh taxied the aircraft to the ramp at the highest allowable speed and parked in the assigned spot. As soon as they had shut down the engines, Walsh keyed his microphone and declared over the interphone, "Alright, ramblers, let's get rambling. I hate this place."

Sergeant Sloan had the rear clamshell doors already open and a special flatbed truck was mating with the aircraft to remove the pallets in the back as both pilots descended the ladder from the crew door.

"Alright, Sergeant, we're working for you now. What would you like us to do?" asked Walsh.

87

"Once this other truck picks up the rest of the pallets, would you gentlemen mind helping to flip the roller panels?"

"Roger that, Sergeant."

Six minutes later, as the last pallet of ordinance rolled out of the cargo hold onto the flatbed truck, Walsh and Lee began flipping the special panels inside the cargo bay. With the roller sides up, a single person could actually load tons of cargo by pushing it forward and locking it into place. With the roller sides down, the cargo area had a flat, non-slip deck that was needed if doctors and nurses were to be walking around mid-flight and attending to wounded. Lifesaving surgery at altitude was not all that uncommon.

Major Hightower had returned from the base operations complex after filing their flight plan to Tokyo. He and Sergeant Turner began assisting the ground crew in assembling the upright stanchions for hanging the litters on when the two pilots completed flipping all the roller panels. As Walsh and Lee began to assist the other crewmembers and the three sergeants on the ground crew in converting the cargo hold, Sergeant Sloan came forward.

"Alright, sirs, will two of you start setting up some side seats. It looks like we are going to have about thirty litter patients and about twenty ambulatory. I want the ones who can walk up front so set up thirteen seats on either side in case there are a few more."

Walsh and Hightower broke away from the group assembling the vertical stanchions and began installing the side seats, positioning an oxygen mask next to each one. As they were finishing the installation of the last side seat, several airmen on the ground crew were bringing aboard the medical equipment necessary to turn the aircraft into a fully-functioning airborne hospital. Walsh noticed that the equipment was coming aboard really fast. All of the airmen on the ground crew were under the rank of staff sergeant and none had ever seen line officers do manual labor before. The entire ground crew quickly realized that these officers were totally invested in getting the job done quickly. An officer who was obviously determined to get the reconfiguration done at lightning speed might just take it personally if he thought an enlisted man wasn't giving one hundred percent.

Nobody wanted to be that guy.

Thirty minutes later, Walsh used a towel to wipe the sweat from his forehead. He glanced at his Timex and noted with pride that the entire offloading and reconfiguration of the aircraft took just a shade over forty-five minutes. He was certain it was a new record by at least an hour. He walked back to Sergeant Turner and asked "Sergeant, are we good?"

"Yes, sir. We're ready."

Across the tarmac, the sound of artillery fire in the distance rolled like thunder and the staccato chatter of small arms fire began to pop through the sticky tropical air.

"Alright, I'm going to let the medical personnel know to begin loading. I want to be gone in the next hour. Lieutenant, I want you and Turner to go up front and run the pilot's and engineer's checklists up to 'starting engines'."

With a raise of his eyebrow for the briefest moment, Lee replied, "Yes, sir."

"Roger that," said Sergeant Turner. Both men turned back to the plane and quickly made their way to the crew door and disappeared into the aircraft. Although it was against a slew of regulations to allow non-rated crewmembers to do any of the checklist tasks for the pilots, Walsh knew and trusted Sergeant Turner completely. If it were anyone else flying as his engineer, he would never have directed a sergeant to touch anything in the front row of the aircraft.

"We'll go let the medical folks know she's ready for their patients," said Major Hightower.

"Roger that."

Walsh and Major Hightower jogged into the base operations building. Seeing a lieutenant colonel standing with a staff of five nurses, Walsh took note of his name before introducing himself.

"Dr. Doelling, we're ready to load your patients. How can we help out?"

"Thanks, Captain. The most helpful thing would be some strong backs to get the litters aboard. There is a nasty bit of business going on at the DMZ and a lot of these guys have only gotten battlefield aid. I don't even know how much work on these kids I'm going to have to do in-flight and we'd really like to get to it. "

"Roger that, Doctor. We'll help and I've got two more on my crew who can lend a hand."

As the doctor and nurses headed toward the plane, Walsh and Major Hightower went out of the building and up to the window of the first waiting ambulance in a line of nearly fifteen others.

"Pull your ambulance as close as possible to the back of the jet, Sergeant," said Walsh to the driver.

As the young man replied, "Yes, sir," the sound and then the slight pressure wave from a rocket detonating close to the airfield reached them.

"Man, this might get ugly," said Walsh as they jogged back toward their plane. As they reached the aircraft, the first of the ambulances had backed within ten feet of the aft cargo doors. Climbing into the ambulance and making his way to the front in a crouch, Walsh saw the young Army private laying in it had bandages around his chest and head that were saturated with blood. Still, the young man looked directly into his eyes and smiled slightly.

Looking back at Major Hightower, Walsh could see the lack of color in his navigator's face. He remembered the first time he had seen the effects of high-speed metal and explosive concussion waves on the human body. It wouldn't be accurate to say that Walsh had become completely desensitized to the sight of traumatic injuries but he didn't have the queasiness about it to the extent that Major Hightower did. Still, the major just pressed on, acting much better than he felt. Taking note of the name on the remnants of the soldier's cut away blouse, Walsh looked at the boy, no older than twenty, on the litter. Manufacturing a grin he didn't feel, and a passable British accent, Walsh said, "Good evening Private Brown. Welcome to British Airways. Will you be flying tourist or first class tonight?"

"First class, sir. It cost a bit more but the service always makes it worth the while," answered the young man. The soldier's voice was raspy and full of weariness.

"Very good, Private."

Using the invaluable skill of humor in the situation, Major Hightower added, "And how would you like your steak cooked?"

"Medium rare please," answered the young man who, at least for the moment, had been effectively distracted from the considerable injuries he had sustained. Having his hands full under the weight of Private Brown, Walsh smiled widely at the injured infantryman. The two senior officers had flown several Air Evac missions together and, despite the sometimes heart-wrenching emotions that accompanied the flights, they both knew the first rule of Air Evac missions: always try to keep the patients' spirits up using whatever means necessary.

As the two pilots hefted the litter into the forward most position in the cargo area, Private Brown asked, "Will you be taking my drink order then, good sir?" One of the five nurses on Doctor Doelling's staff began checking the battle dressings on the private.

"I would be quite happy to but I'd bet you would prefer to have this beautiful stewardess take it for you."

The nurse smiled at the remark with her lips but there was no light in her eyes as she did so. He winced in pain as she lightly touched the area surrounding his chest injury.

"Lemme' take a bit of the edge off, Private," said the nurse as she injected morphine into the boy's forearm.

The young man's eyes began to loose a bit of their focus. Even so, he managed a weak grin and said in a voice that began to quiver with emotion, "That sounds like a great idea, Captain. Thanks...for the lift...you guys."

There were rare and precious times in Walsh's life where he had witnessed the true nature of humanity showing itself. In that moment, within the cargo area of his aircraft, a young man expressing the sentiment, *Thanks for saving my life,* deeply touched his heart. Walsh's eyes began to tear up and, fighting to keep his composure, he managed to reply, "Our pleasure, Private."

Walsh made his way around Major Hightower and Sergeant Sloan, as they placed another litter below Private Brown and he passed the redheaded nurse who had just checked the private's bandages. He remembered seeing her for the first time a year earlier on his first Air Evac mission as pilot-in-command. Then, she had been a slender, soft-spoken girl with red hair and angelic alabaster skin. Her voice, he remembered, was annunciated with a soft South Carolina accent and its softly rounded vowels. There, in the cargo bay, attending to another boy with a shattered body, she was almost unrecognizable from the girl she had been a year before. From the scent of tobacco and the gravel in her voice, it was apparent that she had discovered cigarettes. She had also put on at least twenty pounds and there were worry lines and creases around her eyes that had tremendously aged her appearance. The most shocking transformation however, had been in her eyes. He remembered the first day seeing the most vivacious, emerald green eyes that had since lost all life they once possessed. All of the nurses on the flight had the same look; they had just seen too much. These women had saved countless lives, but had done so at a horrendous price.

 Thirty minutes later, all of the litter patients were stacked in their rows along the walls of the cargo bay and twenty-three ambulatory patients were at their places in the red cloth-web seats affixed to the walls. Walsh and Lee, both saturated with sweat, took their respective seats in the front of the cockpit. Maintaining pilot duties for their flight out of Viet Nam, Walsh took the left seat and Lee the right as co-pilot.

 Acting as 'scanner', Sergeant Sloan stood fifty feet off the nose of the aircraft with a set of headphones that enclosed his entire ears and were attached to the jet by a long wire cord. The headset gave the scanner the ability to link up with the interphone system from outside the jet and communicate over the roar of jet engine noise. Keying the microphone that activated the headset on Sloan's ears, Walsh transmitted, "Scanner, Pilot. Where are we with the ambulances?"

 "Pilot, Scanner. The last ambulance is pulling away now and aft doors are closing."

 "Engineer, Pilot. Where are we in the checklists?"

 "Sir, we have completed all items on pilot's and engineer's checklists up to 'Starting Number One'."

 Reaching above his right shoulder to the overhead panel, Walsh pushed the engine start button and called, "Starting number one."

Keying the radio, he broadcast to the control tower, "Da Nang Tower, Air Evac 60177 is taxiing on runway three-five-right. Do we have flight plan clearance?"

"Negative clearance from Center, 177. Taxi south. Winds are light and variable. Altimeter 2994."

Not even close to the answer I was looking for, thought Walsh. Pushing the throttles forward a quarter inch, the jet began to roll. As they taxied south on runway three-five-right's parallel taxiway, both pilots quickly ran through the remainder of the checklist items. As they turned the aircraft around to line up on the runway, Sergeant Sloan called in on the interphone, "Cabin secure for takeoff."

Just as Walsh was about to radio the tower for a second takeoff clearance request, the inbound rocket slammed into the grassy area between the taxiway and runway only a hundred yards ahead of their position, throwing a geyser of dirt up and leaving a five foot round, smoldering crater in the earth. The sound from the explosion and concussion wave reached the jet, rocking it slightly on the landing gear shock absorbers. Two seconds later, small chunks of dirt and pebbles began pelting the windshield. A frantic voice immediately called over the radio, "Attention all aircraft, Da Nang has gone *RED!* I say again, Da Nang has gone *RED!* Da Nang runways are closed!"

Walsh yelled an expletive and immediately advanced the throttles to full power. The jet began to accelerate down the runway. Over the sound of the engines, Walsh roared, "I'm not sitting here with a plane full of wounded! We're going right now!"

Lee had never dreamed of violating any rules or regulations in regard to flying. As much as he liked and respected his instructor pilot, he was tremendously relieved that he was not the aircraft commander just then. Two more rockets detonated off the right side of the aircraft as the plane screamed down the runway. Twenty seconds later, everyone aboard let out a collective exhalation when Air Evac 60177 took to the skies and out of immediate harm's way.

"Gear up," called Walsh.

Lee raised the gear handle and five seconds later, the *thunk-thunk* sounds of the gear locking into place inside the fuselage were heard.

"Nav, Pilot. We're going to hit the southern tip of Taiwan as our first check-point. What's our direct heading for Heng Chung?"

"Zero-six-zero, Captain. Did we get clearance direct?"

With a slight grin, Walsh answered, "Naw…we didn't get any clearance at all. We're just kinda' going that a way. Did we file for flight level three-three-zero?"

"Yeah. We've got plenty of juice at three-three-zero or above."

Switching his radio to the VHF communication frequency to contact Departure Control, he broadcast, "Da Nang Departure, Air Evac 60177 out of five thousand for three-three-zero. Direct Heng Chun, direct Tokyo. Requesting clearance."

A controller whose voice dripped with irritation responded, "Roger 177. We have radar contact. You do *not* have clearance."

"Understand negative clearance, Da Nang. We'll contact Saigon. 177 out."

Walsh continued through the climb checklist and switched over to the frequency to contact Saigon Control.

"Saigon, Air Evac 60177 out of one-one-thousand for three-three-zero."

Another air traffic controller with a tone just as irritated as the one sitting in Da Nang responded, "177, this is Saigon. Your clearance is *denied*. Your requested altitude is blocked. Hold on the zero-six-zero radial from Da Nang, eighty miles to ninety miles at one-seven-thousand feet. Acknowledge."

Just as Walsh was about to reiterate to this new controller that his aircraft was a medical evacuation mission and he wasn't about to accept a denied clearance, Sergeant Sloan checked in on the radio interphone. It was highly unusual for anyone other than the pilots to communicate on the interphone before level-off because interphone chatter had the potential of creating a missed radio call from the ground or another aircraft. The check-in immediately got Walsh's attention.

"Pilot, Load. Doctor Doelling is going to have to perform

some surgery back here right now. He requests the smoothest ride possible, sir."

Just then, the controller from Saigon Control came across the VHF radio with a more insistent tone than the first time.

"Air Evac 60177, Saigon. Acknowledge!"

"Stand by, Saigon."

Keying the interphone, he responded to Sloan, "Load, Pilot. Smooth it is."

Again the controller in Saigon barked, "Air Evac 60177, Saigon! Acknowledge you are entering holding pattern. Do you read?"

"This dude just doesn't get it. We're a medical evacuation and they want us to fly circles? Forget that," growled Walsh as he keyed his radio again. "Saigon, 177. *Negative* holding pattern. We are out of two-six thousand for three-three-zero, direct Heng Chun, direct Tokyo. We are an Air Evac. I say again we are an *Air Evac* with surgery in progress, I repeat *surgery in progress*. I don't care if Air Force One is in my way. Move them!"

As one of the most basic elements of aviation training, different altitudes were to aircraft like lanes were to automobiles. The westbound 'lanes' above thirty thousand feet were thirty-five, and thirty-seven thousand feet. The eastbound were thirty-three and thirty-five thousand feet. For safety, even-numbered altitudes were considered absolutely forbidden except in dire emergencies.

Over the radio, both pilots heard Saigon Control's response.

"177, Saigon. Three-three-zero and three-seven-zero have a military block on them for the next two hours. I say again, acknowledge holding instructions."

"This guy must be having a little problem with his receiver," said Walsh as he keyed the VHF radio again and broadcast with a tone of absolute finality, "Saigon, 177. I say again *negative* holding. I am leveling at flight level three-*four*-zero. Proceeding as stated. 177 out."

Over the interphone, Walsh said, "Must be an inbound B-52 strike blocking the altitudes. Let's keep our eyes peeled because a thousand feet isn't a whole heck of a lot of vertical separation."

"Roger that," answered Lee.

Lee sat in the right seat, performing his duties as co-pilot and in absolute awe of Walsh's actions. He couldn't imagine himself making any different decisions, but to directly disregard instructions from the air traffic controller was something he would never have dreamed he would witness firsthand.

Switching the radio over to the frequency Starlifter pilots referred to as MAC Common, he broadcast, "Any Charles One-Four-Ones on Common please respond to Air Evac 60177."

A few seconds later, he heard, "Evening, 177. This is 008. How can we help?"

"177 is looking for smooth air from Taiwan to Tokyo. Can you assist?"

"Roger 177, we are at three-five-zero right between Okinawa and Heng Chun. We've had light to moderate chop since about a hundred miles northeast of Okinawa and it's still about a rough as a stucco toilet seat. Best guess is that we are in the bumpy part of the jet stream and will be for a bit longer."

"Thanks 408. Please update us if you have any changes. 177 out."

Walsh called to his navigator to give him a heading to avoid the jet stream. After changing course to that heading, there was not a single bump of turbulence.

An hour later, Doctor Doelling climbed up into the crew loft and came forward to the cockpit. There was still blood staining the disposable surgical gown he wore.

"I can't thank you guys enough for giving us a smooth ride. There was a nasty bit of shrapnel lodged in Private Brown's heart and a bump at just the wrong time, and things could have gone south really fast."

"Thank God for that, doc," said Walsh. He had no idea which soldier was undergoing surgery until the doctor just told him. The feeling of elation knowing the young private would probably make it was better than any feeling he ever knew. That his piloting skill had been a small part of that equation brought a joy to his heart that would stick with him for days. Turning to Lee, he saw his student pilot grinning ear to ear.

"We had the easy job, doc," said Lee.

"Roger that," added Walsh.

**Travis Air Force Base
San Jose, California
96th Airlift Squadron Building
1730 Hours
Friday, September 14th, 1969**

Chapter Nine

The colonel twirled his silver pen between the fingers of his right hand as he sat across from Captain Walsh and asked, "Are you absolutely sure you can't stay around? I was just about to recommend you for assistant squadron operations officer?" asked Colonel Larry Schauer. Behind closed doors, the need to address each other by their rank was dispensed with.

Colonel Schauer had always liked and respected Chris and thought of him much like the son he never had, although he'd never say so. Being an effective commander of a military unit meant avoiding the appearance favoritism even if it existed. If asked, most men in the 96th Airlift Squadron would have thought the exact opposite of the colonel's estimation of Walsh based on the eardrum-splitting reprimands he received from the commanding officer for his frequent liberal interpretations of Air Force regulations. The Vesuvius-like oral eruptions from the colonel could oftentimes be heard on the opposite side of the building, two hallways and seventy-five yards away in the flight planning room, and were fodder for jokes from anyone hearing them. The exchanges were largely for show and once the door was closed, it was a completely different conversation between the colonel and captain. Colonel Schauer considered Walsh an exemplary model of an aircraft commander and aviator who could think and act under pressure in the best interest of his men and the mission even if a few regulations were dented on occasion. That morning, Schauer knew by his colleague's tone that he had absolutely zero chance of changing Walsh's mind.

"Larry, I would if I could but I really have made up my mind. It's time for me to go see what I can accomplish in that world outside the fences here."

"So what are your plans once you leave all this luxury?" asked the colonel with a smile on his face but a definite tone of disappointment at knowing a valued fellow pilot and friend was leaving.

"Well, I've been working on an idea for starting a company that wouldn't be much different from what we do around here but I'll need experience first. You remember Mike Larson? He works for that Flying Cougars outfit and says he can get me on there. I figure I'll join them for a little while and learn all I can. I'll write the business plan along the way and try to sell my idea to some rich investors and start my own air cargo company.

"Yeah but the civilian world doesn't do things like we do. It's a completely different animal, Chris."

"That's what I'm counting on, Larry."

Colonel Schauer knew it was time to sign the separation papers neatly arranged on his desk. As he grimly nodded and began to sign the paperwork officially turning Captain Chris Walsh, United States Air Force, into just Mr. Chris Walsh, he said, "Well, this Air Force is losing a heck of a good man and a great pilot. I really wish you all the best, Chris." Both men stood and shook hands.

"Yeah, Larry. I'll miss you and all the guys."

"So you recommended Lieutenant Lee for upgrade to aircraft commander, huh?"

"I'd recommend that guy for upgrade to base commander if I thought he would get it. I'd fly with him anytime. I've never seen a cooler customer under pressure."

The two men exchanged promises to keep in touch that both knew weren't true.

Walking down the hall, Chris performed his last duty as an

officer in the United States Air Force and signed out of the official squadron log.

"So you're really doing it, huh?" asked a voice from behind Walsh.

Turning to see Major Hightower standing behind him with a hand offered for a handshake, Chris took his navigator's hand and answered, "Yeah, John. It's true. I've got a few more days around here but then I'm heading west."

"There's not much more west left from here."

"Well, if you went much further, you'd get wet. I figure I'll see if I meet any movie stars or take up surfing or something to pass my time when I'm not flying for Flying Cougars."

"Bunch of undisciplined civilian-types trying to do our job in the long-hairs' world," said Major Hightower with a shake of his head.

"Yep, may be, but I won't get shot at or have to watch the crews hose blood out of my cargo hold anymore."

"Yeah, roger that. Well, take care of yourself, Chris."

"You too, John. I'll keep in touch," lied Walsh.

Outside, he climbed into his 1961 Buick Wildcat that he had bought for three hundred dollars from another pilot who had left for Viet Nam two years earlier. The vehicle had no rear window and because its blue book value was less than nothing, he had no intention of throwing good money after bad by fixing it up. Still, it had been a reliable pile of bolts for two years. To deal with the occasional rain showers and lack of rear window, he had simply drilled holes in the floorboards to allow any rainwater to drain out of the backseat. It was a perfect vehicle for leaving in the 96th Airlift Squadron building parking lot for weeks at a time. Based on the increasing quantity of smoke emanating from the tailpipe, he knew there was a seal problem in one of the cylinders and the days of the Buick were quickly drawing to a close. Not wanting to be stranded on the side of the highway, Walsh intended to be the owner of a new Chevy Mustang by close-of-business the next day. Earlier that afternoon, he had taken one on a test drive with the salesman at the dealership a mile from the airbase. His bank had a healthy cushion of cash from being smart with his money while in the Air Force. Since he was going to pay cash, the salesman even agreed to let him abandon the Buick on the lot.

Five minutes later, Chris pulled into the parking lot of the officer's club and went inside, immediately spotting Lieutenant Lee at a table, nursing a beer. As he took a seat at the table, Lee asked, "So you really did it?"

"Yeah, the old man signed them right in front of me. I'll be here for another three days finishing up some paperwork, including my official recommendation for your upgrade to aircraft commander."

"So you're sure you are going to get on with that cargo outfit?"

"My buddy said it's a lock. I just think getting the lay of the land in civilian cargo aviation is the smartest thing before trying to start my own company. You know I fully expect you to come on board if you ever get tired flying for Uncle Sam."

Just as Lee was about to say something, Chris noticed his eyes locking on something behind him. When he turned his head to see what had commanded Lee's attention so thoroughly, he saw the source of distraction and couldn't fault his friend in the slightest.

Taking a seat at a table across the room was a breathtakingly attractive female major with classic Nordic features including blonde hair that, although pinned up in an appropriately conservative military style, seemed to glow with its own luminescence, and a pair of aquamarine-colored eyes.

Accompanying the major was a stern-looking brunette captain who would be more Chris' type if it wasn't for the perma-scowl she seemed to wear perpetually fixed on her face. He remembered once hearing an officer newly assigned to Travis approach her at the bar and ask the captain what her sign was. That her response had been, "Exit, Major," had come as no surprise. Chris knew both women from his flight physicals. Just about every single man on the base knew Doctor Erika Jensen, the major, was the youngest physician working for Colonel Stevens, the lead Flight Surgeon on the base and she was often in the company of Captain Wendy Riley, the brunette, who was in charge of the emergency room nurses stationed at Travis.

"My goodness," murmured Lee.

Laughing at the relatively tame reaction to Major Jensen's

appearance, compared to many he had heard in his two years stationed at Travis, he reached across the table and firmly put his hand on Lee's shoulder.

"You certainly have impeccable taste, Lieutenant. Major Jensen is a lovely woman but with a…bovine excrement detector sharper than a scalpel. I've seen her shoot quite a few expert pilots down in flames. If you make an approach, you better be darn sure you have your flaps and trim set just right in case you have to go around."

"Gosh, Captain…uh…Chris, I didn't say I wanted to ask her to marry me. I just thought she was pretty. Besides, I'm being rude. We were talking about your future. I apologize for the distraction."

"Hey, man. It's totally understandable. In fact, I've got to head back to my place and start packing up."

They both stood and gave each other a strong handshake. In the moment, Lee wanted to tell his mentor and closest friend in the Air Force how much he was grateful for, but the words were unnecessary.

"I'll call you once I get settled in Los Angeles."

"I know you will. I'll…," said Lee as his voice cracked.

Feeling the emotions welling up in him as well, Chris smiled and headed them off by saying, "I'd actually give a strapping young buck like you even money on getting a date with the major. It's just the brunette anti-aircraft cannon sitting with her you'll have to neutralize first."

They gave each other a quick man-hug and Chris headed for the door. As he reached it and turned back, a huge smile broke across his face. What he saw his protégé doing was one of the bravest things he had seen in a long time. Lieutenant Lee was standing a respectful distance from the table where Major Jensen and Captain Riley sat, saying something he couldn't hear. Remarkably, the major was actually smiling and, in what could only be described as a miracle, Captain Riley seemed to have a slight upturn to the corners of her mouth as well.

Chris thought, *Attaboy, killer. I just hope it's not stall, spin, crash, burn, die.*

Just as he reached the door, he turned to see Major Jensen pull a chair out for Lieutenant Lee.

I really should start going to church again because I've clearly just witnessed and act of God, he thought as he walked through the lot to his car.

After fifteen minutes of conversation, the fact that Erika Jensen and Jack Lee had grown up a few miles from each other came to light.

"You've got to be kidding! I went to St. Catherine Labouré!" said Lee.

"Our Lady of Perpetual Help!" exclaimed Dr. Jensen with the tone of complete shock that coincidences in life with infinitesimally small probabilities generate.

"Two kids from the same home town? Oh, well then it *must* be fate. If you two will excuse me, I'll go get fitted for my bridesmaid dress," said Wendy. Even though her intent was mild ridicule, she already sensed something powerful occurring between Major Jensen and Lieutenant Lee. She had spent enough hours watching Erika decline offers of company from a myriad of men to know she had never seen her best friend look at a man in the same way she was looking at the handsome pilot across from her.

Lee heard what Wendy said and momentarily flashed a warm smile at her then turned his attention back to Erika. It was a bizarre feeling but something felt completely logical about Captain Riley's comment. He *really* hoped Wendy was right.

**Travis Air Force Base
Airbase Flightline
San Jose, California
1540 Hours Local Time
Saturday, December 6th, 1969**

Chapter Ten

"Thanks for all your solid work," said Captain Jack Lee to his co-pilot, Lieutenant Brad Schinstock. Lee enjoyed moving his legs and stretching his back as they walked across the tarmac toward the base operations building. One of the things Lee really loved about living in the high desert was the moderate temperatures throughout the winter months. It was a dry, comfortable seventy-two degrees as they walked from the jet.

"Pleasure flying with you," answered the young lieutenant as they walked across the tarmac.

From the direction of the squadron building came a high-pitched, "Baby, over here…it's me!"

Standing just outside the squadron building a hundred yards off, a redheaded girl wearing a tee-shirt and very short shorts jumped up and down, holding a six-pack of beer, smiling ear-to-ear. The lieutenant looked at Jack with an expression just short of pleading, playfully slugged his aircraft commander in the shoulder and said, "If you don't mind, boss, is there any possible way you'd consider…"

"I'll close the flight plan, Schinstock. Get out of here," said Lee.

"You're a great guy to fly with, Captain. Let's do it again soon," exclaimed the lieutenant.

"Yeah, yeah…"

The lieutenant sprinted ahead, past the waiting crew bus, and across the hundred yards to the squadron building in impressive time. His helmet bag danced around in one hand and his garment bag flapped in the wind behind him like a superhero's cape.

"Looks like Lieutenant Schinstock has some plans for tonight, Captain," said his navigator, Major Glenn Schulman, as both officers watched the lieutenant drop his bags and lift the exuberant girl high into the air.

"Yeah, Glenn, it sure looks that way," answered Lee with a weary tone.

Two days earlier, the C-141 Starlifter they had flown into Hawaii experienced a blown hydraulic pump on the number four engine as they were inbound to Hickam Air Force Base. There had been no spare available that day, delaying Lee's return to Travis by a day. The equipment failure had been particularly unfortunate for Lee because, had he returned on Friday when he had expected to, he and Erika had a date night planned.

"I'm so sorry, angel. It's a stupid hydraulic pump on the engine and the first sergeant here says they won't have another until the re-supply tomorrow."

"Oh, Jack, I totally understand. I'd really love to see you this weekend but I'm on duty Saturday afternoon until 0430 hours Sunday. My boss is down in Texas at Brooks attending a conference and I'm basically it for my unit this weekend."

"Maybe we could go to Mass together on Sunday?"

"Great. Just let me know what Mass you want to go to when you get back here and we'll talk then."

Stupid hydraulic pump, thought Lee as he had hung up with Erika the previous afternoon. It would have been their twenty-third official date. He had been keeping count.

After closing the flight plan and being dropped off at his quarters, Lee showered and dressed for a run. After so many hours in the jet, he needed a run to get back to feeling human. Lee locked the door to his quarters and stretched a few minutes to limber up. Heading west down his street, he passed the base chapel, and wound his way through some other residential streets until he reached Airbase Parkway and headed west toward the main base entry gates. As he continued along the main road, he began to hear a number of emergency sirens coming from somewhere east of him on the base. A security police car screamed past him down Airbase Parkway. Lee looked back and didn't see any smoke coming from the runways. He'd had enough stress-inducing situations over his last ten-day mission and made the conscious choice to ignore the commotion.

    A few paces short of the sentry shack at the airbase entrance, one of the gargantuan new C-5A Galaxy cargo jets rumbled overhead, the sound waves from its four twelve-foot-tall General Electric TF-39 engines drowning out all other noise including the cacophony of sirens, for several seconds. A football field-sized shadow momentarily turned midday to dusk as the avionic leviathan lumbered overhead. Looking up at the jet, it was almost impossible to believe something that large could remain airborne. Although the C-5A was a very impressive sight to behold, Lee counted among his blessings the decision to turn down the opportunity to be part of the first cadre of pilots to fly that monster. A former 96th Squadron pilot who had made that fateful jump to the Galaxy program had related a harrowing story of a little engine mounting problem over beers one night.

    "We were on a test flight out of Dobbins and had just released brakes. As we began to roll, we heard...well, felt a *bang* that stopped our hearts dead in mid-beat. The number three engine just popped off, pylon and all and all we saw on that side of the jet was a wall of flame. We thought we were going to fry to death, right there in the cockpit, forty feet off the ground. There are only three huge bolts that hold those big, screaming beasts to the wings and the rearmost one decided it was a perfect time to shear off. The freaking engine flipped itself entirely over on the wing and sliced the wing completely off. When it did, thirty thousand pounds of JP-4 went spraying all over the place. Not my favorite aviation memory."

    "Well, at least that didn't happen at thirty thousand feet, brother."

    "Amen to that, my friend," his colleague had said, taking a

long pull off his beer.

As Lee remembered that conversation while he jogged past the guard shack, he just shook his head as he continued to run, thanking God he wasn't forced to transition into those jets. He had heard other complaints from pilots about the unprecedented amounts of ramp time the C-5A required. According to guys that knew, the Galaxies needed over sixteen hours of maintenance time for every hour of flight time. The community of transport pilots that flew the Galaxy had given her the nickname "FRED." The acronym was definitely not a term of endearment. The "F" stood for an expletive Lee never used and the other three letters stood for "Ridiculous Economic (interchangeable with 'Environmental') Disaster."

It was typical military pilot humor.

Stuck waiting hours or, on rare occasions, an entire day for his C-141 Starlifter to be repaired over his past year flying in the 96th Military Airlift Squadron, oftentimes at remote military bases, Lee had considered the Starlifter a fickle piece of machinery before hearing stories from Galaxy pilots. If he had been a "FRED" driver, he could have easily been grounded in Hawaii for a week.

At the mile point in his run, just outside the base, Lee picked up the pace. As he often did while running, Lee had a little chat with God, thanking Him for a list of things, not the least of which was another safe return to the U.S.

"We're getting a bad one. ETA ten minutes. Six year-old boy struck by a hit-and-run driver. Medics say he's not doing well," said the charge nurse, Captain Wendy Riley. "They're not sure he's going to make it here."

"Trauma Two," was all Dr. Erika Jensen said in response. It had been remarkably quiet month right up until then. In April, Erika had seen everything from broken bones, a few cases of alcohol poisoning, and an endless procession of snotty kids with high fevers from a spring outbreak of a nasty flu virus. There were also the occasional self-inflicted injuries resulting from someone doing something inherently brainless. The airman that had attempted to open a can of pork beans with a K-Bar knife and had taken his thumb almost completely off had been her particular favorite. They had managed to reattach his thumb. She had heard through the grapevine that the other men in the 60th Maintenance Squadron were continuing to mercilessly give him the thumbs-up since his return to limited duty.

Five minutes later, the ambulance backed up to the doors and everyone on staff in the ER could tell by the medics' expression that it was hopeless. The minute she saw the boy, her heart sank. His beautiful green eyes were completely fixed and dilated when she shone her pen light on them.

"Call it at 1653 hours," declared Erika five very intense, long minutes later. There had been no hope whatsoever. The child's entire chest cavity had been crushed under the weight of the truck that had run him down. Trying to keep up a professional demeanor, she looked down at the fractured little body and fought back tears as she said, "Get the chaplain."

"Yes, Ma'am," responded Captain Riley as she was already picking up the phone to do just that. A very profane series of thoughts about the driver responsible for this tragedy was kept to the confines of Riley's mind with the utmost effort.

"Where were this kid's parents while he was running around in the street?" demanded Erika as the anger over the circumstance that brought the child into her ER began to take the place of the adrenaline that was beginning to wear off.

"Doc, the kid was in his own front lawn," said one of the two paramedics that had brought the boy in. "The SPs already have the airman responsible in custody. We arrived on scene and there were tire tracks across the lawn. The family lives in the corner house where Wyoming curves past Michigan Street and the guy missed the turn completely."

"How fast was this idiot going?"

"Ma'am, he was drunk."

"Please tell me that's not true."

"Ma'am, I brought up the police frequency when we were inbound with the patient and heard the SP broadcast the subject was 10-55. That's…"

"Drunk." She began to absolutely seethe with anger.

Five minutes later, Erika and the young base chaplain, Father Gregory, began the long walk to the waiting room. There had been two instances during her civilian medical career where she had the unenviable duty of informing next-of-kin, but never the mother of a child.

Ten people in varying states of emotional distress sat in the waiting room, the mother of the child easily identifiable by the blood-stained white tee-shirt she wore. Two security policemen in the room were asking questions in quiet, sympathetic tones for their official report when everyone looked up and collectively stopped breathing, absolutely frozen in shock for a moment at the appearance of the doctor and the chaplain. Without having to be told, little David Jacobs' mother knew her son was dead.

It was all Erika could do to force the words out, "I'm so sorry."

The bloodcurdling scream reverberated throughout the emergency room. It broke everyone's heart.

Just as Erika was hanging up her office phone with the base morgue, Captain Riley knocked on her door and stuck her head in the office.

"Major, you're not going to believe this but the airman that ran over that kid is on the way in with an abdominal gunshot wound."

"What now?" she said, shaking her head. Over the past ten minutes she had been making calls to put in motion the mechanism to bring a trained social worker, a staff member of the judge advocate, and numerous other trained professionals to help the family deal with the ramifications of losing their little boy. With each call she made, having to relate that an innocent child boy was the victim of vehicular homicide, Erika became more incensed. Although she knew it would be totally impossible, and beneath her dignity to do so, the impulse to tell Riley to put the guy in a room and conveniently forget about him crossed her mind.

Erika stood and marched across the emergency room to Trauma One with Captain Riley. She could hear the gunshot wound patient moaning from within the room that was being guarded by three very angry looking security policemen.

"We were dragging this guy out of his pickup truck and he went for Sergeant Davis' weapon. The guy couldn't even talk. We thought he was too drunk to see straight and there was no way he'd make a boneheaded move like that, but he got the pistol clear of the holster and I had to drop him," said the muscular security policeman whose nametag identified him as Captain Vianna.

With supreme effort, Erika restrained herself from blurting, *That's not entirely a bad thing.* Donning the disposable smock and gloves, she approached the gurney and immediately recognized the patient. Erika's anger finally got the best of her. Realizing she had personally attended to this guy two other times since coming to Travis eighteen months earlier, Erika turned to the security policeman and said, "I know this jerk!" She began going through the process of assessing his vital signs and the wound. As she did so, she thought, *What are you doing back in my ER, you moron? You finally did it this time, Airman. You killed a kid, got yourself gutshot, and if we save you, you're going to buried under Leavenworth. What a useless waste.*

"Doc, we know this guy pretty good," said Captain Vianna. "We've dragged his butt back to base knee-walking drunk six times this year. I personally brought him in here last year, near dead from alcohol poisoning. I don't know how, on God's green earth, he hasn't been discharged yet but I guess this will fix him, but good."

As Erika angrily snapped the latex gloves off her hands and flung them into the receptacle, she said, "The last time this guy was brought in, I put in my official report to his commanding officer that he needed some sort of help. I diagnosed him with chronic alcoholism. His blood and liver panels were those of a sixty-year-old and I told him then that if he kept up with the booze, he'd be dead before he was forty. Apparently my warning didn't mean much to his CO because look what we've got now."

"Where am I? What are you doing to me?" pleaded the airman through gritted teeth as he began to struggle against the restraints he had been strapped to the gurney with.

"You're in the emergency room, Airman. You've been shot."

"Sh..shot?!? How…what's going on?" pleaded the kid as he

came out of the alcohol-induced blackout he had been in.

"You fought with the SPs and grabbed one of their guns."

The senior security policeman lost his temper. "And it's the last time for you, pal! You killed a kid! You ran him over on his own lawn and if you live, I'm going to personally see to it that you live twenty-three hours a day for the rest of your life in a concrete box in the middle of Kansas!"

"A kid…? I kil..killed a…," choked Airman Brian Walls, when he suddenly began to gasp for air and the heart monitor suddenly emitted a shrieking whine. The airman began to convulse, violently straining against the gurney restraints.

"He's in v-fib! Crash cart now!" ordered Erika.

Ten minutes later, for the second time in one shift, Erika turned to Wendy and said, "Call time-of-death at 1722 hours."

It was too much for Airman Walls to survive. The lethal combination of three times the legal blood-alcohol limit, the trauma from the gunshot, and the sudden realization that he had irreparably destroyed the rest of his life pushed Airman Walls over the cardiovascular brink.

As Erika exited the trauma room, the effects of watching two lives utterly wasted in the span of an hour was more than her ability to keep a stiff upper lip could take. She ripped off the protective gown over her scrubs, shoved it in the receptacle in the trauma room, walked to her office ignoring several nurses asking questions, and slammed her door as hard as she could. A crack formed in the center of the door glass. Staff in the ER looked at each other with expressions of silent shock.

As Lieutenant Lee was about to jump in the shower, the phone rang for the second time in as many minutes. The first call had been a friend in his squadron telling him the news about the child that was sweeping like wildfire across the base. Picking up the phone for the second time in as many minutes, he answered and was highly surprised to hear Captain Riley's voice. Standing in a towel, he simply listened to her whisper into the phone. He could hear the din of numerous voices in the background.

"Look Jack, I could get in real trouble for telling you this but some really bad things went down here today. Did you hear about the kid?"

"Yeah. I just did."

"Well the guy that hit the kid was brought in too after being shot by the SPs. Erika lost both of them. I've never seen anything like it and she's taking it really hard. The CG's chief-of-staff was just in with her for an hour and I'm sure that was no bowl of cherries. All she's been doing for the past two hours is dealing with the JAG people, the SPs, the brass, and a whole bunch of other folks involved in this disaster."

"I really appreciate you telling me."

"I'm not sure exactly why I called you but I was just hoping you might try to do something to, you know, cheer her up or something."

"Do you think she's still on till 0430?"

"Not a chance. General Corbett had his chief-of-staff call in Erika's relief early so she could focus on completing her report for this incident and then he ordered her off-duty until tomorrow. I just left her office and she was just completing the last few sections and should be done in an hour at the latest."

"Wendy, I'm grateful. Thanks for...trusting me."

"I'm not sure exactly why I do, but...well, I do."

"Thank you."

Lee hung up, threw on a pair of jeans and a tee-shirt, and sprinted out the door to the lot of the bachelor officers' quarters, and jumped into his black 1969 Chevy Impala. Six minutes later, he pulled the powerful muscle car into the lot at the David Grant Medical Center and began driving around, looking for Erika's easily-spotted red Corvette Stingray. In the sea of grey, black, and Air-Force blue cars throughout the lot, he quickly found her car in the staff parking, found the nearest spot he could, and walked over to wait for her.

It wasn't long.

The look on her face was easily identifiable as full of stress and anger. Lee had never seen her so upset. She kept walking with her head down and didn't even see him until she almost walked directly into him.

"I heard it was a tough day," he said as she looked up. Upon seeing him, Erika stopped in her tracks. She had to look at him for a moment before it registered that he was really there. Through a wave of emotion that she'd been suppressing to maintain her appearance in front of her staff, Erika began to try to ask, "How…?" when her eyes filled with tears. Lee went to her, wrapped his arms around her, and stood silently holding her as she sobbed.

"It was just so pointless. I mean we knew this guy was headed for trouble the first time I saw him. Nobody around here listens…" she finally said when she regained her ability to speak.

"I'm so sorry you had to go through this, angel. I'm so sorry. I wish I could take the pain from you but I can't."

"I know, sweetheart, but I'm just so angry that I did everything I could to warn that kid's CO about him and it feels like I totally failed. I mean I know there is a God but sometimes I have a hard time seeing that. What kind of God kills a six-year-old kid?"

"I'll tell you what I believe. I don't think God killed that child or that sad kid with the drinking problem. In fact, I think things happen all the time that break God's heart. What killed that little boy appears to me to be a very sad man with a bad problem who couldn't feel God's love enough to not drink like he did. That's what I believe caused this awful thing today. We humans have an ability the angels don't. We have the ability to turn our back on God and go on doing things our way."

"But what am I supposed to do now?"

"I have an idea that works for me when I get angry about things. It might sound a bit weird."

For the first time in hours, Erika smiled slightly and asked, "What is it?"

"Well if you want to do something to help you deal with the feelings from this whole awful thing, would you be willing to go somewhere with me? Right now?"

Erika was about to say that she really wanted to go back her condo and get some sleep but suddenly the words she heard in her head were, *Go with him.*

"I…sure," she said.

Lee took her hand and walked with her to his car, opened the passenger door, and after starting the engine, slowly pulled out of the parking lot. Driving across the base, he continued to hold her hand, gently caressing it. The simple act was very calming and Erika began to feel the anger inside her begin to subside. Five minutes later, Lee parked in front of the base chapel, and walked hand-in-hand with Erika inside.

"Why don't we spend some time praying for all of the people affected by this tragedy today?" whispered Lee as they knelt in a pew.

"That sounds like a good idea," said Erika with a thin smile.

"I know this will sound a bit weird but I was thinking of praying especially for the sad airman who made such an awful mistake that cost so many people so dearly today. I think that guy could use some prayers."

Erika looked into his eyes, seeing he really meant that and, for a moment, she fought the instinct to disagree. It seemed so counter to her instincts to pray for the guy that caused all the trouble, but as Lee's words bounced around in her head, praying for the dead airman just made sense in her heart. She silently nodded.

For the next thirty minutes, Jack Lee and Erika sat, praying in the empty chapel. As they stood to leave, Erika realized that she no longer had a shred of anger toward the airman. Looking over at the handsome pilot next to her, Erika could swear she saw a glow to his face when he looked back at her.

It hit her just then. She really loved this man. She had known all along, during their six months of dating, that Jack was special but in that very moment, she knew without a doubt that any man who could help comfort her very soul was a treasure.

Again she heard the voice from within, *Go with this man.*

She smiled, reached over and took Jack's hand, and as their fingers intertwined, she thought, *I will.*

To look out at this kind of creation out here and not believe in God is, to me, impossible."

-John Glenn from Space Shuttle Discovery

Part Two:

New Headings

The 1970s

Photo provided by Melissa Stipes

Final Delivery / Will Dempsey

**Los Angeles International Airport
Los Angeles, California
Flying Cougars Airlines Cargo Terminal
8:55 A.M. Pacific Time
Monday, March 15th, 1972**

Chapter Eleven

Chris Walsh glanced at his Timex watch as he signed in at the front desk at the cargo terminal, steeling himself for the tirade he knew he was going to receive from Jerry Mitchell, the vice president of operations for Flying Cougars. Chris had called in sick for the entire week prior. Returning to work on that Monday, Chris was without a shred of evidence that he had seen anything resembling a doctor to satisfy the stringent company policy requiring medical documentation for any sick days. As Chris was about to leave his apartment that morning, he rolled his eyes, knowing exactly who was calling. For the next five seconds, Chris was treated to some of Jerry's trademark blustering. Before Chris could fully annunciate the word, "Hello," Jerry had barked, "Report to my office immediately when you get here and arrival better be at precisely at 0900 hours."

Click!

There hadn't even been a, "goodbye," or, "see you then," or any other manner of concluding a telephone conversation with a semblance of courtesy. There was just an abrupt hang-up.

Idiot! thought Chris as he placed his phone back on the cradle and finished packing his peanut butter and jelly sandwiches into his lunch box.

The air cargo operations of the hybridized airline/delivery service was the most costly to operate of the entire business and senior management was under tremendous pressure from the board of directors to make it profitable. When a pilot gave the impression he wasn't giving one hundred percent, he was quite quickly shown the door.

Chris had seen how tenuous a pilot's job security could be at Flying Cougars firsthand. His old Air Force buddy, Mike Larson, had been let go the week before. Mike had been the one to pave the way for Chris to come on board with Flying Cougars two years earlier when Chris had left the Air Force.

Within the human resources office of Flying Cougars was a file in which a final warning write-up for not completing paperwork resided. That documentation sat atop a slew of other formal reprimands in Mike's file. Mike was sloppy in his paperwork, sharp in his flying, and also a hair-trigger temper. In the last twelve months, Mike had been on final warning twice. Once for punching a ground crewman who got smart with him and, within a week of making it past the year probation period, was back on final warning for throwing his pilot's briefcase across the flight planning room when his flight schedule was changed at short notice. The briefcase had accidentally hit another pilot. The straw that broke the proverbial camel's back happened four days earlier. While being disciplined by Jerry once again for a relatively minor policy violation, Mike had informed the man ten years his junior with a receding hairline and a tasteless plaid suit, precisely what his personal and professional estimate of Jerry was, including those observations in expansive terms. Also included in the assessment was a stream of profanity which had sealed Mike's fate in regard to being on the payroll of Flying Cougars. When Mike had walked into Jerry's office that morning, had the ice he was standing on been any thinner, it would have been called water.

Mike had sounded quite self-assured over several drinks the night he had gotten fired. Drunk bravado was all it was. Right or wrong, Jerry had a job to report to the next morning and Mike didn't. Even if Mike's assessment of Jerry's character as an unqualified, untalented, and unnecessary paper-pusher was somewhat accurate, Jerry had pushed the right paper through human resources to bounce Chris' only close friend in the company out the door. The night Mike was let go at Flying Cougars and took the bitter edge off of being thrown away with an elephant-paralyzing number of drinks, Chris had helped his friend out the door of the bar and into the door of a cab.

The next morning, Chris heard renewed hope in his friend's voice as it came through his telephone.

"I gotta go buddy. I've got an interview with an outfit that flies supplies up in Alaska. At least nobody will be shooting at me.

"Great, Mike. I'm sure everything happens for a reason, right? Maybe getting set free from the most penny-pinching company in modern history might be just what you needed to find out what you really want to do," said Chris.

"Well, pal, just hang in there and don't let them give you any lip," said Mike.

"Roger that, buddy."

Arriving at the door with Jerry's name and title affixed on it, Chris rapped on the door jamb in an intentionally civilian pattern and pushed the door open. Although he had been repeatedly told by Jerry that any visit to his office was to be announced by two knocks and a wait for an invitation to enter, Chris just didn't feel like it. Jerry's already considerable scowl deepened as he began to annunciate, "Enter," even though Chris was two steps into the office at that point. Chris *hated* hearing the little tyrant address him as a senior officer did back when he was in the Air Force. Once, on a hop from LAX to Miami International, Chris and Mike had chatted about the affected military manner the thirty-three-year-old, whose father-in-law had founded Flying Cougars, seemed to cultivate even though he had never served in anything more militaristic than the Cub Scouts. Mike had once jokingly suggested holding a mock court martial for the terribly unpleasant Jerry on charges of "conduct unbecoming of an invertebrate."

"I'll get right the point Mr. Walsh. If Mr. Larson's luck hadn't run out last week, yours would have today," said Jerry from behind his well-worn laminate wood desk. "I don't know why you think you can just take a week's vacation whenever the mood strikes, but we have a business to run here."

"I understand Jerry. I was…"

"Let me make this perfectly clear Mr. Walsh," said Jerry, cutting him off in mid-sentence with a hand held up to signify complete disinterest in anything Chris was going to say. "We pay you a handsome salary to fly our planes for us. If you don't like flying for us, feel free to put in an application with one of the airlines? I know the pay is better and cannot, for the life of me, understand why you want to fly for us when you could be sunning yourself in Hawaii or seeing New York."

For a moment, as his boss said it, the images of beaches and sophisticated and lovely ladies in Manhattan sounded appealing. Then, before the impulse to say something that would have made Mike proud won out, he remembered why he had chosen to come on board at Flying Cougars in the first place.

Chris had taken the job to learn everything he could about the operation of a cargo carrier from the inside out. He knew the pay was better with the traditional commercial airlines than at Flying Cougars. He could chat up stewardesses any time he wanted at the numerous lounges within the commercial aviation area of LAX, and the Air Force had shown him more exotic destinations than most people would see in a lifetime. The decision to come on board the growing cargo carrier was very calculated. Unfortunately, his drive to start his own company had begun to fade as the day-to-day grind of working for Flying Cougars took its toll. For a time, he had considered bringing Mike in on the plan to start his own company. Unfortunately Chris had quickly seen that Mike's temper was a tremendous liability and, as long as they had gone back together, friendship or not, Mike just wasn't dependable enough to trust with Chris' entire future. There was also the small challenge of finding financial backing as well as writing the business plan, marketing and advertising strategy, operational plans, and every other element of starting a company from scratch entailed. Chris knew he couldn't just lease a plane and hang his shingle on an office next to the airport. His vision of a global air shipping empire needed true professionals and, more importantly, a mint full of cash for start-up funds. Chris had worked long into the evening at the public library and his apartment on sheer faith on crafting a plan on paper. Even with a well-developed business plan, Chris knew building a team of staff professionals would be nowhere as overwhelming a task as acquiring the needed mountain of startup cash. By his most conservative estimates, to start a shipping company with the vision he had would require a minimum of twenty million dollars of capital for the operating budgets of the first two fiscal years.

"I suggest you think long and hard about whether you want to continue with us Mr. Walsh," said Jerry. The words snapped Chris out of the internal movie in his mind that he was playing about his dream cargo carrier. Looking at Jerry and beginning to hear him again, Chris heard his superior say, "You've got the Phoenix run tonight and I suggest you use the time on that trip to consider how important a future with Flying Cougars really is to you." Without any further comment, Jerry returned to reading some paperwork on his desk. No, "That's all," or "We're through here." There was just a return to his paperwork as if Chris was so insignificant an item on Jerry's agenda that day that a formal end of the meeting and dismissal was unnecessary. Chris wrote off the impoliteness as the sort of posturing made by a guy who had authority and no talent for using it.

"Thanks for your time, boss," said Chris as he walked out of Jerry's office. As he reached the end of the hallway, Chris began thinking about where his post-military career might take him from there. He was fairly convinced his days at Flying Cougars were numbered. The uneasy feeling of knowing yet another chapter of his life was closing without the slightest inkling of what door might open for him was weighing heavily on Chris' mind walking down the long corridor that led back to the main office area.

"Chris, there was a call for you when you were in his royal highness' office," said Jennifer Wilcox, the office manager as she handed him a small, pink telephone message slip. "Somebody named Jack Lee from Chicago left a message."

Jennifer was a woman that had obviously been a knockout back in the days of Jerry Lee Lewis and Buddy Holly but had put some mileage on during the era of Jefferson Airplane and Joan Baez.

"Thanks, Jennifer. You look nice today," answered Chris with a warm smile, as he took the message slip from her.

Wonder what Jack's calling about? pondered Chris as he left the offices and headed for the crew lounge where the two other men he would be flying with on the short flight from LAX to Phoenix that night. He decided to call his old co-pilot from the relative privacy of the crew lounge telephone and see what was on Captain Lee's mind.

As he entered the door marked 'Crew Lounge', a radio was playing the program *American Top Forty*. Casey Kasem was saying, "And now for the third week in a row at number one, the bittersweet story of love lost down by the sea: *Brandy by the Looking Glass.*"

Chris sung the lyrics under his breath as he completed the flight plan paperwork. It was a catchy tune that reminded him of visits to his grandparents on the Maryland shore as a child. Like most guys, Chris didn't mind singing in the privacy of his car or shower but when the two other members of his crew, First Officer Benny Smith and his engineer, Glenn Strain, walked in, his musical mumblings immediately ceased.

"How's it going, Captain?" asked Benny. He knew Chris had been tight with Mike. It was an awkward moment for Benny, knowing that he had been assigned to the crew as a result of the captain's closest friend being shown the door by Flying Cougars. Benny was quite relieved when, with a small smirk, Chris shot back,

"Never better, thanks."

Benny took it as a good sign that flying together as a new crew would not be an exceedingly painful transition.

"We met last year at the annual party up at old man Jennings's house," said Chris to Benny, extending his hand.

"Yeah, I sort of remember that," replied Benny. "You'll have to forgive me if my recollection is a bit fuzzy. Open bars tend to have that unfortunate effect on me."

Smiling, and shaking his new first officer's hand, Chris said "I can understand that. I've sampled the local brew on six continents and I have no guess how many islands while flying for Uncle Sam," and they shared a laugh.

121

By what Chris considered a cruel twist of fate, his pedantic, self-righteous boss, Jerry Mitchell, had somehow wooed the heart of one Ms. Emily Jennings ten years earlier at the tenth anniversary company party. That would bear no relevance to Chris' life whatsoever except that Emily was the eldest daughter of one Mr. Alan Jennings, the former W.W. II Marine pilot who had founded Flying Cougars twenty years earlier with a single surplus Douglas DC-3. The fleet of planes had grown to nearly fifty Lockheed L-1011s that flew passengers and cargo across the world, mostly to complete government contracts. Flying Cougars had been one of the main civilian carriers utilized by the Pentagon to fly American boys to the exotic destination of Viet Nam. Flying Cougars also distinguished itself as the first company to offer three-day delivery to anywhere in the country and numerous points in Europe, weather permitting.

"If you guys want to get your details squared away before departure, I've got to make a quick phone call and then we'll head out," said Chris. Glenn and Benny both nodded and began to prepare their paperwork at the little table in the middle of the room while Chris went to the telephone and dialed his former co-pilot and student.

"Captain Lee, it's me, Chris calling back. How in the heck are you, killer?"

"Chris, please call me Jack. I know it's going to take a bit of getting used to with all this undisciplined civilian name-calling but I separated from the Air Force in January."

"Really? So what are you doing with yourself these days?" asked Chris.

"Well, when I'm not peddling medical devices, planning the wedding seems to be the only thing my free time is allocated to."

"Wedding? You can't possibly mean….?"

Jack's excitement barely contained itself as he tried to say, as coolly and offhandedly as possible, "Well, yeah Chris. It's my pleasure to inform you that Dr. Erika Jensen is about to become Dr. Erika Lee."

Chris' excitement bubbled over and he shouted, "No way! No possible way! You somehow managed to corral Major Jensen? I knew you had talent kid!"

"Well, it was actually Lieutenant Colonel Jensen. She was promoted to light colonel six months before we decided to resign our commissions."

"That's fantastic, pal! So when's the wedding?"

"Just under three months from today. Saturday, June fourteenth. Do you think that might be enough lead-time to free up your calendar so you could attend?"

"You can absolutely count on me being there," said Chris.

"I'm thrilled to hear that. Let me ask you a small favor if I could?"

"Sure?"

"Do you think you might be able to come in a day early? I was hoping Thursday instead of Friday. I've got something completely unrelated to the wedding I want to talk to you about and I promise it will be something that will interest you."

Chris thought for a moment and said, "Yeah, I'll find a way to make that happen."

"Great, well then I'll be seeing you in a couple of weeks. Just call me if anything comes up."

They said their goodbyes. Chris hadn't seen Jack for nearly three years. They had talked a handful of times since he had left the Air Force but the conversations had been no more substantial than all 'old buddy' conversations always were. Jack always asked how Chris' plans for his own company were going and Chris always told him he was still doing the research and Jack always encouraged him to keep at it.

Married! Wow! Well, it couldn't have happened to a better guy, thought Chris.

An hour later, after strapping into his seat in the cockpit, Chris asked his first officer and engineer, "So did you guys bring your golf clubs? I hear there is a new golf course just outside the airport and it's supposed to be great." Chris had taken up golf since leaving the Air Force. Although Jack Nicklaus had nothing to worry about, he had developed into a pretty good player, holding a ten handicap at his home course. He always stowed his clubs aboard planes he flew whenever possible and there was going to be a layover between flights.

"Actually, Captain, there is a nice young lady that works at the hotel we're staying at that I have every intention of getting to know better," said Glenn with a grin.

"Yeah, well, when James Dean here is making time with the catering manager at the Hilton, I'll join you on the links," said Benny.

"Great," said Chris. The crew completed their checklists and obtained clearance to taxi to Runway Two-Nine-Left. As he sat in yet another Lockheed aircraft, preparing to fly cargo to an expectant customer, Chris thought, *The more things change, the more they stay the same.*

Five minutes later, Chris advanced the throttles and the jet accelerated down the runway. Out the right side of the cockpit windshield, the distinctive dome-shaped main terminal of Los Angeles International Airport zipped in and out of view as they lifted off. The sprawl of Los Angeles dropped away beneath them as the jet rose through some scattered cloud banks. Catalina Island off the coast quickly came into view. As Chris pondered the question of his future, and the jet rose through twenty thousand feet, a hole in the clouds materialized. Suddenly, the view of the fiery orange sun dipping into the Pacific Ocean was awe-inspiring. The view instantly made all Chris' worries about where he was going in life vanish. It seemed as though an inexplicable feeling of calmness was just flowing into him. The sensation lasted a few moments until he began to dwell again on the drain working for someone else was causing on his enthusiasm for flying.

Coming around to the south and then banking onto an easterly heading that would take them on their hour and a half flight to Phoenix, Chris knew that driving airplanes for Flying Cougars was taking all the joy out of being a pilot. The feeling of exhilaration from lifting off the runway, as the whole world sprawled itself out in front of him, just wasn't there anymore. He knew his days at Flying Cougars were numbered. Glancing at the view again of the golden sunlight shining through the break in the clouds gave him an inexplicable sense of peace.

Whatever it is, it's got to be better than this, he thought.

**O'Hare International Airport
Chicago, Illinois
Cargo Operations Terminal
12:50 P.M. Central Time
Thursday, June 12th, 1972**

Chapter Twelve

One of the benefits of being a pilot for Flying Cougars was a free ride in the jump seat of any available cargo flight. Chris deadheaded along on a delivery run from Las Vegas to Chicago, arriving at the cargo terminal an hour ahead of schedule thanks to a speedy ground crew in Las Vegas and a considerable tail wind. After exiting the cargo terminal, Chris began making his way toward the main airport entrance.

"Hey there, brother. I got in a bit earlier than expected so I'll just grab a drink at the bar here just off the main entrance," said Chris into the pay phone. He had caught Jack just as he and Erika were about to leave her home in the north shore suburb of Glenview for the airport to pick him up.

"Alright, buddy. We both can't wait to see you. Erika needs to be back at her house by four to meet with the florist and finalize menus with the caterers so we'll be there as fast as we can."

As Chris looked over at the bar, a woman with long, auburn hair was cleaning a highball glass with a towel and looking back at him with a pair of mint-green eyes. He smiled and she rewarded him with a quick wink before turning away to arrange something on the counter behind her.

"Lemme' make a suggestion. Don't set any land speed records getting here. I'll be making myself quite comfortable at this Houlihan's place just inside the main terminal entrance," said Chris.

"Roger that, my friend."

Chris hung up, picked up his two bags, and made a direct approach to the bar and the woman he felt a powerful compulsion to make the acquaintance of.

After three flying stories and two exchanged phone numbers, Chris sat at the bar, drinking in the words spoken by Keely Kennedy, the bartender. A bomb could have detonated behind Chris and it would be even money whether he would have noticed. She was telling a few bartending stories of her own, each relayed with the pleasant lilt of a woman born and raised on the Emerald Isle. As she finished telling Chris about a quaint little bar she knew in the Lincoln Park area, the chemistry between them almost palpable, Jack and Erika walked in.

"Miss, is this old man bothering you?" asked Jack playfully. His face wore the expectant joy that seeing old friends after a considerable time apart generates.

At the sound of Jack's voice, Chris' mind returned to his body sitting in his barstool at the little airport bar. With a mile-wide grin, he stood and hugged his old co-pilot hard, lifting him off the ground with moderately alcohol-fueled enthusiasm.

"I guess you must have finally figured out precisely how to set your flaps and trim, my boy," said Chris while winking at Erika.

Knowing quite well what the Air Force pilot-speak meant, Erika laughed and said, "Well, Captain Walsh, as your former flight surgeon, I'm a bit concerned. My trained medical eye tells me that there is a pronounced absence of precious metal encircling the fourth digit of your left hand. Are you to have me believe that a charming, eligible pilot like yourself hasn't found a suitable co-pilot yet?"

Chris looked back at Keely and, in a moment of childish enthusiasm replied, "Well, I'm working on it." For a half-second, he locked eyes with Keely, feeling like his eyes were magnetically connected to hers. He didn't know, until then, that such deep level of attraction was possible.

"Uh, Keely, I'd like to introduce you to my former co-pilot, Captain...," said Chris as he paused for a moment and turned to Jack and asked, "It was captain when you got out, right? I mean you didn't break any of their airplanes and get busted back to lieutenant or anything, right?"

"Yeah, buddy, it was captain."

"Well then, I'd like to introduce you to Captain....uh, Jack Lee and his incredibly talented, yet tragically nearsighted fiancé, Dr. Erika Jensen."

Keely stopped cleaning her glass and her head cocked to the right. She asked, "You wouldn't happen to be a relation of the Dr. Erik Jensen that invented the cardiovascular stent are you?"

Erika turned to Keely and said, "Yes, actually. He's my father." With a quizzical look, she asked, "Are you in medical school? How do you know about him?"

Keely's hands came to her mouth. Her eyes began to glisten with moisture and she took a moment to compose herself before answering. Jack and Chris just looked at each other in reaction to the unexpected show of emotion from such a seemingly benign question.

"My father came over from Castlebar last year to see a specialist at Northwestern. Too many years of cigarettes and Guinness had done quite a number on his heart. He was told that all his arteries were so far gone that there was no hope. They told my daddy that he should start making final plans until your father came up with the stent that saved his life."

Erika's eyes also slightly misted over in reaction to the unexpected emotion from Keely. The emotion was understandable. Dr. Erik Jensen's device had, in fact, saved Liam Kennedy's, as well as dozens of other people's lives within the first year of the device passing the rigorous process of FDA approval and being available to heart surgeons.

Turning to Jack with a radiant smile, Erika said, "You once asked me why I chose medicine."

Chris, somewhat uncomfortable in such emotionally-charged scenes, instinctively used his sense of humor to lighten the mood.

"You see, now you've gone and done it. You've wasted all your tears and the wedding isn't even until Saturday," he said to Erika.

Keely dabbed her eyes dry with a towel from her apron and said, "My goodness! You two are getting married this Saturday? Christopher, why didn't you tell me that you were here to go to a wedding?"

"We're not altogether sure he's actually aware of the concept of marriage," joked Jack while giving Chris a light elbow to the ribs.

Glancing at Keely, Chris said, "I had planned to tell you all about it over dinner."

Keely beamed and said, "Alright there, mister pilot. Go ahead and have fun with your friends. We'll continue our conversation later. Dr. Jensen, please convey my gratitude to your father for saving mine."

Erika shot a glance at Jack. He nodded back immediately and then they both looked at Chris with smiles across their lips.

"What?"

Erika turned to Keely and said, "Would you happen to have any plans for this weekend, Ms...?"

Chris looked at Keely, then at Erika, then back to Keely with a sheepish expression, realizing he didn't even know her last name.

Keely smiled and let Chris off the hook by peeling off a guest check from her tablet and, writing on it said, "Kennedy. Keely Kennedy. Just like your president. See, Mr. Pilot, it's just that easy to spell."

Jack and Erika laughed at the passing of the awkward situation and Keely winked at Chris as she began to hand the paper to him once she finished writing her phone number on it. Just as it was about to touch his fingertips, Keely playfully snatched it back, held it up out of his reach and said, "Just to make sure you really are a pilot, let me test your vision. Can you read those numbers clearly?"

Jack and Erika laughed again as Chris dutifully recited her phone number.

Erika then said, "Well, Ms. Kennedy, I'd love to offer you the opportunity to thank my dad personally and we need someone to keep our dear Chris out of trouble."

Keely smiled broadly, displaying a set of movie-star white teeth and said, "I'd be honored. I'll get someone to cover my shift Saturday night."

"Alright, it's decided then. You'll escort our good friend Chris here to the wedding and make him look good." said Erika with a mischievous grin. Matchmaking and romance always seemed to be on the minds of women during a wedding. She could recall at least three of her friends that had met their future spouses while at a wedding.

"You three drive safely out of here," said Keely.

"Thanks, Keely," said Chris as he reached for his wallet.

"On the house, mister pilot," she said, giving him a mock salute with two fingers.

Chris smiled back, picked up his baggage and began to follow Jack and Erika out of the little airport bar. Not quite sure exactly how the events of the past few minutes had happened, he heard Keely call out to him as he reached the door of the bar.

"Hey, mister pilot...did you forget the tip?"

Chris stopped, turned back to her, and before he could say something, she said with perfect bartender timing, "Here's a tip: you better call me tonight."

Chris just laughed and returned her salute.

Walking through the airport, Chris and Jack talked animatedly about sports teams and other trivial subjects as Erika quietly listened to the banter, not wanting to interrupt the reunion. They continued through the airport as she listened to the sort of testosterone-fueled chatter that men engage in when not sure exactly what to say to each other.

As the three friends exited the main terminal, they were stopped in their tracks by a loud shouting match going on outside. A group of long-haired teenagers wearing tie-dyed shirts, beads, torn bell-bottom jeans were loudly jeering at two young Army sergeants in their Class-A uniforms as the sergeants were trying to exit the airport. The sergeants appeared to be close to the same age as the group of counter-culture youths accosting them. By the looks on the faces of the sergeants, only a wafer-thin layer of restraint prevented them from inflicting severe violence. The sergeants never expected that, for all the sacrifice they had made enduring the brutal combat they had survived, they would return stateside and be met with such an unbridled level of hate from the love-professing protesters.

"Get out of my way mister. You and your friends aren't prepared for the consequences if you keep this up," said the larger of the two sergeants although the smaller stood a good six feet tall. The biggest of the hippies was a stringy guy with a malicious sneer his only fearsome feature.

"What are you going to do, baby killer? You going to kill us just like you did the children over there?"

After a twenty-three hour trek across two continents and ten thousand miles, any air traveler would have been quick to lose his temper at mild inconveniences like lost baggage. If that air traveler had just spent a year in the most hellish combat ever seen in modern history, the last thing he would be expected to handle well would be vastly offensive, inaccurate indictments from people who neither had the intestinal fortitude to serve in combat, or a shred of truth about what was really going on in the war. Having expected to be welcomed home like a hero in the same manner their fathers had been after World War II but instead being met by a group of people screaming at them for their efforts, the verbal assault was undoubtedly shocking to the soldiers.

"You baby killers! Why don't you go back to Viet Nam and commit some more war crimes in the name of America!" yelled the stringy guy who seemed to be the biggest mouth of the group.

"Uh oh!" said Jack as the two sergeants dropped their bags simultaneously, immediately taking up a hand-to-hand combat stance.

With a voice that neither her groom-to-be nor Chris could ever remember hearing, Erika bellowed, "Sergeants! Do *not* engage these sad, pathetic children in their own games! You *will* pick up those bags, bid these misguided individuals a good day, and will *smile* as you do it!" Any drill sergeant would have been proud of the cadence, forcefulness, and timbre of Erika's voice as she attempted to stave off the imminent slaughter.

The two sergeants turned to see the face that had just issued the command voice they heard, fully expecting to see some female Army officer who had randomly happened upon the scene standing there. When they only saw Erika in her bright yellow sun dress glaring at them, they stood dumfounded for a moment, looked at each other, and burst into laughter.

Erika was a presence regardless of her tone of voice. She had spoken the soldier's language in just the right way to snap them out of attack mode before things got horribly ugly.

"Yes Ma'am," said the larger sergeant.

The two soldiers picked up their bags as the also speechless hippies said nothing. Before walking off, both sergeants snapped to attention, gave a sharp salute to their detractors, and marched off. Just then, an airport policeman exited the terminal and walked purposefully toward the group.

"Officer, I believe these youths have no tickets or any business at the airport," said Erika. Being strikingly beautiful did have its advantages. The police officer, sensing the tension in the air, and wanting to be the hero to the pretty damsel in distress, ordered the hippies to produce tickets or leave the airport immediately. It had become a regular and unwelcome occurrence that war protesters staked out the airport to take their frustration with the war out on the unfortunate soldiers returning home from fighting it.

The stringy youth began to mouth off, "Officer, as a public facility, I have every…"

The cop had no interest in a debate and lost his temper.

"Listen real good, people. Get your shiftless, pot-smoking rear ends out of my airport right now or I'll throw all of you in jail for failure to comply with a lawful order!" yelled the cop as he began to finger his police baton. The group of protesters looked to their foul-mouthed leader for guidance. The stringy guy grudgingly turned and walked toward a bright orange Volkswagen bus in the parking lot, his flock in tow. Chris wondered how many returning servicemen had to endure the insults and disrespect of war protesters during the course of the day. He thought that it was a wonder there weren't hippie corpses lying in the street. In a final, pathetic act of defiance, the skinny leader of the youths shot his middle finger at the cop from the driver's window as they drove past, and yelled, "Stupid pig!"

"That was a close call," said Chris as he shook his head.

Jack turned toward the cop and said, "Thanks officer."

With a self-satisfied tone, the officer looked first at Erika and then at Jack and replied, "My pleasure. Drive safely and enjoy your time in Chicago."

Chris, Jack, and Erika crossed the road into the parking lot.

"Baby, you amaze me," said Jack.

"Those poor kids wouldn't have stood a chance against two combat-hardened soldiers. Someone would have gotten hurt badly," said Erika. "I took an oath to do no harm and if I can, prevent harm from being done."

Jack was constantly amazed by the woman he was to marry in two day's time. Without having to say anything more to express it, he pulled her close and kissed her quickly on the cheek.

She stopped and kissed him back on the lips. The embrace lingered a moment longer than Chris felt comfortable witnessing. He couldn't muzzle the remark on the tip of his tongue and said, "Ok, you two. Get a room."

Erika ran her hand through her long hair and continued walking toward the car with a clearly flushed face as Jack said, "In two days, you'll have to burn the building down to get us out of one."

"Ugh."

They reached Jack's car in the short-term parking lot. It was an immaculately-kept white Cadillac. As Chris placed his bags in the spacious trunk, he realized his former co-pilot must be doing quite well working for Erika's father. They had talked a bit in the past about the medical device company Dr. Jensen had started to manufacture and distribute the groundbreaking new cardiovascular stent.

"Looks like you've come up in the world," said Chris.

"Well, selling medical devices to hospitals makes me a nice paycheck but I think there is something I'd enjoy doing more. We'll talk about it tonight after dinner at the future in-laws' house," replied Jack as he started the powerful engine of the Cadillac.

"I've got a reservation at the Holiday Inn off Chicago Avenue in Evanston," said Chris.

"Nonsense, Chris. You are going to stay in my guest house.

We knew you would argue if we told you ahead of time, so just get over it now, smile, and say, 'Yes Ma'am,' just like those nice young sergeants did," said Erika.

"Yeah pal. I'd have put you up in my spare bedroom but my apartment is just full of boxes right now. There's an awesome view of the lake I'll miss, but the view I'll get to wake up to the rest of my life makes it all worth while," said Jack as his and Erika's hands intertwined.

"You guys are so cute, I almost can't stand it," said Chris with a grin.

"Yeah, we know," retorted Erika.

Jack drove the smooth-riding car onto the ramp to the highway as Chris sat looking out the window.

I haven't seen these guys in three years and in the first ten minutes they've arranged my date and averted a bloodbath right before my eyes. This should be a weekend to remember, thought Chris as he sat quietly in the back seat, watching the neighborhoods and industrial facilities of western Chicago scroll past.

The comfort of the plush seats, the smell of the opulent leather, and the purr of the engine lulled Chris into a state of magnificent relaxation. He began musing about the young Irishwoman he'd just met and hopefully would be seeing quite a bit of that weekend. There had been many opportunities in his life for relationships, but for some reason, he had just not given them any effort. Most women he dated had realized quite early on that Chris was married to his airplanes and they would be, at best, a mistress. There was, however, something about Keely that had stirred a feeling in him that he was completely unfamiliar with.

They drove along the Kennedy Expressway and then headed up the Eden Expressway into the North Chicago suburbs. The urban buildings and stores gave way to trees and grass along the highway the further north they went. Taking the exit for Glenview, they drove along a picturesque road that bordered a nature preserve until they made a left turn onto Glenview Road. Headed west, they began to pass through affluent neighborhoods with impressive homes on either side of the road. They passed a grand-looking golf club with a sign in calligraphy script that read:

North Shore Country Club-members only. Just past the golf club, they turned right onto a road that had extremely large estate homes with fences and gates obscuring them from view entirely. At the end of the road, they stopped at a wrought-iron fence, and Jack keyed a code into a pad mounted on a small stand. The two ornate, steel gates opened inward and they drove up a short drive to an impressive French chateau-style house that had a courtyard and secondary guest house on the opposite side of the drive.

Man, I know she's a doctor but I had no idea, thought Chris.

Knowing what his long-time Air Force mentor must have been thinking, Jack said, "Don't let the house fool you. I'm still the same guy you used to drink with at the Drifter's Reef."

Erika, who had grown up accustomed to the finer things in life, thought it wholly unnecessary to add comment. She continued to go over a list of wedding arrangements to be completed, that she had written in neat handwriting on a leather-bound jotter pad.

Chris pulled his luggage from the car and followed Jack up a flight of stairs on the outside of the guest house and into the quarters he would use for the weekend. The inside was tastefully decorated with furniture and wall hangings that would have been quite acceptable at any five-star boutique hotel.

"Here are your quarters, Captain. We'll meet at seven for a drink before dinner. By the way, don't feel like you absolutely have to invite the girl from the bar. Matchmaking is more Erika's thing than mine, but whatever," said Jack.

"Thanks for the room Jack. I can't tell you how happy I am for the both of you. Couldn't happen to a more deserving guy," said Chris.

Jack smiled and, with a slight tone of weariness to his voice, said, "You know, I could go on for the rest of my life working for Erika's father, and we'd have just about the perfect life, but it's not what my passion is. I think you can relate."

Chris was familiar with the excruciating drudgery of doing a job he didn't love.

"Well, get yourself settled in, relax, and if you want to go anywhere before dinner, you can take Erika's Volvo. Jack produced a key from a key ring and handed it to Chris. Drawing the curtains back, he pointed to a midnight-blue station wagon in the three-car garage along the western side of the drive.

"She's not the sexiest set of wheels on the road but she'll get you there in one piece," said Jack. Just then, the distinctive sound of afterburning turbofan engines broke the tranquility of the suburban utopia. A two-ship flight of McDonnell Douglas F-4 Phantoms flew directly over the house.

"Headed to the naval air station on the other side of town," said Jack as he looked out the window. Turning back to Chris, he said, "You know, they say that you've lost the taste for flying when a plane goes overhead and you aren't compelled to watch. I've never lost the compulsion and never will."

Standing in the doorway, Jack said, "I know the air cargo service was your idea and you've been working on it for a long time now, right?"

"Yeah."

"And you keep saying it's a viable idea but you need the capital to get it off the ground, right?"

"Yeah?"

"I want to talk to you about making it a reality. Selling medical devices to the second-most confident group of professionals is killing me."

"Hey man, me too, but I've been working like a dog to try to get the plan together and find some willing venture capitalists that share my enthusiasm but nobody seems to buy into it. Unfortunately, you're right. My main problem is that I don't have a few million bucks lying around and don't have the slightest idea how to begin to find investors."

Jack smiled and closed the door behind him.

Chris decided to take a small nap before dinner. After arranging his clothes from his light-blue hang bag in the closet and setting out his sundries kit, he lay down on the bed. As he turned over, the matchbook with Keely's number on it fell out of his shirt pocket onto the cool twelve-hundred thread count sheets. Picking it up, he made a quick decision, picked up the phone on the nightstand, and dialed.

"Houlihan's," said a lovely voice with a sing-song, Irish brogue.

**Residence of Dr. Erika Jensen, MD
3452 Fairway View Court
Glenview, Illinois
6:57 P.M. Central Time
Thursday, July 12th, 1972**

Chapter Thirteen

Jack, Chris, and Erika sat comfortably on Erika's Nytt Hem Swedish couch, enjoying small glasses of Scotch before heading out to Erika's parents' home for dinner. At Jack's feet sat his pilot's briefcase. When he had laid it down at the foot of the couch as they sat for drinks earlier, Chris asked what Jack needed it for.

"You'll see after dinner," said Jack. Chris watched as he winked at Erika and she reciprocated. "So what's the E.T.A. of your date this evening, Chris?"

"She should be here any minute. I think my directions were pretty good," replied Chris just as the intercom from the front gate buzzed. Jack smiled and said, "Well, directions used to be Major Hightower's specialty but she apparently arrived here all the same." Erika went across the living room to the panel on the wall, pressed the button, and said, "Keely, come right in, I'll open the gate."

"Thanks loads, Doctor," was the accented reply that came through the little speaker on the wall.

Ten seconds later, the puttering sound of an underpowered engine resonated from the drive.

"Sounds like a nest of hornets. What the heck is that woman

driving?" said Chris in reaction to the sound. They stood, went to the front window, and looked out. Keely emerged from a baby blue car touched with rust along the wheel wells and in various spots on the rest of the body. Salt on the roadways during the brutal winters in Chicago took the same toll on many a vehicle. As she emerged from the car, Chris sharply inhaled just audibly enough to make Jack snicker a bit. Keely was nothing less than a vision of breathtaking beauty.

Both men looked at each other and almost in perfect stereo synchronicity, said, "Ford Pinto."

Erika countered with, "Yves St. Laurent."

Before the two men could enter into juvenile commentary about the car or Keely, Erika opened the door and invited her in.

"Keely, come in, welcome. We're so glad you could join us this evening," said Erika as she gave a little hug to Keely.

Looking over at Chris, standing by a coffee table with Jack, she replied, "Oh, the pleasure is all mine," as she favored Chris with a demure smile. It was a moment Chris knew he'd remember on his death bed. Never much lacking for something to say, Chris was utterly speechless as she walked over toward him. Her auburn hair done up tastefully, the simple, yet form-fitting dress and designer shoes she wore made her look like she should have arrived in a chauffer-driven Rolls Royce as opposed to the sputtering little go-cart with the bad safety record sitting in the driveway.

Coming out of the intoxication her presence induced, Chris remembered his manners and asked, "Keely, can I offer you a drink?"

"I'd love to but who is driving this evening?" she replied.

"It's well in hand, m'lady," said Jack, affecting an amusing old-world manner. "Erika's father is sending his driver to collect us. It is about fifteen minutes to his house. They live in a little place on the shore out in Evanston."

Keely considered that comment momentarily. If Jack meant the home they were going to was on Lake Michigan, it was most definitely not a 'little place'. There were no little places on the lakefront. That strip of land, commonly called 'The Gold Coast' in the North Chicago suburbs was the province of CEOs, politicians, surgeons, trial lawyers, luminaries, and all other manner of obscenely wealthy people.

"Well that's fair enough. I'll have what you gents are having. Neat."

The four sat sipping thirty-year-old Macallan single-malt scotch over the next hour, chatting animatedly and waiting for the driver to arrive. At precisely eight p.m., the buzz from the gate intercom came from the wall panel. As pilots, Jack and Chris instinctively looked at their watches and saw the driver was, pleasantly, exactly on time.

"Right on the hack," said Jack with a nudge of Chris' ribs.

"You Americans with your odd speech mannerisms," said Keely. You know, we spent hundreds of years developing a perfectly adequate language throughout the British Isles and you Yanks do your red-letter best to hack it up. Good show, that." Erika nudged Keely, her co-conspirator in the prior hour's conversation. The two were becoming fast friends.

"Keely, if you are going to hang around pilots, you just have to get used to their secret code words. They might just initiate you to join their little boy's club," said Erika.

Jack had just enough alcohol in him to loosen his tongue and said, "Baby, after we're married, there's a club I'd like to initiate you into. We'll charter a plane out of Palwaukee Airport, and I'll issue you your club membership card at just slightly higher than flight level five-thousand."

At the uncharacteristically racy comment from Jack, Erika blushed and said, "Alright, honey, that's quite enough out of you. Bartender, this man is cut off!"

Earlier, while Chris had taken a short nap, Jack had driven to his downtown apartment in a high rise building off North Sheridan Drive, packing up more of his things that now resided in the garage. Although Jack and Erika had briefly discussed the idea of living under the same roof, but sleeping in separate rooms, prior to their wedding, it had only taken the mere mention of it to Father McNamara for that idea to be squashed.

"You really want to test your human infallibility that strongly, huh?" the kindly priest had asked in a pre-marital counseling session. It was the only conversation on the subject necessary for both of them. As a result of their upbringing and formation of values that resulted in the common goal of a chaste courtship, Jack and Erika knew that their love was truly founded on a relationship with God. They both believed that without that fundamental focus, any true sacrament of marriage was impossible. It was, at times, excruciatingly painful to conduct themselves in a chaste manner but they both knew waiting to celebrate their love in the physical arena made it possible for the true intimacy they shared to grow. Neither one, regardless of the personal cost, was willing to jeopardize that gift. It was that understanding that made Jack's uncharacteristic comment all the more hilarious to Erika.

As she smiled back at her bridegroom, Erika understood where he was coming from. It seemed like the hours approaching their union were dragging on forever.

A moment later the doorbell rang and the four stood and went to the door. Erika opened the door to a distinguished-looking man with short, grey hair, wearing a dark driver's uniform, holding his cap. Harold, a man well into his sixth decade, had the polished manner of a professional chauffer.

"Good to see you, Harold," said Erika as she gave him a little hug.

"It is always good to see you too, Dr. Jensen," said Harold. Returning to the side of the Cadillac limousine, he opened the doors and said, "Ladies and gentlemen, your car awaits."

Keely said nothing but thought to herself, *Now this I could get used to,* as she put her arm through the crook of Chris' elbow for the short walk to the car.

Twenty-five minutes later, after crossing through Wilmette and passing increasingly affluent neighborhoods, they came to the residence of Dr. Erik Jensen, MD. He was not only the former director of Cardiovascular Medicine at Northwestern University Hospital, but the founder and president of the phenomenally successful medical device company, Cardiotech.

The Jensen estate was entirely obscured from view by an ivy-covered brick wall and occupied nearly one hundred yards of the frontage. The wrought-iron gate bore a crest of arms and a stylized "J" formed in the center. Harold depressed the button on the intercom box.

"Yes?" responded a cheery female British-accented voice.

"I have Dr. Jensen's guests for the evening."

"Very good," replied the voice coming from the speaker and the gates immediately swung inward. It took another twenty seconds to drive the length of the drive and reach the mansion. Marble columns supported the portico and the architecture bore a striking resemblance to a more famous home on Pennsylvania Avenue. Harold, after placing the car in park, once again opened the doors and wished his four passengers a lovely dinner.

"I'm at your service whenever you'd care to return to your residence, madam," said Harold.

The front door opened inward and a cherubic, smiling woman with an English accent opened the door exclaiming, "Dr. Jensen, Mr. Lee, do come in. You and your guests are expected."

"You're a dear, Maggie," said Erika.

Chris offered his elbow to Keely and she gracefully slipped her arm inside his. Seeing the gesture, Jack smiled at Erika and they intertwined their arms as well before entering the entryway.

Dr. Erik Jensen and his wife, Marie entered the foyer. Dr Jensen immediately planted a kiss on his daughter's cheek as Marie hugged Jack. Jack turned to the elder Jensen and said, "Erik, Marie, this is the man who taught me more about flying in the Air Force than anybody before or after."

"So you're the pilot extraordinaire that Jack's been talking about, young man? Well, I'm sure we'll have lots to talk about this evening," said the elder Dr. Jensen.

Chris nodded politely and said, "Dr. Jensen, I'd like you to meet Keely Kennedy.

Keely's green eyes twinkled and she wore a brilliant smile as she extended her hand to the doctor.

Shaking her hand, Dr. Jensen said, "The pleasure is ours to have you as our guest this evening."

"Oh no, Dr. Jensen, the honor is all mine. My father, Liam, is sitting in his study back in Ireland today and eating healthier foods because you gave him a second chance when every other doctor told him he was done for. Your stent saved him."

Jack and Erika smiled broadly, saying nothing to spoil the

moment.

"Mrs. Jensen, if you don't mind...," said Keely as she planted a kiss on Dr. Jensen's cheek and gave him a hearty hug.

Chris, after a few seconds of the hugging, said, "Now then, I was under the impression you were *my* date?"

The group laughed as Mrs. Jensen said, "I think dinner should be ready momentarily. Shall we head to the dining room?"

They feasted on roast beef dinner with Yorkshire pudding and a port-merlot sauce served by Maggie and another young girl that helped around the house. The conversations ranged from the Watergate scandal, the economy, and, when it inevitably came up, the war in Viet Nam. Both Chris and Jack told stories of their experiences flying cargo into airfields that were, on more than one occasion, under rocket or mortar attack. The rest of the group listened in amazement at the flying stories from two men who had been there.

"How much longer do you think this dreadful thing could go on?" asked Keely.

"As long as it has to," said Jack in a tone that, without having to explain himself, made it perfectly clear that he believed in what America was trying to accomplish in the war-torn peninsula on the other side of the world.

Sensing the possible point for heated debate, Marie decreed, "Alright, I'm invoking executive privilege: only lighter topics from here forward."

"Agreed," said Erika as the topic changed to the wedding arrangements and what challenges Marie had been having with the catering service that was hired to orchestrate everything for the lavish reception at the estate.

As dinner was concluded, the group stood. The plates were being cleared by the younger house staff girl while Erika and her mother took Keely off to the patio to enjoy an after dinner drink.

"You gentlemen have some things to discuss so we'll enjoy a bit of girl talk," said Erika with a wink. Jack excused himself and in a moment returned from the front reception area with his pilot's briefcase. The three men went to Dr. Jensen's study where the two story room had floor-to-ceiling shelves filled with medical journals and all manner of texts. In the middle of the room sat a beautiful mahogany table and three chairs.

From his pilot's briefcase, Jack retrieved and spread out several documents on the table, smiled at Chris, and began.

"Chris, we'll get straight to the point. I've been doing some research and preparation for this over the past year. You know that most major cargo transportation providers, including the one you work for, fly passengers first and then cargo transport as a secondary income source. I know we talked about the same sort of idea in the Air Force but I think there is a vast, untapped market of people who would be willing to pay more to guarantee overnight shipping to anywhere. The concept I'm talking about removes passengers entirely from the equation. I'm thinking of an entire fleet of aircraft completely dedicated to cargo transport only."

"Jack, I completely agree, but there's the small problem of the cost of leasing aircraft, not to mention the facilities that need to be leased or built to support such an operation. I'm sure you've looked into that and the cost is pretty astronomical. Based on my most conservative estimates, to start a company with a fleet of ten jets and meet operating costs for the first year would require, at a minimum, twenty million dollars. I can't think that this could work with cheaper, prop-driven aircraft like it did in the fifties when Flying Cougars started out. The world is going much faster so the cargo has to as well."

Dr Jensen placed his wine glass on the table and said, "Gentlemen, I've looked over Jack's business proposal," as he waved his hand across the impressive quantity of research, pro forma business statements, and other assorted documents that Jack had lain across the large antique table. Continuing, he said, "I agree that the start-up costs would be quite enormous but that's where I think I can help."

Chris looked at the reams of paper, picking up various documents, knowing the assembled work represented hundreds of hours of preparations. Although back in his Los Angeles apartment, his own collection of paper dreams for a cargo company sat on his desk, it was nowhere as complete or polished as Jack's.

"You sell medical devices for Dr. Jensen here, right?" asked

Chris. "I mean how did you ever have the time to put all this together?"

"He's actually our best account executive. There's nobody that I've ever known that could win people's trust so quickly," said Dr. Jensen with a proud, fatherly grin. Continuing, he said, "And although I was a bit skeptical when my Erika told me she'd fallen for a pilot, I quickly learned that she'd made a good choice."

Nodding, Chris said, "Jack, I know you could probably sell pigs for cows, and I really believe the concept is viable, but it still comes down to money, and Dr. Jensen, it's clear to anyone that you have been quite successful, but twenty million dollars?" exclaimed Chris.

It was obvious, by the opulence of his estate that Dr. Jensen was fabulously wealthy but Chris couldn't possibly know that the elder Dr. Jensen's net worth, due to shrewd investment of profits from his medical company, left the good doctor just ten million dollars short of joining the small community of billionaires in America. Erik had more money than he could spend in ten lifetimes and wanted to diversify his holdings. Chris hadn't been privileged to the many hours of discussion that Jack and Dr. Jensen had engaged in, talking about the idea Chris had hatched while he and Jack used to streak across the sky together at the controls of Air Force jets.

"No disrespect whatsoever, Doctor, but what sort of investment were you thinking about here?" asked Chris.

With a completely straight face, Dr. Jensen replied, "I've spoken with my financial people. Based on estimation of start-up costs and first five years of operation, I'm willing to allocate upwards of a little over fifty million to the venture. If the business model for overnight shipping service is as sound as I believe, we will begin to show profits in year three. Based on Jack's calculations, as well as some assessments my people have done, I am convinced that my money will be well invested if the marketing is done perfectly and the company is positioned as the preeminent cargo transportation provider in North America."

Chris' eyes went wide in shock at Dr. Jensen's declaration. Looking to Jack with an expression of disbelief, Jack simply nodded, telling Chris everything he needed to know about the validity of the offer.

Chris speechlessly looked over the impressive work Jack had done on the calculations and market analysis. It left him in awe of his friend's determination to make their dream of an air cargo company a reality. He picked up the pro forma business statements and formal proposal entitled, "Velocity Express—the Most Efficient and Profitable Cargo Carrier in the World," and thumbed to the indexed page that laid out start-up costs. The numbers were astronomical.

Jack looked into Chris' eyes and said, "What do you say, partner? Working for Flying Cougars is killing you and, with all due respect, Erik, I just can't bear to visit one more doctor's office for anything other than a physical."

Dr. Jensen, with a warm smile turned to Chris and said, "Jack tells me that this is all your idea anyway. Why not come aboard and make it happen?"

"Your starting salary will be fifty thousand dollars a year until the company begins to generate a positive profit stream, at which time your compensation will be re-evaluated based on a variety of performance goals," said Jack.

It was amazing that for the past six weeks, Chris desperately wanted a way out of his work situation. Had anyone told him this opportunity would unfold, he would never have believed it. In one miraculous day, the entire world had seemed to open up to him.

"Dr. Jensen, may I use your telephone a moment?" asked Chris.

"Be my guest."

Jack suspected that he knew who was going to be the recipient of Chris' call.

After three rings, Chris said, "Hi Jerry, this is Chris Wal….Yeah, I know this is your home number. I…yes, I know…I….Jerry, we need to talk about who is going to take my flights after July. I'm giving you my official notice. Yes, I'm serious. I'm sorry that puts you in a bind but don't lose too much sleep over it. I won't be asking for a reference letter."

Velocity Express, Inc.
2200 Airway Drive
Chamblee, Georgia
9:30 P.M. Eastern Time
Monday, March 2nd, 1973

Chapter Fourteen

The outlays of funds were terrifying to Chris, occasionally creating anxiety just short of true panic attacks. He couldn't understand how Jack, equally invested in the success of the venture, seemed to possess such an aura of calmness. Sometimes, after late-night planning sessions in his room at the Buckhead Marriott, documents spread across every flat surface, Chris found sleep at best, elusive, and oftentimes impossible. He and Jack had been staying in adjoining rooms for the past three months, working tirelessly to create Velocity Express. As with most long-term guests at fine hotels, everyone on the hotel staff knew Chris and Jack by name as well as Jack's wife, Erika, whenever she popped down from Chicago for a visit.

Erika, busy with her work at Northwestern University Hospital, flew in every few weeks and spent some precious hours with Jack between trips to the local shopping malls before hopping a flight back to her responsibilities at the hospital. She had begun quietly making inquires at Atlanta hospitals for staff openings.

After meeting with government officials in several cities considered potential locations for Velocity Express, Chris and Jack had chosen Atlanta for numerous reasons including a favorable tax concession, a vibrant city with growing infrastructure, and very friendly people. The most important consideration, however, had been the fact that the airport had rarely been snowed in or iced over. In a business that was going to be completely dependent upon the ability to put jets in the air, weather patterns had been the most important decision factor.

When Keely and Chris made the final decision over the phone one night that she was going to move down to Atlanta, Chris thought his comment about two double beds in his room would be met with more enthusiasm than it was.

"Oh, babe, I really love you but I don't know if this is going to work…," said Keely with a tone of disappointment.

"But sweetheart, what do you mean? Didn't I tell you there are *two* beds. What could possibly be the problem?"

"Honey, I really want to come down there but if we can't afford a separate room for me, I just can't come."

Chris told Keely he'd call her right back.

"Hey Jack, It's me. I really need to talk to you about something. Do you think you might consider taking me on as a roommate in your room?

For a moment Jack hesitated but when Chris told him the reason, Jack exclaimed, "Oh, well why didn't you say so? Yeah, we can share a room. Good choice, buddy."

Chris didn't feel the need to tell Jack it wasn't exactly *his* choice. Taking an instant liking to the charm of Atlanta, Keely ended her lease at her Lincoln Park apartment. Within a day of arriving at the front desk of the Marriott to register, she had been hired at a popular Irish pub named Fado off Peachtree Street.

Jack occasionally needled his friend, asking when Chris was going to ask Keely to marry him. "You know, pal, if you really want to marry her in the Catholic Church, don't you think it might be useful for you to finally go through Confirmation? It was a theme of discussion a few times after Chris revealed his parochial education ended in the sixth grade. Jack never pushed his own religious convictions on his best friend but felt it important, as was his responsibility as a Catholic, to attempt to encourage his best friend's spiritual growth. Chris couldn't possibly know right then that his full return to the faith was always among the prayer intentions when Jack and Erika said their family rosary together each morning. Jack wasn't cognizant of the fact that Chris had been watching his friend closely. The manner with which Jack conducted himself in all areas of his life was a more powerful demonstration of fully embracing his faith tradition than Jack could have ever accomplished with words. Still, Chris had some lingering prejudices about organized religion but it was hard to argue with the dignity and kindness he watched Jack treat everyone he came in contact with.

Among the endless details to attend to in starting their shipping empire, there had been leasing contracts and meetings with representatives from the aircraft manufacturer Dassault for ten of their jets, meetings with attorneys and the accounting firm to set up the corporation, searching with real estate agents to lease offices and a warehouse for Velocity Express, and a myriad of other details that had to be seen to before Chris and Jack's company was to become a reality.

Staffing the company that only existed on paper had been challenging at times but there was a team spirit emanating from the core group that created a sense of excitement each day. The greatest package delivery company in the world had yet to deliver a single package but Chris and Jack had confidence that once they officially opened for business the following week, Velocity Express had a great chance of being a success. The office and warehouse that were the official headquarters of VelEx, as the company had begun to be referred to by the founding staff members, was located in an industrial area adjacent to Peachtree DeKalb Airport. Already, forty people reported to work each weekday, making efforts to generate business from the sparsely-furnished office. Strategy planning meetings lasted until nearly eleven a.m. and then the bulk of the staff, mostly sales professionals, manned the phones each afternoon, attempting to sell the service of overnight delivery by cold-calling businesses. Many calls were met with the disbelief that any company could guarantee overnight delivery to any point in the United States, but the salespeople were adept at explaining the new concept to potential customers. The marketing department, consisting of Tom and Jill Morgahan—a husband and wife team who had previously worked for a global soft drink corporation—were invaluable in defining market opportunities for the fledgling business. It was nothing short of miraculous that Chris and Jack had been able to steal them away from their very healthy incomes at their former internationally-iconic employer. Tom had always been fascinated with airplanes and the soda pop world just didn't hold the luster it once did for him and Jill. Money wasn't the couple's driving influence anymore and the Morgahans wanted to work for something they believed in. Jack was quite convinced the coup of acquiring them for Velocity Express was divine providence.

On that warm, breezy Atlanta evening, Jack and Chris were meeting with their director of sales, Erin Urquhart. Her youthful appearance and casual attire that included a brightly-colored paisley blouse and wide bell bottoms worn to the late night planning session belied her brilliance. Erin, in a stroke of creative genius that wouldn't necessarily be expected upon first glance at the twenty-eight-year-old, came up with the tag line that would forever define the identity of Velocity Express. Sitting at one of the long sorting tables that had been installed along the wall of the large warehouse, Chris, Jack, and Erin talked about shaping the company identity.

"So we are going to provide the service of guaranteeing overnight delivery to customers and, for this, we will charge them a premium for the expediency, right?" she asked.

"That's the basic idea," answered Chris.

"You've read the business plan for creating a very profitable niche in the shipping industry. If we guarantee delivering packages overnight, the value in it for customers is that it will save businesses critical time that might just give them an edge over their competition," continued Jack.

Erin looked around the hangar and said, "I get all that and of course I really believe the business model is sound. I wouldn't have signed on with you guys if I didn't believe in Velocity Express, but what I'm trying to do here is help us define an *identity*. What is it exactly that we do here?" Erin asked.

"We save customers time," offered Jack.

"Yeah, we guarantee them their package will be there on time," chimed in Chris.

"One hundred percent of the time according to our brochures," added Erin. "A bold claim but I believe, with this 'hub and spoke' system you guys have come up with, we can pull it off."

The plan was simple: collect packages across the country at offices situated in close proximity to regional airports, bring them all into the central location in Atlanta during the middle of the night, and send them onto their destination city on the jets, utilizing various ground transportation services in those cities. Each delivery would generate a signature form, confirming the time of receipt and copies of those forms would be available to the original customer.

The creative gears spun in Erin's head. With a tremendous grin, she looked at both men, and said, "I've got to go to the printer tomorrow and redesign the brochures."

Jack and Chris first looked at each other and then back at their director of sales with incredulous expressions. Erin simply sat with a twinkle in her eye. With a Cheshire cat grin she remained silent, thinking, *Come on guys, just go ahead and ask, already!*

Chris cleared his throat and asked, "Just out of curiosity, what exactly do you think the cost of trashing the thirty boxes containing the ones we already had printed comes to, Ms. Urqhart, and secondly, what the heck do we need to do that for?"

"First, the cost is exactly seven hundred and thirty two dollars, Mr. Walsh. I paid the printer's invoice myself, and in answer to your second question is that there is a critical flaw in the brochures. They say what we do but they don't contain our *identity*. I mean, in those brochures we definitely tell them what we provide in so far as services and prices but it still doesn't differentiate us from the United States Postal Service."

"And what would?" asked Jack.

She looked at both of the men, hanging on her next phrase like two boys waiting to open Christmas presents, and said, "On time…every time."

"On time, every time," mumbled Jack as he contemplated the simple genius of the phrase. "That's it. On time, every time," repeated Jack while looking around the cavernous warehouse that still had cobwebs in almost every corner and empty sorting tables just waiting to be used. He began looking at the ceiling of the building, mumbling it over and over in an increasingly louder voice. Erin, catching the *My Fair Lady*-esque rhythm, even exclaimed, "I think he's got it!"

"Erin, when you re-order the brochures tomorrow, I want you to get them to print us one of those huge banners: the ones as wide as bed sheets. And I want it long enough to string across the ceiling. Letters five feet tall in Air Force blue and our logo on the end of it!" exclaimed Jack with bubbling enthusiasm that Chris didn't appear to share.

Chris, ever mindful of the financial implications of every decision relating to the business asked, "So what do you intend to do with our three hundred dollar banner…string it behind a plane and fly over Atlanta?"

Erin laughed and said, "No, we'll get to work on that next week."

"I want it hanging across the ceiling right there," said Jack, pointing to the section along the back wall of the corrugated steel home to Velocity Express' Package Operations Facility.

The day they had signed the lease to their office and the warehouse, the agent handed them the keys to a rusty padlock securing the front door. In very ceremonial fashion, the two men had slid back the big door, beers in hand, and officially named the dust and grunge-filled structure, giving a big, important title to a dirty, vacant warehouse. They were confident that when actual service started, the sorting tables would be at least partially filled with packages needing delivery. The sales staff burning up the phone lines had already secured thirty-eight customers who agreed to allow Velocity Express to shuttle some items across the country for them. It wasn't nearly enough business to even cover the cost of one jet flight but Chris and Jack knew it was going to be a process to build the business. Empires didn't materialize overnight and the business plan didn't project profitability until at least year four.

"I'll place the order for the banner as well, Mr. Walsh," said Erin as the sound of a vehicle pulled up outside the building. The rumbling from the tailpipes brought a smile to her face.

A moment later, a tall, slender man, with long, brown hair wearing jeans, cowboy boots, and a leather jacket with fringe tassels hanging the length of the sleeves walked in the door like he owned the place.

"Hey, baby, we're just finishing up," called Erin across the warehouse as she turned to Chris and Jack who just smiled at her.

"Run along Ms. Urqhart and have a good time this evening," said Chris. Glancing at her date, he continued, "In fact, as long as you get the details worked out with the printer tomorrow morning, why don't you come in around noon-ish."

Erin shot Chris and Jack one of her megawatt smiles, grabbed her handbag from the table, and went across the warehouse into the arms of her boyfriend Sean. The pair exited the building, hands intertwined.

"I think we're about done for the evening as well," said Chris. Keely had worked the early shift at the bar and should be headed back to the hotel right about then.

Chris and Jack walked out of the warehouse and, as Jack locked the door, they both turned to see a custom conversion van pulling out of the small parking lot.

"Think we'll see her by noon?" asked Jack.

Chris looked out onto the tarmac outside the hangar. Three of their leased jets sat where seven others would be joining them by week's end, the tails bearing the Air Force blue Velocity Express logo. They had chosen the official color of Velocity Express to give a sense of dependability and nod to their military aviation careers. The psychology of the color was also to assist them in garnering government contracts which, as both men knew, there existed a gold mine of lucrative business if they could truly operate an overnight delivery service. The following morning, they were to take delivery of two more executive jets from Dassault with interiors that were designed to function like the insides of a military cargo jet—exactly as the two men had envisioned them sitting in the Drifter's Reef in the middle of the Pacific Ocean, four years earlier.

Velocity Express Offices
Peachtree DeKalb Airport
Chamblee, Georgia
6:55 P.M. Eastern Time
Monday, May 13th, 1973

Chapter Fifteen

S orting tables running the width of the VelEx hangar were full of packages of all shapes and sizes. Eighty employees stood over each one, checking and double-checking that they were labeled correctly and had the appropriate paperwork accompanying them. Everyone in the hangar, especially Chris and Jack, was possessed with the sort of collective energy a theatre company would have just before the curtains rose on opening night. The sales staff, operations people, accounting clericals, pilots, and aircraft maintenance staff were all helping the ten newly-hired 'package specialists'. Everyone, regardless of their normal responsibilities, was participating in getting the jets loaded and the excitement was palpable. As the din of a hangar full of employees sorting four hundred and twelve packages surrounded them, Chris and Jack continued to work the phones to the package couriers in the fourteen cities that the ten Dassault Falcon jets would be touching down in that evening and the next morning.

"Hey, Chris, we've got a problem here. The dispatch supervisor in Cleveland says his driver can only wait for our jet until eleven p.m.," said Jack as Chris was completing a call to a courier service in Los Angeles.

"You tell them that if they don't wait until midnight, as we agreed to in writing, I will see them in court," replied Chris. Orchestrating what was nothing less than a highly complicated airlift operation was, at best, frustrating. An hour earlier, Chris learned that one of their ten leased jets was experiencing a problem with a pressurization sensor and was grounded.

Jack had briefly flown into an uncharacteristic rage when he discovered that it was the newly-installed sensor that was malfunctioning and the maintenance technician had replaced a perfectly functioning one with the faulty one. Technically, the old sensor could have been replaced anytime in the next week and would have been within the scheduled maintenance parameters for the annoying component. Any other day would have been fine with Jack just as long as it wasn't the first day of actual service of their fledgling company. Just as quickly as Jack lost his temper, he apologized to the lead mechanic, Tim Baldwin.

"Sorry Mr. Lee, I thought I was just doing the right thing when I looked at the maintenance logs and saw the pressurization sensor was due for replacement. The new ones really do work ninety-nine percent of the time," said the terrified aircraft mechanic in response to Jack's tirade. Tim was the most experienced of the three full-time aircraft maintenance techs hired by VelEx. Jack closed his eyes, took a deep breath, and regained his composure.

"I know you were, Tim. I'm sorry. We're just a little on edge around here tonight."

No kidding, thought Tim as he relaxed his shoulders and said, "No problem Mr. Lee. You know as well as I do that us worker bees hate nothing more than to take a perfectly functioning part off a plane and replace it with another part that may, or may not, prove functional. Scheduled maintenance bites in my book, but it's my job."

"Well, thanks for doing your job so proficiently," said Jack with a smirk, his tone slightly needling the mechanic.

Without skipping a beat, Tim continued, "Besides, the worst thing that could happen with a failed pressurization sensor is only that the entire flight crew could die of oxygen hypoxia and our jet slams into the earth at some random location." The dark humor was just what Jack needed to slap him back to reality.

"You are quite an amusing guy, Tim. I'll be keeping my eye

on you, mister," said Jack as he laughed for the first time that day, letting off some of the tension resulting from the need for everything in his world to go exactly right that night.

"We're going to have to add New York to ship eight's flight plan tonight to make up for the bird that's out-of-commission," said Chris.

"I'm making that happen right now," replied Jack as he watched four employees load the table piled high with packages bound for New York's LaGuardia Airport being taken to the eighth jet on the flight line in front of the VelEx hangar. The flight plan paperwork lay in a manila folder on the table in front of him, having been updated to include the new stop along with Portland, Maine and Nashville, Tennessee. Ten jets in all were lined up exactly as military jets would be on the flight line at a U.S. airbase but instead of fighters, bombers, cargo jets, or other military aircraft, these ten were executive jets made by Dassault. The only visible difference between the aircraft was their tail numbers. The distinctive VelEx logo was painted on the sides of all ten aircraft, nine of which were taking to the skies that night. The planes were originally designed to be comfortable executive jets that would take very important people to very important places. But instead of a wet bar, fine walnut trim, and leather seats within the fuselages of the ten jets, the only seats were in the cockpit. Where the passenger area would have been was nothing but the aluminum floors and numerous tie-down ringlets to keep the packages secure during flight. The military-like precision with which the jets were parked gave a sense of comfort to both Chris and Jack on a night when the multitude of things that could go wrong would most likely have put either of the men in a mental ward if they stopped to ponder them for any length of time. Of the fifty million dollars Dr. Jensen granted access to, Chris and Jack had already utilized nearly half the money on start-up costs. Launching VelEx was a high-stakes poker game the men were playing and with a fifty-million dollar bet on the table, the business world was calling their hand that night. If they could successfully get every package to their destinations by the following day, as promised, it would be a royal flush and they would have proven an entirely new and viable way for widgets to move around the country. The alternative would be a debt owed to Jack's father-in-law that neither man would be able to repay in ten lifetimes.

"We've reloaded the New York packages onto ship eight and I'm going to go to the office to file the new flight plan," shouted Jack over the increasing noise of the first departing jet spinning up its engines. He and Chris stood silently for a moment, watching the jet begin to taxi away from the VelEx hangar. By four a.m. Eastern time, that jet would land in Dallas, Phoenix and finally Los Angeles. Eighty-three packages to be handed off to three different courier services in the respective cities lay within that particular jet.

The sound of jet engines always got Jack's blood pumping forcefully but with everything riding on that night's successes or failures, the effect was amplified tenfold. For a moment, while watching that jet taxi out to the runway, a wave of adrenaline washed through his body.

An hour and a half later, nine VelEx jets were airborne, each one streaking across the United States with packages of varying sizes, shapes, and contents. The contents ranged from a box of medical records being sent to an attorney bringing suit against a California hospital, to a nine carat, D-color, internally flawless diamond ring valued at nearly one hundred thousand dollars.

Chris had met the owner of that package while playing a late-afternoon nine holes at the North Fulton Golf Club near Jack's house three weeks earlier. Rick Barr, a prominent Atlanta jeweler was, after having met Chris on the golf course, trusting VelEx to deliver overnight.

"So it's completely insured? I mean you guys can insure something like that?" asked Rick, three weeks earlier as he lined up his nine-iron shot to the green.

"We will insure anything on our aircraft that's not illegal contraband," Chris had replied that day, acquiring another customer while lowering his golf handicap.

"Well if you guys can really deliver, I could do some great business with clients that live out-of-state," said Rick. "I'll call you this week if I think I can use you."

One of the many details that had required ironing out over the prior three months was negotiations with insurance companies to find just the right fit of coverage and premium costs not only for the aircraft, but for the items of varying value they were going to transport. Chris and Jack had met with insurance brokers from numerous firms specializing in the various policies they would need. After one such meeting with a particularly aggressive broker who was convinced they needed some of the most expensive coverage premiums they had heard quoted yet, Jack joked, "I think I'm going to start bringing some sponges and towels to these meetings." Nodding, Chris had picked up the ball and continued, "Yeah, I haven't seen so much drooling since I babysat my cousin's kid few months back."

    The insurance policies were all finally in place along with more business licenses, corporate legal paperwork, accounting statements, personnel files, aircraft documentation, FAA registration, and a host of other lengthy, boring, but absolutely necessary tomes packed full with micro script legalese that were required to create their company, most of it housed within the Velocity Express offices attached to their large hangar.

    Chris and Jack knew it was time. From a box, Chris pulled out a bullhorn and, to the fifty-plus employees who were finishing up their assigned duties, he depressed the button and announced, "Ladies and gentlemen, if you can get to a stopping point, Chris and I would like to have you come over here for just a moment." Erin Urqhart, their sales director smiled, nodded at the two bosses standing together, and quickly slipped out a side door to the hangar as Chris began.

    "I cannot tell all of you how much all your hard work means to us. This night is the culmination of a dream Chris and I had while schlepping cargo across seven continents and untold numbers of islands for Uncle Sam a few years back."

    At that, a number of employees chuckled.

    "None of this would have been possible if God hadn't sent us eighty of the finest, hardest-working people in all of Atlanta as well as the nearly three hundred people staffing our offices we've opened in our first trial cities," said Jack.

    Chris slapped Jack lightly on the back and continued, "We

don't know if our packages are going to get to their destinations tomorrow as promised or if Jack and I are going to be eating a ton of humble pie and apologizing to our customers, but one thing is for sure: whether we are a stunning success or a dismal failure, it has been our distinct honor to work with all of you to make Velocity Express a reality."

Right then, a large custom conversion van rolled around the front of the hangar, coming to a stop and backing in slowly. As soon as it came to a complete stop, Erin threw the back doors open and popped open a bottle of Veuve Clicquot champagne from the six boxes of bubbly inside. They had asked the owner of the Downwind Restaurant, which was attached to the airport administration building, if they could keep the boxes chilled in his cooler that day until it was time for the small celebration. He had happily agreed, having gotten to know Jack and Chris well over the prior three months as they would often eat in his place while discussing details about bringing Velocity Express to life. Erin's boyfriend, Sean, began unloading the boxes of champagne onto sorting tables while Erin played hostess and set the plastic glasses out and poured.

"I think you might be just a little too drunk to drive yourself home," said Jack as Chris finished off his fourth glass of champagne.

"No problem," said Chris as he glanced at his watch which did appear a bit blurry to him. Even so, he could see it was nearly eleven p.m. "Keely is coming to collect me in a few minutes but there is one thing I am not too drunk to think about," he said as he placed the plastic champagne glass forcefully enough on the table to separate the base and plastic goblet. Both components rolled off the table onto the hangar floor.

"You know Chris, I love you like a brother but I'm not willing to hear any talk about such things. You aren't married to the girl," said Jack.

"No, no, no...I wasn't talking about *that!* I meant something about how we set up this business that is eating at me."

"Oh, in that case, what's on your mind, Captain?" asked Jack. Even though their military days were behind them, Jack often referred to Chris in that manner as a term of endearment.

"You know, with all the last-minute calls to the courier services in every city, it occurred to me that we are taking a pretty big gamble on outsiders to complete our job. I mean it is *our* job to ensure the packages get to where they are going, but I'd feel a lot more confident if I didn't have to play childish games to make sure there is ground transportation waiting for our jets when they arrive,"

Jack instantly saw the logic in it. "I have to agree. We really need to look into acquiring our own assets to deliver the packages once they are on the ground," he said.

"Well, all of that might be academic if we don't deliver tonight, but I've got a good feeling everything is falling into place," said Chris.

"So are you going to do your checkout flight in one of the Dassaults this weekend?" asked Jack. Jack already had his certificate to fly the jet they were using. Both men had no intention of staying out of the flying part of the company. It had been their love of flight that inspired them to start the venture in the first place.

"Yeah, I'll be qualified by the time you get out of bed, sport. I'm meeting Jacob here to take a check-ride with him at 0630 hours so if you don't mind, will you stop off at the engraver and have my desk nameplate changed to add a slash and the word 'pilot' after my name?"

"Sure, old man. I'll have time to finish that chore right after I finish my five miles around Piedmont Park. Care to join me before you climb into the pilot's seat?" retorted Jack, knowing that Chris hadn't put fitness as high a priority as he had during their post-military lives. It was true that Chris hadn't run an entire mile since leaving the Air Force. Chris wasn't slovenly by any stretch of the imagination but there was a layer of extra flesh around his midsection that was completely absent from Jack's chiseled physique. At the respective ages of thirty-one and twenty-six, Chris bore a resemblance to a pro golfer and Jack to a pro football quarterback.

Chris was about to try to nip at his friend again, using his mildly-impaired wit. Before he could start with some remark about the growing number of fanatics in the United States that ran when nobody was actually chasing them, Jack said, "I think your ride's here," motioning over Chris' shoulder. Chris turned to see Keely smiling, dangling keys in her hand playfully as if to call a small child to its mother with some variety of toy.

"How was everything at the bar tonight?" he asked as she hugged him.

"Now look at you. You're exactly the sort of man my mother would be so happy I'm with, God rest her soul."

"Oh, how's that?" asked Jack

She smiled broadly, kissed Chris on the cheek and said, "My dear Christopher, you have just had the most important day of your entire professional life, with more money riding on today than you might make in ten reincarnations, and here you are asking me how my little barmaid job went. You're totally selfless. That's you."

"You are much more interesting than flying a few packages around. That's old hat for us," said Chris as he placed his arms around Keely's waist and kissed her. "Our little package and airplane business can wait."

Keely could hear the stress in his voice and hugged him again.

"Our soon-to-be package, airplane, and truck business," said Jack.

"Right."

They said their goodbyes and headed toward the parking lot. Jack walked out to his Cadillac and Keely and Chris waved goodbye, walking a few more parking spaces to where their Oldsmobile sat. Chris had drunk just enough champagne to make him mildly intoxicated but he leaned on her more out of emotional exhaustion rather than drunkenness. As they pulled away from the large hangar and suite of offices, Chris looked at the newly-installed sign bearing the company name on the hangar and the glowing declaration of the existence of VelEx elicited a mix of emotions: excitement of Velocity Express coming to life that night as well as the uncertainty of whether they could deliver as promised.

"On time, every time," he muttered as he began to doze off in the passenger seat.

They drove out of the airport, heading south on Clairmont

Road before turning onto Dresden Road and heading into the Brookhaven area of North Atlanta. The homes had all been built in the post-war years and were a mixture of architectural styles. Chris had rented a home in a charming neighborhood called Drew Valley where the houses all sat atop little hills away from the street. The builders had kept as many trees as possible when the homes had been built during the years immediately following World War Two.

 Only six minutes from leaving the airport, Keely turned the car into the driveway and pulled into the carport. Chris awoke to the sound of the vehicle being put in park and rubbed his eyes. It had been an exhausting day and the only thing he wanted to do was to head to bed. Ten minutes later, Keely was in the shower across the hall where her room was. Although fully well knowing what their agreement was and the fact that she had been quite adamant about waiting to become physically intimate until marriage, there were times it was something he had a hard time digesting. He knew in his heart of hearts, however, that he was certain she was the woman he wanted to spend the rest of his life with, at any cost. As he lay on the bed in that place between awake and asleep, the conversation he and Jack had a month earlier began to replay.

 On an early April afternoon, Jack and Chris sat in Jack's living room watching the final round of the Masters golf tournament. Erika and Keely, wholly disinterested in golf, were out shopping for furniture for the new house Jack and Erika had just purchased. When the final putt was sunk for the tournament win, Jack had placed two glasses of beer on the table, and turned off the television. It had been a particularly grueling day the Friday before as a result of the four hour negotiation session with the owner of a large ground delivery service in a major city they planned to offer delivery service to.

 "Man, I'm so glad I don't have to spend one more minute talking with that guy. Can you believe the rates he quoted us? Anyway, I can't wait to spend some time alone with Keely tomorrow night," said Chris as he took a sip of his beer.

 Something about Chris' tone make Jack look up from some papers on the table.

Sensing his friend's scrutiny, Chris said, "You know, I know she's Catholic, and I am too. I mean not like *you,* but still…and I know what the Church says about waiting for marriage and all that, but I gotta tell you, I don't know if I'm really capable of waiting until then," said Chris.

Jack looked at his friend for a few moments and said a silent prayer knowing what he was about to say wouldn't be what his best friend wanted to hear. As he said the prayer, the thought came that being a friend meant that it was important to tell someone the truth even if they didn't want to hear it. With a tone of concern, Jack said, "Well, isn't that what *she* wants to do? Remember, Chris, real relationships aren't about *you.*" As he said it, Jack's mouth formed an unintentional smirk that annoyed Chris immensely. The flash of irritation passed but the impact of Jack's words was impossible to ignore. In a conciliatory tone, Chris said, "I guess she really wants to wait because every time we've been alone together, she usually deploys the air brakes just when things get a bit warm. She's got these funny rules about lying on a couch together or allowing me into her bedroom at all."

"Have you two thought about the pre-marriage counseling offered at the church?"

Chris sat silently for a moment, looking down at the floor and then looked up with a pained expression.

"I think she might want to do it but we haven't talked about it directly. I just sort of assumed she'd tell me if she wanted to."

"Let me ask you something Chris. Do you love her?"

"Of course I do. You know that."

"I do know that so if you'll indulge me a minute, I'd like to give you a gift."

"Gift away, partner."

"Alright then. Let me tell you then that I really believe you have found a spectacular woman who has a healthy approach to courtship. She's not saying no to you because she doesn't love you or because it's any easier for her. I'm convinced she's doing it to keep the relationship healthy."

"Healthy for who, exactly?" grumbled Chris, not thrilled with the whole conversation to that point but still listening to Jack. Something about what his friend was saying, however, was registering with his heart but having an awful difficult time making it the eight inches vertically to his head.

"Let me tell you, Chris, that the ones willing to emotionally superglue themselves to men very quickly-which is what having sex outside of marriage always does-are usually afraid you will leave. They often feel that if they don't go down that road with you in short order, you aren't staying. The ones that are willing to wait usually have a healthy appreciation of their own worth and are willing to relinquish a perceived power that can be used to manipulate a man to stay around. My father always told me that the less I need you, the more I can love you because it becomes less about me filling a void with someone else and more about being a loving, caring man to her."

"I hear you. I mean we aren't sleeping together and I'm pretty darn sure we aren't going to."

Jack's face bore the look of skepticism for a moment before saying, "Well, my friend, I personally think that the idea of same house but separate rooms has an inevitable expiration date. It's not *if* but *when* the mood, timing, circumstances, or emotions will all line up perfectly for you two to compromise on the excellent decision you've both made…or at least she's made and you've honored. You two are big boys and girls. The decision to live in sin is yours, but like I said…"

Chris sat for a moment trying to come up with just the right words to convince his friend of his willingness to try when a particularly close call a few nights earlier came to mind and took the wind out of the sails of the argument he was about to present.

Jack smiled and said, "Look, pal, I'm not sitting here on some lofty plane looking down on you, her, or anyone else. What I'm trying to do is give you a gift. Believe me, I'm human too and don't think there weren't moments when Erika and I were courting when it was close, but we didn't sleep with each other and I'll be eternally thankful for the grace to do that."

"Yeah…but I didn't grow up like you did. I told you that I stopped going to church when I was thirteen years old. Actually because this girl, Amy Hall, skipped Mass and Amy Hall was gorgeous, come to think of it."

Jack smiled and said, "Chris, what I'm talking about is in line with what the Church teaches but it's not about Catholicism. I actually learned about how to court a woman in a healthy way from my uncle Scott. You interested in what he taught me?"

"Sure."

"Ok, well, when I was sixteen, I spent a couple of weeks down in Nashville with my aunt and uncle. One afternoon, I was at the ice cream shop and…"

"You were at an ice cream shop.? I can't believe it."

Jack smiled. "Yeah, well, while I was sipping on my root beer float, this gorgeous girl named Rachel walked in and sat down next to me. Immediately I liked her and she liked me. We took a walk around the square and sat on a bench for what seemed like days, talking about everything and nothing…you know how those conversations are."

"Oh, yes. I do," said Chris.

"Everything was going great but I got a really weird feeling when Rachel asked if I wanted to go down by the creek with her.

"What was wrong with that?"

"It wasn't what she asked but how she asked it. You know what I mean?"

"Oh, yeah."

"Well, by coincidence, Uncle Scott was in town running an errand and happened to see me sitting on the bench with Rachel. We were just holding hands and I never saw Uncle Scott but when I got home, he was sitting on the porch with two glasses of iced tea and asked me to have a seat."

"Yeah but you were just holding hands, right?"

"Yeah, but that wasn't the point. Rachel was a beautiful girl who never felt like she was beautiful. Her daddy had a bad drinking problem and Uncle Scott said she had been hurt by him. I never asked exactly how but in a small town people talk. Uncle Scott knew some things about Rachel and her family. To this day, I don't know what happened to her but she's still in my prayers. But what Uncle Scott asked me was, 'Jack, what do you want in so far as the ladies? I mean do you want to get the most notches in your gun belt or do you want the relationship of a lifetime with one spectacular woman?'

"Knowing you, I think I know your answer."

"Thanks, buddy, I appreciate the compliment and you're right. I answered that I wanted the second option of course. He asked if I knew how to find a healthy girl who is capable of giving and receiving love. I gave him the same puzzled look you are giving me right now and he said, 'Look, you meet a girl you like and you take her on three dates and don't do so much as kiss her on the cheek. On the third date, she might be of the mind to be a little more affectionate if you haven't yet. At that point you look her right in the eye and say the following, 'Look, I find you exceptionally attractive. I wouldn't have asked your permission to take you out if I didn't but for me to be able to participate in this, I have to stay out of this arena until I know its right, which for me is marriage.'"

Chris looked at Jack with a pained expression because what his friend was telling him was ringing true but also went against every fiber of his being. Seeing it, Jack smiled and said, "I know that look. I gave the same look to Uncle Scott but let me tell you why it's important. Item one: The healthy ones capable of love will appreciate that because they think enough of themselves not to need to seal the deal using sex."

"Hmmm."

"Item two: The ones who have some growth to do before they would be capable of a loving, committed relationship will run screaming because you have just taken away the only weapon they really had to keep you under their thumb. If they need to control you, and use you, they can't possibly love you."

It sounded right and Chris' arguments began to shatter.

"Item three: If it doesn't work out with her and you haven't gone to bed together, it's much less painful to go separate ways. Chris thought it sounded completely logical.

"Here's one more reason that I'll throw in for free. If you can't say no to it now, how are you going to avoid other temptations once you are married? When the priest marries you, he'll ask if you accept the vows to be with each other for the rest of your lives freely. Freely means you have the capacity to say no. If you don't have the capacity to say no, you don't have the freedom to say yes."

Chris stared at the ground for several moments until he looked up at Jack with a sad expression and said, "You know, it must be easier for a guy like you. I mean I'm not what....well, haven't been what anyone would consider a saint in that department."

"Chris, it's not easy for *anyone*. It wasn't for me either. No matter what you may have done in the past, we have a loving God that is eager to forgive us, provided we just *try* to do better. The other piece of that is He knows we can't without His help so the next time you are feeling amorous toward Keely and know it's not appropriate, just take a few breaths and pray for His help. Believe me, pal, I did it on countless occasions."

The truth of what his friend was saying registered and Chris thought of the conversation he was going to have with Keely that night. It seemed such a shame after just getting moved into the new house but Chris knew Jack was right. He fully intended to talk to Keely that week about their living arrangement when he had left Jack's house that night a month earlier.

The conversation hadn't happened yet.

As he drifted off to sleep, Chris thought, with a sense of self-satisfaction that, for the first time since meeting Jack, his friend had been wrong about something. He and Keely had successfully avoided the increasingly powerful urges to, as Jack would say, fall into sin. Chris had, on more than one occasion, subjected himself to frigid showers to quell the feelings. Besides, if his plan for tomorrow night went the way he hoped, it would make everything legitimate.

"If she was my fiancé, who could say anything if we ended up..," he began to tell himself when a voice from within spoke so quietly, he tried to ignore it.

If you can't say no, you can't say yes.
"Yeah, yeah, but..." he muttered.
It's not giving yourself freely if you can't say no.
"Who asked You, anyway?"
You did.
"Ugh..."

**Residence of Chris Walsh and Keely Kennedy
2372 Poplar Street
Atlanta, Georgia
8:00 A.M. Eastern Time
Tuesday, May 14th, 1973**

Chapter Sixteen

Sitting at the small kitchen table, Chris and Keely held hands and sipped from their coffee cups. Chris used his free hand to close the Bible on the table. Even on the morning that would decide the fate of Chris' entire professional and financial future, he and Keely kept their morning ritual intact. Reading the daily scriptures and discussing their relevance in their own lives over breakfast gave a start to their day that Chris treasured. Keely had introduced Chris to the discipline the first morning they moved in together and he would be forever thankful that he had been blessed with such a remarkable woman. As he closed the Bible, he thought, *I mean what's the problem here. We even read the Bible together. I think Jack is making a big deal over nothing.*

Like many of the spiritual gifts Keely had bestowed on him, Chris was not originally enthusiastic about reading the Bible but he could tell it was important to her so he went along with it. It felt odd at first but after a few days, he knew sharing the experience with Keely gave him a great sense of increased intimacy with her that he had never shared at such a level with any other woman he had known. That held true this morning despite the monumental impact the next few hours would have on his life. As he closed the Bible after reading and talking about several verses from the Book of James, Chris' concern about whether planes and boxes were on time was, at that particular moment, the furthest thing from his mind.

Warm, golden sunlight shone in through the small part in the curtains Keely had hung in the small, wooden-floored rental home.

The backyard was heavily wooded as all back yards in the quaint neighborhood were, but there was a space between two huge fir trees that, for twenty minutes each spring morning as the sun rose, cast a perfect beam of sunlight through the kitchen window. The light's golden color amplified as it passed through the pine tree pollen that had adhered to almost every outdoor surface including the window glass.

As Chris watched Keely gaze out the window, the joy of being with her touched his heart. A sense of peace washed over him sitting next to her and it was often, in the quiet, unspeaking moments between them, that Chris felt love for Keely that went beyond the capability of his vocabulary to describe. Those were the most precious moments that needed no explanation. He touched her cheek gently. She turned toward him, smiled and reached for his hand, intertwining her fingers in his. Little things like that made his heart leap. A happiness that had virtually no rival in his life erupted from his heart in that moment. He cherished those times with her. He squeezed her hand and as she stood to get another cup of coffee, she rewarded him with an angelic smile, kissing him on the cheek. Suddenly realizing the time and the fact that Chris hadn't left for the office yet, she exclaimed, "I'm shocked you weren't in the office hours ago. Aren't you going to even call to find out how things are turning out?"

"There are things in life eminently more important than a silly little fifty million dollars…like this," he replied as he stood and put his arms around her, catching a whiff of the coconut-scented shampoo she used. Suddenly, he felt some stirrings, and the reality of the conversation he had replayed in his mind the night before became abundantly clear. In that moment, he knew there was going to have to be a change in their living arrangements but he just couldn't bring himself to broach the subject. Something his father used to say came to mind just then. "Good is often the enemy of the best."

Oh, man, he thought.

Just then, Keely smiled in the particular manner reserved only for him in those moments and he realized he was willing to do anything to be with her. As he was about to bring up the conversation about their living arrangement, the phone rang, abruptly ending his impetus to have the talk.

Chris rolled his eyes and picked up the phone.

"This better be good," he growled jokingly into the phone, knowing exactly who it would be calling.

"If I had bad news, Captain, that sort of greeting would not be appreciated," heard Chris from the phone, the quiver of Jack's excitement barely concealed. Jack knew Chris was just being Chris.

"So what's the score?"

"So far four hundred and ten packages have arrived as promised, according to the couriers. That's every single one with two exceptions that will be delivered by midday in Chicago and Los Angeles. Those two packages, already handed off to the couriers, have caused a minor hiccup."

"What's the story there?"

"High Road Cartage in Chicago had one vehicle break down and they are sending another truck and driver to finish the delivery. Same thing in L.A."

A huge smile broke across Chris' face. Keely's hand was clasped in his as he beamed at her and squeezed her hand to tell her everything was going well. Chris jumped up from the table and did a football touchdown dance, getting the telephone cord wrapped around his neck in the process.

Hearing Keely's laughter at the dance spectacle, Jack asked, "I didn't interrupt your breakfast did I?"

"You, my friend, are just way too thoughtful. You call me up to tell me that it looks like Velocity Express is a living, breathing company and you're concerned that you might have interrupted our toast and eggs? You are truly a prince, buddy!"

"Thanks, partner. So what time do you want to get together today and start exploring the idea of our own ground transportation?"

Chris looked at the clock and said, "I'll be in the office in an hour. We'll take a look at everything that went right and what didn't yesterday and try to map out some ideas as to where to go from here." He sat and listened for a response from Jack for a few moments and when there was none asked, "You still there?"

"Yeah, I'm still here. I'm just watching two of our birds taxiing up now." He paused for a moment, and then he asked, "This is real, isn't it?"

"Yeah, it's real. See you in an hour."

Chris hung up and listened as a jet flew overhead. He didn't know whether it was one of Velocity Express' aircraft but the sound was exhilarating nonetheless.

"It went well, I take it?" asked Keely as she headed for the bathroom.

"So well that I think we might just be in business, sweetheart. I think that this calls for a celebration tonight. What do you think of me taking you to that new Greek place, Kyma, off of Piedmont? Say eight o'clock reservations?"

She turned from the bathroom and said, "Babe, that's a great place but a bit on the pricey side. You're not exactly a millionaire after the first day of business."

Chris' face registered a bit of disappointment at her bringing him back to earth in regard to financial discipline when his head was clearly at much higher altitudes.

Countering with, "So you'd rather have Chinese delivery?" his tone let her know he had no intention of allowing the wind to be let out of his sails. It was a momentous day for them both and he fully intended to celebrate. In his heart, he knew the time was perfect for something else as well.

"Alright, honey, I'll wear my little black dress you like so much," she called from her bathroom.

As Keely continued to do her morning beautification rituals in her bathroom mirror, Chris stood, went to his room, opened the dresser and felt for the little box under some socks. Finding it exactly where he had hidden it three days earlier, he called across the hallway to her, "I'm really looking forward to tonight, baby. It's been a while since you and I enjoyed a nice dinner out alone."

Keely had been a professional bartender for over a decade and reading people and their tone of voice was a finely developed skill she possessed. There was something to his tone that she immediately picked up on. From down the hall in her room, she called out, "Are you up to something, you clever boy?"

Terrified that she was onto his surprise, he answered flatly as possible, "I just thought we'd enjoy some quality time together. We hardly see each other any more with my working to get the company up and running and you working at the bar so many hours. I just thought…"

"Alright, babe, I believe you," she said as she went back to scrubbing her face, knowing he was trying way too hard to sell her. She knew that when Chris didn't feel comfortable discussing something, he always began to babble on incessantly. She wasn't exactly sure what Chris had planned, but there was one thing she prayed it might be. Chris dressed for work in front of the mirror, putting on a pair of jeans, a crisp, white Brooks Brothers shirt, and no tie. As he buttoned the last button, Keely came to the doorway of his room and, in a tone of voice that immediately sent a shiver up his spine, said, "I do love you so, Mr. Christopher Walsh." When he turned around, the smile he wore couldn't have been any brighter.

"And I do love you Mrs. Keely Wal…," said Chris. His brain, upon hearing what just came out of his mouth, completely stopped working for a moment and froze. Keely looked into his eyes. She could tell by his expression that he was teetering between embarrassment and the terror of verbalizing the thought from which the slip had originated. They had done the lover's dance around the topic for months. He began to try to correct himself.

"I, uh, meant…"

"Shhhh…..it's alright, babe. I know you had a long day yesterday. Those neural synapses must not be firing just right," she said with a mischievous grin as she put her finger to his lips. It was a very feminine gesture that she had used on more than one occasion to silence his babbling.

He kissed her on the cheek to put a pleasant bit of punctuation on the exchange and he headed to his bedroom to finish dressing. Five minutes later, after placing the little box first in his pocket, then in his briefcase, and finally settling again on his pocket, Chris walked down the hallway to the kitchen where she had a cup of very strong coffee laced with healthy portions of milk and sugar waiting for him. He quickly downed the coffee and gave her a hug.

Feeling the object in his front pocket of the pair his Levis jeans against her thigh when they embraced, a wave of joy washed over Keely. She couldn't be sure of her suspicion but somehow she instinctively knew what it was. The protrusion was small, square, and a size that would fit her dream perfectly. For a second, she almost asked, "Is that a ring box in your pocket or are you just happy to see me?" but realized that it would not only be grossly inappropriate but could potentially ruin a momentous occasion if she was right. Her occasional impetus to bring such suggestive comments into the conversation was beginning to increase in frequency and intensity but she had managed to refrain each time. It was getting more difficult to push those impulses from her head but she had made a promise to herself and God to not go there until marriage. She made a mental note to talk to Father McNamara about it.

Chris, oblivious to yet another telling bit of foreshadowing, walked out the door to his car, tossed his briefcase in the back, and then slipped the little box in the glove compartment while watching the kitchen window to see if she were looking. Again dissatisfied with the location, he removed it and put it, once again, in the briefcase along with notepads and copies of that day's flight plans for the day's planned delivery flight operations.

As Chris walked into the office, the excitement was palpable. Staff members were working the phones, following up on delivered packages with customers and farming for more business. Each person, as Chris walked by, smiled or gave a thumbs-up, or some other sign that all was running very well.

"We've just booked another two days of aircraft full to capacity," said Jack as he hung up the phone on his desk when Chris walked into his office.

"Well that's just remarkable. I cannot believe we made this happen," said Chris with a grin.

Jack looked at his partner with a peaceful, contented look that seemed out of place in the frenzied activity.

"You know, *we* didn't really do this. We may be the instruments for bringing the pieces together, but something this good couldn't possibly be the work of two characters clearly as flawed as us. We have to have a little help from the One who makes everything possible."

"You know, I'm really beginning to believe that," said Chris.

Standing in Jack's office, fidgeting with the little box in his pocket, Chris could barely contain his excitement about the news he was about to share with his partner. Jack noticed a slight detachment from the conversation he was trying to have with Chris about operational concerns, paused, looked at him and asked, "Hey, where are you? I just asked if you had seen the fuel bills from the California and New York runs last night. It looks like they really are trying to take us to the cleaners at those airports."

Snapped out of his thoughts about what he planned that evening, Chris apologized. "Sorry, Jack. I'm just a little distracted."

"Well, find another time to be distracted because we do have several things to get done today including revisiting your idea of acquiring our own ground transportation."

Chris couldn't contain himself anymore. From his pocket, he removed the small, black box, opened it, and held its contents forward for Jack's inspection.

"Oh my goodness!" said Jack. "That thing is beautiful! And it's about time!"

"Well tonight, God willing, Keely will accept it from me and agree to be my wife."

Beaming with happiness, Jack exclaimed, "That's fantastic! Your timing couldn't be better. There's a new priest at the Cathedral that I've heard is great at pre-marital counseling."

Chris looked at his best friend and said, "Uh, I thought you only had to go to counseling if a marriage is falling apart."

Jack looked at his friend and with an exasperated tone said, "Correct me if I'm wrong but hasn't your intended bride-to-be been a Catholic her entire life?"

"Yeah."

"And despite you two living precariously under the same roof before marriage, hasn't she been going to church with my wife and me every Sunday while you slept in?"

"Well…yeah."

"So pal, have you given any thought as to exactly where you two will be married?"

"Well, my plan was to do it on the beach at that little golf resort we went to down in Ponte Vedra, Florida."

Jack just rolled his eyes and said, "We really need to talk again."

As he said it, Chris had no argument left in him. He knew that Keely's devotion to Catholicism, which had grown even stronger since the friendship between her and Jack and Erika had begun nearly a year ago, would not permit him to just skate by on the matter.

"I'm assuming you'll want to be married in the Catholic Church?" asked Jack.

"Alright, alright…," said Chris with a tone of exasperation. "Let's just see *if* she says yes first and *then* we'll talk about the rest of this deal, ok?"

Can't anything be simple? thought Chris as he picked up the fuel invoices and began to look over them, returning to the moment at hand that involved running the newest air cargo carrier in the world.

Chris and Keely pulled into the front drive of the newest Greek restaurant in Atlanta on Piedmont Road. The stark, white building looked as if it had been plucked from the island of Santorini, exactly as the owners intended. As Chris tried to hand the keys to the valet, he was so nervous that he dropped them on the ground. As the valet attempted to pick them up, Chris bent to get them at the same time and they bumped heads.

"Sir, I've got it. Really," said the young man as he rubbed his head.

Before arriving at the restaurant, Chris' plan was to wait until after dinner but he found it impossible to wait one more moment.

He suddenly realized, as he looked over the menu, that he had absolutely no appetite. Just after the waiter placed the bowl of various olives on the table and retreated to give them a chance to look over the menu a little more, Chris stood, walked over to the side of the table next to Keely, and got down on one knee. Immediately other diners took notice and as he cleared his throat, Chris could hear their excited whispers. As soon as he had knelt down, Keely began to tear up, her breaths short and her hands covering her mouth

"Keely, I don't have any fancy words but just want to tell you that I cannot imagine any other life than one with you. Will you marry me? Will you be my wife?" Holding forth the ring in the box, the colors of the rainbow flashed in Keely's eyes as the light from above hit the stone. For a moment she was completely unable to speak, totally overwhelmed with emotion and when she could, she grabbed his hands in hers and managed, through the tears of absolute joy, to say, "Yes, yes….oh sweetheart, yes! I so want you to be my husband! I…yes, yes!"

Tables all around broke into applause.

As Keely threw her arms around him, he held her tightly and everything seemed frozen in that moment. As he held the woman he loved more than life itself, an odd childhood memory popped into his mind. He suddenly recalled a lecture from seventh grade parochial school. Sister Veronica told all of the kids in class that day about two types of time: *Chronos* was the linear time that we kept with clocks. *Kairos* was always God's time and was always now. Sister Veronica said that if you did something that was pleasing to God, it was always in God's time and was forever.

They held each other in an embrace that seemed an eternity.

**Cathedral of Christ the King
Peachtree Road
Atlanta, Georgia
6:03 P.M. Eastern Time
Friday, May 29th, 1974**

Chapter Seventeen

During their first pre-marital counseling session, Father John McNamara got straight to the point.
"Are you two already sleeping with each other?"
"No, Father," said Chris with a tone of pride.
"That's fantastic to hear. I know it's difficult, but you will be so happy that you haven't when you marry."
Had he kept his mouth shut, Chris might have escaped without further discussion but with an air of confidence, Chris proclaimed, "Yes, Father, I'm sure you are right. We sleep in separate rooms right now."
"Oh, wow," said Father McNamara as his face fell. Looking him directly in the eye, the priest said, "Guys, do you two *really* want to test yourselves that much? Well, that has to come to an immediate end right now if you want to have the slightest chance of making it to your wedding day. That's not a theory. That's my experience in counseling hundreds of couples. Every time a couple has lived together, as the wedding day approaches, there comes this idea, 'Well, what's the harm? We're going to be married next week anyway.'"

Chris began to utter the word, *But,* in protest but inwardly, it was a relief to hear it from their priest. He had intended to have the conversation with Keely for months, receiving subtle but frequent reminders from Jack that it was the right thing to do, but Chris never could bring himself to get around to it. Father McNamara stood, went to his desk, retrieved a small, blue booklet entitled *Clean Love in Courtship,* and handed it to him.

Looking over at Keely, he was somewhat relieved to see that she looked as uncomfortable as he did.

"Chris, let me ask you something. What is the reason for marriage?"

A man often with an answer for anything, Chris began to respond with the brilliantly-articulated, "Uh…well…"

"Relax, my son. Let me put you out of your misery," said Fr. McNamara with a smarmy grin Chris winced at. He instinctively knew what the priest was about to say was not only true, but not something he wasn't going to want to hear. "The entire purpose for marrying this child of God," continued the priest, "is to help her to get into heaven. Her purpose in marrying you should be the very same. Yes, going forth and multiplying is called for but not until *after* you both are joined in Holy Matrimony. Marriage is a sacrament. Any playing at it before you make the commitment is a grave insult to God's plan for us. You catch my drift there, sport?" Father McNamara, in his early forties but still extremely youthful looking and considered one of the more 'hip' priests by the children he taught at the school, had a gift for carrying God's message in a manner that would be easily heard by the intended recipient.

"So, if you are ready to make confession, it would be a great start," said Father John.

Chris looked at Keely and then back to Father McNamara, not having foreseen this turn of the conversation.

"My dear, would you be kind enough to wait outside while we have a little chat," said Father John. Keely quietly stood, thought, *Oh, grand,* and then walked outside Father John's office.

"We'll get to you in a few minutes," said Father John as she closed the door.

That evening, sitting in the little home they rented, Chris and Keely talked about what Father John had said.

"I think he's right, honey. What's a year?"

"Well, fourteen months anyway, if we do it in June next year. But yeah, I agree. I had been meaning to talk to you about this anyway but just couldn't bring myself to say it. Jack and I talked about it a while back but I really didn't think that it was really that important until now. I was afraid that if I moved out, you wouldn't think I loved you and you might leave. I didn't think I could talk to you about it."

"Oh, sweetheart, please don't think you can't tell me something. Please, baby. I'll love you no matter what."

Chris went over to her chair and she stood. They held each other for a while and kissed. In the moment, they both felt the draw they knew they absolutely needed to avoid. With a flushed face, she took a deep breath and said, "Alright then. It's time for you to go," playfully pulling his arm to lead him to the door.

Chris smiled and said, "Yeah, it really is."

Chris called Jack and was surprised at how receptive Jack was to an unexpected guest that night. When he was about to fall into the bed in the guest room, he noticed a card on the bed. Opening the card, there were only two words on the inside: "Good choice!"

The following morning, Chris and Keely met for breakfast at a landmark diner just off the campus of Oglethorpe University called The Original Pancake House. There was a sense of peace and joy they shared about the state of their relationship that hadn't been there before. A few hours later, Chris signed the lease on a little apartment a half-mile from the airport. Since they were still obligated to the rental house for a year, Keely asked a new girl at work to be her roommate to share the cost. Chris was comforted by the thought that Keely wasn't living alone in that house. When Chris came in to the office and threw his key to his new place on Jack's desk, Jack was overjoyed at hearing the news.

"I'm telling you Chris, this will change your relationship immensely. You'll be amazed at what it does for your character. I really didn't hold a lot of hope out for you two until today."

The small voice of truth deep inside Chris knew his friend was right.

The following month, Chris began to attend the formal classes of the Rite of Christian Initiation for Adults. Chris had attended parochial school up until seventh grade when his family had moved from Washington D.C. to Dallas, Texas for his father's job It had been a transitional period for the family and there wasn't a parochial school within reasonable distance or cost. When he began attending public school that year, his parents, Tom and Clara, had made an effort to continue his religious education with evening classes for children. But when his teacher, exasperated by Chris' total disinterest in the lessons, called his mother for the fifth time in as many weeks, Tom and Clara finally decided to let Chris make his own decisions regarding his participation in religion. Discussing it one evening, they had come to the conclusion that it should be Chris' decision to make Confirmation and, until returning to the church at the age of thirty-four, Chris had been a member of one of the largest segments of Catholicism: the fallen-away Catholic. As a willful teenager, Chris hadn't made any attempt to adhere to the tenets of the Church of his childhood a priority in his life. For the better part of two decades, Chris hadn't made seeking a relationship with God a priority until the slow transformative process began with Jack Lee entering his life.

Chris remembered a conversation at a restaurant with Keely a few months back. "I know I've been a total failure at times in my past relationships but I really am trying to live by the things we believe. You know I love you completely, don't you?"

"I do know that, baby. Love is how God gets our attention," answered Keely.

It was one of a number of treasured moments they had shared during their courtship that had left Chris with no doubt that she was the woman he wanted to spend the rest of his life with.

Before making the decision to formally re-join the Church, as Chris had never made the Sacrament of Confirmation, he had talked it over with his spiritual director, Father McNamara. During his monthly appointment with Father McNamara, the priest informed Chris that because he had made all of the other sacraments while in parochial school, he was technically eligible to make his confession and make Confirmation without attending R.C.I.A.

"You know what, Father? I've been pretty much away from the Church for over two decades. If I'm signing up for this way of life, I think I should be pretty well versed in what that really means."

"Excellent decision," the priest had answered as he handed Chris a copy of *The Baltimore Catechism*, and said, "Here's your first assignment. Read this."

Oh man, homework. Great, thought Chris.

The time spent attending Rite of Christian Initiation for Adults, or RCIA, classes each Sunday morning before Mass, discussing the readings and Gospel, had been transformative to Chris' thinking about a great deal of things. After a while Chris just began to hear things he had never heard before. It wasn't that they hadn't been said around him all his life but that he hadn't had the capacity to actually *hear* them.

"When the student is ready, the teacher will appear," said Jack one morning over coffee as Chris tried to describe the experience.

"It's like being back in Catholic school again, but this time I'm not in Sister Sean's office three times a week," he had said, much to Jack's amusement. As his class sat in the large, 1930's-era cathedral each Sunday, listening to the readings, the Gospel, and finally the homily, Chris began to see it as a precious time where the never-ending work of running Velocity Express could be put on the back burner. The other effect on his life that returning to the Church had given him was an enhanced sense of closeness to Jack and Erika who, after Sunday Mass, would join up with him and Keely for lunch at any number of the restaurants along Peachtree Street in the lower Buckhead area.

On an early Sunday evening, while enjoying dinner over at the Lee house, Chris and Jack sat talking about their faith and what had been discussed during that morning's R.C.I.A. class. The ladies chatted and cooked in the kitchen. The cozy house, overlooking a golf course in the Chastain Park area, had a small kitchen. Jack always asked if he could help his wife in any way and she always answered, with a smile, that she appreciated it but two was company and three was liable to cause an accident. Jack winked at Chris and then said, "Hey, I want to show you what I did with that back room." They both stood and walked down a hallway. Jack opened the door and motioned Chris to come inside. The room had a gorgeous bay window overlooking the park and an orange sun was setting over the thick canopy of trees that appeared to stretch all the way to the downtown Atlanta skyline. The room's furnishing consisted of a few shelves with an old, family Bible and other spiritual meditation books. On the wall was one cross made from palms from the prior year's Palm Sunday with a rosary hanging around it. Hanging in the center of the other wall was an ornate, beautifully-crafted crucifix.

"When my father was in the Navy, he had that cross blessed by Pope Pius XII while he was visiting the Vatican," explained Jack when Chris had asked about the cross. There were two rocking chairs and a small table between them in the middle of the room that faced the window.

As they sat down in the chairs that evening, Chris had asked, "What else are you going to put in here?"

"Nothing. This is exactly how this room is supposed to be."

"But this has the best view in the house. Don't you want to make this into an office or something?"

Jack had smiled and said, "Wouldn't you give God the best room in your house when he came to visit? This is my prayer room. I figure if God gives you a house, you should give him a room. Don't you?"

"I hadn't thought about that."

"You know, Chris, I can see a total change in you over the past few months. You're more relaxed at work and I know you and Keely stand a real chance of making your relationship work now."

"Man, I used to think you were a little over-the-top with the whole Catholic thing, especially when we were in the Air Force, but when I look back at all that has happened over the years, I can't really argue that there is a God."

"Did you always think there wasn't?"

"You know, I've always believed in *something* but I wasn't really able to say it until now. I just couldn't see myself adhering to the rules of the Church because they seem so restrictive."

"That's a common argument to what being Catholic calls for, but can you say that anything you've been doing in your faith has really restricted you, or do you find that trying to do what God calls us to do actually gives you freedom?" asked Jack

"When you put it that way, I'm not wasting time trying to figure out the rules to know just how much I can get away with. Yeah, it really is freeing."

"Let me ask you something else. Was there ever a time in your life that you really felt the close presence of God?"

Chris sat for a second, knowing his answer and debating whether or not to share it. Knowing he could tell Jack anything in the world, he chose to describe the one experience that stood out among all others.

"I've never told anyone about this when I was in the Air Force...or since because if they believed me, I'd probably still be in Leavenworth Prison, or at the very least have a dishonorable discharge on my record," Chris answered.

Jack, deeply concerned, just nodded.

"During flight training at Moody, it was my last flight in the T-38 before they assigned me to the C-141. I took off and was somewhere between the Okefenokee swamp and Jacksonville, eighty miles off to the east. It was an absolutely perfect day for flying. For some reason, I got a wild hair to see just how high I could take her."

Jack, having been through the exact same training began to realize where Chris' story was going. The service ceiling of a T-38 Talon jet was forty-five thousand feet. To take it above that was a direct violation of numerous provisions of the Uniform Code of Military Justice but at the time, radar didn't have the capability to accurately determine altitude.

Chris continued, "I nosed her up and began an instrument climb. When the needle pegged at fifty-two thousand, three hundred, I knew it was all she had." He looked at Jack who sat spellbound, looking into his friend's eyes.

"I looked up from the instrument panel and above me, the sky was black. When I turned my head to the west, I saw the curvature of the earth. I mean I *really* saw it and not just a little." His voice cracked slightly as he described the view. Jack smiled as he listened. Having flown the exact same jet in pilot training, Jack knew that at that altitude, there was barely enough air passing over the air surfaces of the jet to keep it in stable flight. If something had gone wrong at that altitude, it wasn't likely Chris would have survived an ejection. In that minimal atmosphere, his blood would boil with nitrogen bubbles much like scuba divers experience the lethal condition known as "the bends."

"I looked at this beautiful, blue and white ball floating in space and looked out into eternity. Right then, I felt this warm sensation like it was just being poured over me and felt a peace wash over me that I've never experienced since. For the next few weeks, the feeling stayed with me."

"That's *exactly* what I'm talking about!" said Jack. "It must have been something like that that inspired the line in the poem *Hight Flight*, that talks about touching the face of God."

Chris had never thought of the experience as spiritual. He knew then that it most definitely had been. The line in the poem reverberated in his mind. *To slip the surly bonds of earth and touch the face of God.*

Fellini's Pizza
Peachtree Road
Atlanta, Georgia
8:45 P.M. Eastern Time
Friday, August 19th, 1974

Chapter Eighteen

Jack seemed distant and glum all day. With more packages to deliver than ever, and two of their jets down for maintenance, it had been a challenging week for the entire VelEx staff. But, when Jack's sullen mood carried over into their customary Friday night dinner at Fellini's Pizza, Chris knew there had to be more to the dour mood.

"Hey, man, what's going on with you? If you're not making fun of my olive and jalapeño pizza, I know something is up. Spill it."

Jack let a long breath out and said, "I'm really ticked off at Erika right now." He took a long pull off his beer.

"Wait a minute…you mean that there's trouble in paradise? I've never seen you so much as raise your voice one decibel toward her. What could she-who-can-do-no-wrong have done to put you into this kind of mood?" asked Chris. It was true; he had never heard anything remotely resembling a disparaging remark from Jack about Erika.

"You know when we rent that little cabin in the mountains that Erika and I go to every winter, there's more to it than just relaxing and enjoying the view. We can talk for hours without interruption from hospitals or VelEx or anything else that regularly comes up at home. We actually prepare topics before going to the cabin that we want to talk about and discuss them. Basically, we check to make sure we are on the same page in all the important areas of our marriage. Erika calls it our 'one-couple retreat'. This last time, I thought we were pretty clear on the decision to try to get pregnant."

"Really? That's great," Chris exclaimed, his eyes wide with excitement. "I'm so happy for you both."

Jack leaned back in his chair, took a deep breath and said, "Well, that *was* the plan. This morning when I brought up the natural family planning stuff, she tells me she might be offered a teaching position in the medical school and it wouldn't be such a good idea for her to get pregnant right now."

"Wow, I'm sorry to hear that," said Chris. For a moment, he chewed a bite of his pizza with no intention of prying further but he was struck with a thought that compelled him to continue, "But does it make sense that she wants to wait? I mean, would teaching at Emory make her happier than what she's doing now?"

Jack swirled the remnants of his beer around in the bottom of the bottle. Suddenly, he looked up at Chris, sighed, and then a sheepish grin broke across his lips. Jack appeared to say to the ceiling, "Ok, ok…I get it."

"Get what?"

Jack looked back at Chris and said, "That I've been an idiot about this all day long. I was so wrapped up in what *I* wanted that I didn't even give Erika a chance to talk to me when she saw I was upset and tried to explain this morning. All I did was grab my things and tell her that I needed to get to the office."

"Well there's nothing wrong with wanting to be a father, right? Correct me if I'm wrong but aren't you the one that always says that children are the way God brings new souls into the world?" asked Chris.

"Yeah, that's true, but it is equally important to be a good husband to the wife you are going to enter into the partnership of parenting with. If I'm so wrapped up in what *I* want, and how being a father might make *me* feel, then I'm not ready to be a father."

Chris just looked at his best friend, silently impressed.

"Hey, man, I hate to cut this short but I have to go see my wife about an apology I owe her," said Jack as he stood from the table.

"No worries, buddy. I'll see you at 0700 at the office?"

"I tell you what; can you move the planning session to ten? I'd actually like to take Erika to breakfast tomorrow morning if that's alright with you?"

"Not a problem at all. You know, I gotta say I wish I could think about these things like you do. I mean I try to do the right things with Keely and I haven't really messed up too badly yet…"

Jack stopped pushing in his chair, smiled, pulled it back out, and sat back down. He leaned into the table and looked Chris directly in the eyes and said, "Let me tell you something. You are the best friend I've ever had. You listen to my garbage when I need it and don't think for a second I don't think you are a great man for Keely. I'm not some sort of genius about these things… that should be perfectly clear by our conversation tonight. What I know for sure though is that you have done some huge things to grow in your faith and it shows in every area of your life, including how you love Keely. I've never judged you, my friend. That's not my job. If you see things that you might find helpful in the way I do them, that's just God using me to be helpful to you."

"I just don't know how you do that all the time…talking about God in relation to the simplest—or sometimes not so simple things—but not making me feel like an idiot or less than you."

"Chris, you are an amazing guy with a real love for Keely. I've watched you do a lot of things that were just for her, regardless of the cost to you."

"Yeah, well isn't that what being a good fiancé is about?"

"I'm not talking about taking her nice places or buying her gifts. I'm talking about the things I've seen you do that were tough for you. Like last fall."

"Oh, yeah."

The prior fall, Chris was in Los Angeles to finalize the purchase of a trucking company to complete deliveries in the area. It was a pivotal move in the expansion of VelEx, Chris' meeting with the owners was scheduled for the following morning. As he approached the frond desk of the Beverly Hilton hotel, he received a note from the front desk clerk that read, "Chris, call me. Urgent. Jack."

Keely had been in a car accident when a teenager in a pickup ran a red light trying to keep up with a carload of cheerleaders ahead of him. The impact sent her Datsun 260Z into a fire hydrant at nearly forty miles per hour. Her left wrist was broken and she had friction burns from the seatbelt. Chris handed the phone back to the desk clerk and, without so much as a word of explanation, picked up his bags and made a beeline for the cab stand outside. Despite Jack's assurances that Keely was going to be fine, he bought a ticket on the first available flight home.

When Chris called the offices of Joe and Jimmy Letourneau—the owners of Costal Couriers—from the airport to explain the situation and ask to reschedule, the brothers decided the fair offer from VelEx wasn't enough, given the delay.

"Mr. Walsh, we'd love to do business with you but we have another offer from Flying Cougars and they said they could close the deal with us by tomorrow…and they're willing to match your offer and increase it by five percent."

"Are you kidding me? I just told you my fiancé was in a car accident and you're choosing now…this day…to play hardball with me and renegotiate a practically done deal. A deal for which I have a letter of intent drawn up by your attorney."

"Well, Mr. Walsh, I feel your pain but this is business, not personal," Joe had retorted with a tone Chris promised he would somehow make the man pay for.

The fact that Chris' former employer might get their hands on a business operation that would be crucial to VelEx deliveries in Los Angeles made it an expensive loss. That these guys were using his fiancé to put the screws to him made it personal.

Chris took a deep breath and managed to pray a silent prayer: *God, help me not say anything else.*

"Goodbye, Mr. Letourneau. I'm going home to my fiancé and I might be in touch," said Chris through clenched teeth. He placed the phone in the cradle and headed for his gate at Los Angeles International. As he walked to his gate, he could see a

Flying Cougars Lockheed L-1011 lifting off on Runway Two-Five-Left. He had piloted Flying Cougars jets off that very runway hundreds of times and it was quite likely that he had flown that very jet he was watching climb into the California sky. His own Eastern Airlines flight was nearly an hour away and he wished that he could be in the cockpit of the jet that instant so he could get back to Keely faster.

"Yeah, that was an unbelievable day," said Chris.
"But you were willing to walk away from an important deal to be by Keely's side when she was hurt. That's beyond just being a good fiancé—that is what real love is all about. When you feel a real responsibility for someone, not just enjoyment of the emotions the relationship creates, *that's* love.

The entire fiasco with the Letourneau brothers that day had been a blessing in disguise. When the offer from Flying Cougars fell through the next week, Chris returned to the bargaining table armed with a piece of information he didn't have the day of Keely's accident. Thanks to a phone call from Glenn Strain, his old colleague at Flying Cougars who was ready to jump ship, Chris now knew that the Letourneau brothers were so deep in debt that they needed to unload the business to avoid personal financial ruin. Having already signed Glenn on as VelEx's newest pilot over breakfast, Chris sat down with the Letourneau brothers in their office. He opened the discussion barely concealing a smile.
"Gentlemen, our offer is now a hundred thousand less than what we talked about. I figure if you guys want to pick the day that my fiancé is in an accident to try to squeeze a little more cash out of us, I'm going to return the favor. It's not personal, mind you. It's just business."
The Letourneau brothers had seethed with silent rage as they signed the documents in front of the attorneys.

"So does Keely have any idea about tomorrow night?" asked Jack as they walked to their cars behind Fellini's.
"Nope, not a clue."
There was a concert the next evening at the Chastain Park

Amphitheatre a few blocks from Jack's house featuring a band Keely had adored since she was a teenager. Chris had purchased the front-row tickets the day they had gone on sale, six months earlier.

On Saturday, Chris spent all day doing things he really didn't find that interesting such as shopping with Keely at the open air mall at Lennox Square for fall clothes. Not being a student of the world of fashion, he played a mental game by challenging himself to come up with questions about the different styles Keely modeled for him. That day, Chris had discovered the difference between a wedge and espadrille shoe. He secretly planned one Saturday a month to do things that she enjoyed without telling her it was his plan. What he had discovered was that the time invested in learning about the things Keely was passionate about paid huge dividends in their relationship. Not only did Chris feel like he was engaged to the most remarkable woman he'd ever met, but he was discovering that intimacy wasn't just based on physical affection or the warmth of emotions being with her created. He felt that he really knew the woman he was gong to marry as an equal and as his best friend.

As they drove back to Keely's house, he said, "Hey sweetheart, I know we said we would go out to Kyma tonight but I really would love to take a nice walk with you. How about we go take a lap around Chastain Park before dinner? I could move our reservations to nine?" He knew she loved taking walks with him but hoped the location didn't give his plan away, given she was such a fan of the band performing tonight. Thankfully, she didn't piece it together or, if she had, she didn't let on.

"That would be lovely, baby. Thanks for asking!" she said excitedly. An hour later, after Keely unloaded her purchases into her house and changed for the evening, they drove over to Jack and Erika's house in the neighborhood surrounding the park and parked their car in the Lee's driveway. Noticing all the people walking along the sidewalk in the direction of the concert venue, Keely was about to ask when she turned to see Chris grinning, holding a pair of tickets in his hand.

"I love you so much, baby!" she said, wrapping her arms around his neck and kissing him.

As Chris and Keely took their seats, the sun was setting below the tree line, casting a warm, golden-orange light across the amphitheatre. Onstage, the seven-man band known as The Association began strumming the guitar chords that everyone knew as the beginning of their hit song, *Never My Love*. A round of applause from the audience met the opening notes, bringing smiles from the band members that Chris and Keely saw clearly from their front-row seats.

As Chris sat holding Keely's hand, the opening lyrics suggested the question as to whether a lover would ever grow tired of his beloved. He looked over at Keely, squeezed her hand, and knew to a certainty that the answer was an unequivocal, *Never*.

Keely leaned over and kissed Chris on the cheek. The look of peace in her eyes as they met his brought absolute joy to his soul. She leaned her head on his shoulder as the band played. As they listened to the music, Chris reflected back on all the events and conversations that contributed to the formation of his thinking and beliefs. He could see the hand of God in all of it and said a silent prayer of thanks for everything that made him certain Keely was his soul-mate.

It wasn't because Keely was beautiful, which she was. It wasn't because she possessed an intellect and wit that kept Chris captivated and engaged in conversations, which she definitely did. It wasn't the unfailing kindness he had watched her show to people from all walks of life in countless situations during the time he had known her, which she had. Chris knew in his heart of hearts that his love for Keely was no longer based on the childish notions of love he had grown up with and, regrettably, had carried into early adulthood. Those erroneous ideas that love was based solely on the emotions generated from his involvement with the women he had previously dated had provided him with painful lessons at the end of two prior significant relationships. Looking back on those experiences, he could now see that were it not for the pain of those experiences, he might never have been drawn to finding a different solution.

Thinking about what Father McNamara had said at the conclusion of their last pre-marital counseling session, Chris smiled at the memory.   In his characteristic brogue, Father McNamara looked Chris directly in the eye and, with an intensity in his expression Chris hadn't expected, said, "If you only remember one thing from our discussions here, remember this: Love is about wanting good for those you love more than for yourself."

"Amen," whispered Chris to himself as he put his arm around his bride-to-be.

**Cathedral of Christ the King
Peachtree Road
Atlanta, Georgia
1:39 P.M. Eastern Time
Saturday, June 6th, 1975**

Chapter Nineteen

With a jubilant smile, Father McNamara proclaimed, "I now pronounce you husband and wife. You may kiss the bride."
    With that pronouncement from the kindly pastor, Chris lifted Keely's veil away from her face, radiant with joy. Chris' cheeks streamed with big droplets, much as he tried to hold them back. It had been just about all they could do to get through their vows, both choking back waves of emotion, neither caring in the slightest that two hundred friends and family members sat watching them. Many guests were also moved to tears as well.
    Something about Johann Pachelbel's classic piece of music, *Canon in D* had always stirred powerful emotion in Chris. The eight notes of the music, as they overlaid each other and grew from a single violin to several violins and cellos woven into an increasingly complex and beautiful medley, touched something deep within his very soul. It was secretly his favorite piece of music ever. Often, when the daily grind of running the company would reach critically stressful levels, losing himself in that six minutes and eleven seconds of musical perfection created by the Chicago Philharmonic Orchestra would ease him back into serenity.

Fifteen minutes earlier, Chris watched with awe as Keely walked down the aisle with her father, Liam, to the melody of that piece of music. The sight of her started the water works and, as Father McNamara performed the marriage, both he and Keely had gone downhill from there but neither of them cared. For anyone, pledging all their love in this lifetime first to God and secondly to the woman before him would be moving but that morning, Chris felt the presence of God almost as strongly as he had at fifty-two thousand feet in the cockpit of that fighter jet ten years earlier.

On that morning, as Chris and Keely became husband and wife, the experience was made all the more meaningful to Chris by his growing faith in God. Chris knew he was entering into a deeper relationship with God through the privilege of partnership with a spouse.

The rice flew so thickly for a few moments that it looked like a blizzard. Stopping at the limousine, Keely and Chris had to shake the little grains out of their hair for almost a full minute before collapsing into the car. Twenty minutes later, they arrived at the posh Capital City Club. After another half-hour of guests arriving and finding their tables, the band began to play and the announcement was made, "For their first dance as husband and wife, Mr. and Mrs. Chris Walsh."

The dance lessons they had been taking were evident to all who watched as Chris confidently swept his bride into his arms and guided her across the floor. It was one of many things they had done together over the year-long engagement to enrich their relationship. The most important of which had taken place a month earlier when Chris formally rejoined the Church at the Easter Vigil Mass. Months of preparation had gone into Chris' Confirmation and sharing every detail of it with Keely gave him a sense of purpose in a marriage that had always eluded him.

"Do you think we looked that happy on our wedding day?" Erika asked Jack, holding his hand and watching their closest friends dance elegantly across the floor.

"I don't know if we looked like that, but I sure felt like they look. Still do…always will," answered Jack.

She looked at him and thought, *I love this man so.*

"You know, I am so glad they made it to this day. If Chris hadn't rejoined the Church, who knows what would have happened."

Erika saw how happy Jack was for their friends. It was, to her, his most attractive quality. Certainly, he was aesthetically-appealing to any woman with his chiseled features and athletic body but his total other-centeredness was what had really drawn her to him. Anybody could be a pretty-boy. The nice guys were few and far between and Erika was sure she married one of the best.

"You really did some good work there, sweetheart," said Erika.

Jack smiled and said, "I just carried the message. God did this, not me."

Erika smiled and nodded. Jack's remark triggered a memory of something she remembered Father McNamara saying during a homily a few years back: "I don't ever get to be the living water. On my best days, I might get to be the pipe."

The band played the final notes of *Your Song* by Elton John and, to a wave of applause, Chris led Keely off the dance floor, back to their table. An hour later, after nearly all two hundred guests had come by the head table to congratulate them, the newlyweds sat watching their families and friends enjoying themselves. Many guests were beginning to talk with slightly elevated tones, clear evidence that the open bar was serving its purpose. As Chris sat with his new bride, a tall, slender man in a handmade Seville Row suit, handsome features, and slightly graying blonde hair approached the table. Chris smiled and stood to greet the club member who had sponsored the reception. Capitol City Club was very private but at a member's request, it was available for such functions as wedding receptions and company parties at the discretion of the board of directors.

"Congressman, it's fantastic to see you again and we cannot thank you enough for making your lovely club available for this," said Chris.

"Well it's great to see you both too," said Congressman Paul Miller, the second-term legislator who had left a high-paying law career to enter public service seven years earlier.

"I apologize for not being able to attend the ceremony but we just landed forty-five minutes ago. There's been some serious maneuvering going on to try to get the funding for our boys fighting over in Vietnam slashed and I'm darn sure not going to keep our kids fighting without the tools to get the job done," said the Congressman.

"Amen to that, Paul," said Jack.

"So you guys really are becoming the kings of cargo, huh?" asked Congressman Miller.

"I wouldn't say it quite like that, Paul, but we seem to be on the right track. The only thing limiting us now is regulation of air carriers. It's just too costly to pay the same rates for insurance and other factors that the passenger airlines do. Our risk exposure is nowhere near what theirs is. Also, it's almost impossible to get certificates to operate in certain areas that the airlines have lobbied really hard to control. We'd love to take a step up from the small executive jets we've been using to the larger Boeing 707's, but the current hoops to jump through make it pretty unpalatable," said Jack as Chris nodded in agreement.

The politician seemed to ponder that for a moment before asking, "How much of a difference to your company would it mean to be deregulated as a non-passenger carrier solely moving cargo and making getting certificates for operation a heck of a lot easier?"

"It could change our entire ability to turn a profit, Paul. I mean it could make or break us as a company," said Jack in a deadly-serious tone.

"Well, you might know that I sit on the House Committee on Public Works and Transportation and we are just beginning to draft a bill that might be of some interest to you gentlemen."

Jack and Chris simultaneously nodded and listened with intense interest. Being unable to transition to larger jets from the fleet of thirty-five Dassault Falcons had been a major obstacle to Velocity Express' growth. Using larger aircraft required a mountain of certifications and overcoming geographic restrictions imposed by the FAA and Department of Transportation. The unfortunate reality was that the volume of packages being delivered by VelEx were beginning to cost more per package as more small aircraft were needed to service the demand. VelEx was certainly in its ascendancy in its second fiscal year of operation, and was on track to show a profit an entire year earlier than projected in the original business plan. The problem was that they were becoming a little too successful for their ability to provide service. Up to that point, there had been relatively minor problems with delivery, especially since they had purchased courier companies or started their ground delivery operations in cities to bring the actual delivery of packages to the final recipients in-house. In recent months, however, both Chris and Jack began to see that their fleet of jets was being stretched thin. They knew they needed bigger jets for VelEx to survive.

Seeing the smiles, and a potential opportunity to help out some very up-and-coming constituents, Congressman Miller looked over to the ladies and said, "Ladies, I apologize for talking shop on this most blessed day." Turning back to Chris and Jack, he continued, "Why don't you call me next week when I'll be back from D.C., and we'll schedule a time to come to my office and look the entire situation over?"

"You're my first call Monday morning, Congressman," said Chris.

"Great, now let's have a little fun," said the Congressman as he extended his hand toward that of a beautiful redheaded woman that sat alone at the next table while the first bars of *Play That Funky Music, White Boy* began to play. Chris smiled at his bride and asked, "Would you do me the honor of accompanying me to the dance floor?"

Keely just smiled and nodded as she stood. She thought, *Yes, love. For the rest of my life, I'll accompany you anywhere.*

Piedmont Hospital Women's Center
1938 Peachtree Road
Atlanta, Georgia
2:44 A.M. Eastern Time
Wednesday, November 16th, 1975

Chapter Twenty

"Honey, I know we decided on natural childbirth but as a trained......*aaaahhhhh!*"

Dr. Erika Lee would have preferred to have had their little girl at Emory University Hospital where she worked but there was no baby factory at Emory and Piedmont was the closest to where she and Jack had been enjoying dinner when the first strong contraction hit.

"Babe, what are you saying?" asked Jack as the nurses continued to monitor her vital signs and prepare her for childbirth. Erika tried to use the breathing techniques both she and Jack had practiced during their natural childbirth classes but they just weren't having the advertised effect when the rubber met the road

"Honey, I'm saying....*aaaaaaaahhh!* I'm saying that as a trained medical professional, I've reevaluated the risks of having meds for the pain and in my .....*ooooohhh!*"

"You just keep breathing there Dr. Lee. You are doing fine," said one of the nurses.

"Professional opinion I......*oooohhhhhhhh!*"

"Just breathe sweetheart, like in the classes. You can do it." As the pain overtook her, Erika looked up at her husband and spoke in a voice that he had never heard before. "Give me a freaking epidural right now or I'm going to stand up in these stirrups and kill everyone in the room! Starting with *you*!"

When Chris had picked up the phone an hour earlier, and groggily answered, "Hello?" Keely had instinctively known what the call was about. Sitting up and listening to her husband's reaction to what Jack was telling him over the phone, Keely had immediately gotten out of bed and began dressing in a sweatsuit and sneakers. When Chris had said into the phone, "Good luck buddy, call me when you are a daddy," Keely feigned a threat to throw her shoe at him.

"Get your lazy rear out of bed, Christopher. Tell him we'll be there in thirty minutes, and start dressing, mister!" She always used the full, "Christopher," when she was serious. Chris always thought that was cute.

"Guys, I know it's late but thank you so much for coming," said Jack, wearing operating room scrubs. He had stepped from the delivery room for a moment when he saw Keely and Chris outside the delivery room door.

"We wouldn't have missed this for the world," said Keely.

"So get in there and don't come out until you're a daddy," said Chris.

Jack nodded, lifted the facemask over his nose and mouth, and headed back into the delivery room.

"Wow, I've never seen Jack look so nervous," said Chris.

"He's going to be just fine. So what do you think about them standing on this side of the door someday?" asked Keely.

"That would be wonderful, baby," said Chris

"Really, sweetheart? Are you sure you mean that?"

Chris turned to her, studying her expression. There was intensity in her tone that made Chris pause for a second to consider how to answer. "Yes, baby. I mean that completely. The company is running really well now and I think we should definitely talk about that."

Keely wrapped her arms around Chris' neck and kissed him.

Chris was so thrilled for the Lees. He distinctly remembered the day when Jack had walked into the office, bursting at the seams with joy. Erika had worked out a deal with the university to hold the position with the medical school for eighteen months to allow them the time to have their first child. She would continue her work at the hospital as long as possible into the pregnancy and have plenty of time to prepare her course curriculum. Her reputation as a brilliant physician and fantastic communicator made her highly desired by the dean of the medical school—enough so to let her join the faculty on her terms.

An hour later, Jack stood next to Erika, speechless, holding his daughter, Grace Elizabeth Lee, for the first time. Erika cried gigantic tears of sheer happiness.
"She's got my eyes and your nose," said Erika in a tone of exhausted joy. Her voice was weary from the effort that delivering the nine pound girl had required.
As tears of his own began to crest on his eyelids, Jack felt a level of happiness he had never experienced in his life before as he lovingly gazed at the beautiful girl he and his wife had brought into the world. Erika tore her eyes away from their new daughter, looked up at him with a look of pure adoration and said, "Honey, I love you so much."

Jack walked into the waiting room beaming with joy. "It's a girl and she's...." was all he managed to say before Keely threw her arms around his neck and hugged him with a strength Jack didn't know she possessed.
As the three of them walked down the corridor, Jack talked in excited tones with Keely.
"You know, we've done all the classes, read all the books, and I think I'm usually a pretty competent guy but I have to say that now that she's really here, for some reason I feel totally unprepared to be a dad."
Keely stopped in mid stride, Chris almost walking into her, and grabbed Jack by the shoulders, spinning him toward her.
"Jack, look at me."
Chris smirked at that.

Keely said, "There isn't a single person on the face of the earth that I can think of who would make a better parent than you. You have an endless capacity for love which I see every time I've ever seen you with Erika. Relax. You'll be just fine."

She grabbed Jack and gave him another big hug. She could hear his anxiety subside a bit in the form of a long exhalation. He hugged her back.

"Hey, where do I rate in the parental potential category, babe?" asked Chris with a tone of mock injury.

For a second, Keely studied Chris' face and it appeared for a moment she was about to say something but changed her mind. Suddenly she smiled and said, "You are also good father material, my love."

Jack looked at both of them, a feeling of utter gratitude for having such good friends in his life.

The three of them arrived at the end of the wing housing the maternity ward and nursery. Erika had been placed in her own room to recover from the childbirth. Jack said, "Let me go in first and see how she's doing." Jack slipped quietly inside the room but reappeared in a few moments with a slight smirk.

"Mom is a little tired and, as she put it, 'isn't quite ready to receive callers just now', but she was quite sure little Grace Elizabeth would appreciate a visit."

They went to the nurse's station to get specific directions to the nursery. Despite the ridiculously early morning hour, a young nurse wearing maroon hospital scrubs and a big smile greeted them. The name on the tag was quite Italian but the accent was most definitely Scottish. Stefania Massa laid some paperwork down and said, "I'm going to take a stab in the dark and guess the lovely lady we put in four-o-two is your wife," as she looked at Jack.

"How did you know?"

Stefania giggled and answered, "I'm a consummate professional. Besides, you are presenting classic APP symptoms."

"What?"

"Acute paternal panic. A classic case if ever I've seen one."

"Clever nurse," said Chris.

"That's why they pay me the big bucks."

With that, Nurse Stefania looked at Keely and said, "*You* look like you have your wits about you so I'll give the directions to the nursery to you." The two women, originally from the same part of the North Atlantic, laughed a conspiratorial laugh as the nurse gave the directions.

"She is so beautiful," said Keely as Jack just stared at his new daughter. Turning to the both of them, Jack said, "We intended to ask you together but when I was in with Erika a moment ago, she told me to ask you now."

"Ask us what?"

"Would you two be willing to be Grace's godparents? I know you understand what I'm asking you guys."

Without a moment's hesitation, Chris said, "Definitely, absolutely. We'd be honored," while Keely hugged Jack.

"We'd be honored…Just as long as… you'd be willing to be… ours," said Keely in a halting manner that instantly registered with Chris as being odd. She looked over at her husband and then at Jack and back at Chris. Her curious smirk developed into a gigantic smile as she watched the light of realization come into Chris' eyes.

"Oh, my G… " exclaimed Chris, stifling the last word of the phrase even in light of the monumental revelation. More than once, Jack had gently reminded him that use of that phrase was considered to be using the Lord's name in vain and inappropriate. Somehow, in the midst of the moment, Chris had the presence of mind to look at Jack, wearing a sheepish look. Seeing the discomfort on his best friend's face, and knowing its origin, Jack smiled, clasped his shoulder, and said, "Relax, man. I think that's the first time I've ever heard you almost say that, and it would have been borderline appropriate.

"But…"

"What I mean is that I'm glad to see you are giving credit where credit is due."

"Oh, I get it. Thanks, Jack. Thanks for…everything."

Chris turned to Keely and lifted her completely off the floor as he kissed her and held her in his arms.

"Easy now, Hercules. Let's be gentle with the mom-to-be," said Keely as she giggled with joy.

Chris was overwhelmed with the happiness he felt in his heart. Looking into the mint-green eyes of his soul-partner, he pulled her to his embrace and whispered in her ear, "I love you so much, baby"

"I love you more, husband."

"Aeronautics was neither an industry nor a science. It was a miracle."

-Igor Sikorsky

Part Three:

Climb to Altitude

The 1980s

Photo by Johanita Akers

Final Delivery / Will Dempsey

Residence of Chris and Keely Walsh
1475 Moores Mill Road
Atlanta, Georgia
7:55 A.M. Eastern Time
Tuesday, July 4th, 1980

Chapter Twenty-One

"We'll, let him sleep a bit more but get him up in thirty minutes," whispered Chris to Johanita. "We don't want to be late to the airshow out at Dobbins." The young nanny nodded in silent agreement as Chris carefully closed the door to his son's room. The thirty-minute sleep extension allowed Chris just enough time to wrap his present before the birthday boy would be up and about. As he walked down the hall, Chris marveled at how quickly the four years had passed since Thomas Francis Walsh entered their lives.

Chris applied one more piece of tape to put the finishing touch on the gift wrapping job. He began to smile in anticipation of his child's reaction. He knew the gift inside was exactly what the boy had asked for

"Daddy, I want a jet—a Phantom—and the landing gear have to go up like yours," the child had declared a few months earlier.

"He's definitely your son," Keely had joked, smiling at how most three-year-olds would have simply asked for a toy plane. Not Thomas Walsh. He had to have operational landing gear.

A year earlier, on the cusp of Thomas' third birthday, Chris got the first evidence that airplanes were going to be a big part of his son's life. Standing outside a hangar at the Lockheed Aeronautics facility in Marietta, Chris saw the look in Thomas' eyes as a SR-71 Blackbird flew overhead. The roar of the most powerful jet engines in the world almost drowned out the screams of excitement coming from Thomas' mouth. Chris knew there was pilot's blood pumping through the kid's veins.

    Cary Johnson, the aeronautical engineer whose team had been responsible for the design of the jet that had just lifted off, simply smiled at the boy's exhilaration. Chris had met Cary at a local charity golf tournament and, discovering the quiet man worked for Lockheed, a discussion of planes ensued that lasted the entire eighteen holes. As the C-141s Chris and Jack formerly flew were one of a number of avionic products built by Lockheed Aeronautics, there was plenty to talk about. Cary was the director of a team of designers and engineers known as 'Skunkworks' that worked on the most classified aviation projects in the United States. When Chris had asked Cary, the master aircraft designer never mentioned specifically what he did at the company other than to say that he worked on a design team. When Chris asked what they were currently working on, Cary had smiled and said, "Some upgrades to some engines but nothing really interesting right now," and had left it at that. Truth be told, which Cary couldn't without violating numerous laws, he was the head of the team that was responsible for the black jet that had just flown overhead as well as the remarkable high-altitude U-2 spy plane. There were other projects that he had worked on that would never make it into the realm of public domain knowledge but men like Cary simply did their extremely challenging work without needing credit. An aircraft that performed its missions flawlessly was all the reward Cary ever strived for. At the end of the eighteen holes, Chris and Cary had become fast friends.

    "I'd be happy to show you around sometime," offered Cary. He was a kind man, but the offer wasn't completely uncalculated. Knowing that Chris sat at the head of one of the fastest-growing companies in the United States, and that Velocity Express relied on the use of jets, he knew it was very smart to foster a friendship with his playing partner. When an upgrade for the Lockheed L-1011 was being retrofitted onto jets and Cary had called Chris at his office to invite him out to Lockheed for a look at the production line, the idea suddenly occurred to Chris that it would be a great day to bring Thomas along and introduce the boy to airplanes up close. At that time, Chris and Jack were weighing the pros and cons of purchasing the Lockheed jet or a newer version of the Boeing 727.

Cary had told Chris, "As long as the boy isn't afraid of loud noises, I can't see why it would be a problem. I'll inform the security office that y'all will be coming out and arrange your visitor I.D. card."

"Thomas afraid of loud noises? That boy *is* loud noises," said Chris, to Cary's amusement. Thomas was generally well behaved for a child and really only acted out on the rare occasions when he wasn't allowed to play with his extensive collection of toy planes.

That July morning, on Thomas' fourth birthday, Chris knew the plan for the day would absolutely send his little airplane fanatic into orbit. Sitting at his desk with a final piece of tape still sticking to his finger, Chris folded the last side of the wrapping paper around the box containing the model jet. It did, indeed, have retractable landing gear and it had been a major hunt for a manufacturer that made such a product. In reality, the model was quite expensive, but the German firm guaranteed it was the most realistic representation of the plane in the world.

The sound of his son's feet drumming down the long, hardwood floor on the corridor that led toward his office let Chris know the birthday boy was awake.

Into the room bounded a shirtless Thomas, just as Chris slipped the gift under his desk, out of sight. Johanita trailed behind with Thomas' shirt in her hand.

"You be a right proper boy and let me get this on you," she said, her words falling on completely deaf ears. Thomas leapt up into his father's lap with wide, expectant eyes.

"Young man, didn't you just hear what Johanita said to you?"

The little boy turned his head around, finally noticing his nanny standing with his shirt that had a picture of an F-4 Phantom screened onto it. Finding a manufacturer that made iron-on images of airplanes had been another project that Chris had tackled earlier that year and Keely had carefully applied the decals to a collection of children's tee-shirts. Little Thomas had an entire wardrobe of such shirts and was, unless absolutely forced to, unwilling to wear anything else. Johanita made a valiant attempt to fashion a stern look on her face but the slight smirk ruined the effect. There was something about Thomas' enthusiasm and vivaciousness that made it hard for anyone to stay annoyed with the boy, even when he was bouncing off the walls, which was often.

"Sorry, Jo Jo," said Thomas as he began to slip off Chris' lap. Suddenly, noticing the brightly-colored box at his father's feet, Thomas yelled, "Ooooh! Is that for me? Is that a plane?!?"

Just then, Keely came into the room, having been awakened by the racket that had made its way past their bedroom door moments earlier. Wearing a plush, white cotton robe, she held her rosary and a cup of coffee. With his wife there, Chris decided it was time to let Thomas have what the boy was to believe was his birthday gift. The bigger gift was to come later.

"One….two….three….Happy birthday to you, happy birthday to you," sang Chris, Keely, and Johanita. The ladies sounded melodic, Chris more spasmodic but they got the annual job done to Thomas' delight as he lovingly held his new toy jet.

"Alright kiddo, take your new toy and get a move on. We have to meet the Lees in an hour," said Chris. Mimicking the *ssssssscchhhhhhoooooooooo* sound of jet engines, Thomas flew his jet out of the room above his head, running down the hall. Johanita just giggled and followed the boy out of the room. When Johanita was gone and their laughter subsided, Chris put his arms around his wife, and placed his lips gently against the back of her ear.

"I love you so much, baby," he whispered.

"Any more of that and we are going to be late," she whispered back as she prudently kissed him on the lips and headed out of the room to make herself ready

The phone rang.

"Hello."

"Chris, Jack. I just got a call from Dobbins and our bird just arrived. They gave it a spot right next to our seating area exactly as planned."

"Great, great…," said Chris somewhat distractedly as he watched Keely walk down the hallway. She was, and always would be to him, the most beautiful woman God ever placed on the planet.

"So, we'll link up at your place in about forty-five minutes then," said Chris, remembering he was in a phone conversation.

"Roger that. See you guys then."

Keely emerged from the bedroom thirty minutes later wearing a pair designer jeans and a green Izod shirt with her hair done up in a colorful headband. She walked past him to grab her handbag. Chris, appreciating her well-sculpted figure within the designer jeans whispered, "Oh, la la…Sassoon."

Keely rolled her eyes, smiled, kissed him on the forehead and said, "I didn't realize you watched ladies jeans commercials on a regular basis, love," as she checked the contents of her handbag.

"I didn't realize that there were things about me that you didn't realize, love."

She stopped inspecting the pockets of the handbag at that remark, and rewarded him with a smile and a slightly lingering kiss on his cheek as she headed for the garage.

The sound of a throaty engine resonated up the driveway a few seconds before Chris and Keely could see the car. Erika pulled into the Walsh driveway with Jack in the passenger seat of her new white Porsche. Keely walked up to her window and said, "Now this is pretty."

Erika smiled. "Yes, it is."

"Grace isn't coming?"

"Grandpa Erik and Grandpa Marie have her for the day. They insisted in taking her to get new clothes for her first day at kindergarten, answered Jack."

"Understandable," said Keely.

Chris, Keely, and Thomas rode north on Interstate 75 in the family Mercedes toward the suburb of Marietta with Jack and Erika right behind them until a few miles into the drive, Erika decided to demonstrate the power of her new vehicle. Chris just whistled as the Porsche shot past their Mercedes like they were standing still.

"Don't even think about it," said Keely.

Reaching the appropriate gate of the Dobbins Air Force Base the Air Force Security Police officer noted the hanging tag specifically for corporate sponsors dangling from the rearview mirror. Chris was told, "Please proceed to the lot marked for sponsors on the left, sir."

As they drove toward the correct lot, Thomas began to bounce up and down in the back seat as he watched a group of Marine Corps Skyhawk A-4 attack aircraft fly overhead in formation, the sound of their engines momentarily eliminating the ability to hear anything else.

Erika stood by her car with a smirk on her face, twirling her keys on one finger. "What took you guys so long?"

The four began walking to the main area of the air show as Chris repeatedly had to tell Thomas not to run ahead. Once on the main airbase tarmac, the group walked past dozens of military and civilian aircraft. A collection of booths selling all manner of aviation-themed souvenirs had been set erected along a quarter-mile stretch of concrete. Thomas, still flying his toy jet in his hands above him, was in as close to heaven as he would get in this lifetime. The numerous parked aircraft, including the large VelEx Boeing 727 at the very end, near a row of grandstands, were static displays allowing the public close-up experiences with vehicles they usually only saw from thousands of feet below.

"Hey, Son, do you want to see the inside of one of my planes?" asked Chris.

"Please, please, please!"

After walking up the stairs and through the cargo hold of the big jet, father and son descended the steps back down to the tarmac. As they reached the bottom, Chris saw his friend, Cary Johnson, approaching.

"Chris, Keely, how are you two?" asked Cary as he spotted the assembled group walking toward the reserved grandstands.

"Fantastic, Cary. It's great to see you again. I'm sure you

remember my partner Jack and his lovely wife Erika.

"Sure do. Nice to see you guys again," said Cary as he turned to see Thomas running straight toward him, making jet noises with his model F-4 Phantom.

"Boy, do I remember this little man," said Cary, as he swept Thomas up into his arms and over his head, much to Thomas' delight.

"It has retractable landing gear! Wanna see?" yelled Thomas just as the sound of the engines from the Skyhawks drowned out every voice in the vicinity with a low-altitude fly-by.

Seconds later, as the ability to hear anything returned with the jet formation passing, Cary smiled and took the plane into his hands, immediately appreciating the accuracy of the details on the model.

"Are you enjoying this, Thomas?" asked Cary.

Thomas' expression said all that was needed to let anyone know he was in Nirvana.

"You think we should do it now or would it put the poor boy into cardiac arrest?" whispered Cary to Chris.

"I think there's no time like the present," responded Chris.

Just then, the base commander, Lieutenant General Mike Warner, stepped past the two security policemen standing at the entryway to the reserved grandstand. Both SPs executed crisp salutes. Cary knew the general well and had arranged a special experience for Thomas.

"So, this is the future pilot," said the general as he bent down to shake Thomas' hand. Thomas, eyes wide as saucers, simply stood grinning.

Keely smiled and said, "Thomas, tell the general here what your favorite plane is."

With a huge grin, Thomas held his model jet forward for the general's inspection.

"With a deep, pleasant laugh, the general said, "Mine too, Son. In fact, I flew one not too many years ago." Just then, a voice from both men's past came from behind the general.

"Well, they told me you were starting to make something of yourself, Captain, and I see the intelligence was accurate," said Colonel John Hightower. Neither Jack nor Chris had seen their former navigator in nearly ten years and the day was made all the more magical for it.

Noting the eagles on his former crew member's shoulders, Chris exclaimed, "Colonel Hightower, how long have you been in Atlanta? This is fantastic!"

"I just was reassigned to the general's staff as his logistics officer last month. I've been a bit swamped but knew I'd see you both here," said Colonel Hightower.

"Well, isn't this a glorious day. Future pilots, new friends, old friends, and the beautiful sound of turbofan engines roaring overhead," said the general.

As if on cue, Chris, ever the enthusiast for the dramatic, said, "General, I cannot think of a single thing that might make this day any more exciting."

Turning toward Thomas who, even at his early age understood the significance of the man with the three stars on his epaulets talking to him, General Warner said,

"Young man, there's something I'd like you to see."

Taking the boy's hand and winking at Chris and Keely, the general began to lead the boy toward a jeep with two flags attached to the hood. Embroidered on each flag were three silver stars. A local reporter for the Atlanta Constitution newspaper sitting in the grandstands, noting the unusual pair, took a few photographs, wondering what a lieutenant general would be doing with a young civilian boy in tow. A minute later, the reporter got his answer. The jeep was driven a hundred yards out to the flight line, where eight blue and gold jets sat in a row waiting for their pilots, surrounded by ground crew. Switching to a long-range lens, the reporter captured the images of a young boy being given the experience of a lifetime.

"Son, even though these birds belong to the Navy, we won't hold that against them," said General Warner as Thomas gawked at the number one F-4 Phantom II jet of the United States Navy Flight Demonstration Team, more commonly referred to as the Blue Angels. The air show still had another hour-and-a-half, and the Blue Angels were the last and most dramatic part of the show. The Blue Angels show always began with the unit support aircraft, an immaculately-kept C-130 cargo plane with the Blue

Angles' paint scheme, taking off nearly vertically from the runway using RATO rockets attached to each side of the plane's fuselage. The acronym stood for Rocket Assisted Take Off and they definitely assisted the large propeller-driven plane into the air, almost straight up. Following a few fly-bys of the large plane, the Blue Angels would conduct a precision ground ceremony where the pilots and their ground crews would take to their planes, start the engines, exchange salutes, and take to the air. The choreography on the ground was just as precise as that of the aerobatics in the air.

A voice from behind Thomas, as he looked up at the gleaming blue jet, spun the boy's head around.

"I heard a rumor that a special boy was having a birthday today," said Commander Tom Janis. The naval officer was in his navy-blue flight suit, wearing mirrored aviator glasses and immaculately-polished boots. Thomas, at that point completely overwhelmed, just inhaled with wordless awe.

"What would you say to a look inside there, Mr. Walsh?" asked the pilot.

Thomas exclaimed, "Really?!?"

The general and commander both enjoyed a good laugh at the boy's youthful innocence and excitement.

Commander Janis lifted Thomas up and placed him several steps up the foot and handholds on the side of the jet, and followed the boy up the side, insuring that if Thomas lost his balance, he would easily catch him. With impressive form, Thomas climbed into the jet as if he were a seasoned pilot, just as Commander Janis was about to instruct him about how to enter the jet.

Commander Janis stood on the side of the jet, pointing out the various systems and controls to Thomas who just sat, drinking in the commander's words like they were directly from God's mouth. To the birthday boy, the pilot standing to the side of Thomas was nothing short of just that.

As Thomas was totally immersed in the experience on the flight line, the reporter from the newspaper captured plenty of wonderful images of Thomas Walsh's first up-close experience with a fighter jet.

"If you do well in school and keep your grades up, you might get to fly one of these someday," said Commander Janis as he helped Thomas down the ladder.

"I will. I will!"

As General Warner returned Thomas to parents, Chris shook the base commander's hand and said, "General, I'm completely in your debt for doing that. If I can ever do anything for you, don't hesitate for a second to ask," as he handed the base commander his business card.

The reporter, who had a good sense of what had transpired, approached the group, made an introduction, and produced a business card with the newspaper logo atop. After talking with Chris and Keely for a few minutes, and jotting down the details, the reporter asked permission to file a story about Thomas' experience.

"What was the best part of getting to see the jets that close?" asked the reporter to Thomas.

"Thomas, the nice reporter asked you a question."

Thomas tore his eyes away from a jet overhead, smiled, and said, "I'm going to do that. I promise!"

The group burst into laughter as Chris thought, *I have no doubt you will, kiddo. I bet you do whatever you set your mind on.* He looked at his son, appreciating where the boy had been blessed with his mother's angular facial features. It was easy to see the resemblance despite the layer of childhood softness to them. He could see the inquisitive glimmer in his son's blue eyes.

The next day's Atlanta Journal Sunday Edition had a page-two story with a picture of Thomas in the cockpit along with the headline: "Future Pilot Gets Birthday to Remember." That article would sit framed in Chris' office forevermore next to a signed photograph of Commander Janis next to Thomas in the jet.

**Capital City Country Club
Atlanta, Georgia
2:15 P.M. Eastern Time
Friday, April 3rd, 1985**

Chapter Twenty-Two

"The green is over there, Jack Nicklaus" muttered Congressman Paul Miller, after slicing his ball way right, and yet another of his new Titleist golf balls found their way to the watery realm of smallmouth bass and snapping turtles.

"Don't be so hard on yourself, Paul. How much sleep could you have possibly gotten last night?" asked Chris as he lined up his hundred-yard shot to the green with his pitching wedge.

"I got plenty, thank you very much. The red-eye flight isn't the problem. The problem is I spend all my time on the Hill trying to make things easier for guys like you to do business and how do you repay me? By picking my pockets clean on the golf course. That's some arrangement."

Chris found the congressman's frustration mildly satisfying and not entirely untrue.

As Chris judged his shot, he said, "I seem to have a vague memory of the good people at the Re-Elect Miller 82' office receiving a slip of paper imprinted with VelEx's name containing a good number of zeros."

"I have a pretty good recollection of that as well, my friend," replied the Congressman, momentarily distracted from his lackluster performance on the golf course by the thoughts of healthy campaign contributions. One common joke around the

Hill was that any legislator that carried a handicap of ten or better was spending far too much time on the golf course and not nearly enough time representing their constituents. Congressman Paul Miller was in absolutely no danger of that sort of accusation.

Chris wound his body to the top of the swing and then unwound like a spring. As the clubhead swept through the dimpled, white orb sitting atop the neatly-manicured grass, it cleanly clipped the ball off the turf with a solid *thwack*. The short wedge club launched the ball high into the clear, blue spring sky as Chris held the picture-perfect follow-through position that would have looked appropriate on a pictorial in *Golf Magazine*. Reaching its apex, both men watched the ball fall toward the green, heading directly toward the flag.

"Go in!" yelled Paul as the ball landed five yards directly in front of the flagstick, bounced once, and began to roll toward the cup.

Chris voiced the exact same sentiment. "Get in the hole!" he commanded the inanimate object that neither had interest in his plea nor the capacity to care. It was a common delusion of golfers that coaching a 1.68" diameter synthetic-rubber sphere about their wishes had any effect on the sphere's movement whatsoever. Still, it seemed to offer golfers a comfort that they actually could control something that they intellectually knew was a fallacy. That shot, however, seemed to defy this obvious reality. It rolled directly up to the pin, hitting it dead-center, emitting a barely audible *click* before falling into the hole.

Chris, momentarily not believing his eyes, said nothing.

Paul, however, screamed, "No freaking way! That's an eagle!"

As the fact registered with Chris, he turned to Paul and said, "Well, the ball had to go somewhere, didn't it?"

Always a cool customer.

They both jumped into the golf cart and headed down the concrete path toward the green so Chris could retrieve the ball from the cup. Paul had effectively conceded the match and any bets they had on the back nine holes with that *coup de grace*.

Chris pulled the golf cart to the parking area on the path adjacent to the eighteenth tee box and looked at his watch.

"We've got to get through in about five minutes if I'm going to be on time to pick up Thomas from school."

"Fine, we'll play the last hole for five dollars. Speed golf too. Just hit when you are ready."

Chris stepped to the tee box, placed his ball atop the little white tee peg, and assumed his stance, rhythmically waggling the club behind the ball. The adrenaline from the miraculous shot on the last hole still pumped through him. As Chris' club impacted the ball, with a very loud *crack,* Paul thought, *There goes five more dollars.* Chris absolutely pounded the ball. It arced into the sky, appearing to want to fly forever, finally returning to earth several seconds later, continuing to roll nearly fifty more yards. As the ball finally came to rest, it was just shy of three hundred yards from where both men stood.

"Must be the club," said Paul, making reference to the new type of metal club head Chris was using. Paul addressed his own tee shot and made his best swing of the day, sending the ball directly down the center of the fairway. It didn't have nearly the energy that Chris' had but was a fine shot nonetheless, coming to rest forty yards behind his playing partner's.

Five minutes later, both men walked off the green. Chris just missed a birdie putt and Paul took three putts to get his ball into the hole. The congressman reached for his wallet.

"Keep your nickels and dimes there, Congressman. I know what you guys make," said Chris.

"Yeah, well here's your twenty bucks nonetheless, buddy. I know how much therapy costs for you pilots."

Chris smiled, pocketed the money and again looked at his watch, noting he would be just on time if he immediately left the course and headed for the Christ the King School to pick up Thomas. He had scheduled three full days away from all responsibilities related to Velocity Express to spend time with his son. The business was doing extraordinarily well, having produced gross profits of nearly two hundred million for the prior fiscal year. New acquisitions of jets and courier companies combined with implementation of a computerized system for tracking packages had been expensive but the investments were paying dividends ten-fold. The company would survive a few days of his absence and Jack had been encouraging just such a break for a while. Included on the weekend itinerary was a very special surprise for Thomas that the boy would certainly never forget. Chris and Keely had discussed the idea a few times in the past but she had previously felt their son might be a bit young for what Chris had in mind. That was, until one evening when Chris invited the man that was going to help with the surprise over to their house to assuage her concerns.

"Mrs. Walsh, I am certain there will be no undue stress on the boy when we take him up. My plane is totally current on all annual safety inspections and I do all the maintenance on her myself. He'll be as safe as if he were sitting there on the couch with you right now," the gentleman had explained.

Chris' life had reached a place where money and success were secondary. Nice possessions were always enjoyable but Chris truly lived to be a father to his son. The boys would spend the night going to see a movie. Saturday morning would be a complete surprise for Thomas then Mass and dinner with Keely on Saturday evening. Sunday, the boys would pack up Chris' Chevy Suburban and head two hundred miles east toward the little town of Augusta, stopping at the historic town of Madison, Georgia and a quaint public golf course. Thomas was not seriously interested in golf—his athletic enthusiasm focused more on the unconventional choice of traditional Japanese karate—but at the age of eight, he was developing into a highly athletic kid who had natural gifts that allowed him to be at least functional on the golf course when they played together. Sunday night would be spent in a little motel room off of the main street in the little Southern town that Chris had to book nearly a year ago. Augusta, Georgia's population doubled the second week of April every year. All around Georgia, the dogwoods and azaleas were in full bloom. No other golf course could be considered as close to a botanical garden as the venerated fairways of Augusta National Golf Club during the Masters Invitational week which was understandable, as the club had been built on the former site of a plant nursery. Chris had never seen the club or the Masters golf championship in person, but had obtained two Monday practice round tickets from an attorney friend who was a member of the club. Monday, Chris would share his first visit to the sacred grounds of Augusta National with Thomas. It was going to be an unforgettable experience.

"Thanks, Will, I'm taking them with me," said Chris to the young golf cart attendant who regularly cleaned his clubs upon completion of a golf round. Noting a slight odor of alcohol on the twenty-something as he handed him three one-dollar bills, Chris thought, *Boys will be boys.* At that moment, however, it occurred to him that the young man wasn't a boy anymore. That it was approaching noon on a Friday, and the young man had booze coming from all pores, it suddenly occurred to Chris that there might be a bit of a drinking problem with the always cheerful bag boy who greeted all the members by name. It was only eleven a.m. but thinking back to some of his wilder days in the Air Force, the joke had been, "It's five o' clock somewhere."

"I'll bring them out to the car, Mr. Walsh," said Will as he began to work on the Congressman's clubs.

"Thanks, Will. You have a good weekend," said Chris. From a little voice inside of him, Chris suddenly had the urge to say a little prayer for the boy. It had become a more and more common occurrence that the little voice of conscience had begun to frequently express itself in him after his formal return to the Catholic Church.

God, please keep this kid safe this weekend, prayed Chris silently as he watched the young man zip away in the golf cart. Anyone looking at Chris that moment would have never thought he was having a little conversation with God, but that he was simply removing his wallet and watch from a pocket on the golf bag. Chris didn't know why, but in certain times in his life, whenever something was frustrating him, he would silently pray for somebody else and whatever had been disturbing him would quickly fade from his consciousness. It was something he had heard Father McNamara suggest trying in a homily one Sunday morning and the idea had stuck. More often, Chris began to find himself doing so even when something wasn't bothering him, like that morning when everything in his world couldn't have been going better if he had written the entire script.

Pulling out of the parking lot of the golf course, Chris turned south onto Peachtree Road, driving past the big shopping center at Lenox Road, and through the eclectic assortment of Buckhead area bars, including the one Keely used to work at. Lining either side of the road was an endless selection of boutique clothing stores, home design shops, and restaurants. Chris pulled into the carpool line in front of the Christ the King School ten minutes later. Wearing his navy blue slacks and light blue uniform shirt, Thomas stood in front of school with another boy and three girls, waiting for their rides. Although girls were "gross" by Thomas' current assessment at the tender age of eight, Chris still jokingly thought, *Ah, my little heartbreaker.*

"We are going to make a big kite with a picture of Jesus on it for the Feast of the Ascension and Sister Joan Marie asked me to help design the kite!" exclaimed Thomas as he settled into the front seat of the Suburban.

"Well if it's something that flies, Sister Joan has the right man."

**Christ the King School
Atlanta, Georgia
11:22 A.M. Eastern Time
January 28, 1986**

Chapter Twenty-Three

The class chattered as quietly as a group of third graders could while Sister Joan Marie fiddled with the RCA television to center the picture on the screen. Two of Thomas' classmates giggled at her efforts until she turned and shot them a withering glare. The giggling ceased instantly.

"So you're experts at the workings of a television, gentlemen?" Then make yourselves useful and make the picture stand still, please. I thank you both kindly," said Sister Joan. Bryan Vincent and Greg Stipes sheepishly looked at the floor as several other classmates laughed at her reprimand. As the two boys twisted the knobs on the back of the set and the picture began to steady, Sister Joan said, "Thomas, I think this is as good a time as any to give your report."

Thomas smiled and went to the back of Sister Joan Marie's desk and retrieved a large moving box. He walked to the front of the classroom and set the box on the desk next to the television set.

"My science report today is on how the space shuttle works. Its official name is the Space Transportation System. It is the first reusable space vehicle in the history of the United States. It can be used to launch satellites as well as for conducting experiments in space that can't be done in earth's gravity."

From his grocery bag, Thomas carefully extracted his largest and most prized model. It had taken two weeks and over ten hours to build. Complete with launch pad, the scale model of the Space Shuttle Challenger was impressive by any hobbyist's standards.

As Thomas arranged his model on the desk, several classmates made, "*ooooh!*" sounds indicating the impression the two-foot-tall model made. Thomas looked around the room at the surprised faces of his classmates and beamed with pride.

"The shuttle achieves orbit velocity by use of two solid rocket boosters and three main orbiter engines," said Thomas as he pointed to the representations of the solid boosters on the model. "Approximately two minutes into flight, the solid rocket boosters are jettisoned and the shuttle relies on the three main engines to take it the rest of the way into orbit."

For the next few minutes, Thomas continued giving a very complete report on the spacecraft.

"Thank you, Thomas. That was an excellent report on the Space Shuttle. Now, who can tell me why this shuttle launch is very special?"

One girl raised her hand and simultaneously blurted, "Because a teacher is riding on it."

"Yes, Stacy. That's right."

"And she's going to teach her class from space," said Kevis. "My dad read about her to us at breakfast this morning!"

"Alright, children, please remember the rule about being called on before answering," said Sister Joan but everyone could tell she wasn't really mad. The class was full of excitement. They had never watched any special events on television in class before.

"You are right, Kevis. There is a teacher on board. Her name is Christa McAuliffe and she's a teacher at a high school in Concord, New Hampshire."

Another student, largely considered the teacher's pet, raised her hand.

"Yes, Jennifer,"

"I read all about her in the newspaper. She was selected from over 11,000 teachers and is going to give two lessons from space and do a tour of the space shuttle she calls 'The Ultimate Field

Trip'."

A few classmates rolled their eyes.

"Thank you, Jennifer," said Sister Joan Marie as several low-volume murmurs of gossip could be heard. Sister Joan Marie was having none of it.

"Now, class, I want total quiet and I mean right now. I want no talking when I turn up the television and if I find any of you not paying attention or chit-chatting, you'll be in Sister Elizabeth's office faster than that rocket will be flying into space. Understood?"

"*Yes Sister Joan,*" acknowledged the class in unison.

The class silently watched the news channel broadcast the last few moments before launch. Listening to the announcer, Thomas felt a wave of excitement at hearing the technical details from the voice of the NASA Public Affairs Officer. The PAO was the official voice of Mission Control for the media and would comment on what was happening with the shuttle as it lifted off.

"T-minus twenty one seconds and the solid rocket booster engine gimbals now underway. T-minus fifteen seconds. T-minus ten, nine, eight…," announced the PAO as Thomas watched the main engine igniters spray a shower of opposing sparks below the three main engines. He turned to Kevis on his right and, despite Sister Joan's warning, whispered, "This is so cool!"

"Seven, six, we have main engine start," said the PAO as three cones of superheated gasses erupted from the main shuttle engines. "Four, three, two, one, and…we have liftoff. Liftoff of the twenty-fifth space shuttle mission! Challenger has cleared the tower."

The entire class applauded and cheered.

"Good roll program confirmed," said the PAO as the shuttle rotated in the air. "Challenger is now heading downrange." A moment later, "Engines beginning throttling down now, at ninety-five percent."

The class continued to watch the shuttle accelerate away from Earth with rapt attention

Kevis leaned over to Thomas and whispered, "Do you want to

be an astronaut? I do!"

"You bet! I'd do that anytime."

"Thomas! Kevis! Do you both have something to share with the class?" came the voice of Sister Joan from her desk.

"Sorry, Sister Joan. Kevis just asked about the solid rocket boosters," replied Thomas.

They both held their breath awaiting the verdict.

"No more of that, do you hear me?" said Sister Joan as Kevis mouthed '*thank you*' to Thomas.

The PAO broadcast, "Velocity twenty-two hundred fifty-seven feet per second, altitude four-point-three nautical miles, downrange three nautical miles."

The news reporter covering the launch broke in to add his own commentary.

"So the twenty-fifth shuttle mission is now underway after countless delays."

The class watched silently for several second into what looked like a perfect launch. The news program switched intermittently from views of the vehicle ascending into space to the family and friends of the astronauts watching the launch in the VIP guest viewing area at Cape Canaveral.

The image on the television suddenly switched to a profile of the Challenger.

Something immediately looked horribly wrong to Thomas.

For an instant, it appeared as if the flames from the main engines and solid booster were climbing up the large, orange external fuel tank toward the crew compartment. A fraction of a second later Thomas sharply inhaled as the entire vehicle was enveloped in a massive explosion. Unlike the rest of the class, Thomas immediately knew it was a disaster and not part of the normal launch events. He shouted, "Oh, no! It exploded! It blew up!"

Sister Joan, who had been looking over some papers on her desk, looked up and angrily snapped, "Thomas, what in the world would make you say such a horrible thing?"

"Sister Joan, it did. It did! Look!"

For a moment, Sister Joan tried to deny it by asking, "But aren't those the solid rocket boosters coming off the shuttle?

Aren't they supposed to do that?"

"Look, Sister Joan. They are still burning. They don't come off until their fuel is completely burned."

She looked and in her heart was shocked at the reality. The boy was right. If there was anyone in the room who would be right about such things, it was Thomas. His well-known expertise on things that fly was why she had selected him to do his presentation on the space shuttle for his semester science project that morning.

"Is he right? Did it explode?" asked one girl.

"I'm not sure," said Sister Joan, not truthfully but not wanting to upset the children.

A moment later, her fear that Thomas was right was confirmed when the reporter declared, "It looks like the, ah, solid rocket boosters flew away from the side of the shuttle in...an explosion."

There was absolute silence both from the television as well as in the classroom for a few moments until the PAO broadcast, "Flight controllers here are looking very carefully at the situation. Obviously...there's been...a major malfunction."

Sister Joan sprung from her chair and went to the television and reached for the power knob to turn it off. Thomas looked at Sister Joan's face as she watched another few moments of the television broadcast. It was now clear that countless pieces of the shuttle were falling from the explosion, many leaving contrails of smoke in their wake. Just as the camera view began to show a long-range shot of items impacting the ocean surface, Sister Joan turned the television off.

Sudenly, Sister Elizabeth, the school principal, came on the school public address system.

"Attention all teachers and students: there will be a special assembly in the gym for the next class period. All teachers will meet me at the front of the gym as soon as you have your students seated. That is all."

"Do the astronauts have parachutes?" asked a student.

Thomas was surprised to see Sister Joan looking at him with a very sad expression on her face, rather than answering. He wasn't used to grownups being sad like that. Sister Joan looked like she was about to cry and it scared Thomas.

"Thomas, do they?"
"I don't think so, Sister Joan."
"Dear God in heaven," she muttered.

Standing at the front of the gym, all of the Christ the King School teachers surrounded Sister Elizabeth, talking quietly enough that the students couldn't hear. Thomas sat several rows back from the front row amidst the three hundred other Christ the King School students. Everyone knew it was a very unusual assembly because the archbishop of Atlanta and every priest assigned to the cathedral stood with Sister Elizabeth. The teachers began walking back to sit with their classes and as soon as they were seated, Archbishop O'Malley went to the microphone and addressed the entire school.

"Students, I asked Sister Elizabeth to call this assembly together today because, as most of you saw in your classrooms, there was an accident with the space shuttle Challenger this morning. This is a national tragedy and to the best of my knowledge, the news is reporting that all seven astronauts were lost in the explosion, including the teacher, Christa McAuliffe. I know seeing something like this must have been very frightening for many of you. We may never know exactly why this terrible thing happened but I thought it important to bring the entire school together to pray for the souls of the lost astronauts and for their loved ones, most of whom were watching the launch live at Cape Canaveral.

Several students began to cry. There was a pall of sadness over the entire gym. Thomas was embarrassed by the wave of emotion that began to make him tear up. Trying to hide it from his classmates, he buried his face in the sleeve of his light blue uniform shirt.

"Please join me in saying a rosary for the astronauts, their families, and everyone at NASA who must be devastated by this tragedy," said Archbishop O'Malley. He held the cross on his rosary beads in his hand.

We believe in one God, the Father Almighty..., began the entire student body of the Christ the King school. Thomas dried his eyes as best he could and joined the hundreds of other voices.

"It's so very sad," said Keely Walsh as she and Chris Walsh sat with Thomas on the living room couch watching the news about the shuttle accident. At eight p.m., an announcer on the television declared, "We now interrupt our regularly scheduled programming for a special broadcast from the Oval Office."

President Ronald Reagan came on the screen. With a somber expression he began, "Today is a day for mourning and remembering. Nancy and I are pained to the core by the tragedy of the shuttle Challenger..."

As the president eulogized the astronauts and the collective sadness the nation was feeling, Thomas couldn't help wonder what it was like for the astronauts the moment the shuttle exploded. Did they feel pain? Were they afraid? Did they feel anything? He dwelled on the thoughts, barely hearing the president's address. Thomas felt his mother's hand on his and looked up at her. She was crying. It was the first time he had ever seen her cry like that. Thomas began to listen again as the president concluded his address.

"We will never forget them nor the last time we saw them, this morning, as they prepared for their journey and waved goodbye and, 'slipped the surly bonds of earth to touch the face of God'"

The screen faded to black and then the station returned to a news broadcast where aerospace experts and officials were giving commentary on the accident and their theories on what might have caused it.

Just before climbing into bed, Thomas looked over at his dresser where the large space shuttle model still sat in the moving box he had brought it to school in. Clearing the top of the collection of sports trophies sitting atop the dresser, Thomas replaced them with the model. He stood, looking at it for a few moments. Then, kneeling by the side of the bed, he silently prayed, *God, I don't know why things like this happen but could you please make sure the astronauts are up in heaven with You?*

"Amen."

**U.S. Department of Transportation Offices
Washington D.C.
12:30 P.M. Eastern Time
Wednesday, February 4th 1986**

Chapter Twenty-Four

Chris and Jack walked out of the Federal Aviation Administration Orville Wright Federal Building feeling euphoric. With the passing of the legislation sponsored by Congressman Miller, Velocity Express had been given a new lease on life. Prior to the deregulation, the numbers had been stacking up against them and costs to operate might have spelled the end of the company within three years. That was until the deregulatory miracle that had happened, thanks in large part to Congressman Miller's efforts on the Hill.

In 1976, Congressman Miller had sponsored a bill known as Public Law 95-163 that, after the requisite amount of political posturing on the Hill, finally passed the House and the Senate in one hundred and ninety-three days. The new law allowed all cargo carriers to obtain certificates from the FAA to operate to any point in the United States, effectively eliminating the monopoly-like control over numerous airports by the major airlines. The bill had saved VelEx by eliminating restrictions on the use of larger jets like the Boeing 707 without having to fight with airlines about where they could use them. Essentially, the law drew a line between people carriers and cargo carriers.

As the two men walked along the sidewalk toward Seventh and Carolina Avenue, where they had asked their driver to pick them up after the meeting, Chris checked his day runner. The following day, Chris and Jack had meetings scheduled at the Federal Aviation Administration's to register six new Boeing 747s that VelEx had signed the lease paperwork for the prior week. The days of using cost-inefficient smaller executive jets were at a close.

As Chris and Jack walked along Seventh Avenue to meet the car from the hotel that would take them back, they heard a car pulling to a stop behind them.

"Excuse me, Mr. Walsh, Mr. Lee?" called a man from a back seat window in a black town car limousine.

"Yeah?" answered Chris warily. Jack stood, saying nothing, and noting the car had a government plate. It was the most common vehicle on the road around Independence Avenue and the Capitol. There were a sea of identical cars ferrying all manner of government officials around the town where the most valuable currency wasn't cash but access to power and decision-makers.

"Guys, I apologize. I didn't mean to surprise you gentlemen but I'm with the DOT and there were a couple of details they forgot to discuss with you back at the office. We only realized it when the paperwork hit my desk as I was on my way out. If you wouldn't mind, I can zip you guys back to my office and get you back to your hotel in fewer than thirty minutes," said the man who extended a business card that identified him as John Wilson, Air Carrier Division of the Department of Transportation.

Chris and Jack inspected the card and, not wanting any paperwork errors to cost them a single second of operating their more profitable larger jets, climbed into the back seat when John pushed the door open for them. Both men were highly surprised to see Congressman Miller sitting in the opposing seat and grinning as they climbed in.

"Guys, I hope you've been enjoying Washington," said the lawmaker.

"Uh, yeah, Paul. What gives here?" asked Jack who immediately knew something wasn't on the level.

"You pilots are such a cautious lot but, in this case, you're right about this not really being about paperwork."

"Did it ever occur to you to just pull up like a normal person and ask to talk to us?" asked Jack, not liking the feel of the situation. Adding to Jack's sentiment of annoyance, Chris said, "I can't imagine a busy congressman like you would just pop in on two of his constituents to see how their visit to the Capitol is going, like some sort of convention and visitor bureau intern."

Congressman Miller turned to the other man in the back seat and said, "You see. We're not talking to dummies here. I told you they are exactly who we are looking for."

Who we're looking for? thought Chris, who sensed that the man with the military-cut gray hair and deeply lined face sitting opposite him was definitely not in the employment of the DOT. The man across from Chris had piercing green eyes.

"Sorry about the little act we used to get you gentlemen in the car but in my experience, it tends to make people a little uneasy if I were to say, "Hi, I'm your personal CIA intelligence officer for your trip to the nation's capitol and if you don't mind too terribly, could we have a little chat?"

"Yeah, I have to say that would be a bit off-putting," said Jack.

"And a bit indiscreet, I'm sure you'll agree," said the congressman. "So let's get down to brass tacks, guys. Kind of an 'I scratched your back' sort of thing here."

"Well, there's nothing to get a conversation off to a good start by lying about who you are. That aside, please feel free to tell us what the Christians in Action might want with us this morning," said Chris, using his favorite and slightly sarcastic euphemism for CIA.

The CIA man said, "Fair enough. I can see you guys are at a disadvantage and don't appreciate it so let's have some proper introductions. I'm Gus Avernus and I'm the deputy director of operations at Langley. I'm not currently a field guy but have done my bit of traveling at Uncle Sam's expense over the years. I know you both are former military aviators so I'm sure I don't need to define the word 'classified', which this conversation is."

This should be good, thought Chris. In his experience with the intelligence types while in the Air Force, they often seemed to be an overly-confident and under-informed bunch. The intelligence squirrels, as he and many others in the military often called them, always seemed to have an almost perverse need to withhold information. Chris didn't expect to get anything in the form of a complete explanation from the professional spy sitting across from him. If it weren't for the presence of Congressman Miller, Chris and Jack would have put an end to the conversation immediately.

"So let's say that there are some boxes from General Dynamics that have to go from San Francisco to Lahore, Pakistan and we don't want to have to use military flights. How would you gentlemen like to take your business to a new level by an expansion into international markets?" asked the Congressman.

"Didn't you guys purchase General Chennault's little airline and turn it into Air America for in the last war? Why don't you use them now?" asked Jack who was becoming increasingly uncomfortable with the entire conversation. The driver, obscured from view by a black partition, took a right turn, heading east on Constitution Avenue, the dome of the U.S. Capitol building looming up ahead.

"Guys, it's a new world and you may or may not be aware of the plight of the *Mujahedeen* freedom fighters in Afghanistan. I'm sure you know the Russians rolled in there with several divisions of troops and the *Muj* are doing their best to keep their country. Well, at least they are trying to slaughter the Russians as best they can. The problem is that without a suitable way for them to combat the Mi-24 Hind gunship helicopters, the freedom fighters come up short in every engagement. What we need to do is to give them an edge."

"And you need us to send them that edge via priority overnight delivery, I'm assuming," said Chris.

"Precisely. The problem is that it is a bit politically delicate for us, meaning the United States, to overtly arm the local boys in Afghanistan. We love giving them toys to fight a big, bloody war of attrition against the Soviets, but to date, we've been packing in all manner of weapons *not* made in the good old, United States of America," said Gus

Continuing the explanation, Paul said, "Yeah, and if you can believe it, we've got an Israeli arms dealer selling Soviet arms to Muslim guerrilla fighters. What a world, right? See, it's kind of a little unwritten understanding we have with the Russkies. They understand that we can back anyone we want that is willing to fight against communism, but the way we do so without escalating these conflicts to an actual shooting war between us and Moscow is by not slapping them directly in the face with it. Proxy wars have become the way of the future," said the congressman.

Let's face it—the entire country is basically functioning in the fourth century. We don't expect it to become some shining beacon of democracy in Southern Asia but the more Russian assets tied up in Afghanistan, there are less of them to deal with on the NATO front."

"Tell them the best news," said Congressman Miller in a tone that was almost gleeful.

"This bloody massacre is not only taking Russian soldiers' lives by the truckload, but also costing the U.S.S.R. an astronomical fortune. Possibly enough to put the Union of Soviet Socialist Republics into a real financial crisis," said the CIA officer.

"In a wonderful bit of irony, the Russian's own AK-47's have been particularly popular with the freedom fighters. That's been good until now but that brings us to you. The decision has been made to give the *Mujahedeen* a man-portable anti-aircraft capability. We call it the FIM-92A but its common name is the Stinger missile. The weapons we have been sending in increasing numbers are usually packed in on the backs of mules. I'm talking real mules. We actually gave them an entire farm load of em' from a Tennessee farm. The problem is that, even though we have been working with the Pakistani Intelligence Service, we don't trust them any further than we can throw them. This is where things require a bit of delicate handling. We need to bring the missiles into Pakistan but we need to do so with a completely clandestine profile when we start giving the Afghani people U.S. ordinance. It's our people, not the Pakistanis, who will have positive control over the weapons systems once they are in-country. Getting them there is half the fun and that's where you might come in."

Chris and Jack sat silently as they rode along Independence

Avenue. Watching the people on the street, Chris and Jack silently mulled over what was being asked of them. Chris wondered how many conversations involving the U.S. putting its fingers into international pies took place inside the hordes of black town cars prowling the avenues in the Capitol. Many, was his suspicion.

Jack broke the silence by looking at the politician and the spy across from him and said, "I'm all for doing my part for God and country but flying jets halfway across the world comes with some hefty costs. Like my uncle used to say, 'Freedom isn't free.' How many flights are we talking about here? Also, guys, there's a little question as to whether this is even legal."

The car was quietly cruising along the eastern side of the Capitol building and Chris took note that they were coincidentally passing the Supreme Court building as Jack voiced that concern.

"Guys, there is a mandate from extremely high up to get this done. I'm not at liberty to elaborate right now but you agree to help us, you won't ever sit in a courtroom for being of service. What I'm offering is a very fair compensation package for your services. Also, your business is one of the most heavily regulated industries in the country. You never know what good influential friends can do for you."

"Jack and I obviously have to give this a bit of thought, if you don't mind," said Chris.

Gus smiled and gave his final pitch. The car took another left onto Constitution Avenue. Gus flipped the tumblers on a locked attaché case on the floor of the limousine. From the case, Gus handed Chris a purchase order for two Boeing 727s that the agency had purchased specifically for the operation. "It's understandable that you want to think about it but if you decide to help us with this, you'll be able to use these jets for VelEx regular business when not working for us and we'll pick up the tab for their operating costs and flight crews as well. That will indirectly add a few million dollars to your bottom line each year," said Gus with an entirely emotionless tone.

The car took the turn off onto Pennsylvania Avenue, heading to the northeast.

Chris looked at Jack and then back at Gus and said, "Ok, I get the fact that if we help, this is highly classified. I want it in writing that if we assist you guys with this operation, the people in these buildings will never come knocking on our doors with warrants." As he said it, Chris jabbed his thumbs toward the J. Edgar Hoover building on the right of the car and then at the Department of Justice building directly on the left.

"Your meeting tomorrow at the FAA was scheduled for ten a.m. We've rescheduled it for one p.m.," said Congressman Miller. Jack and Chris looked at each other. Jack was about to ask how he knew their schedule but then looked over at the CIA man and squelched it.

"What would you do that for?" asked Chris with a timbre of barely-contained irritation to his voice. The entire idea of him allowing VelEx to help with a CIA smuggling operation wasn't unthinkable, given the terms, but he was getting the feeling he was being railroaded into agreeing

"Because the man who lives in that house only has a small opening in his schedule to see you both at nine a.m. sharp," answered the intelligence officer. The most recognizable building in the country loomed behind the wrought-iron fencing at 1600 Pennsylvania Avenue.

Chris and Jack shot each other a look of shock.

"We'll pick you up outside the Watergate at eight a.m. sharp if that's alright with you. Please be on time," said Congressman Miller.

"We always are," said Chris.

"That's one reason we picked you," said Gus.

Both men continued to look over the aircraft documents the CIA officer handed them. Moments later, the limousine pulled under the portico at the Watergate Hotel.

Congressman Miller shook both men's hands before they could get out of the limousine.

"Enjoy your evening, gentlemen. I don't know if you have specific plans for dinner this evening, but I'm getting together with a few people at The Monocle at eight. You would both be welcomed guests if you care to join us."

Chris and Jack looked at each other. Jack shrugged and Chris said, "Sure, Paul. See you then."

As the driver opened the back door, he never looked directly at Jack and Chris but rather at the people on the sidewalk and the cars passing on the street. His suit did not fully conceal the compact machine gun slung under his left arm or the radio earpiece that snaked up from his collar into his ear.

Chris nodded in thanks. The driver didn't nod back.

"I don't know about this, Chris," said Jack.

"Yeah well, they did make a convincing argument. This is not some trivial favor they are asking. It would be a big chip in our pockets if we ever needed some serious help from the government."

"But if it is so legitimate, then why all the cloak-and-dagger stuff using us to help them smuggle things for them."

"I'm pretty sure it falls under the category of what our host tomorrow morning calls 'plausible deniability.' Why don't we see what the...I can't believe I'm saying this...the president, has to say about all of this and then we'll make the call. Did you ever think when we were flying over the South China Sea on final approach to Da Nang twenty years ago, that we would ever be summoned to the round room at the White House?"

Jack looked at his friend for a moment, then at the street at the passing cars, with a contemplative look on his face. Turning back to Chris he said, "I have to admit that if they can guarantee no possible legal ramifications in writing, this could be a miraculous opportunity, but I never though I'd be in the ordinance shipping business again."

"If it's legal, then I have to think it's good business if you can get it."

The doorman opened the door for both businessmen as they entered the luxury hotel's lobby.

Chris thought about the ramifications of getting involved in that sort of business and felt a mixture of excitement and trepidation.

God, what should I do here? prayed Jack.

Atlanta Shotokan Karate
1705 Stuart Road
Atlanta, Georgia
11:15 A.M. Eastern Time
Saturday, October 12th, 1989

Chapter Twenty-Five

Keely and Erika sat, spellbound, watching thirteen-year-old Thomas take his rank examination to pass for first degree black belt. Over the past four years, Keely had watched as many of Grace's soccer games as Erika had Thomas' karate lessons. When, two years earlier, Grace had come to watch one of Thomas' karate lessons after one of her soccer games, she had also been fascinated by what she saw. Soon, both Thomas and Grace spent three nights a week, for two hours, learning to move in highly efficient ways across the hardwood floors of the thirty by eighty foot dojo. Grace, with lanky but powerful legs for a young girl, stood with the other students across the back wall of the school. Around her hips, holding her white, cotton training uniform together, called a *gi,* was a green belt, signifying her as a student with mid-level experience. She had passed five rank examinations of her own to that point but Thomas, with a two-year head start on her, was four ranks and soon to be five above her.

Thomas stood motionless on a small tape mark in the middle of the floor at the formal stance of attention called *yoi.* Around his waist was a brown belt. Although there was no outward movement of his body, internally, Thomas was coiling the core muscles of his body in preparation of an explosive move from what appeared to be a totally motionless state.

At the front of the dojo floor, sitting at a table, were two Asian men of differing age. The younger, in his early forties, was the main instructor for the school and held the rank of *yon-dan,* or fourth degree black belt. Yoshi Kanazawa had come to the continental United States from Hawaii in the early nineteen seventies and studied for years in Los Angeles with the elder man seated at the table. Hidetaka Nakayama was sixty-one years old and was considered the highest ranking instructor of traditional *Shotokan* Japanese karate in the United States, holding the rank of *hachi-dan,* or eighth degree black belt. Once a year, Sensei Nakayama would visit the various schools throughout the United States that were members of the American Traditional Karate Federation.

When directed by Nakayama to begin his *kata* with the bark of the command, *"Hajime!"* Thomas began the exam with an explosive first movement of *Bassai Dai,* which he had been assigned. The name of his form translated in English to mean "to storm a fortress." Most brown belt students were assigned that *kata* in Shotokan, and Thomas had trained hundreds of hours to learn the intricacies of it under Kanazawa for the past year. The effectiveness of the training was clearly evident by the excellent precision, sharpness, and powerful movement Thomas exhibited.

In traditional Japanese Shotokan karate, the emphasis was not on winning pretty medals, titles, or trophies. Although tournaments were conducted, each competition was thought of much like a testing laboratory where a student could see how well the application of his technique and timing stood up under the added pressure of simulated combat. As a student progressed through the ranks, a different *kata* would be learned and trained. Each *kata* grew in complexity of movement and intricacy of the skills they taught by their practice. They were like an encyclopedia of all of the possible techniques a *karate-ka,* or practitioner of karate, could utilize. The forms were practiced thousands of times throughout a student's life to refine their understanding and mastery of the specific techniques the form taught. Thomas finished the last move of his *kata,* then returned to his starting position and with his feet together, he bowed toward the table where the two instructors sat, appraising Thomas' skill.

"It never fails to amaze me how much this looks like ballet," said Erika as Thomas completed the *kata,* he had been practicing for the past year at his rank. Erika's observation that the outward appearance of karate was similar to ballet was quite accurate but the objective of the two arts was on opposite ends of the spectrum. Ballet explored the potential of the movement of the human body to express a multitude of emotion and thoughts. Karate sought to teach the practitioner the most efficient ways of using the entire mass of the human body to focus shocking impact force into a very small area, thereby delivering a lethal blow, called *ippon* in Japanese, literally meaning "finishing blow." The three main sections of rank examination were the *kata,* then *kihon,* or basic technique demonstration, and finally *kumite,* or actual application of techniques against an opponent. Thomas' opponent for the rank examination was Sensei Kanazawa's senior student, Sensei Brad Webb. Webb stood along the back wall waiting for his participation in the examination to be signaled by Kanazawa. Brad, who held the rank of *san-dan,* or third degree black belt, trained with the chief instructor the longest of all of his students. Brad was more than happy to serve as an opponent.

"That was awesome," whispered Grace to another mid-level student named Theresa.

"Yeah, I bet he passes."

"Hai, kihon!" barked Nakayama, meaning for Thomas to move to the left side of the floor to go through the basic technique demonstration portion of the exam. Thomas immediately moved to the indicated place to the left of the instructors at the table. There, he again stood at the *yoi* position which was a variation on a military position of attention. His hands closed into fists in front of the knot in the brown belt he wore. Thomas' back was straight and his posture suggested an immediate readiness for movement, although absolutely motionless.

"Hai, hidari zenkutzu-dachi, gedan barai, hajime!" commanded Nakayama Sensei. The phrase translated into

English as, "left front stance, downward block, execute now!" It was the basic starting position for almost all traditional karate techniques. Over the next three minutes, Thomas moved up and down the floor, forward and backwards, demonstrating the basic syllabus of punching, blocking, striking, and kicking techniques.

Upon completion of the last combination, Nakayama Sensei said, *"Hai,* in-place kicking," and motioned with his hand back to the spot where Thomas had started and finished his *kata* earlier.

In place, Thomas executed a front snap, side snap, side thrust, roundhouse, and back kick, all with his right leg and without his kicking leg ever touching the ground. This was done twice with both his right and left legs and was an impressive demonstration of balance, coordination, and focus.

"That's my boy," said Keely to Erika with a proud grin. Erika smiled and Keely continued, "In a few years, Grace will be doing the same thing." Grace had taken her own rank examination that day and, although not nearly as lengthy or complex, she had been the strongest and most developed of the colored-belt students during her exam. From the table, Sensei Nakayama picked up a pencil and motioned for Thomas to approach the table. Assuming left front stance, with his right arm and fist tightly against his side, he waited for Nakayama to extend his arm, pencil held upright, and stop. Immediately, Thomas launched a reverse punch, his fist coming to a sharp stop less than an eighth of an inch from the pencil's eraser. Over the next ten seconds, Nakayama moved the pencil to various places to test Thomas' ability to focus and reacquire a target. The last punches weren't quite as sharp as the first, but still acceptable for a first-degree black belt.

As the final portion of the exam began, Nakayama Sensei motioned to Brad, the third degree black belt. Immediately the senior student came onto the floor and stopped on one of two pieces of tape that had been applied to the floor ten feet apart, standing in the ready, or '*yoi*' position. Thomas went directly to the opposite mark on the floor. Brad, twenty-eight years old, had been teaching the class the first night Thomas came to train, six years earlier and the two had trained together for thousands of hours over the years. They had as friendly a relationship as would normally be between a teenager and a twenty-something but regardless of any past conviviality between the two, Brad had no intention of not testing Thomas to the fullest. Both students bowed to the table where both instructors sat, then to each other, and immediately dropped into *kamae-te* or fighting stance.

"Attack," said Nakayama as he pointed to Brad and then, "Defend," to Thomas then a sharp, "*Hajime!*" Brad launched forward with a stepping punch to Thomas' head. Keely cringed at the act, as any mother would do while watching such a powerful attack on her son. Stepping back, Thomas executed a perfectly-timed and effective rising block or *age-uke* then, like a spring unwinding, released a reverse punch directly into Brad's solar plexus. During the normal day-to-day training in traditional Japanese karate, emphasis on control of technique was paramount. The idea instilled in each student's mind was to execute techniques that, if the spatial distance was an inch closer, the technique was a finishing blow that would deliver hundreds or thousands of pounds per square inch. The discipline to control a technique through body dynamics was one of the cornerstones of the art, differentiating it from other combat arts like boxing. During the rank examination, it was expected that there would be a bit more impact than normal and when Thomas' punch landed with an audible *pop* sound, Brad's eyes narrowed for a split second at the impact. To any observer, Brad's facial expression foretold an even more aggressive attack but in reality, underneath the intensity of his focus, Brad thought, *Nice. Good job, kid.* The two traded attacks, defenses, and counterattacks over the next two minutes, each time both Erika and Keely expected to see a terrible injury from what appeared to be lightning-fast, uncontrolled violence. The truth was that both athletes demonstrated an extreme degree of control over the powerful techniques as they completed the final portion of the black belt test.

When both Brad and Thomas stood at attention, bowed to the table where Senseis Kanazawa Nakayama sat, and backed off the floor while still facing the instructors, Keely and Erika just looked at each other in utter amazement. Each woman was in awe of the intensity of the test Thomas had just endured.

"I'm exhausted," said Thomas who, with heavy breaths and sweat dripping from his face, sat down next to Grace in the back of the dojo. She smiled at Thomas and gave him a pat on the back and whispered something into his ear that neither mother could hear. Erika looked at Keely and with a slight smirk, winked. Both mothers were of the mind that there was slightly more chemistry between the two youngsters than either of them was willing to demonstrate in public.

After formally ending the rank examination, Thomas clambered into the back seat of the large navy-blue Chevy Suburban next to Grace, who sat reading a crime novel. Keely looked back at her son who was growing into a strong young man right before her eyes.

"You were wonderful today, Grace. I'm so impressed," said Erika from her front passenger seat.

"Thanks, Mom," replied the girl who, although trying to keep a respectful tone, had a slight edge of annoyance. Grace was an intense reader who hated intrusions. Even a compliment fell into the intrusion category when she was engrossed with a book, which was often. Thomas sat in his seat, reviewing in his mind the rank examination, looking for where he could have done better and wondering if he had passed. As he laid his head back, the warmth of the car and the rhythm of the engine sound lulled him to sleep. As Thomas dozed off, his arms uncrossed from where they had been on his lap and one hand fell on the seat next to Grace. She, seeing it there, briefly reached out and touched his hand with her fingertips before looking up at her mother who was fixing her makeup in the rear view mirror. She hadn't seen. The sensation of Grace's fingertips on his brought Thomas out of his nap. As he opened his eyes slightly, he saw Grace looking down at his hand. When her gaze came back to his face and their eyes met, she blushed instantly when she saw him smiling back.

Keely pulled into the driveway at the Lee residence to drop off Erika and Grace.

"Thank you so much for driving today. I appreciated the chance to get some work paperwork done. Thomas, you were so great today. I was so impressed! Weren't you, Grace?" said Erika as she stuffed the papers she had been writing on into her large attaché bag.

"Yeah, he wasn't all that bad. Adequate would be the word I'd choose to describe your exam," quipped Grace with a playfully mocking tone as she winked at Thomas.

"You were...awesome... yourself," said Thomas. He experienced an odd feeling as he said it, lacking the normal confidence he had with the girl he had thought of as a sister—right up until that car ride.

He knew something had fundamentally changed in the nature of their friendship that day.

Thomas had never seen her before the way he did now. It was as if he had awakened to something that he couldn't explain but the awakening wasn't unpleasant in any way. It was just different. He gave Grace a small wave and she smiled back as she stepped down from the SUV.

Grace stood watching the truck pull onto Northside Drive.

Erika searched her bag for her keys and, not finding immediately finding them, called over her shoulder, "Grace, do you have your key?" When Grace didn't reply, Erika turned to ask again, only to find her daughter was not behind her. Instead, her fourteen-year-old was standing motionless at the end of the drive. Seeing the look of longing and blank smile on her daughter's lips as she watched the SUV drive off, she knew. The realization hit the normally cool physician with the subtlety of a freight train: Her little girl had her first crush on a boy.

"Grace, honey, would you like to come in and have a cup of tea with me?"

Grace turned to look at her mother and smiled a slightly embarrassed smile and said, "That would be really awesome, Mom."

"When my brother and I built the first man-carrying flying machine, we thought we were introducing into the world an invention which would make further wars practically impossible."

-Orville Wright, 1917

Part Four:

Air Superiority

The 1990s

Photo by Will Dempsey

Final Delivery / Will Dempsey

Residence of Jack, Erika, and Grace Lee
2231 West Wieuca Road
Atlanta, Georgia
7:34 P.M. Eastern time
January 16th, 1991

Chapter Twenty-Six

Snow flurries fell with a mix of light rain in the early evening darkness outside the window. That morning, on his way into the newly constructed VelEx Package Sorting Facility on the perimeter of Hartsfield Atlanta Airport, the local radio weather guy had said the temperature wouldn't reach thirty-five degrees that day. It hadn't. As Jack and Erika sat together on the couch in the front room, a pair of headlights shone through the window. Jack patted Erika on the knee, stood, and went to the door. Before he could ring the doorbell, Jack opened the door and welcomed Thomas Walsh in from the biting cold wind that blew outside.

"Come on in, Thomas. Grace will be down in a second."

"Thanks Mr. Lee," said Thomas as he brushed wet snow from his hair and placed his book bag on the tiled floor.

"Did you hear on the radio?"

"Hear what?"

"The war has started."

"No way! Are you serious?"

Jack gestured toward the living room where Erika sat with the remote control, flipping from channel to channel. On almost every one, there was a reporter trying to paint a picture of what was happening in Baghdad with very limited solid information available.

"There is supposed to be a press conference from the Pentagon in an hour but what the news is saying now is that planes have been dropping bombs and the Iraqis are shooting up the skies over Baghdad," said Erika.

"Apparently there are a few reporters in Baghdad holed up in their hotel rooms, trying to feed information about what they are seeing out their windows," said Jack.

Thomas watched the screen and his heart raced when he saw what looked like a million points of light coming from the ground in an eerie, green, night-vision shot from a camera.

"Anti-aircraft fire has been literally filling the skies, but we haven't seen anything explode in midair," said a reporter with white hair and a beard. Cutting back to a view from the window, the camera view showed an explosion on the ground that was clearly several miles off but no less spectacular for the distance.

"Well, it was only a matter of time. The deadline was up to pull out of Kuwait yesterday."

"Yeah, but if they are using the F-117s, then there isn't too much to worry about for our pilots," said Thomas with a tone of invincibility common to teenagers not yet truly experienced with the ways of the world.

Jack looked at him and said, "Iraq has some of the most sophisticated anti-aircraft defenses in the world. Just look at that anti-aircraft fire. I bet you can't find more than a handful of places in the world with that many triple-a guns and missile defenses. It's a dangerous environment."

"Yes, sir," said Thomas, quickly losing his smug grin. "Uh, have you ever seen it in person? I mean anti-aircraft fire?"

Erika had heard the question as he considered his response. In the nearly twenty years Erika and Jack had been married, there had been very little conversation about the dangerous moments during his flying experiences in the Air Force.

"Yes, on a few occasions I was shot at from the ground. Nothing like the pilots are having to contend with tonight, though."

Grace came downstairs wearing a pair of jeans and a new style of tee shirt that actually changed color with varying body temperatures.

"Did you know we are at war? Your dad just told me," said Thomas

In a tone that was unusually harsh for the normally cheery, upbeat young lady, Grace said, "Good! Have you seen the pictures of what his army has done to the Kuwaiti people not to mention the chemical weapons he used on the Kurds a few years ago? What else does he have to do before someone stops him?"

Grace's parents and Thomas looked at each other in utter amazement. Not one of them could ever recall hearing her say something nearly as condemning as that before. She noticed the looks on their faces and followed the statement with, "Have you seen the pictures of the atrocities that man and his army of thugs, murderers, and rapists have done to the Kuwaiti people? The man ordered the murder of the Kurds in Northern Iraq with chemical weapons. What else does he have to do before someone stops him?"

Just then, the reporter on the news channel said, "We now go live to the Pentagon where a press conference is just starting."

An Air Force general with four stars on his epaulets stepped to the podium with the oval image of the Pentagon on the front and began the press conference in the military briefing style he had countless times before. It was the first time he had given such information on national television.

"As you'll see in this video, the laser-guided bomb flies directly through the airshaft, taking out a communications center," said the general. The reporters in the briefing room watched silently. The aspect of the building changed slightly as the plane that had dropped the weapon flew over the target. In the center of the screen, a dot held its place directly over the image of the airshaft. Three seconds later, a small, dark momentary shadow merged at high velocity with the spot on the screen where the airshaft was. A fraction of a second later, all four sides of the building erupted outward in sprays of fire, concrete, and glass. From inside the briefing room, microphones picked up the murmur of the reporters openly surprised by what they had just seen.

"In this next video, you'll see a precision guided weapon penetrating an underground bunker," continued the general.

"How in the world did they come up with bombs that will do that?" asked Grace.

Thomas, who had a subscription to *Jane's Defense Weekly* and was quite informed about all things to do with military aviation, took the opportunity to let everyone in the room know it.

"It's not exactly new technology, Grace. They actually developed these back in the Viet Nam War. They take this little optical device called a seeker head and screw it on to the front of a regular bomb. Then they put some controllable fins on the tail so when they drop it from a plane, they can guide it to the target with a laser."

"Well, if the plane has a laser, why doesn't it use that instead of a bomb?" asked Erika.

"Mrs. Lee, they don't have any lasers being used as an offensive weapon right now but I hear they are working on it. The laser I'm talking about is mounted on a pod underneath the plane that focuses an invisible beam on a target. The pilot locks the computer controlling the laser on it. Once the pilot locks the target in, the pod will continue to paint that target with the laser as he flies overhead. The bad guys can't see the laser focused on them but the guidance unit of the bomb can see it. The weapon basically tracks the laser beam from the time it's released until it impacts the target. The little fins on the bomb alter its trajectory based on where the guidance unit on the nose 'sees' the laser."

"Thanks, professor," said Jack as he mussed Thomas' hair playfully.

"One of my tennis team partners is a reporter on CNN. I'll be sure to tell her that if they ever need another talking-head expert on military stuff, you're eminently qualified. I'm not so sure that's a good thing," said Erika.

"Oh, Mom," said Grace as she sat down on the couch, looking through her homework. Erika, sitting next to her, looked at her beautiful daughter and then at Thomas and thought, *When did the world change into a place where fifteen-year-olds can explain advance weapons systems?*

If Erika had inspected her daughter's homework carefully, she would have seen that it was already completed. Thomas had also done all but an hour of his before coming over. The homework was just an excuse. Both parents knew there was some attraction between the two. Erika was much more in-tune than Jack to notice the little things like the way Thomas and Grace looked at each other or how much time they spent talking on the phone, but over the last six months, Jack would have had to be utterly blind to miss the blooming romance.

"Well, you want to get cracking on the math homework?" asked Thomas.

"Yeah, I don't want to watch any more of this right now."

The two teenagers went off to Grace's room. Not wanting to embarrass them, Jack fought the urge to say, "Leave the door open," but when he looked down the hall, he could see his young lady had done just that.

Jack and Erika continued to watch the television for the next hour, flipping through the channels. The last time the United States had been involved in such a major military conflict, Jack and Erika had been a part of it. The war in Viet Nam had gradually escalated and there hadn't been a definitive point where one could have said, "We are now at war." This new war, being fought in the hot, desert night, thirteen thousand miles away, was all the more shocking with its extensive video coverage. Erika could not remember having such a clear understanding of what was going on twenty-five years earlier, watching nightly news reports on the black-and-white television in her dorm room while in medical school at Northwestern. It wasn't until her time in the military that she had been given more insight into the human cost of war than she ever would have wanted.

That night, in their cozy 1930's-era home in Atlanta, an endless procession of images of war traveled across the screen: military officers giving cut-and-dry facts about the air campaign and plenty of talking heads on the cable news stations explaining everything from how Saddam Hussein came to power to how stealth technology worked.

As Erika began to tire of the news, a flurry of little *tick* sounds began to come from the windows. Jack stood and went to the window, observing that there was a sheet of ice covering everything. The streets were totally iced over.

"Hey, Thomas, could you come on down here a second?" he called down the hallway to Grace's room. Thomas poked his head around the door jamb.

"Yes, sir?"

"I think you might want to call your parents. As Jack said it, Erika changed the channel to a local weather reporter describing the drop in temperature that was freezing the roads over and creating highly hazardous driving conditions.

"And if it's not a medical emergency, I strongly suggest staying inside tonight. Stay tuned tomorrow morning for school closings of which I'm sure there will be plenty," said the man with the mustache on the television.

Thomas went to the window and then turned to Jack.

"It's only a bit of ice, Mr. Lee. How bad can it be?"

"You've had your license for all of about two months there, sport. I know you've never driven in this sort of weather and tonight's not the night you are going to start."

"Yeah but…"

"Hey, Thomas, I know you saw *Top Gun*. Don't push a bad position there, *Maverick.*"

Thomas grinned, nodded, and said, "Yes, sir."

"I'll call your parents right now and you can sleep on the couch. We'll see what the weather does tomorrow."

Erika went to a closet and gathered a blanket and pillows. After placing them on the couch, she said, "Honey, I'm headed to bed. I have a big meeting tomorrow morning at the hospital."

"I'll be there in just a minute."

Grace walked into the room and said, "It's really nasty out there."

"Yeah, well, I'm crashing on your couch tonight."

Grace looked at her dad and then at the window where the ice continued to pelt the glass, its surface completely coated with an opaque shroud.

"Alright, but just remember I've got first dibbs on the bathroom tomorrow morning. That's just the way it works in this house. Goodnight, Daddy. Goodnight Thomas." She turned and headed into her room, closing the door.

"So, Thomas, make yourself at home and if you need anything from the kitchen, help yourself.

"Thanks, Mr. Lee. Goodnight, sir."

Jack headed off to bed and Thomas turned the television back on to the news coverage of the war. Watching the continuous stream of videos showing bombs obliterating buildings and vehicles was totally captivating. He even tried to determine the meanings of the small numbers and codes in the periphery of the videos.

"Downward looking infrared radar," mumbled Thomas.

An hour later, he turned the television off as his eyelids became heavy and the deep yawns became more frequent. Laying his head down, Thomas was asleep in seconds. His dream began to take on a familiar theme, Grace and him holding each other and kissing. The dream always had the feeling that someone was watching and they had to be quiet.

Years later, he wouldn't be able to remember if it was hearing some small sound, the brush of her hair against his face, or the soft feel of her breath against his cheek that woke him. As he opened his eyes to find Grace, close enough to see the tiny flecks of green in her blue eyes despite the low light, she smiled the angelic smile he adored.

"What...?"

"Shhhhh."

She pressed her lips against his and the kiss was better than the one in the dream.

Grace pulled away and put her hand on his face, exploring his features with the tips of her fingers. She smiled, sighed, and went back to her room.

Thomas sat in the dark for a long time, reliving the kiss before drifting back into a deep sleep.

**VelEx Corporate Campus
Hartsfield Atlanta Airport
Atlanta, Georgia
5:57 P.M. Eastern Time
Wednesday, December 23rd, 1992**

Chapter Twenty-Seven

The Velocity Express corporate campus consisted of three separate buildings in a row, set back from the parkway with a thousand-car parking lot in the front. From the centerline of each section of the lot was a covered walkway, making more pleasant walks to and from vehicles during inclement weather. The campus buildings were rectangular, eight-stories high, and covered with blue mirrored glass. In the upper left corner of each building, the corporate logo was prominently displayed. In the opposing corner, were the roman numerals I through III. At night, the outlines of the buildings were contrasted against the darkness by yellow neon lighting tubes. Everything from the maintenance of the landscaping to the ornate fountain in the center drive was given the attention to detail afforded to five-diamond resorts.

As Chris was collecting some things into his attaché case to head home, the phone rang on his desk. Seeing it was Bryan McNeil, his vice president of information management systems, he answered. He had been hoping for a call from Bryan's office with good news.

"Hey, Bryan. What can you tell me?"

"Well, Mr. Walsh, I have some great news. One of our systems analysts discovered a major flaw in the software code for the COMPAS Project. The series of tests we've just completed indicates my analyst's correction of the software has it operating perfectly!"

Chris exclaimed, "Yes!" as if he had just watched the Washington Redskins make a touchdown. The COMPAS project had required an investment of millions of dollars but he and Jack had been sold on the concept of a real-time computer system that could manage the flow of vehicles, packages, pilots, drivers, and all aspects of moving things across the planet. Still in its testing phase, COMPAS, which was an acronym for Customers, Operations, and Management of Packages Accuracy System, was two months overdue, and costing more money as days went by.

"How in the world did they find the problem? I thought you said we went over every possible glitch?"

"You are not going to believe this, but one of my staff actually spent the past three weeks going over every single line of code for the entire program. Mind you, there are over a million lines of code."

"Who did you give that plum assignment to?"

"Well, actually I didn't. She just decided to do it. She called me at home last night saying she found the problem. I came in, looked at what she found, and approved the correction. We've spent the past six hours running test scenarios and I'm confident enough to say that we are prepared to launch the system."

"Well, that is fantastic!" exclaimed Chris, glancing at the clock, mentally calculating how long giving an important pat on the back to the programmer would take, balanced against his and Keely's dinner plans for that evening.

"So, how long will it take you and this programmer to be in my office?"

"Uh, well, sir, I guess we could be there in ten minutes?"

"Great. I want to meet this analyst who just put us back in the game!"

"Yes, sir."

Chris hung up the phone and called Jack's office.

"What's up?" answered Jack on the first ring.

"McNeil just called me and said they have finally fixed the problem with COMPAS. He said he's confident that we are ready to launch it!"

"Thank God for that. It was beginning to feel like we were just dumping cash into a black hole and all we were getting in return was a room full of Einsteins sitting at desks and tapping keys."

"I asked McNeil to come up and bring the programmer that found the code problem. Should be here in ten."

"Want me to come over?"

"Yeah, I think that would be nice."

Jack walked into Chris' office and the two began to talk about their holiday plans. Chris' secretary rang the intercom and announced Bryan McNeil and one of his staff were there to see him.

"Send them in."

"Yes, sir."

The door opened and in walked Bryan and a young Asian woman who looked overwhelmed to be summoned to the office of the CEO. In one arm, she held a ream of green and white lined computer paper. Over the other, she held what looked like a brown, paper lunch bag. Chris looked at her I.D. badge and noted her name was Sarah Balcos.

"Hello, Ms. Balcos. Bryan here says you are the savior of our computer system!"

Sarah looked to Bryan and he smiled and nodded to encourage her to take credit due.

"Well, Mr. Walsh, it really wasn't that big of a deal. It was my job to fix the problem and I fixed it."

"No more data transfer errors uploading information from the bar code scanners?" asked Jack.

Sarah flipped the computer paper open to a particular page with three lines of computer code circled in red ink, and answered, If you look right here, you will see that the values in the…"

Chris laughed and said, "Sarah, if you say it is good, we believe you."

Sarah smiled.

"Mr. Walsh, Mr. Lee, I just want to tell you how hard Sarah has worked on solving the problem. As Bryan continued to gush about Sarah, she blushed. Continuing, Bryan said, "Every morning I've found her going over the code when I arrived and still doing so when I left. Honestly, I thought the prospects of discovering an error in over a million lines of code remote at best, but clearly I was wrong."

Sarah looked from Chris to Jack and then reached into her lunch bag, pulling out a small, worn teddy bear with a missing eye button. She held it up and said, "Mr. Walsh or Mr. Lee, I doubt you'll remember me but Father Jalandoni told me who you were when I was old enough."

Chris and Jack shot each other a wide-eyed look, both men utterly speechless.

Bryan's eyebrows shot upward at the scene he was watching unfold in front of him. There was something very significant about the bear but he hadn't a clue what she could possibly mean. As a man who prided himself on always knowing what was going on, he was very unsettled.

"Uh, Mr. Walsh, I'm kind of at a loss here. Is there something I should know about?"

"I can't believe it's...really you!" exclaimed Chris.

"I can," said Jack. Turning to Bryan, Jack continued, "Actually, Bryan, I could tell you but I doubt you'll believe it. Ms. Balcos, how long have you worked for us?" asked Jack.

"I've been on Mr. McNeil's team a little over two years, since I finished my masters in computer science at Georgia Tech."

"And in all that time, you never mentioned to your boss about what happened?"

"I never told anyone. I felt it would be horribly bad office politics. I just kept my little bear in my bottom drawer as a reminder of why I wanted to work for you. Father Jalandoni helped me with the cost of coming to the United States when I was thirteen and arranged for foster parents through the Archdiocese here in Atlanta. He told me that without your help, he wouldn't have been able to send me here. So, you see, when I knew there was a problem that was hurting your business, I became committed to finding the solution no matter what it took."

Glancing back at the credenza behind his desk, Chris looked at the most prized piece of correspondence he would receive the entire year. With several colorful stamps and a Philippine postmark, the Christmas card from Father Jalandoni at the orphanage had a note of thanks and the scribbled signatures of every child in residence. From the time VelEx began generating serious profits, Chris made it a priority to quietly send a large check each year that would pay almost all expenses for every child in the orphanage. He considered the gift he received in his heart from doing so to be better than anything he could physically possess. Nobody except Jack, Keely, and his personal CPA knew about his philanthropic effort. He felt a warm glow in his heart every time he saw the Christmas card from the other side of the world. Miraculously, his altruism of nearly a quarter-century before had apparently caught up with him, the very teddy bear that was the inspiration to start Velocity Express had returned.

"Ms. Balcos, I'm, well…I don't know what to say."

"Mr. Walsh, you don't need to say anything. I'm grateful for my chance to work here."

Bryan and Sarah left Chris' office a few minutes later.

Jack and Chris agreed on a sizeable Christmas bonus for Ms. Balcos before Jack headed for the door. As he reached for the doorknob, he turned back to Chris and said, "You know, all business aside, that woman just gave us a gift that we don't have enough money to repay her for.

"Yes, she did."

As Jack began to close the door to Chris' office, he asked, "Do you think this is just one more huge coincidence in our lives?"

"I'm…done…with the concept of *coincidences.*"

Jack smiled from ear-to-ear.

"It's not hard to see God's hand in things when you're looking," said Jack with a smile as he closed the door to Chris' office.

As soon as Chris was alone, he picked up the phone and called Keely. As he began to speak, the enormity and significance of what just happened touched Chris' heart and through a wave of emotion, he began to say, "Baby…you'll never guess in a million years …what just happened here."

**Cessna Flying Center
Peachtree DeKalb Airport
Chamblee, Georgia
9:07 A.M. Eastern Time
Friday, May 6th, 1993**

Chapter Twenty-Eight

Thomas walked around the gleaming white plane with red and blue stripes lining its fuselage, running his hand over its surfaces. Feeling every rivet and seam along the fuselage and checking the operability of the flaps and rudders by manually moving them up and down, he had performed the same pre-flight inspection of the Cessna 172 numerous times before, but there was a special feeling this morning. His two-and-a-half-hour flight was going to take him and his passenger from Atlanta to Craig Airfield on the south side of Jacksonville, Florida. The flight would provide the final two hours needed in his logbook to complete five solo cross-country hours and finish all the qualifications he needed to get his FAA Private Pilot's Certificate. Thomas was thrilled to be knocking out the final requirement that morning. The only thing he enjoyed more in life than being at the controls of an airplane was spending time with Grace. On that morning, Thomas was going to do both, simultaneously, for the first time. Grace stood off to the side of the plane and smiled as she admired his thorough pre-flight check of the aircraft.

"Do you look at every square inch of the plane before takeoff every time you fly?" asked Grace who, wearing a pair of shorts and tee shirt perfect for the beach, watched him inspect the plane.

Her comment was in a joking tone but truth be told, she was highly impressed with his maturity and attention to detail.

"Yeah, basically I do. But maybe a bit more today."

"I trust you."

He stopped for a moment and looked at her. She still gave him butterflies in his stomach when she smiled at him. Grace's long, blonde hair was tied up in a ponytail and her smile was radiant. Her eyes were magic—he always got lost in her eyes. Feeling much the man for his young age, Thomas smiled and said, "I know you do." Thomas and Grace had officially been a couple for nearly two years since he awkwardly asked her to accompany him to the spring dance at the Christ the King School over sodas at the Atlanta Diner. The fact that they had spent as much of their free time together as possible for years still didn't eliminate the nervousness Thomas felt the first time he asked Grace to be his date. Their first public dance together, with the nuns and chaperones looking on, had elicited a few joking remarks from a few of Thomas' guy friends along the wall. The remarks had been instantly halted with a grin and the retort, "Well boys, joke all you want but I'm dancing with this angel and you're dancing with cinder blocks. Keep up the good work, boys." Truthfully, every one of the group of eight boys watching would have given their left arm to be dancing with Grace.

The relationship between the two teenagers had been a lifetime in the brewing. Thomas had grown into a slender, yet muscular young man with his mother's classic dark Irish features and his father's facial structure. Though Thomas had been given attention by several of the girls in his class, to him there was nobody who held a candle to Grace. She possessed a combination of beauty, intelligence, and a genuine kindness in her heart that gave her the dominant place in his.

In three hours' time, they were to meet Grace's parents at the regional airport on the south side of Jacksonville, Florida. The Lee and Walsh families were all enjoying one more weekend together at a beautiful beachfront resort before Thomas and Grace left for their respective colleges. Jack, Erika, and Keely had left the prior evening and had already checked in to the Ponte Vedra Inn and Club that had been a favorite getaway spot for both families for years. Chris had to finish up some business that weekend and was going to fly the company jet down to join them on Sunday.

Thomas and Grace knew their time together was drawing to a close though they didn't talk too much about their impending separation. As all high school sweethearts that face collegiate separation do, they had promised to stay true to each other. Thomas had accepted an appointment to the U.S. Air Force Academy and was leaving for Colorado Springs in a few short weeks. His Basic Cadet Training would take place during the summer prior to any academic coursework and would be almost identical to the basic training all active-duty airmen went through but Thomas wasn't worried. He knew he had what it took to get through the ordeal.

Grace had her choice of ten different schools, three being ivy-league grade, and had chosen Georgetown University in Washington. She intended to enter the pre-law curriculum and, after graduating, head to law school. She had, however, no intention of practicing law. She intended to enforce it. Grace knew she wanted to join the Federal Bureau of Investigation. There were very few pieces of literature, fiction or non-fiction, in existence about the FBI that Grace hadn't read. Grace had visited as often as possible with VelEx Director of Security, Greg Ruskin, at his office and listened to the stories of his thirty years with the FBI.

Thomas had graduated a year early because of the credits he earned through advanced placement courses and through numerous credit-by-examination tests so, although Grace was a year older than Thomas, their college careers were beginning at the same time. With her perfect grade point average, Grace had graduated valedictorian of their class. Never receiving a grade less than an A, her grade point average was only a few hundredths of a point higher than Thomas'. Were it not for Thomas' extensive extracurricular karate and flying activities, they might have had a dead even tie. His pair of B+ grades during the prior four years had relegated him to second-best in the grade point average race but he wasn't overly concerned. Thomas was absolutely certain that, with his grades, pilot experience, and determination, he would be sitting in the cockpit of the most advanced fighter/attack aircraft in the world upon graduation from the Academy: the F-16 Fighting Falcon.

"November Four-One-Two Charlie, you are cleared for takeoff runway two-seven left. Contact departure control on 126.5"
"Roger, tower."
With Grace at his side, Thomas' exhilaration at advancing the engine throttles and the plane beginning its taxi was amplified beyond the joy flying normally gave him.

When Chris had driven Thomas and Grace to the airport for their flight an hour earlier, it had been a surreal experience for Chris. He hadn't been back to the original VelEx building since the company had relocated. Looking around the hangar, he could still visualize twelve Dassault Falcons with the Velocity Express logo paint schemes on the tarmac. Also absent were the pilots, ground crews, package sorters, and other administrative staff running around that had known Thomas since he was an infant. When the new offices, colossal package sorting facility, and VelEx terminal had been completed down at Hartsfield Atlanta Airport four years earlier, all those people had gone with the planes to their new home. It was comforting coincidence that the next tenant in the former VelEx offices and hangar was the Cessna Flight Center training school. Cessna had leased the very building in which Thomas had spent so many hours around airplanes as a child, to be their location for their flight training school. Chris' familiarity with Thomas' flight instructor gave an added sense of comfort to Chris who, although ultimately confident in Thomas' piloting ability, still had a bit of parental nerves allowing his boy to go through the rite of passage for every pilot. He had joked with Jack the night before that it was like giving your child the keys to your car for the first time but the car's top speed is almost two hundred miles per hour.

"He'll be just fine, Chris. The boy has the gift," said Jacob Sanderson, the flight instructor that had been coaching Thomas through all the necessary stages of getting his FAA Private Pilot's Certificate.

"I know he will, Jacob. I had to wake him up last week after I found him asleep at the table with his head on the FAA rules manual."

"That kid wouldn't know the meaning of 'average' if you tried to explain it to him. You know he absolutely aced the knowledge and practical tests."

As the instructor spoke, both men stood watching the plane with Thomas at the controls and Grace in the front passenger seat accelerate down runway two-seven-left and after ten seconds, Chris' son and his best friend's daughter lifted off into the clear Georgia sky all by themselves.

"You know, Jacob, if I had half the enthusiasm for life that kid has when I was his age, who knows what I could have accomplished by now."

Perplexed by such a comment from a man that had achieved more in life than most could accomplish in ten, Jacob looked at Chris and said, "Ah, Mr. Walsh, I don't exactly know what you mean by that but from where I'm standing, it doesn't look like you did too badly."

"Yeah, but that kid is really going places. I mean there's nothing he can't do."

"Name one thing you'd like to do that you haven't."

Chris looked at the older man and smiled.

"I know you'll think it's stupid, but I'd like to do something to help people. I mean something big that might bring the world closer together."

"Correct me if I'm wrong, Mr. Walsh, but from what I've read in the papers, VelEx is one of the most generous companies in the world when it comes to charity. Didn't you guys fly all that food and supplies to the earthquake victims in Mexico?"

Chris watched as a large corporate jet touched down. In a slightly weary tone, he answered, "Yeah, but we've also tried to help other places and it didn't work out so well."

Jacob didn't know exactly what Chris was talking about but the tone of the comment didn't invite further discussion. He just smiled and extended his hand.

"Well, Mr. Walsh. I guess after this, Thomas is a fully-fledged pilot. The next flight training he'll be getting will be on Uncle

Sam's dime so I guess I'll just say it's been an honor to teach your boy."

Chris turned back from watching the jet taxi and shook Jacob's hand.

"I really appreciate it, Jacob. I've got to run but if you ever need anything, and I mean anything, you give me a call. That's the home number." Chris wrote the number on his business card and said his goodbyes. A minute later, Jacob watched Chris pull out from the parking lot in his black Chevy Tahoe, onto Airport Road.

Grace looked out the cockpit window watching Atlanta and the surrounding communities to the south roll by.

"Look over there. Those are the VelEx offices," Thomas said as he banked to lower the starboard wing and pointed out Grace's window. She looked down for a moment, nodded, and then back at Thomas. Watching him confidently do the pilot things he was doing made her feel totally safe.

Thomas finished his tasks and, after leveling the plane out at ten thousand feet, he turned to her with the boyish, mischievous look she found so endearing.

"This is your captain speaking. We expect clear air between here and Jacksonville and expect our flight time to be just over two hours. That should put you at the terminal right at about eleven twenty a.m. We know you have a choice when you fly and would like to thank you for flying Walsh Airlines."

"So when you are in the Air Force, do you think they'll let you borrow one of their jets so you can come see me at Christmas time?"

"I'll steal one if I have to."

Grace reached into her large Dooney and Bourke handbag and retrieved a small gift wrapped box.

"I was going to wait until tonight to give you this but I just couldn't wait."

Thomas took the gift and deftly removed the wrapping from it with one hand while keeping the other on the yoke. Carefully removing the lid of the small box, his heart leaped when he saw what was inside.

"That's a real pair of United States Air Force wings. I want to pin them on you when you become a fighter pilot in a few years. Look on the back... carefully along the bottom."

Thomas turned the wings over and, holding it close to his eyes, read aloud the words that had been engraved in tiny micro-script along the bottom edge, "...And touch the face of God. Love, forever, Grace"

Thomas glanced down at the wings again and was in awe of how thoughtful Grace was to have taken the time to have the inscription etched on something that would be so meaningful to him.

"Our secret," she said.

"This is the best gift I've ever gotten."

"Well, I'm glad you could read it. Kind of a test. I just wanted to make sure you've got pilot's eyes there, handsome. Otherwise I would have made you fly this thing back to the airport and found some other cute boy to fly me to Florida."

He laughed and then he reached back behind his seat to where his backpack sat on a rear passenger seat.

"I was going to wait to give this to you on the beach this afternoon but it just feels right to do it now."

From his backpack, he removed a small, blue-green box. Her heard skipped a beat when she saw it was just the right size for a ring. A few weeks earlier, they had looked at the diamond rings at the Tiffany's at Phipps Plaza. The saleswoman was gracious enough to take time to show the rings, fully well knowing that the kids on the other side of the counter were just playing grown-up in a teenager, fantasy sort of way. The saleswoman was quite happy to indulge the two young people and was very surprised the next day when Thomas came back into the store by himself.

He couldn't possibly be asking me to marry him! thought Grace. After removing the white bow and opening the box, she gazed at the beautifully-engraved gold locket on a chain that sat inside. She took the locket gently from the box and opened it, finding a picture of them together that had been taken a few months earlier at the spring formal dance.

On the back were engraved the words: "With God's Love and mine, Thomas."

Grace immediately clasped the locket around her neck. With a tone that caused his heart rate to race, she asked, "So, handsome, does this thing have an autopilot?"

He looked at her with an uncertain expression and said, "Well, yes, I guess. Why?"

"So we won't crash if I kiss you."

She leaned over and kissed him. For a few moments, Thomas uncharacteristically threw caution to the wind, kissing Grace while flying the plane. The joy of their closeness pushed the thought of their impending separation completely from his head. Something deep inside him knew, however, that physical distance between them couldn't mean the end of their relationship. He took comfort in that conviction.

"Well, that's a first. I've never kissed a boy at ten thousand feet before," said Grace as she, with flushed face, sat back in her seat.

"Funny coincidence, me neither," answered Thomas as he fought to slow his breathing again.

Chris sat in his home office, talking with Congressman Paul Miller, who had arrived just as Chris pulled into the drive.

"So the kids are off to Florida," said Paul as they each drank a beer on the back patio of the residence.

"Yeah. I'll be joining the family later. So what can I do for you, Paul?"

"Well, it's been a while since the Afghanistan thing you guys helped out with."

Chris unconsciously frowned slightly as he said, "Yeah, and all I've got to say about that is that you guys never got back all of the Stinger missiles after the war. Do you guys even know where they are because that *Taliban* government that popped up after the Russians pulled out hasn't been known as a shining example of democracy and tolerance. Also, from what I've been reading, the guys we were helping in that little war are the largest producers of the poisons that are killing kids on our streets here?"

"Yes, well that does, unfortunately, fall into the category of something called blowback. There are some high prices in war sometimes," said Congressman Miller with a tone of sincere regret.

"Well, I don't think VelEx wants to help arm any fourth-world armies anymore if that's what you are here for. I'm sorry and I appreciate what you've done with Thomas' appointment to the Air Force Academy and everything else, but seriously, Paul, we armed the largest, most ruthless collection of thugs and drug lords in the world with one of our most sophisticated anti-aircraft weapons."

"I'm not here to ask you to help with covert arms shipments. I promise. We just have some projects where we need to insert people into certain places. You guys can fly into almost anywhere in the world without raising an alarm."

"Oh. I see."

"I'm not asking because I get perverse pleasure from playing cloak-and-dagger games, Chris. I'm asking because there are some things going on in the world right now that we think could be really big."

The two men sat on the porch, talking for the next hour.

As he stood to leave, Congressman Miller asked, "So are you and Keely going to be at the dinner next month?"

"Yeah, we just received our invitation. I had the pleasure of meeting the president at a fundraiser dinner two years ago at the Marriott. The only other time I've ever been to the White House is with you, remember?"

"Of course I do. Different man in the office today but he's one of the real white hats. Pilot too, if you remember."

"Yeah, the first time we met, we talked about his flying days in the Navy. Did you know the island he was rescued from when his plane went down was inhabited by cannibals?"

"Actually, I did. Just so you know, he mentioned meeting you at that fundraiser last week when I met with him in the office. He said he likes you a lot."

Chris looked at his friend who he knew from experience wasn't a man to just craft fabrications for effect. Even so, with a tone of skepticism he asked, "You mean to tell me that you actually had a discussion with the president of the United States and my name came up?"

"VelEx, well, I mean you personally did contribute a hundred thousand dollars to his campaign didn't you?"

"Yeah, but so did about a thousand other CEOs."

"But how many of them have gone the extra mile for God and country like you?"

"He knows about that?"

Congressman Miller laughed at what seemed gross naivety from a man he knew to be brilliant and very world-savvy.

"The guy is a former director of the Central Intelligence Agency and there isn't a person alive with a higher security clearance. Yeah, Chris, he knows. Don't worry pal, it's just a social dinner with all you captain-of-industry types. Don't be surprised however, if you get a note inviting you to accompany a nice Secret Service agent to the West Wing while you are there."

Chris knew if the Congressman was hinting at a private chat in the Oval Office, it was as certain to happen as the nose on the end of his face. His question was why. Chris wasn't particularly thrilled with the outcome of the last conversation in that office. Seeing the perplexed and concerned look that had developed on the face of one of his most wealthy and influential constituents, Paul smiled and used his soothing, trust-winning politician voice and said, "Just go and have a good time. Nobody puts on a party like the folks at sixteen hundred Pennsylvania Avenue."

United States Air Force Academy
Catholic Cadet Chapel
Colorado Springs, Colorado
9:15 A.M. Mountain Time
Saturday June 19th, 1993

Chapter Twenty-Nine

As the Walsh family walked to the Air Force Academy Cadet Chapel earlier that morning, the warm rays of sunlight had seemed to add a glow to the building, creating a beautiful spectacle back dropped by the dramatic Rampart Range towering over the campus to the east.

Looking around at the other young men, Chris knew Thomas belonged. Like Thomas, the other kids who had attended the special Mass for the new Catholic selectees to the Academy were bright-eyed with the mixture of excitement and nerves common to all new university students at any school in the world. Not one of the incoming cadets had any delusion that the next four years at that ultra-competitive institution weren't going to be the biggest challenge of their lives to that point.

As Chris and Keely walked several yards behind Thomas from the chapel to the Terazzo, viewing the dozens of iron statues of planes and significant Air Force leaders and aviators, Thomas realized he had significantly outpaced his parents and turned around with a sheepish grin. Chris felt Keely grip his bicep and, looking into her eyes, knew she was on the verge of tears. He smiled and pulled her close, hugging her and letting her dry her eyes on his shoulder. He smiled at her and over her shoulder he watched Thomas for a moment. He could see the look of confidence in his boy's eyes. Thomas had been sizing up the other selectees and knew he belonged in the group of the best and brightest students selected to the elite university that would create the future leaders of the greatest air force in the world.

Chris thought back to the homily given during the Mass.

"The bad news is that each of you incoming cadets know that the challenges you will face over the next four years will push you beyond anything you've ever experienced. The good news is that nobody comes here by accident," Colonel Joe Peek, the Catholic chaplain, had said during the services.

Chris watched Thomas walk up to a young Asian man and tap him on the shoulder. When the other boy turned, it was first with a look of question, and then suddenly both their faces erupted with laughter, smiles, and an exchanged high-five. They clearly knew each other from somewhere but Chris couldn't figure out how. He had never seen the other boy during Thomas' high school years and was pretty sure he knew most of Thomas' friends.

"Have you ever seen that boy before? Thomas seems to know him," he asked Keely.

"I have to say he looks quite familiar but I cannot figure out from where," she replied.

Just then, Thomas pointed back toward his parents as an older man, who looked like a grown-up version of the boy Thomas was talking to, joined two new Academy cadets. Suddenly, Keely made the connection.

"Karate! That's it. They know each other from his karate tournaments. That boy's father is the instructor for the group of karate students in Dallas; a doctor of some sort if I remember correctly.

Thomas, the other boy, and his father began walking up to Chris and Keely.

"Hey, Mom, Dad, this is Mike Chang and his father, Dr. Alex Chang. Do you remember them from Dallas?"

Chris stuck out his hand and shook Dr. Chang's hand while Keely greeted his son.

"You're the karate instructor for that area. We met you during the national championships last year, right Dr. Chang?"

"Please, call me Alex. And yes, I am. This young man of yours was quite the phenomenon from that competition. I'm certain Sensei Kanazawa must be quite proud of him."

Keely smiled at the compliment and responded, "If I remember correctly, your son Mike here almost won the entire men's *kata* event."

Due to business responsibilities, Chris was rarely able to attend Thomas' out-of-town karate events. He was at a bit of a loss for conversation about Thomas' karate interests but had watched enough classes and belt tests in Atlanta to know his son was quite skilled at the art. "It is quite a neat coincidence that both of you ended up here. That's really fantastic. Now you both will know somebody right off the bat," said Chris.

Thomas and Mike smiled, both clearly happy to know there was at least one other person they each knew who was about to begin the same grueling challenge.

"Hey, I called the athletics office a few weeks ago and found out they don't have any karate club here," said Thomas.

"Yeah, they have a judo club but no karate."

"You think if the academics don't kill us, we might start one?"

"I like the way you think. I already asked my father if he'd approve and he said if it didn't interfere with my studies."

"We'll see how things go. I'm not going to let anything get between me and one of those," said Thomas pointing to a familiar winged object in the corner of the parade grounds.

The two boys continued walking a few paces in front of their respective parents across the campus, physically punctuating the fact that they were entering a new, adult phase of their lives.

Dozens of families were milling about the Terazzo and down the "Bring Me Men" ramp that led down to the parade ground from the Terazzo level. At each corner of the area, four real airframes of fighter jets were placed for décor as well as tangible reminder of the tools of the Air Force trade. Thomas felt a jolt of excitement while staring at an F-16 Falcon in the southwest corner. It was part of the atmosphere of the Academy that constantly reinforced the idea to each cadet that the sole purpose of their time in Colorado Springs was to give them the skills to allow the United States to own the skies in any military conflict.

Turning back to his father, Mike asked, "Can we go check out the Thunderbirds Overlook, Dad?" as he looked at his Breitling watch. It was another two hours before they had to be in place on the parade grounds to begin the official in-processing for new cadets.

"Sure," answered Dr. Chang. Turning to Chris and Keely, he asked, "Would you care to come with us. I want to see the airfield before I have to set this kid loose on this place."

"Absolutely," answered Chris.

The overlook was a scenic vantage point across the campus where people could watch the small gliders and propeller aircraft take off and land at the Academy airfield. It was at that airfield that many cadets received their first hands-on experiences with aircraft. Thomas had a jump start, already possessing his private pilot's license, but that qualification wasn't uncommon. Seventy-three other new cadets in the fall of 1993 possessed the same FAA rating.

As the group stood at the Thunderbird Overlook, a yellow glider silently and gracefully returned to earth as another was being towed into the sky behind a Cessna 172. Next to the group, mounted on a twenty-foot pylon, was a T-38 Talon painted in the red, white, blue, and black scheme of the Thunderbirds aerial demonstration team.

"Ever been in one of those?" asked Mike

"The Cessna, a bunch, the glider, no. Not yet. What about you?"

"Neither. I wanted to take flying lessons before coming here but never had time with debate, math club, and volunteering at the hospital. Oh, and of course, karate."

"Wow, I thought I had a full schedule before getting here."

After touring the rest of the campus at a leisurely pace, the three parents stood in the middle of the parade ground saying their goodbyes before Thomas and Mike would board a bus to head to another area of the Academy for official in-processing.

"You'll be just fine. I know this place has a reputation for being a tough deal, but I know if there is anybody who has what it takes, it's you," said Chris.

Like every young man and woman being separated from their families for the first time, Thomas tried to keep his composure. However, his emotions ran over when Keely gathered him into a hug, not letting go for a full thirty seconds. He quickly wiped any evidence of tears on his sleeve before turning back to his father.

Looking at Thomas, Chris could still see the little boy bounding into his office every birthday, searching for the inevitable new toy airplane.

A voice boomed over a loudspeaker.

"Attention incoming cadets. Those with last names ending in A through E form up right here!" commanded a senior cadet, referred to, in Air Force Academy vernacular, as a first classman.

Keely and Chris stood motionlessly as Thomas nodded once, turned, and made his way toward where the new cadets were forming up.

He didn't look back.

Thomas marched up the ramp with his group to one of the waiting busses. He had just taken his seat on the second row when the bus was rocked slightly by a three hundred pound first classmen bounding up the steps.

The senior classman stood next to the driver and smiled.

"Welcome to the Academy. My name is Cadet Basso. It's nice to see you. You are going to love it here," said the hulking cadet in a perfect uniform complete with white dress gloves. The bus pulled away from the curb to take the short drive to the campus proper as Cadet Basso continued to offer words of comfort to a few of the cadets who were crying but doing their best to stifle it. The bus pulled away from the curb and began to enter the interior of the Academy campus. As they began to take a turn around a stand of trees, Thomas sensed the change in the first classman's body language a split second before a demonic-like verbal assault was unleashed.

"Alright you pathetic, sniveling, little children, every last one of you get on the first third of your seat! In case you weren't paying attention, I'm Cadet Basso and you will do *precisely* what I tell you to do *precisely* when I say it! Welcome to *my* United

States Air Force Academy! God help the person on this bus who I have to waste my valuable breath on to repeat an order. Do I make myself one-hundred percent clear or do any of you crybabies need me to get a translator? My 'sniveling baby' is a little rusty!"

Thomas made the mistake of glancing over at the girl next to him out of curiosity of how a girl might take such a ferocious berating.

Oh, no, he thought as, in his peripheral vision, he saw the eyes of the huge cadet go wide as saucers. Before he could snap his head forward again, the man was within one inch of his face screaming at the top of his lungs.

"You got a little crush on miss pretty thing here, cadet? I'm *highly* offended. You would prefer to look at her rather than keep your useless eyes forward on me?!? Do you not find me as attractive, you worthless waste-of-space? Make that mistake again and I promise that you will live out the balance of our time together in a level of misery you couldn't even imagine exists!!!"

Thomas kept a perfect bearing forward as he heard the soon-to-be most unfortunate person on the bus snicker. The laugh lacked any humor but more the nervous laughter of someone completely unprepared to process the ranting of Cadet Basso.

God help that guy, thought Thomas.

After unleashing a barrage of bellowing, disparaging remarks on that poor soul, Cadet Basso continued up and down the bus for the next five minutes it took to reach their destination, making absolutely certain that everyone aboard knew who was in charge.

"Every last one of you, get on your feet and get off of my bus in the next twenty seconds!" screamed Cadet Basso.

Within seventeen seconds, everyone was off the bus. It felt to Thomas like they had gone from the frying pan into the fire. Now there were eight different first classmen screaming in the face of whatever cadet was unfortunate enough to catch the attention of the senior cadets. They were being ordered, in no uncertain terms, to find a place on a twenty-by-twenty yard square that had been painted on the concrete. In perfectly spaced intervals, there were painted the silhouettes of two grey feet at forty-five degree angles. What Thomas and every Air Force Academy cadet would come to know as 'The Feet' would be their location for the next hour learning exactly how the Air Force expected its future leaders to stand at perfect attention. It would be a place they would become intimately familiar with over the next few weeks of the first phase of Basic Cadet Training.

I gave up my entire summer for this, huh? thought Thomas as a screaming first classman pointed out the numerous hanging threads on the last civilian attire Thomas would wear for the next eight weeks.

"Mister, if your uniform ever has as many cables hanging from it as does your useless civilian clothes here, you won't last in my Academy very long!" yelled another first classman upon close inspection of Thomas' attire.

Later that evening, Thomas lay on the top of the perfectly-made bunk in his dorm that would be home for the duration of the first phase of Basic Cadet Training. It had taken more than thirty tries and three hours of making and re-making his bunk until it finally passed inspection. As he drifted off to sleep, he thought, *I can handle whatever they throw at me.*

It seemed like he had only just closed his eyes when an obscenely loud broadcast of *Welcome to the Jungle* by the band Guns and Roses shocked him into consciousness at precisely 0430 hours. The high-decibel broadcast was joined by furious pounding on the doors by first classmen screaming for everyone to get out of their rooms, ready for inspection, in the next sixty seconds. The barrage of noise on his senses didn't deter Thomas from being the first one out of his room. Seeing a first classman glaring at him just outside the door, he was shocked by the result of his expedient preparation.

"Seems like we have a real overachiever here, guys. You know the penalty for forgetting to be a team player, Flash Gordon? Get down on your face and give me push ups until the very last one of your little friends here decides to grace us with their magnificent presence!"

As he began to pump out push-ups, Thomas thought, *I'm going to be a fighter pilot...I'm going to be a fighter pilot...I'm going to be a fighter pilot!*

**Georgetown University
Washington D.C.
Fall Career Fair
11:35 A.M. Eastern Time
Wednesday, September 19th, 1997**

Chapter Thirty

Grace Lee strode past all of the recruitment tables at the career fair toward her single objective. Wearing her most conservative navy blue suit, sensible shoes, and a strand of Mikimoto pearls, Grace carried her résumé in a neat, leather-bound notebook. Grace was interested in talking with only one organization. A handsome man standing behind the U.S. Treasury Department booth gave her a million-dollar smile. She politely returned the gesture with a nod, and his face fell as she strode by, heading for a table directly ahead. Two women from the U.S. State Department assessed Grace's fashion sensibility as she walked by. Grace was singularly focused, carrying only one résumé in her portfolio along with one set of reference letters. She passed recruitment specialists of lobbying firms, private companies, almost every major governmental agency, all branches of the military, and even the United Nations without a break in stride. Grace was singularly focused. She walked with a sense of purpose and intensity that neither special agent at the Federal Bureau of Investigation booth could ignore as she approached. Grace noticed the square bulges from underneath the pair of agents' suit jackets and the gold shields held in the leather credential holders attached to their belts. On the wall behind the booth was an organizational crest she knew so well that she could draw it in perfect detail from memory. She had, in fact, done just that, inside the covers of a notebook during a particularly uninteresting lecture on marketing statistics. The two special agents of the FBI watched her approach, sizing her up and neither, upon first impression, could find fault.

"Hello there. I'm Special Agent Jenna Thompson and this is Special Agent Chad Harris." Grace thought Special Agent Thompson was somewhere in her mid-thirties and, despite her attractiveness, wore no wedding band. Her hair was worn in a short bob and around her eyes were the slight lines that gave her the look of a woman who had experienced life intensely. Extending her hand first to Special Agent Thompson, Grace wondered for an instant if she was getting a look at herself in fifteen years. She turned to Special Agent Harris. He had an appraising, intelligent look to him. Harris gave her a polite smile and handshake. His left second finger did have a gold band around it and she wondered for a moment what sort of woman he was married to. She could easily see he was keeping his expression as noncommittal as possible and she was impressed by it. Grace was accustomed to men turning on the charm regardless of the situation and it bored her to tears. These two—especially him—made no special effort to win her. The Bureau was ultra-selective in its recruitment and it was time to put her best foot forward.

"So what attracted you to the Bureau, Ms. Lee?" asked Special Agent Harris. When he opened his mouth, the smooth voice that came forth gave her the impression that he could get whatever information he wanted. She could imagine him in an interrogation with someone accused of espionage and easily getting the spy to admit to every nefarious activity he had ever committed.

Grace looked him directly in the eye and answered, "The Bureau is entrusted with the task of investigating the most significant crimes in the country. You catch bank robbers, serial killers, kidnappers, terrorists, and espionage agents who are trying to hurt Americans directly or the security of the entire country by their illegal actions. I believe that I meet the basic requirements for a new agent and I'd like to serve."

Looking up from her résumé, Special Agent Thompson asked, "How do you know Greg Ruskin?" in response to the reference letter he had provided her.

"He's a friend of the family."

"He's also one of the most highly-decorated agents in the history of the Bureau. He was teaching counterintelligence at the Academy when I went through."

"You're Jack Lee's daughter," added Special Agent Harris flatly.

Grace's hopes of avoiding that conversation vaporized.

Special Agent Thompson looked back at the Velocity Express letterhead and inwardly cursed herself for not immediately making the connection. Although most agents were not only skilled investigators but also uncannily well-informed about a multitude of things, Special Agent Thompson hadn't benefitted from a personal phone from the FBI director to her desk like Special Agent Harris had that morning.

"There will be a young lady that will be coming to see you this morning named Grace Lee."

The director had given Special Agent Harris a brief summary of the young lady's family and background.

"I want your first impression by close of business."

"Yes, Mr. Director."

Special Agent Harris headed recruitment for the Bureau and was considered the finest judge of whether someone was FBI material or not. He was the preeminent talent-spotter. Everyone from the cadre of training agents at Quantico up to the director trusted his instincts implicitly. Regardless of Grace's grades, intelligence, and background, if she didn't pass his muster, she'd never be offered a training slot.

"I noticed that when you walked in, you didn't stop at any of the other booths, Ms. Lee. There appears to be only one résumé in your portfolio."

The observation sent a chill through her. It was exactly why the FBI was her only choice. She had much less anxiety about passing the bar exam in two months than she did about answering Special Agent Harris' question.

Returning his gaze, her eyes locking on to his, Grace simply answered, "That's correct, Special Agent Harris."

The corner of his mouth upturned a fraction of an inch. Special Agent Thompson, looking up from the résumé once again, said, "I'm sure you know, Ms. Lee that the next step is to submit an application package."

From her portfolio, Grace extracted a fully-completed application package and handed them to Special Agent Harris.

"I'd actually be grateful, if either of you had a few minutes, to look over my application and make sure I haven't neglected anything." She knew it was perfectly in order nonetheless.

Harris looked at Grace for a moment, smirked, and said, "I've got to man the table here but if you'd care to take a coffee break, Agent Thompson, I'm sure you'd be happy to look over Ms. Lee's application package to make sure it's complete. I'll be expecting it on my desk next week and there's nothing I hate more than incomplete paperwork."

At that moment, while still maintaining her composure, she felt like doing a football touchdown victory dance. She had accurately sized up Special Agent Harris as a gatekeeper and it seemed he was willing to open the gates to her lifelong dream. At least it appeared that the FBI was willing to give her a shot. She had no worries whatsoever about the required background check and there hadn't been a challenge yet that Grace hadn't found some way to overcome. Former agent Ruskin had often told her stories of the pressure-cooker environment of the FBI Academy and, as she had listened, Grace couldn't wait to step up to the plate and see if she had what the instructors at the Quantico, Virginia facility would be looking for.

Special Agent Harris sat at his desk going over Grace's application package. Looking over her high school and college transcripts, he noted that they were virtually flawless in every aspect. Still, he had met many men and women over the years that possessed genius-level book smarts but totally lacked the ability to creatively apply that brainpower. Opening his e-mail, Special Agent Harris typed a concise report to Director Freedman.

"My first impression of Grace Lee is that she meets the

requirements for initial acceptance to the Academy. Pending the outcome of her background check, my recommendation is to offer her a slot in the next class upon completion of law school."

"Daddy, I don't know," said Grace to her father on the phone. "They took my application package but the agent that was running the recruitment table knew you were my father without me saying anything. Do you think that will hurt my chances? I mean do you think they'll just think of me as some rich guy's daughter who wants to play FBI agent?"

Jack listened to the concern in his daughter's voice that night as he sat with Erika in their living room. They had just finished their evening bible reading and discussion when she called. It was such a great feeling that Grace still came to him to let him do the one thing he enjoyed most in life: being her father. He knew his daughter was a grown woman now but she would always be his little girl.

"You'll be fine, sweetheart. I promise I didn't do anything to interfere. If you get in, you did it all by yourself. Either way, I'm the proudest dad in the world."

"Do you think I'm really good enough?"

"You are good enough to do anything, sweetheart."

"I love you, Daddy."

**Apartment of Second Lieutenant Thomas Walsh
Six miles from Luke Air Force Base
Glendale, Arizona
0447 hours, Mountain Time
Thursday, February 14th, 1998**

Chapter Thirty-One

Driving out of the parking lot of his apartment onto the street, Second Lieutenant Thomas Walsh was pleasantly surprised by the sight of three meteorites streaking in rapid succession across the clear desert sky. The sun wouldn't be peeking over the Papago Buttes and Camelback Mountain for over two more hours. At that pre-dawn time of the morning, with lights from the city a minimum, Thomas could gaze upward, directly into the heart of the Milky Way Galaxy. The first time he had seen the universe at high desert altitude, he couldn't believe that there were so many stars.

Wearing his olive-colored Nomex flight suit with the unit patch of the 309th Fighter Squadron prominently on his shoulders, Thomas drove through the empty streets of Glendale and the current of excitement he always had before flying was present with a heightened intensity. Thomas had finally become exactly what he aspired to be since childhood: a "Viper" pilot. Although the official name for the General Dynamics F-16 was the "Fighting Falcon," those that got to strap one to their backs called them "Vipers" because of their cobra-like shape and the similarity of appearance to the fighting spacecraft on the 1970s sci-fi television program *Battlestar Galactica*. On that still, desert morning, Thomas was finally going to strap into an F-16 and take off on his first simulated combat mission. In a little over two hours, he would start the engine of the powerful and agile jet, taxi out to the end of the runway, set the brakes, advance the throttle to full military power, release the brakes and, following his flight lead down the runway and launch into the Arizona skies to fly his first simulated mission with real weapons loaded onto the jet.

In the twenty months since graduating from the Academy, Thomas had first flew a desk at Vance Air Force Base in Oklahoma for almost a year filing flight plans and accident reports before finally reporting to Moody Air Force Base in Georgia for basic flight training. Flying first the Cessna 172 again and then the T-6 Texan to demonstrate basic airmanship skills, Thomas finally got his hands on his first high-performance aircraft, the T-38 Talon, just like his father had a generation before. After looking at a manufacturer's plate on the underside of his jet one day, and seeing the jet he was flying had been manufactured twenty-seven years earlier, he realized that he just might be flying the very jet his father had taken to fifty-two thousand feet.

"Just remember, Son, radar has gotten much better since my days. They know what altitude you are at and won't just take your word for it anymore," joked Chris to Thomas over the phone that night.

"Roger that, Dad."

"If you want to see the curvature of the earth, I suggest you get into the astronaut program."

"Yes, sir."

The morning the duty assignments were posted had been one of the most eagerly-anticipated days in Thomas' relatively short military career. When he saw he had been assigned to the fighter track or, in Air Force speak, "high performance," he exchanged high-fives with another classmate that had also discovered he was getting fighter jets. All of that preparation had brought Thomas to Luke Air Force Base to really get down to the business of learning the skills that would make him a true fighter pilot and, more importantly, a lethal asset for projecting American power.

    Taking the on-ramp to the southbound lanes of Loop 101 and knowing there would be very few cars on the road at that morning, Thomas goosed his little Toyota up to ninety miles an hour. His rate of speed paled in comparison with what he would attain a few hours later but it was still a minor amusement. Taking the Northern Avenue exit, he drove west along the road toward the airbase and opened the sun roof of the car, letting the clear air of the desert pre-dawn fill the vehicle. Thomas arrived at the main base entrance straddling the aptly-named Thunderbird Road. Luke Air Force Base had been the original home to the Air Force Air Demonstration Team, commonly referred to as the Thunderbirds, before their move to Nellis AFB in Nevada during the 1960s.

    Turning his headlights off in compliance with security protocols, Thomas slowly drove toward the guard shack. The security policeman at the gate gave him a quick look over, snapped a salute that Thomas returned, and allowed him access to the base. Just inside the base, Thomas pulled up next to a VelEx drop box in a parking lot and picked up a package from his front seat. As he deposited it into the box, he smiled at the thought of the recipient opening it two days later.

    Thomas arrived at the building that housed the 309th Fighter Squadron offices. When Thomas walked into the flight planning room, he wasn't surprised to see Lieutenant Mike Chang already pulling together the materials to plan his training mission flight.

    "Get a little extra beauty sleep there?" jibed Mike who had arrived two minutes earlier.

    "How much of that could I possibly need?" shot back Thomas.

    Mike grinned and went back to the business of planning his flight with maps of the target ranges to the south arrayed in front of him. Thomas went to a combination-locked safe on the wall and extracted a classified book that detailed various known capabilities of foreign fighter aircraft. Looking over the details of the Russian top-of-the-line Mig 29 Fulcrum, Thomas memorized the details that would be covered in preflight briefing. Although the odds of a Mig 29 flying within five thousand miles of their flight that day were infinitesimally small, part of the process of becoming a fighter pilot was to learn the intimate details of potential enemies.

"Hey, Thomas…you pumped?" asked Lieutenant Chang.

Thomas turned around from scanning the three-ring bound foreign threat book and just laughed.

"Yeah, I thought so. I mean did you really think we'd finally get here?"

Without a second of hesitation, Thomas looked at his friend whom he had shared all of the forging experience of the Academy with, and simply said, "Yeah. I did." Just then, the third member of their flight, Lieutenant Casey Eaton, joined them. Casey had been the product of an Air Force R.O.T.C. program at a small school in central Texas.

"Morning, Casey," said Thomas

"Morning guys," replied Lieutenant Eaton without a shred of embarrassment over being the last of their flight to arrive at flight planning.

"Now here's a guy that really doesn't need the beauty rest," joked Mike. The three officers had enjoyed a beer out at a popular college bar near Arizona State University one night and the attention lavished on Lieutenant Eaton from a number of college girls had been astounding. With his blonde hair, blue-eyed, boy-next-door looks and a physique chiseled by years of gymnastics, the girls' adoration had come as no surprise but was still impressive to watch.

"Might want to light the afterburners on your mission planning. Briefing starts in fifteen," said Thomas.

Lieutenant Eaton smiled and extracted his paperwork, already completed, from his pilot's briefcase.

"Took the liberty of nailing this down last night," said Lieutenant Eaton.

Mike just looked at Thomas and shook his head, admiring the strategy and thinking how he would do the same in the future. Over the next fifteen minutes, the three pilots continued to plan the details of their first simulated combat sortie at the controls of the F-16. Their first month as members of the 309th had been exclusively academic work and time in the flight simulators. Their first five flights in an F-16 had been in the front seat of the F-16D variant two-seater to review basic piloting skills of the jet with an instructor pilot in the rear seat. The three fighter pilots had successfully completed their line check qualifications flying solo the week before with an instructor pilot in another jet shadowing their every move. Their training was now moving into the next, higher-paced phase where they were going to be taught the deadly art of using their jets to destroy enemies both in the air and on the ground. The F-16C was the only jet in the Air Force inventory that had two roles: highly maneuverable air superiority aircraft and ground attack platform. When they had completed the paperwork, Mike asked Thomas to look over his work and vice-versa. Nobody wanted to be embarrassed by having his mission planning paperwork be called shoddy by their instructor.

"Looks perfect to me," said Mike, looking over Thomas' work.

"Call it good," said Thomas about Mike's.

"Roger that," added Casey

The three men headed to the briefing room with a current of energy running through them even though it was still nearly two hours before they would actually climb into the front seat of the F-16C with live ordinance on the jet's hardpoints and launch rails.

Major Phil Lancelot looked at his watch and when it flipped to precisely 0500 hours, he looked up at his three students for the morning's mission and said, "Time hack o-five-hundred hours. Today we will be flying out to Range A and letting you get some experience with the weapons systems of the F-16." The Major was an Air Force Academy graduate and experienced combat pilot with over two thousand hours at the controls of the F-16 and over a thousand in the F-4. Major Lancelot had coincidentally been a fellow alumnus member of Thomas' squadron at the Academy—the Viking Ninth Squadron—but that would garner Thomas no extra favor. In fact, despite knowing it, Thomas had never even brought it up. Nobody cared about a pilot's background in fighter pilot training. The only thing that mattered was how well he flew.

The briefing continued over the next hour and a half, covering radio frequencies, weapons release procedures, discussion of the foreign threat material that had been digested earlier, and several practice run-throughs of emergency procedures for an engine shutdown at altitude.

"The F-16 has a glide ratio of one-to-one, meaning that if you fly the aircraft perfectly, you will lose one thousand feet of altitude for every nautical mile of ground you cover. If your nearest airfield is eighteen miles away, what's the minimum altitude you pray you are at if the engine dies on you, Lieutenant Walsh?"

"Eighteen thousand feet, sir."

"Good to see they are still teaching you a little math up at the Academy. Lieutenant Eaton, what is the size of the warhead explosive payload and the effective range of the AIM-9 Sidewinder missile?"

"Sir, the AIM-9 contains twenty-point-eight pounds of high explosive and is effective out to a range of approximately eleven nautical miles."

"Correct, Lieutenant Eaton."

The four pilots continued for another hour discussing everything that should happen on their mission and what to do if things went wrong, which was quite possible with three pilots who had never flown a simulated combat mission before. All three men, in their various ways, silently prayed the universal prayer of all fighter pilots: *God, please don't let me screw up.*

The pre-flight briefing concluded, Lieutenants Walsh, Chang, Eaton, and Major Lancelot headed over to the Life Support building to slip into their G-Suits, helmets, and other flight gear. Thirty minutes later, all four men climbed aboard a crew transportation bus that would drive them out to the flight line. The hangars for the F-16s were small, single jet hangars in rows of four to six structures that were designed to give shade to ground crewmembers to work on the jets in the oftentimes hundred-degree plus temperatures that Phoenix was known for. As it was February, and the time was 0630 hours, the air temperature was a comfortable sixty-two degrees, but the days of oppressive heat, especially on a flight line full of jets expelling superheated gasses, was only a few short months away.

The crew bus pulled to a stop in front of four hangars that housed the jets that 'Cooler Flight' would fly that day. Thomas had been assigned to a jet with the Air Force aircraft number designation 84243, the last three digits boldly displayed on the tail. The large base designation letters LF on the vertical stabilizer identified the jet to be part of Luke AFB's inventory of jets.

First Sergeant Ashley Folkes was supervising the ordinance crew's final tasks of loading missiles on the jet like a stage mother watching over her child. Seeing Lieutenant Walsh hopping off the bus, he walked toward his pilot.

"Morning, Sergeant. How's she look," said Thomas as he shook Sergeant Folkes' hand.

"Perfect, sir," replied Sergeant Folkes with a sharp salute. Thomas began the requisite walk-around inspection of his jet. It was much more of a cursory look to make sure there wasn't anything glaringly wrong with the jet. Those occurrences were rare and pilots needed to trust the professionalism of their crew chiefs. In Air Force parlance, Sergeant Folkes 'owned' that specific jet. He was ultimately responsible for ensuring everything was working perfectly when his pilot would take "his" jet up. So much so, that the Air Force had painted his name, and his assistant crew chief, Sergeant Dave Dresner, on the jet. The crew chiefs and their maintenance crews claimed that they actually owned the jets and the pilots were just allowed the privilege of flying them.

Satisfied that there were no glaring defects in the jet, and trusting that when Sergeant Folkes said the bird was perfect, Thomas mounted the ladder and climbed into the cockpit. That morning, for whatever random reason, a memory from his childhood popped into his consciousness as he entered the tight space that was commonly called a cockpit but which fighter pilots referred to as their "office". The memory of a Navy officer helping him into the first fighter jet he ever climbed into at an air show so many years before flashed across the landscape of his mind. It brought a smile to his face as he sat, being assisted in connecting his oxygen and restraints by Sergeant Folkes.

"Looks like somebody is eager to go fly," said Sergeant

Folkes, noticing the grin. Thomas simply gave a thumbs-up to the sergeant and returned his attention to the task at hand which was an involved, complicated process of setting the controls and instruments in the jet in preparation for flight.

As the powerful Pratt and Whitney engine two feet below Thomas' cockpit came fully on line, Thomas heard their flight leader, Major Lancelot, call in to the tower. As student pilots in the four-ship flight, there would be no communication from them. They would simply listen and follow their flight leader's orders. The call-sign for Major Lancelot had a few versions of its origin but the one Thomas believed was the most accurate involved a small, portable cooler the major had in the cockpit and an unfortunate oversight in not bringing a "piddle pack" for in-flight relief. Most Air Force call signs had an embarrassing incident as their inspiration, but absolutely nobody with half a brain would be the one to openly question the instructor pilot about it.

"Tower, Cooler Flight of four, taxi," transmitted Major Lancelot.

"Roger Cooler Flight, taxi to runway three-six left."

Advancing his throttle slightly, Thomas began to follow in the third position behind Major Lancelot and Lieutenant Chang, with Lieutenant Eaton taxiing behind him. The four jets came to a stop in an area several hundred yards from the hangars where ordinance crews waited to arm the bombs and missiles aboard the jets. Noting the Sidewinder missiles on the wingtips were not the day-glow orange of practice weapons but real weapons gave Thomas a tremendous jolt of excitement. To that point, he had never actually carried live weapons aboard. It was a seemingly small detail but it was tangible evidence of how different the training pace was going to be from that point forward. As he raised his hands so that the ordinance crew could clearly see they were free of the controls, they quickly went through their process of flipping the switches and freeing the wires on the bomb fuses to make them live weapons.

Two minutes later, after rolling out to the end of the runway, the four aircraft positioned themselves in a diamond shaped echelon formation and set their brakes. All three students heard Major Lancelot broadcast, "Cooler One, ready for takeoff runway three-six left."

"Roger Cooler one, cleared for takeoff. Contact departure on channel four."

In unison, the four pilots advanced their throttles and powered their engines up to full military power, meaning a setting just below full afterburner. The superheated tongues of exhaust shot from the rear of the jets, generating hundreds of decibels. When Major Lancelot broadcast, "Release," the pilots simultaneously released their brakes and, like four drag racers, shot down the runway. Twelve seconds later, the small, agile jets leaped into the Arizona sky and the expanse of Phoenix began to unfold beneath them.

Keeping his assigned position off his flight leader's starboard wing, Thomas heard Major Lancelot broadcast on the Departure Control channel specific to Luke, "Departure, Cooler One, flight of four airborne at five thousand. Enroute to range one."

"Roger Cooler One. Report visual with range one," replied the tower.

At altitude, the sun was casting its first morning rays across the desert as the flight of jets roared over the White Tunks mountain range, heading for the Sonoran Desert National Monument. The early morning light bathed the craggy features in the soft, reddish glow of desert mornings. The desert was known for mild temperatures throughout the winter but spring always brought strong winds. Occasionally sustained winds would top fifty miles per hour and with those winds came ferocious dust storms. The prior week, one of those had blown through and the atmosphere was still highly laden with silica dust. The benefit was that sunrises and sunsets glowed with a brilliant ruby redness that non-desert dwellers would never experience.

As they passed through twenty thousand feet, Thomas could make out Interstate Eight, four miles below, looking like someone had taken a pencil and drawn it on the earth. The feeling of being exactly where he was, doing what he was doing, with these pilots, was a euphoria he lived for. As the four jets streaked along their southwesterly heading, Thomas thought, *I hope Grace enjoys her birthday gift.* Her twenty-fifth birthday was in three days. He trusted his package would be there the following day. The gift was somewhat whimsical but something she would understand. Inside the little blue and yellow VelEx box, he had placed a small metal model of an F-16, a replica pair of pilot's wings, and a unit patch of the 309th Fighter Squadron. The wings he still wore on his Class-A uniform were the ones with the tiny inscription on the back she had given him so many years before. She had talked about how exciting and challenging the work she was doing at the FBI was, but kept details to a minimum due to the sensitive nature of her work.

Thomas still remembered the scent of the Chanel perfume she always wore. Twice in the past week, he smelled someone wearing it—once in the grocery store and once at the Starbucks just off base. The scent always immediately made him think of her.

He always looked forward to their weekly telephone conversation and lately, his favorite part of the day was checking for electronic computer messages on the new service "America Online" they had signed up for.

Turning his full attention back to the serious business at hand, he took a deep breath, let out a small sigh into his oxygen mask, advanced his throttle slightly, and broke the sound barrier.

287

**Cathedral of Christ the King
Blessed Sacrament Chapel
Atlanta, Georgia
7:52 A.M. Eastern Time
Thursday, October 12th, 1998**

Chapter Thirty-Two

Chris and Keely walked into the 1930s-era gothic cathedral for their designated Holy Hour of perpetual adoration at the Blessed Sacrament Chapel. The custom of praying in front of an exposed consecrated host was a tenet of the Catholic faith that virtually every priest in the world participated in, and would laud the benefits of.

Chris had been putting it off for years, despite what he had heard repeatedly about the practice. Smiling at how wrong he had been about the value of Eucharistic Adoration in his life, Chris remembered the first time he begrudgingly mentioned to Jack that he was going to give it a try, five months earlier.

Pouring over financial documents one morning in the Velocity Express board room, Chris finally put them to the side and looked up at Jack across the table.

"So when I went to Father McNamara for my spiritual advisement appointment last week, he pretty much ordered me to do an hour of that Eucharistic Adoration thing and Keely was really excited to go with me," said Chris.

Jack looked up from some reports with a huge smile, ecstatic at the news. "I'm so happy you are going to give it a try! Erika and I go the exact same time on Mondays and I wouldn't trade anything for the sense of peace I get from it. You just have to go and do it and you'll know," said Jack.

"Yeah, well, we're going together tomorrow morning. So that's what you and Erika have been doing when I've seen your cars in the lot on the way to work? I always knew you and Erika went to the morning Mass but you guys were doing the adoration thing, huh? That's why you never schedule appointments before ten, right?"

"You got it, pal."

"I can't believe we've never talked about this before."

"Yeah, I can't either," said Jack, reflecting that he should have mentioned it sometime over the prior fifteen years of their sharing their faith within their Church. He felt a pang of guilt for not having encouraged his closest friend to explore a practice that added so much to his and Erika's lives.

Shaking his head, Chris said, "I'm so glad Keely was kind enough to wait until *after* we had left our session with Father John to explain exactly what Eucharistic Adoration means. She told me she could tell by the look on my face that I had no idea what he was talking about but I did a good job faking it. I mean, I felt totally inadequate seeing as how I went to Catholic school as a kid."

"Well, don't feel too bad. They didn't talk about it too much when we were kids, but didn't they explain it when you went through R.C.I.A. before you guys got married?"

Chris looked down at the carpet for a moment before looking back at his friend, pretty certain that the specifics of the devotion had been covered, but Chris sometimes referred to his mind as his personal home entertainment center with everything but an "off" switch.

"Yeah, well, they might have, actually…"

With a warm smile, Jack said, "Well, it's never too late."

Chris had not been entirely keen on the idea of spending an entire hour doing nothing but sitting in a small room with his thoughts. Uninformed about the true purpose and benefits of Adoration, he couldn't know what a profound effect on his life the practice would ultimately have. When he went to Father

McNamara for regular consultation about how to better conduct himself as a Catholic man, the pastor had suggested Eucharistic Adoration as a way for him and Keely to enrich their faith together. Sometimes the suggestions Father McNamara made weren't things Chris would want to do but, over thirteen years, the wise priest had never steered Chris wrong. Still, Chris originally had some reservations about giving up an entire hour of his day when he had a multi-billion dollar corporation to run.

The first morning he and Keely went together, he quickly knew Adoration was an extraordinary experience. Immediately, Chris decided that he didn't ever want to miss out on it again. While sitting in front of the ornate monstrance that held the oversized host within a special cylindrical section in the middle, Chris prayed his rosary and sat quietly, reflecting on his faith and how he could better live his life. It was a time Chris grew to cherish, once a week, to sit in prayerful meditation with his wife and a handful of other devout parishioners. There was someone in front of the Blessed Sacrament twenty-four hours a day, giving the custom the proper name of Perpetual Adoration.

On some occasions, Chris was able to quiet the rapid-fire thought processes long enough to get inspiration about areas of his life. Some of the important inspirations that came to him ranged from how to be a more loving husband to his wife or how to best be a steward of the vast financial success he had enjoyed. Sometimes inspirations about how to be a better father came or even such simple inspirations as to call a colleague to encourage them when he knew that person was going through a difficult time. It wasn't like he thought up the ideas deliberately. As he sat staring at the little white wafer of blessed, unleavened bread in the center of the monstrance, the volume of his own ever-present, internal dialogue faded away and thoughts that brought warmth to his soul entered his heart and mind. Father McNamara once suggested bringing a journal each time he went and to attempt to write down any inspirations he received. After doing that for a month, Chris had looked back on what he had written. He smiled and saw his writing on the pages of the leather-bound journal had nothing to do with acquiring anything for himself. The entire product of his inspirational hours of reflection, in the very presence of God according to the Church, was a series of thoughts about some way to do kind things for others.

Over four consecutive weeks in a row back in July, Chris received inspiration during adoration about how to use the vast financial resources within the coffers of Velocity Express to help others throughout the world. He and Jack's collective personal fortunes were measured in ten decimal places and it took an army of accountants and team of tax professionals to file their personal income tax statements each year. Over the past three months that Chris and Keely had exercised the practice of their Holy Hour together, Chris knew in his heart that the philanthropic projects he and Jack had quietly organized were inspirations that wouldn't have necessarily occurred to him without having spent the wonderful hour each week in adoration.

Although there was no conclusive evidence of a correlation between Chris and Jack's charity and the amazing business success VelEx was experiencing, he was absolutely astounded at the inexplicable spike in business over the last fiscal quarter. In a pretty soft market, there was no reasonable explanation for the upturn in business. In the third quarter, where he had allocated a budget of more than ten million dollars toward sending medical professionals and basic quality-of-life supplies to some of the most impoverished spots in the world, the company had recorded astounding profits. There had been an unprecedented twelve percent jump in net income before taxes in the quarterly financial reports and the stock VLX was being traded at over fifteen dollars a share more than it had been the previous quarter.

It hadn't just been the business windfall of late that had amazed Chris. The thing he loved the most about spending time with his wife in prayer was the sense of peace from the devotion and the joy in his heart he had experienced from the altruistic inspirations of helping others. He just felt closer to God as a result and the peace from spending time in prayer seemed to be making all aspects of his life more fulfilling. All of those experiences over the past several months had given Chris a wonderfully-enhanced sense of God's presence throughout his days.

That October morning, Keely sat on one of the cushioned

benches that ringed the small Blessed Sacrament Chapel, praying her daily rosary while Chris knelt on one of two single-person kneelers directly in front of the tabernacle. Just as he was about to cross himself and rise from the padded kneeler, there was a loud knock at the door. Chris went to the door and peered through the peephole. Seeing a man wearing several layers of clothes, a wool cap, and with a huge, black piece of rolling luggage, he instantly knew it was one of the handful of homeless people that ventured the few miles up from the downtown parks and shelters or possibly had trekked the two miles from the Lindbergh area Interstate 85 overpass, where a community of indigent had set up camp under the bridge.

"Who is it, honey?" asked Keely.

"It's a homeless guy, sweetheart. I don't know exactly what he wants but you guys stay here," answered Chris as he quickly went through the custom of kneeling on the floor, bowing to the Blessed Sacrament, making the sign of the cross, and then exited the small chapel. Poking his head out the next door over from the chapel door, Chris called to the man, who continued to rap in increasingly harder knocks on the chapel door, "Sir, can I help you?"

The man looked over, surprised, and answered, "Yeah, I need help man. Nobody around here will help me."

"Well that's just the door to the Blessed Sacrament Chapel. Have you been downstairs to the office?"

The man looked at Chris with an expression of disgust and retorted, "Yeah, I've been there. They just told me to go over to the Buckhead Christian Ministry or to the Saint Vincent DePaul office up the highway. I mean does it look like I've got my car and driver waiting to take me to that appointment?"

Chris thought the irony of that remark clever and smiled. For a second, the man looked like he was about to say something else of a snarky nature but suddenly he stopped in mid-syllable and stood with an appraising expression. Looking directly into Chris' eyes, he said nothing for several seconds and, as if a switch had suddenly been flipped, the homeless man's face broke into a genuine smile. Sizing the man up as not presenting an aggressive posture, Chris stepped to the cobblestone driveway and walked toward the man, ensuring the door behind him locked. Chris extended his hand as he approached.

"I'm Chris, what's your name?"

"Tim."

"Well, Tim, what are you trying to do. I mean what sort of help was it you were you trying to get at the office."

"Well, I'm trying to get together enough money to buy a monthly pass on the MARTA bus, but I've only got seven dollars collected and they cost thirty-five dollars for the monthly card."

As he stood close to the man, Chris didn't smell the telltale odor of someone who had been drinking heavily. It was difficult to understand why an articulate, intelligent guy like this one would become homeless but something about the man intrigued Chris and he wanted to know more about the man's situation. Chris knew that even if he did have a few dollars in his pocket, which he really didn't, the small sum wouldn't be a real a solution for the man's problems. Even so, Chris was struck with a real desire to be helpful in a significant way.

Chris sighed as he said, "I'm sorry but I don't have a single dollar of actual cash on me. If you want though, I could maybe take you to the bus…"

The man's face fell and he looked down, shook his head, and said, "Well thanks anyway, sir."

The man grabbed the handle of his rolling luggage, hefted the backpack he carried more securely onto his shoulder, and turned to leave. Chris looked at his watch and knew he had an exceptionally important meeting scheduled in a little over an hour. For a man that was obsessive about punctuality, there was a growing sense of unease at the time he was spending with a man who seemed righteously indignant and unresponsive to even the smallest gesture of civility. As he was about to turn to go back inside, however, a small, quiet voice whispered through his consciousness. It was the strangest sensation but it felt like the words were not annunciated in his head but somewhere in his chest. The words he would later describe to Jack that he heard were, *If you want to get closer to Me, work with my children.* He had the strangest warm sensation in the center of his chest as he opened his mouth to speak.

Final Delivery / Will Dempsey

"Listen, Tim. My wife and I are going to breakfast down the street. You know the funny looking place with all the parrot cages outside?" Pointing to his Chevy Tahoe, he continued, "I'm sure we can fit your things into it and maybe you'd like to let me buy you breakfast? After that, I can drop you wherever you want. Really, no kidding. I'd kind of like to hear what's going on with you."

From inside the chapel, Keely had been watching the exchange between her husband and the homeless man through the peep hole in the door. She knew Chris was capable of taking care of himself but it was still unsettling to see her husband in such close proximity to the man who had been banging on the door moments earlier with increasing aggressiveness.

"Is he safe or should I go get someone?" asked the other woman that had been praying in the chapel.

Seeing the expression on the homeless man's face soften and his posture relax, Keely knew everything was going to be fine.

"No, I think my husband is doing just fine." She annunciated the word "husband" with a tone of pride and loving timbre to her voice.

Chris spoke on his car phone, saying, "Michaeline, do me a favor. Something important has come up and I'm going to be an hour late getting in today. Could you please call the members of the board and tell them I apologize to keep them waiting but there's something I have to do."

He listened to her reply.

"Yes, that's what I said. I said *late* by about an hour. Thanks." Placing the car phone back in the cradle in the middle of the console, Chris turned to Keely and said, "Sweetheart, this is Tim. He'll be joining us for breakfast this morning."

Saks Fifth Avenue Department Store
Phipps Plaza Shopping Mall
Atlanta, Georgia
9:37 A.M. Eastern Time
Wednesday, October 3rd, 1999

Chapter Thirty-Three

A little over twenty minutes before the store opened, Special Agent Grace Lee stood with Ian Walters, the asset protection manager, and five other FBI agents, listening intently as her boss went over all of the operational contingencies in place for discretely approaching one Mr. Ali Shamkhani and inviting him down to the FBI field office for a little chat.

"We have no reason to believe this guy is dangerous. He's got no record and, by all appearances, seems to be just what he appears but let's be smooth about this, guys," said Special Agent Mike Cooper, Grace's supervisor.

The subject they were at the upscale store to arrest that day was making it easy for the agents. They referred to this sort of operation as an 'arrest by appointment'. The subject claimed he'd never received the official GIA diamond grading certificate from the Italian jewelry maker, Roberto Coin. There was no crime whatsoever in requesting a certificate for the three-carat round brilliant stone valued at seventy-two thousand dollars, except that it had been stolen in a grab and run incident at the Beverly Hill Saks Fifth Avenue two months earlier. If Mr. Shamkhani hadn't gotten greedy, the necklace would have been gone forever.

However, his phone call to the manufacturer demanding a certificate based on the serial number inscribed on the stone set in motion a coordinated effort by law enforcement that would be executed within the next hour, provided Mr. Shamkhani actually showed up.

"Since we don't know exactly what Mr. Shamkhani looks like, we don't know if he was the actual thief from this tape," said Special Agent Cooper as they watched a video of the robbery in Beverly Hills, "or someone else now in possession of the diamond. I'm guessing it's the second option but there are stupid thieves as we all know."

All assembled in the asset protection office snickered.

The video the assembled agents and police officers were watching of the theft showed a tall and slender man wearing lots of jewelry. He had originally been described as an African American by the salesperson he had robbed in Beverly Hills but, upon closer inspection, it was determined the thief actually had Middle Eastern features.

"Alright people, let's get everyone into position," said Special Agent Cooper.

While her fellow FBI agents posed as customers, Grace would assume to role of fine jewelry department manager. Attaching a Saks pin to one lapel of her Armani suit and doing a radio check into the tiny microphone affixed to the other, Grace fit the part perfectly. The accessory that differentiated her from the other salespeople was the SIG Sauer 9mm compact pistol held in a paddle holster in the small of her back. Grace enjoyed the opportunity to wear one of her fine suits that day as opposed to the ultra-conservative Brooks Brothers quasi-uniform she wore on a daily basis. The collection of men in the room apparently had no idea the suit she wore cost more than most of their monthly salaries. The only person who had made any comment about it was the regional asset protection director, Stephanie Gallagher

"I love that suit," said Stephanie when the law enforcement officers and asset protection staff had gotten together to plan the operation that morning. Within the Atlanta FBI Field Office, only Special Agent Cooper knew her father was co-founder of VelEx and Grace took pains to keep it that way, especially as her first assignment was back in her home town of Atlanta. Wearing the assortment of designer clothes she had in her closet to work would have been politically inept and make her the target of office gossip and ridicule. Unless spending time out with girlfriends on the weekends, Grace toed the party line and did her best to blend in with her colleagues every time she strapped her holster and badge on. Grace had other challenges to being taken seriously in the highly male-dominated environment of the Federal Bureau of Investigation. Cover girl looks were an asset in many ways to professional women but they could definitely be a double-edged sword. That day, however, the FBI was utilizing her looks to blend in perfectly with the staff in at Saks.

With the entire staff of the jewelry department assembled, Special Agent Cooper said, "Real quickly folks, when any man comes in to ask for the manager, you just direct him to Special Agent Lee here who will be sitting at this desk here." He nodded to Grace and asked, "Anything to add, Special Agent Lee?"
Grace nodded back, inwardly grateful for the professional courtesy. She was the one potentially going into harm's way and by acknowledging her and asking for any final input before everyone took their places, Cooper sent a message that he respected her. That was worth more in the FBI than doubling the GS-12 pay she earned.
Grace nodded at Cooper and said, "Let me make this really clear, folks. This isn't a big deal and not anything all that exciting. I trust everyone will just be cool and go about your business. There is almost zero possibility of this getting exciting in any way. We are just going to have a friendly chat with a guy in the back office. We don't even know if he's a criminal. He may have legitimately bought the stone from anywhere but there are a lot of police here to keep things nice and quiet. Any questions?"
"Yes, ma'am, are you currently dating anyone?" quipped a nice-looking young salesman. The real department manager rolled his eyes at his staff member's remark but the laughter it evoked had the effect of relaxing everyone.
"Can you shoot a two-inch grouping of five rounds with a

Glock at twenty-five yards?"

The young would-be suitor's eyes widened at the unexpected retort.

"No, Ma'am."

"Sorry, a girl has to have her standards."

The entire assembled group roared with laughter at that. Grace shot the salesman a smile and a wink and took her place at the desk with a notepad and a few product books from various jewelry vendors to give the appearance of being the department manager.

"You just can't help acting like a five-year-old, can ya? And ditch the gum before the store opens. You look like a cow chewing a cud," she heard the real manager say to the young man as they walked off. She smiled.

It wasn't long before Mr. Shamkhani approached a sales associate at the Cartier watch counter. She knew it was the man the agents were waiting for, not only by his appearance, but by how he carried himself. He had the look of a guy who was trying to get away with something. As soon as the sales woman motioned toward the manager's desk, Grace's pulse quickened despite what she had said while briefing the staff.

"Mr. Shamkhani? I'm Grace Johnson, the department manager," she said as she stood and shook his hand. She looked into his eyes to try to size him up. He was a short, rotund man but was well-dressed with a nicely-tailored suit, Gucci loafers and a fresh manicure. She didn't sense an ounce of aggression potential from the man but she knew well enough to never make assumptions.

"Come on in to my office and we'll match up the certificate with the stone."

"I don't have the stone with me, Ms. Johnson. I've just brought the serial number. You can understand my reluctance to walk around with a diamond necklace in my pocket."

Plan B, she thought. The two male agents, posing as customers in the department would know Shamkhani hadn't brought the stone by the radio transmission from the microphone in her lapel. They were going to let him walk. It was a contingency that had been planned for.

"Well, in that case, let me just get the certificate for you and we'll be all set. I'll be right back."

She walked to the office door, unlocked it, stepped inside, and retrieved the certificate from the top of the real manager's desk. Agents were already positioning themselves to tail the man to wherever he went upon exiting the department store.

"Here you are, Mr. Shamkhani. Can I be of service in any other way?" she said as she handed the man the small passport-sized, laminated document.

"You have been most kind. I'm pressed for time so good day, Ms. Johnson." The man turned and strode away and out the double doors right next to the department.

She retrieved her radio from inside her handbag and turning it on, heard radio chatter confirming they had a visual on the subject pulling away in a Mercedes 500 sedan.

Grace grabbed her handbag and reached the exit at the same time as Special Agent Cooper and two other agents. They were met at the curb by another agent already at the wheel of a Caprice Classic with three radio antennas protruding from the top.

Though they still weren't sure if Mr. Shamkhani was a criminal of any sort, speeding through the twists and turns of the parking lot while the Fulton Country Air Unit helicopter loomed overhead certainly ratcheted up the intensity of the situation.

Mr. Shamkhani pulled into the portico of the distinctive, cylindrical Peachtree Westin and entered the parking garage. Shortly after, two vehicles driven by very serious-looking men pulled up to the garage entrance. One agent, paused a beat to wave his credentials out the window at the approaching valet and then entered the garage behind Mr. Shamkhani. Agents from the other FBI car parked and took up positions at the garage entrance to block any possible escape attempt if the agent was made and Shamkhani tried to flee Grace and the other three agents arrived under the portico thirty seconds later and parked. A valet attendant began to approach and was instantly dissuaded with a flash of credentials from the agent driving. The four agents marched into the entryway of the hotel, up a short escalator, and immediately headed for the check-in desk. A large convention group was checking in and for a second, someone began to protest as they walked directly up to the desk clerk.

"Hey, there's a line, pal" barked one man who looked like he was already having a bad day with his rumpled suit and disheveled appearance. Another flash of the credentials silenced him immediately. Special Agent Cooper flashed his badge and I.D. credential to the supervisor standing at the desk behind three guest service agents, noted her name on her tag as Kim Fish, and said, "Ms. Fish, FBI. Mr. Shamkhani. What room?"

The young lady nodded and stepped to a free computer terminal, tapped her keys furiously, and looked up with a confused look.

"I'm sorry, sir, but there's no Mr. Shamkhani registered."

The agents all shot each other a look. Mr. Shamkhani just went from a guy with potentially bad luck for buying a stolen diamond to something else altogether. Legitimate businessmen didn't check into hotels under assumed names.

"Do you keep vehicle records on the registration cards?" asked Grace, thinking quickly.

"Sorry, no. What does the guy look like?" asked the desk supervisor in a desperate attempt to be helpful.

"Middle Eastern, kind of heavy-set. Short."

"Oh, wait a second. *That* guy. Yeah, he came in yesterday. Hold on a second. I can't remember his name, or at least the name he checked in under, but give me a second. There were some words between him and the valet about him not wanting to valet his vehicle and self-park." She disappeared into the back office and returned a moment later with a computer printout. Scanning the names, she said, "I'll recognize it if I see it. He made me wonder because I looked at his wallet when he pulled his credit card out and it looked like there were three different driver's licenses in the same wallet. I couldn't be sure so I didn't say anything but the one he gave matched the credit card."

"That's why I love front desk people. They pay attention,"

said Special Agent Cooper.

"There it is. Mr. Ali Zaif. Room 322. Do you guys want a key to the room?"

"That would be great. Thanks Ms. Fish. Hey, just a thought but have you ever considered a career in law enforcement?"

"Well, uh, maybe. I'm getting my business degree right now at Georgia State," the young woman with short, blonde hair and pretty features said as she encoded a card key on the key encoding device.

"Give me a call when you're getting ready to graduate," said Special Agent Cooper with a smile as he placed his business card on the desk. It never hurt to cultivate loyalty in the local community.

The agent that had followed Mr. Shamkhani's Mercedes into the parking garage radioed, in a self-disgusted tone, that he had lost visual on the subject when he entered the lobby. Special Agent Cooper instructed him to link up with the other three agents on the third floor. Three minutes later, the five agents stood outside the door, service weapons at the low ready, while Special Agent Cooper used his cell phone to call the hotel and be transferred to room 322.

"Thank you for calling the Peachtree Westin, how may I direct your call?"

"Room 322 please."

"And the last name?"

"Zaif."

"Thank you."

They heard the phone ring inside the room and Special Agent Cooper's face lit up when someone picked up the line.

"Hello?"

"Mr. Jones?"

"Wrong room," blurted Zaif and hung up.

Grace looked to Special Agent Cooper for a cue as to how they were going to proceed. Cooper whispered to Grace, "Housekeeper."

She knocked on the door and called, "Housekeeping!"

"No service. Thank you!" they heard from inside.

Grace slid the key card into the door and the green light on the electronic lock indicated it was disengaged. As she began to turn the handle, she felt it resist.

"I said no serv!…" was all Shamkhani managed before realizing the people standing outside his door were the furthest thing from housekeepers they could be. He tried to slam the door shut with his weight but two agents threw their shoulders into the door, knocking the thickly-built man backwards. Entering the room, Grace screamed in a commanding voice that even surprised her fellow agents, "FBI! Get down! Get down! Get down! Cooper grabbed the man by a handful of his shirt and tie knot and slipped his hip and leg behind the man, using a simple hip throw to fling him to the floor. Before Mr. Shamkhani/Zaif could try to regain his breath, as the fall knocked the wind from him, Grace fell on the back of the man, sticking the barrel of her weapon directly behind his ear and bellowed, "You even twitch funny, pal, and I'll paint your brains all over this carpet! You lay real still. We perfectly clear?"

Two other agents wrenched the man's arms behind him and had him in handcuffs before he could gather his senses.

After cuffing the man, Grace and Cooper pulled him to his feet and sat him on the bed. They began searching the room. Noting the key from the room safe wasn't in the lock, Grace said, "The safe key, where is it?"

He spat in her direction, barely missing her.

"Item one: we'll find the key or get the security people to open it. Item two: you're already in a bucket full of trouble. Spit on me and the next thing you'll be spitting is your teeth. As a bonus we'll add assault on a federal agent charges."

Moments later, one of the agents grinned as he removed the key from where it had been taped to the underside of a credenza drawer. "Think this will do it," said the agent as he held the key up like a prize in front of the face of their subject. What the agents found inside the safe made Mr. Shamkhani or Zaif or whatever the man's real name was exceptionally interesting: A glassine envelope containing a diamond approximately three carats in weight, two separate passports from Egypt and from Iran under two names. In his wallet, there were indeed three separate American driver's licenses. Whatever Mr. X was, a legitimate diamond dealer he wasn't.

"Good job today, Lee," said Special Agent Cooper as they sat in the FBI Atlanta Field Office just north of Clairmont Road, furiously typing reports. Whoever the man was, once his image was sent to headquarters, it began a buzz of activity and some phone calls came from some very senior agents in Washington. A call directly from office of the assistant director of the national security branch of the Bureau had made Special Agent Cooper's ears really perk up. This was no garden-variety thief. The counterterrorism division transmitted a file with some very interesting information about the subject currently in interview room number two who suddenly lost his command of the English language. Mr. X, as it turned out, was a Yemeni national who had entered the country three weeks earlier under his Egyptian identity passport. He was a person of interest with known ties to *Hezbollah* in Lebanon and a player in the tri-border region of South America where that particular terror organization had a lot of operations in play to generate operational funds. Apparently the faux diamond dealer was a guy that specialized in converting valuable things to cash. Although on the radar of the Bureau, he had been smart—smart right up to the point of being in possession of an identifiable stolen diamond.

"Thanks for backing me up, Mike," said Grace.

"You are really a good kid. I think you're going places," he said with a smile as he returned to the endless paperwork the guy in the lockup cage generated.

"Air power may either end war or end civilization."

**-Sir Winston Churchill
House of Commons, 1933**

Part Five:

Violent Turbulence

The New Millennium

Photo by Will Dempsey

Final Delivery / Will Dempsey

**Walsh Residence
1055 Tullamore Place
Alpharetta, Georgia
8:12 A.M. Eastern Time
Tuesday, September 11th, 2001**

Chapter Thirty-Four

"Pray for us, Holy Mother of God, that we may be made worthy of the promises of Christ. Amen," prayed Chris as he and Keely finished their morning rosary prayers together on the back porch. She squeezed his hand. Keely loved their custom of starting their day together in prayer. The air had a slight nip that morning, foretelling of the change of seasons from summer to fall.

Inhaling deeply, Keely stood and said, "I'll fix you some oatmeal and get the omelets started. You should have a good twenty minutes before the driver arrives."

"Thanks, love," answered Chris as he placed his rosary back in its leather pouch and stuck it in his suit pants.

Fifteen minutes later, Chris finished his coffee while looking over lease paperwork for three new Boeing 747-800 cargo jets, the remnants of his breakfast in front of him. Noting the time, he put the papers away in his attaché case, squeezed Keely's hand, lifted it to his lips, and planted a kiss on the back of her fingers.

"I know that look. You haven't even finished your breakfast. You're always like this on days the company is getting new airplanes," she said with a smile.

"Guilty as charged, sweetheart. But we really think this new model of 747 will give us some considerable savings off the bottom line," said Chris as Keely continued to smile across the table at him.

"Admit it, honey. You just like getting new airplanes. The only way I can describe you when you are talking about buying new jets for the company is like a kid on Christmas morning," said Keely as she walked around the table and kissed him on the forehead.

"You know me all too well, baby," he replied as he opened his case and made one last check that he had everything he needed for the quick daytrip to the Boeing production facilities in Seattle. The phone rang on the kitchen wall and Keely, being closest, answered it.

"Thanks so much, Charley," said Keely as she hung up the phone. "Jason is at the gate, honey," said Keely. Chris nodded and took another quick bite of his oatmeal. It would only take his driver ninety seconds to reach his driveway from the gatehouse.

Since first meeting him two years earlier, Chris always requested Jason, the young Georgia Tech aerospace studies student working his way through college driving for a car service. Chris had asked for an 8:15 a.m. pick-up time and at precisely 8:15 a.m., the doorbell rang. *That kid would make a great pilot,* he thought. Chris intended to keep tabs on the young man and ask what his post-graduation plans were.

As Chris' hand was within inches of the doorknob, Keely playfully grabbed his shirt and tie in a bunch, pulled him toward her, and gave him one more kiss. After twenty-seven years of marriage, Keely still rarely let him leave the house without kissing him goodbye and he wouldn't want it any other way. That morning kiss at the door was one of the moments in his day he treasured. Chris opened the door to find Jason smiling at him and a Lincoln Town Car with an open back passenger door sitting in the drive. Jack gave a mock salute to Chris from the back seat.

"Morning Jason, how's school?" asked Chris.

"My fluid dynamics class this semester is probably going to kill me but I'll make it, Mr. Walsh," replied the trim, tall young man wearing black slacks, starched white shirt, and black tie. Chris smiled and nodded in thanks as Jason took his rolling luggage without any further small talk. Jason knew the protocol in his job driving executive businessmen around: speak when spoken to, nothing more was the official Executive Transportation Services policy. Jason was as professional as he was timely.

Sliding into the back seat as Jason placed his bags in the trunk, Chris nodded at his partner and said, "Morning Jack. How do things look for the meeting with the DOT people next month?"

"Looks like everything will go smoothly. Legal says all our ducks are in a row for the hearings. There shouldn't be any surprises," answered Jack as he looked over a file.

As they rode, Jack looked over some documents for the meeting and Chris found himself thinking about how much he was going to enjoy personally visiting the production line of Boeing's huge manufacturing facility. He'd flown dozens of aircraft types during his lifetime but had never actually watched any of the machines being crafted. The new 747-800 aircraft was completely digitized and used computer-aided control systems known to the aviation world as "fly-by-wire". The pilots' inputs to the controls were analyzed by the computer and his intentions were refined by the system to achieve the wishes of the pilot in the most efficient manner. The most noticeable difference between the new 747-800 and previous models was the absence of the engineer's panel in the cockpit. The computer systems automatically monitored all the required areas of attention that used to be the responsibility of the engineer. With no engineer's panel was also, logically, the absence of the flight engineer, reducing the crew required from three to two during flights of less than five hours. There were still numerous planes within the VelEx stable of aircraft that required an engineer for operation, but as computers were becoming more reliable and software capabilities reaching mind-boggling efficiency, Chris mused that one day, the planes he used to ship cargo all over the world might have no humans on board at all.

While winding through neighborhood roads and onto I-85, Chris and Jack about the kids, home improvements and family events. The center partition lowered unexpectedly as Jason spoke, "I apologize for interrupting, gentleman, but I thought you might want to know that CNN is reporting a plane has just crashed into the North Tower of the World Trade Center in New York."

"What sort of plane?" asked Jack.

"They're not sure at this point other than to say that it was a twin engine aircraft of some sort."

"God help the poor guy, but how in the world do you not see the freaking World Trade Center?" said Chris with a mild tone of disgust.

"Beats me, but he won't make that mistake again," said Jack. Gallows humor wasn't uncommon among pilots, underscoring the fact that their very lives could be snuffed out in an instant by one mistake at the controls of the planes they flew. It was just part of the culture.

As the car neared the exit for the airport, the topic of conversation changed.

"Hey, you know who I've been listening to lately on the radio? That Clark Howard guy. He's really a genius about how to be smart with money."

"Yeah, I like him too. You know, he's a guy that you can tell genuinely loves helping people."

"Keely told me she heard about him at the workshop she went to about how to be a steward of your treasure."

"Well, my understanding is that good ol' Clark is doing quite well for himself. It's cool to see how God blesses people that try to give to others."

Chris thought about that. Jack always amazed him with how freely he associated so many things back to God in everyday conversations. Chris admired his friend's attribute immensely and wished he felt more comfortable doing it.

Jason took the exit for Clairmont Road and headed north toward the airport two miles ahead. Peachtree DeKalb Airport always felt like a second home to Chris and Jack. It had been the birthplace of their company before the move to the new facilities down at Hartsfield Atlanta Airport, and where Thomas Walsh learned to pilot his first plane. On the tarmac sat dozens of propeller aircraft, helicopters, and an impressive collection of multi-million dollar corporate jets.

One of the corporate jets sat gleaming in the sun with the

VelEx logo prominently displayed on the tail. The Gulfstream-V sat on the tarmac just outside the Signature Flight Support Center. Chris and Jack loved all of their company's aircraft almost like children but the G-V was one of their favorites. It was a forty-two million dollar mobile office that traveled at almost the speed of sound. Just prior to the airport entrance, Chris saw the little sign with the yellow biplane on it advertising plane rides over Atlanta. Thinking back to Thomas' tenth birthday, and the joy that Thomas had experienced taking a ride over the city, Chris knew it was the best two hundred dollars he ever spent. There was no question in his mind that the experience was what hooked Thomas on flying. Chris always enjoyed the calls he got from his son, Captain Thomas Walsh, F-16 pilot in the 27th Fighter Wing, Langley Air Force Base.

"Thanks Jason," said Chris as he took his luggage from the driver.

"My pleasure, sir. Have a good flight and I'll be here this evening to get you home," replied Jason as he handed Jack his items as well.

Chris looked down at his watch, noting they had exactly fifteen minutes to get checked in and aboard the jet to be precisely on time for their appointment with the chairman of Boeing, Keith Traxler and the Boeing account executive, Tony Oliver, whose primary responsibility was as Boeing's liaison between the aircraft manufacturer and VelEx. Sitting at the head of a company that prided itself on being on time, all the time, it would be wholly unacceptable to Chris to show up late to a meeting to discuss a multi-million dollar aircraft order.

As Chris walked into the terminal, he saw the other two executives who would be travelling with him and Jack to Seattle that morning standing in front of a television screen. Edgar Rolland, VelEx's chief financial officer was instantly recognizable in the crowd of fifteen people standing in front of the television with his mane of ponytailed, blonde hair. Next to Edgar stood the vice president of operations for VelEx, Dianne Price.

Just as Chris was about to tap on Edgar's shoulder, several people in the group gasped and one exclaimed, "Oh, my

God...that was another plane!"

Looking up at the screen, Chris saw his first view of the World Trade Center towers. A huge fireball erupted erupting from a tower in the background while smoke and flames billowed from the building in the foreground.

"Are you sure? Was that a replay of the first plane?" asked one person in the crowd.

"No, look. They're both burning! That was another plane!"

"Chris, Jack, thank God you're here. You'll never believe what's happening in New York!" exclaimed Dianne when she saw them approaching from the door.

"Wait a minute, we heard a twin-engine plane hit one of the towers. By the sound of things, it was some turboprop job," said Jack.

"No Jack, not plane, planes. Take a look," said Dianne with a tone of shock as she continued, "commercial jetliners. Boeing 767s"

Jack looked up at the screen then and gasped at what he saw.

Edgar's phone rang and he immediately answered, "Did you get out? What's going on?" Tears began to fall from his eyes as he listened, his breathing becoming rapid. His face was almost devoid of color. "I love you too, kiddo. Just stay calm and get out when you can," said Edgar. Closing his phone, he turned to Chris and said, "It's bad."

"Oh, my God," said Jack, remembering that Edgar's son, Justin, started working for Cantor Fitzgerald on the hundredth floor of the North Tower after graduating from Princeton the prior spring.

"He says they don't know how they are going to get out of the building. Everything is on fire on the floors below... he said he can see some people are...jumping," said Edgar as huge tears began to spill down the normally unflappable executive's face.

Chris tried to offer Edgar encouragement by saying, "He'll be fine. The fire people with take care of things. They have plans for this sort of emergency." Edgar was obviously in the beginning stages of shock.

"*Nobody* has plans for *this* sort of thing," said Edgar in a tone of total despair.

311

The entire room was bathed in palpable fear and shock. As they stood watching the television, almost none of the eighteen would-be passengers or five staff behind the desk said a word as everyone watched replay after replay of a video of United Flight 175 impacting the South Tower, the North Tower already clearly engulfed in flames throughout the upper floors.

"I wonder if this is Osama bin Laden again," mumbled Chris.

"Who?" asked Dianne.

"The guy who bombed the embassies in Tanzania and Kenya. The same guy who bombed the U.S.S. Cole in Yemen."

It was just an educated guess but Chris was pretty sure.

"God in heaven," said Jack, completely disregarding his normally inflexible rule of not using the Lord's name in such a fashion. Nothing about the day was normal in any way.

The comment, or at least the sentiment, was echoed by numerous people in the passenger terminal. People immediately began to call families, friends, and loved ones on their cell phones. An instantaneous wave of desire to be close to loved ones swept through the room. Chris' cell phone rang. Seeing it was the chairman of Boeing calling, he answered.

"Mr. Walsh, Keith Traxler here. I hate to say it but I think we'll have to pick another day to have you visit. I'm getting word from a friend at the FAA that they are about to ground all aircraft within US Airspace."

"Absolutely, Keith. Obviously it would be best for everyone to stay put where we are. We will reschedule as soon as possible."

Chris' next call was to Keely, who he saw had called his cell phone three times in the time it took to have his short conversation with Keith Traxler. She had been at home terrified at the events unfolding and had a tone of relief when Chris assured her that he wasn't going anywhere that morning. After hanging up with Keely, Chris turned to the other three and said, "Guys, you know we're obviously scrubbing today's trip." Just as he said it, the commentator on CNN broke in the middle of another replay of the second plane striking the South Tower and said, "We now have reports that a third plane has just crashed into the Pentagon. A long-distance shot from across the Potomac

River of the famous angular building came on the screen. A column of black smoke billowed up into the air. Another view from a closer vantage point showed a huge burning hole and the remnants of floors and offices where minutes earlier an impregnable-looking concrete wall had been.

Jack was talking quietly on his phone to Erika, trying to make sense of the whole thing while another network on another of the three televisions cut to a view of the North Tower as the floors above the inferno appeared to be moving. Just as Jack was wondering if heat waves from the fire were causing the distortion from the view of the news camera what he saw in the next second simultaneously stopped and broke his heart. The entire structure began to pancake inward and disintegrate in an image that would forever be burned into his mind and the minds of billions of people the world over.

On a different network, another announcer, with an ashen-white complexion on her face, could barely annunciate what she was trying to tell the viewers. In the most pained voice Chris could ever remember hearing used during a news broadcast, the woman said, "It appears that the North Tower has completely... collapsed...It's just...gone. It's completely gone." As she said it, her voice cracked and the network cut to another replay of the collapse. Chris looked over at Dianne who was talking with her fiancé, tears falling down her cheek. Suddenly, Edgar collapsed onto a bench. Chris, Dianne, and Jack looked at each other for an instant and immediately realized what they had just witnessed. Dianne said, "Honey, I'm fine. I'll call you back," hung up her phone, and went over to place her arm around Edgar to comfort him but Edgar seemed completely oblivious to her as he continually choked through his tears, "Please pick up...please pick up....pick up your phone!"

Chris, tough ex-Air Force pilot that he was, felt a barely-restrained wave of emotion well up in him. It was all he could do to say, "Excuse me a minute," as he walked outside fumbling with his cell phone in a vain attempt to disguise the real reason he wanted to walk away from his group of colleagues. As he walked out the sliding glass doors to the terminal, tears welled up in his eyes. The absolute horror of what was happening hit him felt like a vice squeezing his chest and negating his ability to breathe. After a few minutes and a difficult effort to regain his composure, Chris finally dried his eyes and began to walk back into the terminal. There was something particularly excruciating to watch big, beautiful jetliners used as instruments of mass homicide.

As the doors to the terminal slid apart, Chris could hear a man yelling at the young man behind the check-in desk of the terminal.

"I don't care who you have to wake up! You get the airport administrator on the phone and I want my plane fueled and delivered here in five minutes! My wife needs me at home with her now!" screamed a man at the Signature Flight employee behind the counter.

"Sir, you're not listening to what I'm saying. The FAA has just grounded *every* aircraft in the country. Even if I got you your aircraft, you won't receive clearance from the tower," said the desk attendant.

Jack walked up to Chris and whispered into his ear, "I just got off the phone with Flight Operations. The FAA just executed the SCATANA plan."

"My God," said Chris as yet another layer of fear was added to the already existing horror of the day. As former military aviators, they were both acutely aware of how unprecedented that was. The SCATANA, or Security Control of Air Traffic and Navigation Aids protocols were developed during the Cold War to be used only in a time of attack against the United States. The protocols designated that every civilian aircraft would be directed to land at the nearest available airfield without exception. SCATANA was designed to give NORAD supreme command over the United States airspace in the event of an imminent missile or bomber attack..

The man at the desk continued to harangue the clerk who, obviously already upset, was on the verge of losing his cool completely when Chris looked over at the indignant man, sighed, and walked up next to him.

"Excuse me, sir. I'm Chris Walsh, what's your name?"

The man turned sharply on his heel toward him and growled, "Are you the airport manager?"

Chris smiled as best he could, although he didn't feel much

like it, and answered, "No, I'm actually the CEO of VelEx. These are my people," as he pointed to Jack, Dianne, and Edgar who then sat with a thousand-yard stare on a nearby couch, desperately redialing on the cell phone over and over.

"Well, can you do anything to get these people to release my airplane to me? My wife is terrified at home in Tampa and I've got to get to her right now," said the man with a tone that bordered on pleading.

"I wish that were possible but I don't think anybody is flying anywhere today. I think it's going to be a very long day for everyone," said Chris. The man looked back at the clerk behind the desk, then looked over Chris' shoulder at Jack and Dianne with her arm around Edgar who still sat on a small bench, rocking back and forth and continually hanging up and redialing on his cell phone. Looking down at the ground, his shoulders slumping in defeat. he turned to the young man behind the check-in desk and said, "I'm sorry, Son. I was totally out of line. You're just doing your job."

Chris walked up to Jack and whispered, "We need to get Edgar out of here." Jack nodded and began to call Jason back to the airport. Chris began to sit with Dianne and Edgar and tried to reassure his distraught colleague with words he didn't feel any conviction in. While Jack was arranging their transportation back to their respective homes, an idea suddenly hit Chris. He turned to Jack and said, "Jack, you know, there are going to be a lot of people that will need a lot of supplies to help rescue efforts."

Jack looked at Chris and, with the first hint of a smile since the monumental tragedy had begun, said, "Make the call."

Chris retrieved his cell phone from his pocket and selected a number. It took several tries to get the call to go through because of the extraordinary number of cellular conversations overloading cellular networks throughout the country. When his call finally rang through on the eighth attempt, a woman's voice with a clearly strained sound answered, "FEMA."

"Good morning, ma'am. My name is Chris Walsh. I'm CEO of VelEx. I know he's extremely busy right now but would it be possible to speak with Director DePalma? We would like to help in any way possible."

**Langley Air Force Base
Bachelor Officer Quarters
Hampton Roads, Virginia
2113 Hours, Eastern Time
Tuesday, September 11th, 2001**

Chapter Thirty-Five

Like most people in the United States that night, Captain Thomas Walsh had the television inside his quarters tuned to one of the news channels. Almost everyone in the country that evening, and billions across the world, watched the horrifying and shocking images in their living rooms. Though it was the same video clips of the two jets impacting the World Trade Towers, their collapse, Thomas couldn't take his eyes off the screen. Adding to the unforgettable scenes from New York were frames from a Pentagon camera that had captured images as the jetliner plowed into the side of the heart of the United States military. Now a pilot in the 27th Fighter Squadron, First Fighter Wing, the oldest air wing in the United States Air Force, Thomas felt worse than he could ever remember. Intellectually, he knew there was nothing that could have been done to change the outcome of that awful day but the feeling was that he, and the rest of the community of military aviators, had failed miserably to allow such an unprecedented disaster to occur. Talking to his father on the cordless phone as he stared at the television, Thomas said, "I know there was no way to make a difference by the time we were directed to Washington, but it was the worst feeling flying combat air patrol over the capitol. We didn't know there were no more jets inbound for hours. I just kept wondering when they were going to task us with splashing a jetliner."

As Chris listened to Thomas, his son's voice lost its ever-confident fighter pilot tone and he could hear the little boy who had grown up devouring anything relating to aviation. It sounded like his heart was broken and, truthfully, it was. For Thomas, seeing airplanes used in that way was like discovering infidelity from a loved one. Thomas didn't tell his father at the time because the sentiment was just to painful to annunciate but if he could, he would have said that he just witnessed the most beautiful thing he had ever seen be used to do the ugliest thing he had ever seen.

Chris could hear the same news channel he was watching from his home office broadcasting in the background of his son's quarters, six hundred miles away.

On his office TV, images of a smoldering hole in the ground in a remote field filled the screen with a crawler denoting the location as Shanksville, Pennsylvania. It was only within the last hour that images from the fourth lost jet began to show up on all the news channels.

On the couch next to him, Keely sat with a bottle of water, curled up underneath a blanket. Turning to Chris she asked, "But where is the plane? I mean aren't there usually engines or parts of the wings or tail or something left when a jet crashes?"

Chris looked at the image, saw the hole in the ground, and tried to imagine how a two hundred ton jetliner could be reduced to nothing more than a handful of dollar and plate-sized metallic fragments around the crater. As a pilot, he realized the jet must have plowed directly into the ground at a nearly ninety-degree angle to the Earth. Turning to Keely, seeing the look of shock and dismay at the day's events on her face, he decided she didn't need to know that particular detail.

She looked at him, reached for the phone, and said, "Let me speak to him for a minute."

"Your mother wants to talk with you, " said Chris as he handed her the phone and sat, staring at the screen, not really absorbing any of the images or information anymore. Chris had seen enough of the footage of the day's events to burn the horrible images into his consciousness for the rest of his life.

Keely, with tears on her cheeks, kept saying, "I know, I know. I'm so glad you're safe. I know...."

After a few minutes, Keely handed the phone back to Chris. Hearing Thomas' voice, Chris could tell he'd been sharing a good cry with his mother on the phone. Thomas tried to reign in the powerful emotions to sound strong for his dad, though.

"I'm so sorry you had to go through this ordeal today, Thomas. Just know we are so proud of you."

Thomas' voice cracked again and he tried unsuccessfully to say something. A moment later, in a voice more pained than Chris had ever heard come from his son's mouth, Thomas finally managed to choke out the words, "This is just *wrong*, sir."

"I know it is, Son. I know it is." A moment later, Chris heard Thomas release a big sigh.

"They're giving me and my wingman forty-eight hours leave to cool down after today. Everyone else is on alert right now...just in case they try to come at us with foreign jetliners."

"Is that considered a realistic threat right now?"

"Who knows? Rules of engagement now dictate that if a jetliner comes within two hundred miles of the U.S. and fails to immediately respond over the radio, it will be intercepted by fighters. If it fails to acknowledge the fighter interceptors, it will be shot down. One radio hail, that's all."

Chris thought about that and it suddenly hit him that the United States was at war. Unfortunately, it wasn't exactly clear with whom. Being a man who paid attention to world events, he had a pretty strong suspicion.

"Are you going to see Grace?"

"Yeah, I called her just after debriefing when the air wing commander told me to take forty-eight hours. She's up to her eyeballs over at the Bureau but I'm driving up to see her tonight.

"I'm sure she'll be thrilled to see you."

"I'm sure I'll be thrilled to see her."

After two years of stellar performance in her hometown, Grace had caught the attention of some very senior FBI officials in Washington and was reassigned to headquarters.

During his past eight years in the Air Force, Thomas and Grace had seen each other on two separate occasions when he was on leave while visiting his parents. Sitting on the porch one night at the Walsh residence, talking late into the evening, both Thomas and Grace knew it was still there. Their feelings for each other were even stronger than they were before going separate ways back in college. They were still intensely drawn to each other. Unfortunately, the last time Thomas had seen her, he was about to be deployed to King Khalid Military City to fly side-by-side with the Royal Saudi Air Force for a year.

When Captain Walsh returned from Saudi Arabia and assigned to the 27th Fighter Squadron at Langley Air Force Base in Hampton Roads. Grace had transferred to Washington only a month earlier. While unpacking boxes in her new place, Grace's phone rang one evening after a particularly frustrating day. Her frustration turned to joy when Thomas told her he was about to be stationed two hours south of her. They promised to get together for dinner the moment he returned to the U.S. Since that phone call the prior spring, they had gotten together for many dinners in fact.

"Alright, Thomas. Go see Grace. We love you both."

"Roger that, sir."

Chris placed the phone softly in its cradle and turned to look at Keely. Finding the television remote that had slipped between the couch cushions, Chris dug it out and turned the TV off. She looked at him for a moment as if to protest, and they both realized they had seen enough of the tragedy that day.

"Let's go to bed."

Without a word she stood. When he stood up, she put her arms around him and nestled her head on his shoulder. He held his wife, his hand caressing the back of her head to comfort her, whispering, "It's going to be alright, honey. I promise."

What Chris couldn't know right then, was that it wasn't the first time Keely had ever seen sudden explosive violence take lives. She had seen it firsthand as a teenager but even after twenty-seven years of marriage, she never told him. The events of that day brought all the pain from her past back with excruciating clarity. She needed him at that moment more than anything but couldn't bring herself to talk about the past. Every time she began to, a wave of paralyzing emotional pain overrode her ability to speak.

As Chris lay in bed next to Keely he took comfort in the conversation with Director DePalma of FEMA that morning. VelEx had made available several aircraft to assist in any way necessary to the agency. He prayed there would be some survivors found in the wreckage in New York.

There hadn't been yet.

In Virginia, Thomas left his quarters, walking down the corridor with a white, highly-polished floor leading to the foyer. In the entryway, the unit insignia of the 27th Fighter Squadron was inlaid in the tile. Still wearing his flight suit, as it turned out to be a perfect garment for keeping him the right temperature for riding his motorcycle, Thomas nodded at the airman at the front desk before pushing on the door.

"Be safe, Captain," said the airman as he saw the motorcycle helmet in the pilot's hand.

Thomas stopped in his tracks, snapped out of the string of thoughts about the day's events, and turned to the airman who was no more than twenty. Smiling as best as he could manage, he said, "You too. Don't work too hard tonight."

Thomas exited the building, heading to the lot where his motorcycle sat. Walking out into the cool Virginia night, he noticed the eerie absence of the sound of jet engines and looked skyward to witness the total lack of navigation lights normally blinking above. The little details in life were amplified by the adrenaline still in his system from the stresses of his mission that day.

It was a two hour ride to Grace's condominium in Alexandria at the speed limit. The Kawasaki Ninja bike he owned, however, wasn't made to putter along at a mere sixty-five miles an hour. Thomas figured if stopped by any police officer, his uniform and a quick explanation would get him out of a ticket.

He was right.

Twenty miles south of Fredericksburg, the blue flashing lights of the Virginia Highway Patrol erupted from a stand of trees. Seeing them in his rear view, Thomas quickly throttled the bike down and went from slightly over one hundred miles an hour to zero in a quarter of a mile.

"Sir, I pulled you over because I paced you at a little over one hundred miles an hour. Is there a particular reason you were going that fast?" asked the trooper as he eyed the flight suit.

"Trooper, if you could have pulled me over the first time I had to come this way this morning, you would have paced me at seven times that speed."

"Is that right?"

Thomas looked at the trooper and said, "It wasn't fast enough then."

Both men, wearing uniforms that identified them as guardians of American citizens, albeit in different capacities, looked each other in the eye. The trooper was a sharp young ex-military policeman who immediately knew what Thomas meant.

"My girlfriend lives in Alexandria and I have a forty-eight hour pass."

The trooper processed what Thomas had said and looked over his uniform once more, noting the 27th Fighter Squadron patch on the sleeve.

"Just slow it down a bit...at least until you get out of my patrol sector which ends five miles up the road, Captain."

"Thanks, Trooper."

Twenty-two minutes later, Thomas turned into Grace's condo development. The sound of his bike in her drive brought her running to the front door. Even before he could get his helmet off, she had thrown her arms around him, holding him tightly as they stood silently in her drive.

Karen Pollard, an older neighbor, who had been annoyed at the sound of the bike at such a late hour, went to her window to glare. Upon seeing the tall, handsome man in the flight suit dismount from his motorcycle and take the nice girl from across the street into his arms, her rancor subsided. She thought back to her Ernie who, having taken off in his F-4 Phantom on January 3, 1968 from the deck of the U.S.S. Forestall aircraft carrier, had never came back from a mission over Viet Nam. September 11th had been a melancholy day of such reminiscing about who and what was really important in her life with the shocking demonstration of how lives could be ended or unalterably changed in seconds. She watched as the two young folks, a generation younger than her, went with hands intertwined inside the condo across the street.

"I begged my supervisor and he finally agreed to let me come in by noon tomorrow. I don't know when I'll get to leave," said Grace as she held Thomas' hands sitting at the kitchen table.

"It doesn't matter. I'd have come if only to see you for five minutes."

She smiled a weary smile. It had been a long day but Grace always took comfort in seeing Thomas. It was as if everything in her life could be unpredictable but he was a constant. She always knew she could count on him no matter what.

"We're pretty sure it was Osama bin Laden," she said as she took a sip of the coffee.

"That's the general consensus from people I've talked with too. It wouldn't be surprising to be deployed to Incirlik in Turkey then."

The words out of Thomas' mouth made her heart sink. Their love for each other was growing each day and Grace often thanked God for the gift of Thomas coming back into her life when he did. Secretly, she was willing to give up her position at the Bureau if it meant being with him, but they hadn't discussed long-term plans as of yet. Neither of them had broached the topic of moving into a different stage of courtship quite yet.

"You just got here. I mean I know it's only been a year but the idea of you going off to some foreign land a half a world apart again just doesn't seem fair."

"This was the work of some seriously bad people, babe. If it really was bin Laden, then you know how the U.S. will respond to wipe him off the face of the earth."

She knew what he said was true and, although it sounded right to her, something inside was a little saddened at hearing it out loud. She sighed, knowing the next few months were going to be off-the-charts busy at the J. Edgar Hoover building. Shaking the thoughts from her head, Grace looked at Thomas, smiled, and said, "Well, right now I just want to sit here with you."

Thomas and Grace talked for another ten minutes speculating

about what would happen next in regard to the United States' response to the attack. Nothing of that scope and magnitude had occurred during either of their lifetimes. The fact that, in their respective positions, they had the most opportunity to actually do something about the people that perpetrated the attacks gave both a small measure of comfort but neither wanted to talk any more about it. At Grace's door, Thomas held her and kissed her gently.

"Ok, then, mister. I'll see you tomorrow morning at 0800 hours sharp," she said as her heart raced.

"Count on it," he said as he fished his keys from the leg pocket of his flight suit.

She felt a mixture of joy and sadness as she watched him start the motorcycle.

He hated leaving her but needed to get to the Courtyard Marriott on Washington Street down by the Potomac before he got too tired to drive safely. He always stayed there when he visited.

The next morning, Thomas sat on one of Grace's deck chairs enjoying the smell of coffee wafting through the air. The morning was cool and both of them sat out on her back porch, holding hands and talking quietly.

"There is a nine a.m. Mass at Saint Patrick's up the road if you'd like to go."

"That sounds great but I'd just like to sit here another minute with you if that's ok."

"Absolutely, baby." Thomas sat quietly and finished his coffee. Again, he looked skyward and the normal presence of jets and contrails across the sky was unsettlingly absent in an area with no fewer than ten civilian and military airfields concentrated within a forty mile radius from him.

An hour and a half later, Thomas sat in his flight suit, freshly shaven, holding Grace's hand while the priest concluded his homily. The olive-drab Nomex suit with his unit insignia and American flag velcroed to the shoulders got a few stares from other parishioners as he and Grace had walked down the aisle to a pew. Thomas looked down at Grace's soft, manicured hand in his and sighed. He had a strong suspicion that sooner rather than later, his squadron would be deployed to hit areas where Osama bin Laden and his *Al Qaeda* thugs were suspected to be hiding in Afghanistan. Once again, he and Grace would be parting ways.

    Father Michael O'Grady stood that Wednesday morning before a church filled with more people than he had ever seen in Mass other than on Christmas or Easter. There were certainly more than he had ever seen during a weekday Mass. Most parishioners wore a look of shock, weariness, and fear as they listened to Father O'Grady preach from the pulpit.
    "I know what I'm about to say might not be popular. I am, however, not in the business of popular but in the business of what's good for the soul. I know what I'm about to say would sound like utter lunacy to those living by the rules of *this* world, but we are called to live by *God's* rules and those rules include absolute forgiveness. That includes forgiveness even for those who perpetrated this abomination against the United States. I am not, in any way, trying to minimize what these spiritually sickened people did yesterday. Of course we all pray for those that have lost their lives in this attack. I truly believe though, that the people who perpetrated this horrible attack on us weren't born the monsters they became. Like so many of us, these people have apparently found themselves cut off from the true will of God. The scary proposition about this is that they feel they actually *are* doing the will of God. Does anyone here think that if these lost souls had been truly walking hand-in-hand with the God of forever and infinite love, they would have been capable of these atrocities?"
    Father O'Grady could almost physically feel the immeasurable rage and sadness in the church over the attacks, but he truly hoped he had redirected the consciousness of the congregation from the path of human hatred. He had no delusions about changing the perspective of everyone in Mass that morning but he prayed he could reach some. It was something that the former Navy chaplain had prayed for years about: finding some way to reach the hearts of those consumed with the disease of hatred. He had begged God on more than one occasion to show him how to help break the never ending cycle of violence, retribution, and more violence that mankind had lived with since before recorded

history began.

Sensing a small shift in the collective emotions of the parishioners gathered, he continued, "I don't have any immediate solutions for what happened and what to do next but I'd like to propose something so counterintuitive that you might think I've gone crazy. The rules of our world say that this act requires a terrible price to be paid by the ones responsible."

Heads nodded throughout the church.

Holding up the Bible, Father O'Grady said, "What the rules in *this* book, written by God through the pens of His disciples across the ages say is that we should pray for our enemies. I challenge you to try to pray for the souls of those sad, lonely, rage-addicted people that were obviously not walking hand-in-hand with the sunlight of the Spirit when they chose to fly planes into buildings and an empty field. I'd also like to suggest that praying for them doesn't include advice to our Father about how exactly to fix them. We didn't choose them as enemies. They chose us. I'm not saying you have to approve of what these hate-filled people have done. I'm suggesting that we pray that those who hurt all of us so badly can feel the unconditional love of God. Doing that means I can work past my rage over these events and not become *exactly* like them."

Father O'Grady stood motionless for almost ten seconds to let that sink in. Finally, he motioned for everyone to stand, and said, "Let us profess our faith by saying..." The church began reciting the Nicene Creed.

As Thomas stood there, saying the words he had thousands of times throughout his life, holding the hand of the woman he knew in his heart was his best friend and the woman he couldn't imagine living the rest of his life without, the words of the priest bounced back and forth in his mind. When he thought about the awful experience of the prior day, a part of him wanted nothing more than to be at twenty thousand feet with his thumb poised over the bomb-release button on his stick. His intellect told him that unless the United States eliminated the sociopaths responsible, more attacks were inevitable. From another place within him, however, came a voice. The words were so clear he almost turned around to see if someone had actually said them when he heard, *They kill you and you kill them…when does it stop?*

Thomas looked over at Grace and she, feeling his stare, looked back. As they sat down, her FBI badge mounted on a leather holder sat on her left hip. Her I.D. credentials which gave her access to some of the most sensitive areas within the J. Edgar Hoover FBI headquarters building hung on a lanyard around her neck and a Glock .40 caliber sat in a holster on her hip. Grace had never talked much about her work in any specific terms. The dark nature of her profession had begun to age her appearance slightly. In the past year Thomas had been formally courting Grace, several strands of gray hairs had begun to show up, intermixed in her locks of blonde.

In that very instant, Thomas thought about how quickly life could end. The prior day's events had made that all too clear.

Right then, looking over at Grace, he made a decision.

Thomas and Grace stood, holding each other next to her Tahoe in the church parking lot. Her arms around his shoulders, he smiled at her, their eyes locked together.

"I've got to head back to the base by 1400 hundred hours tomorrow. If you don't finish up too late, can we have dinner?" he asked as she was climbing into her Chevy Tahoe.

"I'd love to. I just have no idea when or if I'll be finished tonight."

"Fine, I don't care what time. Just call me at the hotel if you can. I completely understand if you can't."

"I will, sweetheart."

She slid into the driver's seat of her Tahoe and rolled the window down. As she leaned out of the window to say something, he leaned in and kissed her on the cheek.

She loved it when he did that.

As soon as she drove out of sight, Thomas retrieved his cell phone from the leg pocket of his flight suit and called his father.

"Hey, Son, is everything alright?"

"Yeah, Dad, given the circumstances, you know, everything's fine. So, lemme' ask you something…do you know anybody who knows anything about diamond rings?"

**Residence of Grace Lee
Cambridge Court Condominiums
Alexandria, Virginia
6:55 P.M. Eastern Time
Friday, July 22nd, 2002**

Chapter Thirty-Six

The street outside was lined with mini-vans, family SUVs, station wagons, and one ultra-efficient gas hybrid vehicle. These were the personal vehicles of the FBI agents and intelligence analysts, as opposed to the official vehicles they often used. Had this been a raid on a suspected terrorist, bank robber, or other nefarious individual who had come under investigation of the Federal Bureau of Investigation, the street would have been clogged by a collection of Crown Victorias, Suburbans, and Tahoes with radio antennas protruding from them and the telltale blue and red lights behind the front grills of the vehicles. On this day, agents and analysts of the FBI converged on 1270 Kiverton Place but instead of pistols, shotguns, submachine guns, and the announcement of a federal warrant, they came with covered dishes, bottles of wine, and gifts.

"John, Valerie, come in. I'm so pleased you could make it," said Grace in her most syrupy, southern voice after opening the door for the eighteenth time.

"You look wonderful, Grace! What a cute dress!" exclaimed Valerie.

"So do you, Val. How long now?"

"Next month. The due date is the twentieth but I don't know if this little Mia Hamm in here will wait that long."

Grace laughed in the way all women do when discussing maternal matters. She wore a Lilly Pulitzer sea-green print dress purchased at the boutique in Tyson's Corner. The designer dress, a departure from the conservatively wardrobed FBI agent she normally presented to the world, looked spectacular on the sculpted figure she kept with daily three-mile runs and martial arts training. As she was off-duty, her service weapon and credentials were locked away in a gun safe upstairs in her bedroom. The dress wouldn't have left anywhere to secure them, had she a reason to.

"We wouldn't miss this for the world, kiddo," said Special Agent John Durkin, who had befriended Grace the first day she had been transferred to FBI Headquarters. Durkin was the second-most experienced agent in counterterrorism and without his guidance on how to navigate the political waters at the Hoover building, Grace would undoubtedly have made some serious mistakes. John had personally seen to it that she hadn't.

"You look wonderful, Grace. I absolutely love that dress on you. I'd buy it for myself but, well, you know," said John's wife Valerie as she placed her hand on her stomach. Inside, the third little child in their family was quickly growing.

From behind Grace, a deep but playful voice said, "She looks great even in those Brooks Brothers uniforms all you Bureau people wear. Leaning around Grace's shoulder, Captain Thomas Walsh planted a playful kiss on her cheek. Thomas wore a pair of khaki slacks and a black polo-style shirt with the 27th Fighter Squadron insignia embroidered on the chest. Hanging above the front door was a sign that read, "Welcome home Thomas!" that Grace had joyfully hung that morning.

Thomas had arrived at Ronald Regan International Airport early that afternoon. It had taken almost thirty-eight hours to make his way from Incirlik Airbase in Turkey back to the United States with an aircraft problem in England. After the hour-long drive from the airport to her condo in Alexandria, Thomas had called his father in Atlanta and had a hushed and brief conversation.

"Yeah, Son, I'm bringing it."

"Well, can you provide me a tracking number there, Dad?"

"That's very funny. We're heading to PDK now and should touch down in about two hours. See you in about three."

"Love you, Dad."

"Love you too. Hey, Son?"

"Yeah?"

"I'm so proud of you."

"I know but thanks for saying it."

The entire party was both a reunion for Thomas, Grace, and their respective families, and an opportunity for Grace to get to know the people she worked so many thousands of hours with after the September 11th attacks in a more social setting. Thomas was relying on his father to bring an important item that had been sitting in the family safe since before his unit's rapid deployment to Incirlik in support of Operation Anaconda in Afghanistan. His squadron was rotating back to Langley Air Force Base with a much more combat-experienced group of men than had deployed the prior October. As much as a reunion, the party was a celebration of Thomas' safe return to the United States. He and his fighter squadron had dropped thousands of precision guided bombs on the Taliban fighters entrenched in the most hostile country the United States military had ever operated in.

The Taliban government was disbanded and, in its place, was an infant democracy headed by a politically-connected former CIA operative named Hamid Karazai. Many Americans had been introduced to the bearded, intelligent-looking man during the State of the Union Address the prior January.

As the doorbell rang again, Grace said to John and Valerie, "There's plenty to eat and drink in the kitchen you guys. Make yourselves at home."

"Thanks, Grace. It's a real pleasure to meet you, Thomas. Grace has told us so much about you," replied John.

"Yeah. We're so glad you're back," added Victoria.

John and Victoria headed into the living room to join the forty-plus other friends and colleagues of Grace.

Thomas looked into Grace's sapphire-colored eyes, smiled, and kissed her hand as she was about to head to the door. Grace squeezed Thomas' hand and said, "Duty calls. Be right back."

Grace answered the door to find her neighbor standing on the step. Karen was in her mid-sixties, wearing a black, knit St. John suit and pearls stood at the doorstep.

"Come in, Karen. I'm so glad you could make it. Thomas, this is Karen Pollard. She's my neighbor across the street."

The woman looked at Thomas and, seeing the fighter squadron insignia on his chest, a small smile formed on her lips. It was forced. She looked at the handsome man with the piercing eyes looking back at her and felt a slight mix of envy and longing. Through the feelings, she managed to say, "I'm so happy you made it home safely. Your Grace is a lovely girl. She's told me so much about you." As she said it, there was a slight quiver in her voice.

"Are you alright, Karen?" asked Grace.

Karen looked at her, smiled, and said, "Yes, dear. I'm fine. I was just thinking about Ernie for a moment."

It had been forty years and a day didn't go by when she didn't think about him. Karen still missed him—at times intensely. Seeing the handsome young pilot of the next generation standing before her had reminded her of her bittersweet past.

"Can I get you anything?" asked Grace.

She smiled again, and said, "Well, it is a bit warm. I would love a little drink."

"Let me show you to the kitchen. I'm sure we can accommodate you."

Thomas just nodded when Grace caught his eyes and, without having to say anything, let him know she was going to spend a few minutes making her neighbor comfortable at the party.

Returning to his seat on one of the couches, Thomas listened as two other agents talked animatedly about another painful point in American history.

"Yeah but McVeigh wasn't exactly a brain surgeon. He almost crashed the truck because the cab of the truck filled with smoke from the fuse. Guess he didn't plan that out too well."

"That's what I'm saying. My theory is that he didn't do any of the planning at all. He was just a malleable rageaholic that Terry Nichols used. Everybody keeps calling it the birth of domestic terrorism but I've got my doubts about that."

"What are you saying, Steve?"

"I'm saying that Terry Nichols was ex-Navy. He married a Filipino woman and when we interrogated him, he wouldn't explain why he went to the Philippines by himself a year before the attack in Oklahoma City."

"Why would that be so unusual that he went to the Philippines if he was married to a Filipino woman?"

"Because he went alone."

The younger agent sat for a moment, considering that, and then asked, "And what would that have anything to do with Oklahoma City?"

Thomas sat quietly, intently listening to the conversation as the older, grey-haired agent who worked counterterrorism continued to talk to the much younger agent that worked in the forensic laboratory.

"Because when Filipinos living in the United States go back to visit, they *all* go-the entire family. Terry going alone without his wife was more than unusual. For me, it was a serious red flag. I'm not leveling any specific allegations here or making a definitive statement of guilt but from an analyst's perspective, it wouldn't be completely implausible that Nichols could have gone to the island of Mindanao and met with some bad guys."

Thomas interjected with, "Oh, where the *Abu Saayef* are operating out of, right?" referring to the Islamic terrorist group in the Philippines known to have some association with the larger, more recognizable organization known as *Al Qaeda*.

Both agents turned, noticing for the first time that Thomas had sat next to them. Steve, the older agent, realizing that he might be talking out of school a bit about sensitive Bureau information, smiled and nodded at Thomas, and in an effort to change the subject, said, "So, Thomas, you must feel good getting back home, huh?"

Thomas smiled and answered, "Yeah, it's great to see Grace again. Reminds me what it's all for."

Satisfied that the subject had been successfully changed, Steve started to ask Thomas about his trip back to the U.S. when Thomas cut him off and asked, "So you think Terry Nichols might have been helping Islamic terrorists?"

Steve smiled a moment, formulating his answer and realizing he had been a bit more talkative then he had intended in front of an outsider.

"I didn't exactly say that."

"But you did say he might have met with the *Abu Saayef,* right?"

Steve smirked as he cursed inwardly. He hadn't been discussing anything classified or anything verifiable, but it was still not considered good form in the Bureau to talk shop around just anyone. It wouldn't be considered prudent by FBI standards even if that anyone had a top secret security clearance, was entrusted with operating a thirty million dollar piece of government property, and was one of the thousands of men and women who were going directly into harm's way to protect the United States from regimes that sponsor terrorism. Just as Steve was about to attempt to dismiss the entire conversation again, he was rescued by Grace reappearing from the kitchen with a Jamaican Red Stripe beer opened for Thomas and a small glass of wine in her own hand.

"You looked like you might be a bit thirsty, babe," she said.

Thomas smiled at Grace and took the beer, taking a small sip and enjoying his first taste of beer in over eight months. Not a big drinker to begin with, Thomas never drank while deployed and flying combat sorties.

"I think I'll go refresh my drink as well," said Steve as he stood.

"Me too," said the younger agent Steve had been talking with.

"Good, now there's room for me," said Grace as she came around the couch and sat next to Thomas, leaning against him and intertwining her fingers with his. She gently rested her right foot on his shin and he smiled.

"I love it when you do that," he said.

"Lets everyone in the room know who I'm with," she answered with a warm smile. He looked down at the delicate, French-manicured fingers between his and thought how absurd it was that the same fingers could expertly curl around the trigger of her Glock service weapon and place a group of ten shots within a three inch grouping at fifteen yards. She had displayed that talent once to Thomas at a local firing range. Thomas considered himself a competent shot, but in Grace's hands, a pistol was an instrument played with the same level of skill with which Yitzhak Pearlman drew a bow across the strings of a Stradivarius. Thankfully, she had never had occasion to fire her weapon in the line of duty and she prayed she never had to.

As the party continued, a shuffling stereo system kept a selection of light jazz playing as the conversations throughout the condominium wafted through the air. Everything from family news, vacation plans, and plenty of shop talk dominated the festivity. The doorbell rang again as Thomas was recounting a mission where he and his wingman simultaneously dropped a new generation of guided bomb right down the throat of a cave opening where numerous Taliban fighters had been operating from.

Grace squeezed his hand, stood and went to answer the door.

"We had just received the BLU-119 that uses a new type of explosive. Some little lady up the road at Pauxtent Naval Station had been developing these things to deal with the cave problem."

Patty Vickers, a friend of Grace's from her women's guild at church, asked, "What was the problem with the caves? Couldn't you guys hit them with the same bombs we used in the first Gulf War that went right down airshafts?"

Thomas turned to the young woman and said, "Sure we could hit them but the problem with conventional explosives is that the blast wave dissipates quickly. Even inside a cave. The weapons designers developed a new type of explosive for the bombs where the pressure wave from the detonation kept its force for quite a long way. They are called 'thermobaric' weapons. Basically a bad guy can hide in a cave as deeply as he wants. When we drop one of those things down the opening, it's all over."

From the door, Thomas heard Grace's voice say, "Hi, Daddy, Mom, Mr. and Mrs. Walsh."

Turning around and seeing his father and mother with Grace's parents, Jack and Erika, Thomas smiled at Patty and the others sitting around listening to his combat stories and said, "Excuse me for a second." He stood and went to greet the parents at the front door.

"Hi guys, was it a good...," was all he managed to say before Chris grabbed him and lifted him completely off the ground in a bear hug. "Been working out there, Dad?" asked Thomas with a laugh when Chris put him down.

"Yeah, Son. Actually, I have. Good to see you."

As if it was choreographed, Keely and Erika leaned in and simultaneously planted kisses on Thomas' cheeks. The shows of affection made the tough fighter pilot blush and several of Grace's friends and colleagues easily noticed his face redden. It elicited a wave of laughter from those nearby. As the laughter subsided, Grace reached for the two overnight bags Erika and Keely had deposited on the floor and said, "Let me take your stuff to the bedroom and introduce you around."

Erika reached for hers and replied, "Love, let me carry these. Just lead the way."

"Mom, I'm a federal agent and I can bench press my own weight. In my home, I do the heavy lifting."

Sitting on a nearby couch with his wife, Special Agent Durkin heard the exchange and said, "Dr. Lee, with all due respect, Ma'am, I'd advise you to allow Special Agent Lee to do what she wants. We've all found it goes a lot smoother at the Bureau when she gets her way." Grace, blushing slightly but wearing a large smile, headed down the hallway with the bags to a guest bedroom where purses and other items had been left. Erika, Jack and Keely followed her. Chris hung back and placed his arm around his son's shoulders. As soon as the other three were out of view, Chris reached into his pocket and produced a small, square box.

"Now, Son, if I can just get your signature on this form," said his father with a grin.

Noticing that Special Agent Durkin was whispering to his wife Valerie, and realizing that he must have seen the handoff, Thomas looked at the agent and said, "I trust you'll keep this quiet, right Special Agent Durkin?"

The seasoned FBI agent smiled back and said, "Keep what quiet?"

"Now I'm not sure exactly when you were planning to ask, but before you do, there's one thing you have to do," said Chris.

"What?"

"Go and have a little chat with Jack."

"Oh, yeah. Right."

"Have you said anything to him yet?"

"Not a word."

"Thanks, Dad."

Jack, Erika, Keely, and Grace were coming out of the guest bedroom. The ladies were remarking about how lovely the condominium was looking. Jack was just listening, without much to add to the conversation until Erika turned to him and asked, "Doesn't her place look wonderful, honey?"

Jack looked around and replied, "Sure does. It looks really nice."

All three women shared a girl moment, laughing at the predictably compliant male response to rating the décor.

"Mr. Lee, let me show you the view from the back yard, if you have a second," said Thomas, meeting up with the group in the hallway.

Thankful for the opportunity to break away from the interior décor discussion, Jack said, "Yeah, sure. Let's go."

The two men walked through the kitchen and made their way through the crowd surrounding the granite island and, reaching the patio door, Thomas slid it open. Sitting on a chair outside, by herself, was the neighbor, Karen, enjoying a three-finger tumbler of scotch.

"Hey, Mrs. Pollard, this is Grace's dad, Jack Lee," said Thomas to the older woman. She looked up and smiled.

"Why hello there Mr. Lee. Nice to meet you. If you'd like a seat, I was just getting up to find the powder room."

She stood, smiled, and began to pull on the glass door. Thomas easily slid it open for her. Unexpectedly, Karen reached up and gently patted him on the cheek then walked past and headed inside. Jack watched the kindness and smiled. Thomas slid the door closed again, turned toward Jack, and took a seat with his heart pounding almost as much as during a six-G turn in his jet.

"Mr. Lee, I've been thinking about this for a long time and, well, I'd like to ask you something…"

Without hesitation, Jack said, "The answer is yes. You have

my blessing. Her mother and I have watched you treat Grace with love and respect for twenty years. So the answer is yes. If you intend to ask her to marry you, you have both mine and her mother's blessing."

"Her mom knows?"

"Do you really think a woman like Erika wouldn't figure it out? She doesn't miss much."

With a long exhale of relief, Thomas said, "Thanks Mr. Lee. Now there's one more person I have to ask," he said with a smile.

Jack exclaimed, "You mean right now?!?"

Thomas reached into his pocket, retrieved the box and, looking over his shoulder to make sure nobody else in the condo full of highly-observant people saw, he opened the little box and displayed its contents. Inside sat a size-six platinum ring. Along the shank was a line of small, prong-set diamonds and in the center sat a radiant-cut, three carat stone that brilliantly shimmered in the sun.

With a grin, Thomas stood and said, "I actually had a plan in place for tomorrow morning, Mr. Lee. I think it will be the most appropriate place for it."

"Care to give me any hints?"

"Now, Mr. Lee, I know you can keep a secret but I think I'm going to play my cards a little close to the chest, if it's all the same to you."

Highway U.S. 1 and on-ramp to Highway 495
One mile south of Alexandria, Virginia
8:47 A.M. Eastern Time
Saturday, July 23rd, 2002

Chapter Thirty-Seven

"Baby, are you sure you want to spend your first full day back home in the cockpit of another airplane? I'd have guessed you would have had your fill of it over Afghanistan. Besides, what could possibly be so interesting about flying those little propeller planes when you can hop into a jet that can go twice the speed of sound?"

Grace sat lazily in the passenger seat of her own Tahoe while Thomas took the on-ramp to the 495 Beltway heading east toward the Potomac River. Smiling back at her, he took her hand in his as he listened to the navigation system tell him to continue on the highway for the next three miles.

"It kind of reminds me of what hooked me on flying in the first place. It's just the purest elements of aviation. In my jet, I have to constantly monitor a bunch of complicated computer systems. It may look like a fighter pilot is simply sitting in the cockpit, pushing the rudder petals and stick around, but flying a high-performance jet requires an amazing amount of work from well before I get in the jet till well after I shut the engines down and climb out of the cockpit. Flying a Cessna 172 is just relaxing for me. I just love the fact that closing the flight plan in a Cessna doesn't require a two hour debriefing."

337

A month before his squadron was to rotate back to Langley Air Force Base, Thomas had logged on to his internet Skype account, donned his headset, and had a nice conversation with the owner of the ATC Flight Training School about his intentions. A former Viet Nam era pilot of highly classified electronics intelligence missions over Laos in the EC-47 himself, Jim Strong was thrilled to be talking directly to one of the brave aviators flying over hostile skies during the current war. After hearing Captain Walsh's plan for one of his school's Cessna trainers, Jim was so thrilled he offered the rental for free, only asking that Thomas pay for the aviation gas for the day.

"Mr. Strong, you really don't need to do that. I'll be happy to pay the rental fee on your website as long as you'll have a plane available that day."

"Captain Walsh, you just get down here with the little lady, fuel it up, and I won't hear another word about the matter. Besides, I outrank you. It's Major Strong, or at least it was when I quit flying out of *Bien Tuy* Airbase back before you were born."

"Well that's really kind of you, sir."

"Think of it as my way of saying thanks for taking the fight to those people that declared war on our country, Son."

As Thomas and Grace crossed over the fabled river that George Washington crossed on a frigid night two and a quarter centuries earlier and entered Maryland, Thomas' chest filled with a warm glow thinking of the small box secretly stowed in the very bottom pocket of his Swiss Army backpack.

"So come on, baby, where exactly are you taking me?" asked Grace as they turned onto Airport Drive. On either side of the fence lining the drive were dozens of general aviation aircraft sitting on the tarmac as Thomas scanned the buildings looking for the flight school.

"I told you. It's a surprise. It's classified."

Slipping her arm through the crook of Thomas' muscular arm, Grace cooed in her best southern belle affectation, "You know sweetie, I have a TS/SCI clearance. The only person with a higher clearance level than me sits in the Oval Office. I think you can trust me with the details."

338

"Yeah, but if I wanted to clear you into this operation beforehand, I would have. You know how it goes: need to know and all that. Nice try, honey."

"Never forget for a second that the federal government trusts me with its deepest secrets and relies on my professional ability to piece information together. I bet I figure out what your game is before we even leave the ground."

Thomas smirked.

"I've got a strange feeling of déjà-vu, babe," said Grace.

"You mean the flight to Jacksonville when we were kids, right? I was just thinking about that."

"Wasn't that just an amazing weekend? Do you remember the shark my dad caught on the beach that afternoon?"

Thomas nodded thinking about the huge shark Jack had hooked and landed on the beach during that weekend down at the little resort in Ponte Vedra, Florida almost a decade earlier. A small crowd had gathered around Jack as the surfcasting rod he had been fishing with bowed over under the strain of the two hundred pound fish stripping line off the reel. After an hour of walking up and down the beach fighting the fish, his audience growing as beachgoers and a few beachfront homeowners had come to see what the commotion was about, Jack finally dragged the fish to within a few feet of the water's edge. Thomas remembered the feeling of dread in his stomach as he saw the dark, thrashing shape in the water and the first good look at the ten-foot long bull shark on the end of the line.

"How you going to get that thing out of the water Mr. Lee?" he had asked.

"Out of the water? That thing has teeth! I'm doing no such thing. I just want to get my lure back if I can."

A guy well into his sixties with the leathery skin of a lifelong Floridian beachgoer snickered next to Jack.

"Got any suggestions?" Jack had asked after glancing at the guy with the Southern Kingfish Association tee-shirt, Columbia fishing shirt, and Guy Harvey belt with colorful images of numerous saltwater trophy fish embroidered on it. Steve Hotvet, a local charter fishing boat captain who happened to be walking off the prior night's hangover on the beach took a drag off his cigarette, smiled, and said, "Well, forget about the lure, mister. That's a bull shark and you give it half a chance, it will take a chunk out of you no matter how tired it looks. You want to do this the easy way or the hard way?"

"Easy way."

Without a second's hesitation, the salty old-timer pulled a folding knife, snapped it open, grabbed the line, and with a flick of the wrist severed it.

The shark had lain five feet offshore for almost a full minute, its dorsal fin protruding completely out of the water, as the thirty people assembled had remarked about the size of the fish.

"What would the hard way have been?" asked Jack as the local fisherman looked on with the others.

"Dragging the thing up on the beach by the tail and asking it nicely to spit your lure out. Only thing is that the last time I saw a vacationer land a decent shark, the doctors at the emergency room had quite a time sewing two of his fingers back on. That guy's fish was a guppy compared to this hog right here that you hooked into."

"What about the lure. Won't it make it hard for the shark to feed?"

Just then, the powerful predator sent water flying with a powerful slap of its tail and just like that, it was gone.

"Don't worry. It will rust out in a week. The old man in the grey suit might be down with a sore mouth for a day, but he'll be just fine after that."

Chris walked from the room onto the beach, having just awakened from a perfect afternoon nap.

"What's all the excitement about?" he had asked.

The shark adventure continued to swirl around in Thomas' mind. Another fond memory of the trip bubbled up to the surface of his consciousness as he continued down the main drive of the airport. The pair of aviator's wings that Grace had given him during that solo flight with her was still the very same ones he wore on his Class-A uniform. On the day he had finally earned the status of a 'rated' officer nearly five years later, he had proudly presented them to his commanding officer to pin on his jacket instead of a plain pair purchased at the base PX. The memory of that first flight with Grace as his single, precious passenger brought another jolt of joy to him as he finally spotted the sign above the ATC Flight School and pulled into its lot.

Walking hand-in-hand through the doors of the flight school, Thomas saw a man behind the counter look up immediately in response to the electronic ping of the door chime. Silver-haired, wearing a Hawaiian shirt and well-worn ball cap with the silhouette of an old C-47 screened on it, Jim Strong smiled with the instant recognition of his nine a.m. booking.

"You must be Captain Walsh?"

"Yes, sir. This is my girlfriend, Grace. Nice to meet you in person," said Thomas with the instant tone of familiarity aviators tend to afford each other regardless of whether they have known each other for five decades or five seconds.

"I'm guessing you set this all up a while back," said Grace as she looked at Thomas and flashed her azure eyes with a flutter of the lashes. He smiled boyishly. Turning back to the counter, Grace took note of the proprietor's name on the business card stack on the desk, she said, "Mr. Strong, would you be kind enough to remind me of the destination on the flight plan. My boyfriend here somehow failed to tell my friends whether they were to pick us up at the international airport or the regional."

Standing behind Grace, Thomas quickly gestured with a finger across his lip and a smile at Jim.

"Nice try, missy. A very spirited effort but I've been advised that information about the destination is, and will remain, on a need-to-know basis."

Laughter burst from Thomas' mouth for a second at the coincidental use of the same spy vernacular he had just used five minutes earlier.

"You know, I knew I liked you right off the bat, Mr. Strong. 'Missy' has such a cute ring to it. I'll let you in on a little secret. I usually answer to Special Agent Lee at the Hoover Building."

Realizing he might have stepped on the stunning blonde's toes conversationally without intending to, Jim cleared his throat and said, "Really. I didn't know the FBI had any women like you. Captain Walsh, is she serious?"

From her handbag, Grace produced her credentials and badge.

"Well, I'll be darned. If you don't mind me asking, Ma'am, what do you do for the Bureau?"

"I work counterterrorism."

Jim looked at Thomas, chewed his gum with a reflective look on his face for a moment, smiled and said, "If you'll just fill out my paperwork, Captain Walsh, she's all gassed up. Don't worry about the fuel paperwork. The gas is on me."

"Mr. Strong, I can't do that. You've been more than helpful already," said Thomas as he reached for his wallet.

"Nonsense, Son. I know what you government employees make. All I ask is that you never stop chasing those sociopaths until you warehouse them in a Supermax prison or send them on their magic carpet ride to Allah with high explosive ordinance. Either way suits me fine, but make sure you get the job done. So let me get you guys on your way for a beautiful flight."

"Yes, sir, Major Strong. Count on it."

Grace looked into Thomas' eyes and saw a look she had fallen in love with years before. Here, they shared one of the sorts of moments only those deeply in love enjoy.

Following the owner out to the first plane in a row of identical Cessna 172's, each with the A.T.C. Flight School logo painted on the side, Thomas held Grace's hand. The feeling of repeating history hit her hard when she watched Thomas go through the same pre-flight inspection steps he had when they were high school kids.

"This is usually the point where I tell people about how serious the military gets about screwing up your position within the Air Defense Identification Zone surrounding D.C., but thankfully I'm dealing with a professional so you know how to handle yourself," said Mr. Strong. Thomas checked the flaps on the tail, smiled, and turned to Mr. Strong, taking the clipboard and release form from him to sign for the aircraft.

"Thanks for the reminder nonetheless," said Thomas. He made a mental note to send a thousand dollar check for the rental despite what Mr. Strong had told him. Understanding the man's patriotism was easy but Thomas' sense of ethics just couldn't allow him to take such a generous gift in appreciation for duties both he and Grace had sworn oaths to perform in service to God and country.

Two minutes later, Thomas began taxiing the plane out to the runway, checking in with the tower. After given clearance for takeoff, he took the runway with Grace again. She sat in awe, watching the love of her life doing what he did better than ninety-nine percent of the planet's citizens: drive an airplane. His masterful command of what seemed a complex series of adjustments and inputs to equipment just to configure the Cessna for flight left her feeling very aroused. It was the masculine way in which he just did things. Taking a few deep breaths to calm her heart rate, Grace looked out the window at the scenery that was quickly scrolling by as the plane accelerated down the runway. Just as she began to relax again, the feeling of liftoff sent her stomach momentarily sinking. Right then, however, a wave of endorphins was released from the sensation of utter freedom from leaving the earth that immediately counteracted her fear. It was in that moment that it became so clear to her why some people thought of flight as a spiritual experience and did everything possible to achieve it as often as they could. The thought occurred that she might love to learn to fly one of these planes so she could share the experience with her boyfriend she adored so much. That was, if she could ever put any free time together. With the FBI the lead agency for domestic counterterrorism, she lamented the fact that free time would be as rare as altruistic politicians. Suddenly, Grace noticed an official-looking form sitting near the throttle. Recognizing it as an FAA flight plan form, she could just make out the origin and destination airports listed as VKX and TEB without having to tip her hand and actually pick up the document. Knowing that the VKX must be the code for Potomac Airfield they just left, she began to try to piece together where in the world TEB might be. Suddenly inspired, she pulled her Blackberry from her handbag, hoping she was still at an altitude where she could get a wireless signal. After a few moments of searching for a connection, and happily seeing she had one, Grace smiled to herself as Thomas began to sense something was up. Looking over at her, he asked, "What's with the phone, honey? You know you probably can't make a call from this altitude."

"Oh, just checking my itinerary for next week, babe," she answered coolly. In a few seconds of using Google, she found a general aviation site that immediately told her their destination was Teterboro Airport just on the other side of the river from Manhattan in New Jersey. She remembered talking to Thomas over a Skype connection one night about how nice it would be to spend a day in New York together when he came back. The fact that Thomas had arranged the excursion while serving in combat operations half a world away made her heart leap. Occasionally, when discussing Thomas with another single female agent from her division, her colleague would ask how she knew she wanted to be with a fighter pilot and all the attendant heartache of him being away with his unit. She had a pretty darn good answer to that the next time it came up in the cafeteria.

"So, I guess you didn't quite win the bet, agent ninety-nine. We're airborne and our destination is still a mystery, huh?"

Not wanting to take the wind out of her love's sails, Grace kept her information to herself and answered, "I'm trying to figure out where we are by looking at the ground but those clouds keep getting in the way. You win."

Boy, I hope so, thought Thomas as he realized there was no time like the present. Reaching behind his seat and feeling for the backpack, he said to Grace, "Honey, could you take the airplane for a second while I get a snack from the backpack?"

"Just tell me exactly what to do," she said excitedly, relishing the opportunity to feel in control of the plane.

"Just look out the front of the plane, keep your feet where they are on the pedals, and don't make any big turns. You see the skyline of Baltimore up ahead? Just keep us pointed at that. This will take just a second."

Grace kept her hands on the yoke, turning it slightly to feel what the plane did in response. Just as she began to get comfortable with the idea of being in control, she turned back to Thomas and when she saw the object in his hand, her heart nearly stopped. The sunlight pouring through the cockpit window made the diamond explode with color as the light hit it perfectly at that moment. Instantly, Grace's eyes began to well up with tears and, in a fit of excitement yelled, "Oh God! Thomas…take the plane, take the plane!"

Thomas lightly held the yoke on his side of the aircraft with his left hand and the diamond ring in his right while holding back the wave of emotion welling up inside him as well. Setting the plane on autopilot, he turned to her and said, "Grace, I have waited a long time to ask you this. You are the love of my life and I can't think of one more day going by without telling you that I want to spend the rest of my days in this world as your husband. Will you...."

"Yes! Yes! Forever, yes! I'll marry you!" she blurted as two huge tears streamed their way down her cheeks. Thomas slipped the ring on her finger and she immediately threw her arms around his neck, kissing him. In the moment, he reflected back to the first time she had kissed him in a plane almost exactly like the one they sat in now. The joy inside was the same as that day multiplied a hundred fold. He knew she was the only one for him.

Picking up the radio, he proudly announced over the aviation frequency, "Baltimore Control, this is November Zulu Five-Nine-Three with you at six thousand. It is my pleasure to report that during the course of this flight, at an altitude of five thousand feet, twenty-two nautical miles southwest of Baltimore, my girlfriend, Grace Lee, has just agreed to become Mrs. Thomas Walsh. Over."

"November Zulu Five-Nine-Three, this is Baltimore Control. You have the entire ATC Center here applauding and offering congratulations. Safe flight to your destination."

United States Air Force Academy
Catholic Cadet Chapel
Colorado Springs, Colorado
12:03 P.M. Mountain Time
Saturday, June 15th, 2003

Chapter Thirty-Eight

Sitting in the front row of the Catholic Chapel level of the distinctive Air Force Academy Chapel, Chris, Keely, and Erika beamed with joy and chatted quietly as they waited for the wedding to begin. One floor above the Catholic Chapel was the more commonly-known Protestant Chapel, with its angular walls meeting at a point at the apex of the roof above them, but for what the Catholic Chapel lacked in size and grandeur, it made up for with a feel of warmth. The backdrop of the altar was decorated by a spectacular mosaic depicting the annunciation of the Good News the Angel Gabriel brought to Mary. The chapel was bathed in soft, amber light shining through the main side windows and points of colored light from the smaller, multi-colored secondary widows.

On this warm summer day, Captain Thomas Francis Walsh, United States Air Force, was transitioning from a man usually billeted in the bachelor officer quarters to a married member of the military and his bride-to-be, Grace Lee, was going to become Mrs. Thomas Walsh.

Right on cue, the fifteen violinists and cello players hired for the wedding music began to play the opening notes of *Cannon in D* and everyone turned to see Grace appear with Jack at the nave of the church. As father and daughter began their procession toward the altar, arm in arm, Chris could hear Erika inhale sharply and, although he couldn't see her face directly, knew what was coming. He smiled as the normally cool and collected physician's hands shot up in front of her mouth. Suddenly, Keely turned back toward Chris and he was instantly reminded of the moment he knew he wanted to spend the rest of his life with her. Keely's eyes glistened with tears and her joy immediately touched his heart too. Keely had been holding his hand as they often did in church and squeezed his hand.

For some reason, instead of watching the bride, Chris turned and watched Thomas' face the moment Grace had appeared and was deeply touched by the expression of rapture on his grown son's face. It was so easy to think back to what seemed such recent times when the now six-foot-tall, broad shouldered man at the altar in his Air Force Class-A uniform was a little boy rushing into his office to show him yet another meticulously crafted model airplane.

Flanked by his groomsmen who were all serious-looking military aviators from Thomas' squadron, Chris felt a pang of sadness in finally realizing that his little boy was a man with his own wife and responsibilities. He had intellectually known it for a long time but it was in that very moment Chris really knew his boy was grown.

Grace, in her spectacular white Vera Wang wedding gown and Jack, wearing a bespoke Armani tuxedo like the other two civilian groomsmen, made their way toward the altar. Thomas watched as father and daughter approached and just as they arrived at the front row of pews, Thomas descended from the altar and walked down to meet them.

"I love you so much, Daddy."

"You'll always be my little girl. Now go marry this gentleman, would ya'?"

She smiled and wiped a tear from her eye, then turned to her husband-in-waiting.

With a wink from Jack, which was both an encouragement and simultaneous attempt to stave off the tears beginning to form in his own eyes at the momentous event of passing responsibility for his little girl's well-being to another man, Thomas took his bride-to-be by the arm and led her back to the altar.

As the organ silenced, the Catholic Air Force chaplain,

Colonel Joseph Peek, opened the service and shortly after, one of Grace's bridesmaids, a close friend from the Bureau took the podium and began reading verses from the traditionally selected Catholic wedding readings in the Bible.

"You made Adam and you gave him his wife Eve to be his help and support," the petite, brunette woman with an intelligent twinkle in her eye recited from the podium. As Chris listened, his thoughts drifted away from the nuptial Mass and back to the conversation that had taken place at the reception dinner the night before.

"So, tell me, cuz'...is it hard to think about the people on the ground you are dropping bombs on?" asked a fairly inebriated cousin of Thomas's who was generally considered the black sheep of the family. As he said it, Ethel Walsh's hands flew to her mouth with a look of utter embarrassment on her face in reaction to her son's indelicate and abrasive question. All around the family table of the rehearsal dinner, increasingly disapproving looks from family members and friends were being given at the twenty-one-year-old Billy as his comments began to have more and more confrontational themes. Billy's mother had mentioned twice to the young man to mind his manners and to slow down on the wine, of which Billy had already consumed three glasses in short order before the entrée was served. To her horror, Billy had already been drinking when she had gone to his room an hour earlier to retrieve him for dinner. The smell of liquor was evident on Billy's breath. With a look of embarrassment on her face, once again Billy's mother nudged him and hissed in his ear, "One more stupid remark and we will get up and leave!"

"Come on, Mom, I'm just having fun," answered the boy.

Having been embarrassed enough by the need to admonish her son, and then compounding the shame by his indiscreet and childish reply, Ethel began to push her chair back and stand, clamping her hand around Billy's right bicep.

Thomas, watching the confrontation, smiled quickly at Grace and said, in a tone that was designed to get the immediate attention of the young man, "You know, Billy, that's a fair question. Of course the answer is yes. Every single pilot flying a military aircraft thinks about the lives he might be tasked to end in defense of our country."

"Yeah but the Bible says, 'Thou shalt not kill,' so what gives you or our government the moral authority to kill other people?"

Thomas had heard stories through the family grapevine about the escapades of young Billy and his endless disciplinary actions from schools, minor run-ins with the law, and the clearly authenticated rumor of a drinking problem. As Billy and his family lived in Chicago, the two sides of the family met on only a handful of occasions—mostly funerals—but the scuttlebutt on Billy was that he was a wild child with a short fuse. Thomas once remembered watching an exchange between Billy and another of his cousins, Kelley at their grandfather's funeral where, after she and Thomas happened upon the boy smoking a cigarette outside during the wake, Kelley took the young miscreant to task by jeering, "I bet you spend all your money on cigarettes and drugs. My parents say you are always in trouble."

Being all of twelve at the time of the incident, Thomas remembered Billy's response like it was yesterday. With a tone of utter defiance and contempt, not unlike that used in asking the current question about dropping bombs, Billy had looked right at his older cousin and spat, "You know, if I have to spend another minute hanging around a total bitch like you, I'll need a drink. When I want your opinion, I'll make sure you're quite clear about it."

Near the head of the table, Chris and Keely sat quietly, holding each other's hands, watching and listening to the exchange between their son and Chris' nephew with a sense of sadness for the obviously troubled young man.

Keely, with a little less tolerance for over-consumption of alcohol, stemming from her experiences as a bartender years earlier, quietly whispered into Chris' ear, "That boy shouldn't be here like that."

In a tone that instantly reminded her of Chris' amazing capacity for kindness, and why she loved her husband so deeply, Chris whispered back, "That boy shouldn't be *anywhere* like that. He should be up in his room trying to drink up enough courage to come down here." The way he said it made it clear it wasn't an indictment, but rather compassion for their nephew. A moment later, Chris and Keely watched their son do something they would never forget and would always be one of the proudest moments they would ever have as parents.

Thomas stood and walked over to where Billy and Ethel sat, pulled a free chair from another table, and said to Ethel, "Ma'am, do you mind if I sit for a while?" Billy looked up at the immaculately groomed, powerfully-built man in the Air Force uniform towering above him with a look of the condemned on his face.

"Please do and I'm so sorry about this," she said.

Billy *hated* when his mother apologized for him. It had been that way his entire life. There had always been the loathed parent-teacher conferences with the inevitable question about Billy's father being absent. The apologetic tone Ethel always took explaining her being a widow due to an illness and Billy's almost predictable punctuation on his mother's claim with his own that, "Dad was a drunk and died like a drunk." Being the center of attention was something Billy structured every waking moment of his life to be but sometimes, like now, it backfired horribly.

"Let me ask you something, Billy. Have you ever heard the story of Sergeant Alvin York?"

Pleased that there wasn't a right hook involved in the exchange, and wanting to diffuse the situation as quickly as possible, Billy's attitude did an immediate about-face and he shook his head no.

"I'm not going to sit here and lecture to you, man. If you don't want to hear about him I'm not going to talk just to hear the sound of my own voice, but I think I can answer your question pretty clearly if you'd care to hear?"

"Um, sure."

"Alright, well, Sergeant Alvin York was a good, ol' boy from Tennessee that liked to drink and liked to fight. His mother always tried to get him to change his ways but good old Alvin just had a hard time listening to others. One night he and a friend got into a nasty fight with some guys in a bar and his friend wound up dead. The shock of seeing that sort of snapped him out of the wild behavior and he actually quit drinking and became a

Christian like his mother always wanted."

Great, more of this garbage, thought Billy without saying a word. "So the guy got Jesus and gave up the demon rum, huh?"

"There was more to it than that. The particular sect of fundamental Christianity Alvin joined was very anti-war and discouraged violence of any kind. Unfortunately, at that time, there was a little conflict brewing in Europe that would come to be known at World War I and Alvin got a letter one day requiring him to register for the draft. He went into the Army and during basic training, the drill sergeants discovered that Alvin was the best shot they had ever laid eyes on. Alvin was truly an artist with a rifle but the problem for him was that he didn't want anything to do with taking another life, which is a pretty big problem for a guy about to be sent to war. In fact, he actually applied for conscientious objector status but he was denied."

"What, you mean if you are a soldier, you can just tell the Army you don't want to kill people?"

"Well, yes actually. There is a process that a soldier can claim that because of moral, philosophical, or religious convictions, they refuse to participate in any sort of combat. It can get a bit complicated but in Sergeant York's case the Army wasn't going to hear anything of it. His religion specifically didn't prohibit it so the Army denied his status application. Sergeant York's commanding officer respected his convictions but told him he needed to make a decision about going to fight. He was told that if he couldn't get over his issues with it, he stood to get in serious trouble; possibly a court marshal. He was given two weeks to get his mind straight about his situation. So Sergeant York began reading the Bible and praying about what to do. Eventually, after prayerfully considering the dilemma he was in, he attributed a verse in the book of Matthew to guiding his decision."

"Render unto Caesar what is Caesar's and render unto God what is God's," interjected Chris who had been following with immense interest and pride the way his son was making a point to the young man without trying to sound pedantic or condescending.

Smiling at his father for his help, Thomas nodded and looked at Billy, who seemed to be genuinely interested in the discussion at that point, and said, "Yeah, exactly right, Dad. Matthew, Chapter 22."

"Matthew, Caesar?" asked Billy, not quite getting the message.

"Yeah, I told you that Sergeant York had had a profound sort of spiritual experience when his friend died in that bar fight. In trying to discern what was right for him, he began to pray and read the Bible and in the book of Matthew, he read that verse in Chapter 22. Basically, he took it to mean that you can still follow God's will and serve your country, even if doing so meant you are required to take another's life."

Feeling embarrassment over the question that sparked the whole lecture from his older cousin, Billy said, "You know I didn't mean anything by what I said. I was just sort of talking about nothing. I mean I didn't mean to insult you, cuz'." After a momentary pause, he corrected himself and said, "I, uh, mean Captain Walsh."

"No offense taken, Billy. I know it's a hard pill to swallow and I'm not going to try to make you believe what I believe. I fly over dangerous places where people want to kill me so badly they can taste it so that you can have the freedom to believe what you want. Insisting other people must believe what they believe has been, in my opinion, the cause of every war since man first picked up rocks and clubs before recorded history, including the one we are engaged in right now. The unfortunate fact is that there are some people so spiritually sick that no matter how much a person, or a nation, for that matter, reaches out to them, the only thing they take pleasure in is sitting back and watching the world around them burn. So the short answer I could have given you ten minutes ago could have been, yes, I do think about it every time I'm tasked to drop ordinance on people. Truthfully, in a perfect world, I'd be out of a job."

Billy lost all impetus to debate. "Well, that sort of makes sense to me."

"Well, I'm glad it does but I wouldn't be offended in the slightest if it didn't."

With that, Thomas stood, squeezed Billy's shoulder, and began to walk back to his seat at the head of the table with his bride-to-be. Grace smiled at her fiancé and when he took his seat next to her again, she slipped her foot underneath his ankle and gently rested her hand on his knee.

"I can't wait to be your wife," she whispered in his ear in a tone that gave him shivers.

"I can't wait to be your husband."

Billy sat quietly the rest of the dinner, drinking water.

As Chris' mind returned to the wedding service, he happily sat next to his own wife, watching as Thomas and Grace exchanged their vows. He squeezed Keely's hand once again, noting her eyes were brimming with tears.

"I now pronounce you husband and wife," concluded Father Peek, "you may…"

Laughter erupted throughout the chapel when Thomas didn't wait for the priest to finish that sentence before embracing Grace and kissing her. They stared into each other's eyes for a fraction of a second to relish their first kiss as husband and wife. Thomas then did something Grace would always treasure as a memory. He took her hands, looked to the cross, and said, "Thank you, God, for this responsibility." He said it only loud enough that she and Father Peek could hear.

Father Peek was overjoyed to hear such a spontaneous prayer at that moment. With radiant smiles, Grace and Thomas turned to the assembled friends and proceeded down from the altar to smiles, tears, and a wave of applause throughout the cathedral from all.

As Captain and Mrs. Walsh left the cathedral, eight Air Force Academy cadets that made up the honor guard stood with hands on the hilts of their sabers. Captain Mike Chang, Thomas' best man, gave the command, "Draw swords!" and each cadet smartly drew their sword, crossing the tips with the cadet across from them, creating the traditional military wedding 'arch of steel'. Thomas beamed with joy as he escorted Grace into the middle of the crossed swords, embraced his new bride, and they shared a kiss that lasted considerably longer than the one at the altar had, much to the delight of the onlookers. The kiss elicited several whistles and cheers from the assembled wedding party and guests. As they made their way past the final two cadets with raised swords, Grace was very aware of an unofficial military wedding tradition and suspected it was imminent. Just as the final honor guard cadet lowered his sword to lightly swat her on the derrière, she spun on her heel, smiled with her finger extended, and said, "Ah, ah, ah...I'm a federal agent. That's a felony." The young cadet's eyes went wide and his sword sharply snapped back to its original position while everyone roared with laughter. To let the poor kid off the hook, Grace winked at him. Taking the joke in stride, the young man nodded and winked back.

As the entire group assembled on the cathedral steps, being directed by the wedding photographer, the peace and quiet of the Colorado summer was pierced with hundreds of decibels of engine noise from four F-16s screaming overhead.

"Did you do that, Dad?" asked Thomas as Chris and Keely stood by the limousine waiting to take the newlyweds to the reception at the historic Cliff House hotel at the base of Pike's Peak.

"I made a call or two," said Chris with a grin.

An hour later, after just completing their first dance as husband and wife, Thomas saw his cousin, Billy, sitting by himself at a table, nursing what looked like a glass of ice water. Looking into the love of his life's eyes, Thomas whispered in Grace's ear, "Hey, can you give me a second?" Being a highly-trained observer of her surroundings, Grace had already taken note of the young man sitting by himself and instinctively knew what her husband was thinking. As she watched her husband walk over to talk with Billy, she whispered the words, "I love you so, husband."

"Hey, Billy, how's it going?" asked Thomas as he sat down.

Looking up from his glass of ice water, Billy looked at his cousin with a contrite expression. "Well, um, better, I guess. You know, I just wanted to tell you that I was a total jerk last night and that I meant no disrespect by it. I sometimes say dumb things when I start to drink a bit. Actually, I tend to say a lot of stupid things so...can you maybe not hold that one against me?"

"Hey man, we're family. I appreciate your apology and there are absolutely no hard feelings from me."

"You know, I was thinking a lot after what you told me about that Sergeant York guy. I mean I don't think they'll ever give me the keys to a plane like you but maybe if the people in the military are like you, it couldn't be all that bad, could it?"

Thomas smiled. "Well, I'll tell you the truth. It's pretty bad at first. If you can't do what other people tell you to do without any question, I wouldn't recommend it. You'd be told to do a lot of things you won't want to, sometimes by total jerks, but if you can stick out the hard things, you could go on to college on the government's dime and learn things about yourself and the world you might never have any other way."

"Do you think I could make it?"

"Yes Billy, I think you could."

"It certainly would be a step up from waiting tables at Pizzeria Uno."

"Men never commit evil so fully and joyfully as when they do it for religious convictions."

-Blaise Pascal

Part Six:

An Eye for a Billion Eyes

2011

Photo by Waqas Usman

Final Delivery / Will Dempsey

Incirlik Airbase
Adana, Turkey
0430 Hours Local Time
Monday, December 16th, 2011

Chapter Thirty-Nine

Major Thomas 'Fist' Walsh and Major Mike 'Mouth' Chang climbed into the van in front of their quarters in the middle of the chilly Turkish night. They weren't the only people up and about on the base at that hour, but they were the only pilots scheduled to launch a mission before daybreak. The base was clean and orderly, everything in its place in typical military fashion. Thomas wasn't, however, a huge fan of the surrounding area and thought of it in much less glowing regard. One of the men in Thomas' squadron had once remarked, "This is the place they'll stick the hose in if they ever give the earth an enema."

    The two pilots rode silently in the crew transportation van to the flight operations building, both studying satellite imagery of the target, a cluster of buildings in a remote area of Iran to the south of the nuclear reactor at Arak. The sun wouldn't be up for nearly three hours at the target area. When they reached the building, both pilots exited the bus and walked inside and headed straight to the weather officer's desk. A female major confirmed to both men that there would be absolutely no weather systems to be concerned with in the region. Stepping down the hall into a briefing room, an Air Force intelligence officer with the rank of full colonel and Defense Intelligence Agency officer sat with two red-bordered folders on the table waiting for the pilots. The Air Force colonel locked the door and flipped the red light on outside it to indicate that classified material was being discussed and that no one, under any circumstances, was to attempt to enter the room until the briefing was completed.

"There is actionable intelligence from an informant inside *Al Qaeda*, code named PEBBLE, that Mohammed Abd al Rashid will be located at this farm with other senior commanders of the insurgent resistance. I don't need to emphasize the fact that this is the man we are sure is responsible for the bombing at Aviano Airbase last month," said the DIA man.

Both pilots glanced at each other, a feeling of eagerness to be inbound to the target gnawing at each of their souls. The truck bomb attack at the base in Italy the prior month had completely leveled a high-rise building housing hundreds of airmen, including two pilots from their squadron. The same thing had happened years ago at the Khobar Towers in Saudi Arabia and no one in the Air Force had forgotten. It was payback time in the form of a pair of GBU-82 thousand-pound bombs streaking silently through the Iranian night sky directly into the Iranian building in which the *Al Qaeda* leader dwelt.

"We also suspect that Tariq al Arabi is going to be in attendance and we think he's the guy getting the copper plates across the border into Iraq and Afghanistan," added the colonel. The most devastating variant of improvised explosive device being employed by the insurgents throughout the theatre of combat was the explosively formed projectile or EFP. Using a quantity of explosive in a tube behind the ten-inch wide copper plates created a dart of copper moving at over fifteen thousand miles per hour that would punch through ten inches of steel armor like it was paper, annihilating anything or anyone unfortunate enough to be on the other side. The EFP was such a lethally effective weapon that the United States had developed cluster bombs using the same principle that were used to destroy heavily-armored tanks. Even the new generation of vehicle the US was employing, known as the Mine Resistant Ambush Protected Vehicle or MRAP, which was designed to withstand anti-tank mines, wasn't immune to the devastating, hypersonic dart of molten metal produced by the weapon. Dozens of soldiers riding in heavily armored MRAPs had died as a result of an effectively placed EFP.

Both pilots flying the strike mission that night knew the stakes were higher on that evening's sortie than on any other mission that either man had ever flown. Both majors felt the unmistakable tightening of their abdominal muscles and the adrenaline spike in their spines. The briefing completed, Thomas and his wingman and long-time friend, Major Chang, left the briefing room and went to the life support room. There, they removed the velcroed unit patches from their flight suits. It was standard procedure for military aviators flying a combat sortie. Both men wriggled into their G-Suits that would keep blood from pooling in their legs during any high-G maneuvers, and rendering them unconscious. Although the stealthy aircraft they would be flying would almost undoubtedly pierce Iranian airspace without so much as a shadow of a blip on any searching radar, and extreme maneuvering was unlikely, the F-22s were high-performance fighter aircraft and one never knew for sure. After donning the inflatable g-suits over the air-cooled flight suits that kept the pilots comfortable in a cockpit packed full of electronics, both pilots strapped on shoulder holsters for their Beretta 92 nine-millimeter pistols. Before slipping the guns into their holsters, each pilot pointed the weapon into a water-filled fifty-five gallon drum in the room that would catch any round if they accidentally discharged the weapon. Both men inserted a magazine into the magazine well of the weapon, pointed the muzzle of the pistol into the drum, and pulled the slide back. With a sharp *clack*, the slide rode forward and chambered a round. It was the last piece of equipment either pilot ever wanted to have an occasion to use. If a need to use their sidearm presented itself, it would only be if the pilot found himself on the ground in hostile territory. That was every pilot's worst nightmare. It was an old Air Force joke that claimed, "It is highly inadvisable to eject over the area you just bombed." If there was any reason to use that particular piece of equipment, things had gone very, very wrong. Out on the flight line, it was relatively quiet at that time of the morning but within one hangar, Two F-22s were being prepared for launch by two crews comprised of three tech sergeants and a supervising first sergeant. The crew chief for Major Walsh's jet, Staff Sergeant Tyler Mobley, oversaw the three junior sergeants on his crew that were ensuring every system and component of Walsh's jet were in perfectly operational condition. As crew chief, Sergeant Mobley took his responsibility deadly seriously. A generally good-humored man when off-duty, Sergeant Mobley possessed no tolerance for mistakes when his team was working on 'his' jet. Noticing that one of the young tech sergeants newly assigned to him was making the same mistake he had admonished her for twice already that day, he marched directly over to her with a murderous look on his face.

Sergeant Christy Bonner looked with shock and anger at Sergeant Mobley's hand that had snatched hers from the place on the jet intake where it had rested as she leaned on it, checking some electrical connections underneath an access panel. Pulling her hand from the jet almost made her fall straight onto the concrete floor of the hangar until she caught her balance at the last instant. Sergeant Mobley wouldn't have cared if she had eaten the concrete.

"Hey man, what the...?"

"Sergeant Bonner, let me fix my earlier error as I apparently failed to clearly communicate to you when I told you this an hour ago. Item one: if I have to remind you one more time that human oils can reflect a radar signature on this otherwise perfectly stealthy aircraft, which your United States government spent one hundred and forty million dollars on, it will go into an official reprimand. Item two: you will learn to address me with proper military decorum and protocol. If you ever refer to me as 'man' ever again while on duty, I'll end your career. I'll make your life so unbearable here, you will beg for a discharge. Understood?!?"

Sergeant Bonner, a native New Yorker, had made it through her advanced schools to teach her how to work on the Raptors at almost the top of her class. Unfortunately, a marriage to an abusive man and an increasing intake of alcohol on her off-time had begun to show its effects on her professionalism on the flight line.

"Yeah, yeah, I heard you the first time, Sergeant."

It was the absolutely worst tact to take with the man ultimately responsible for the airworthiness of the most expensive fighter/bomber in history. Moving to within an inch of her face, and with his rage barely suppressed, Sergeant Mobley hissed, "If you have to hear it again, it will be from the colonel's mouth, not mine, Sergeant." He made a decision right then to request a transfer for her as soon as he could get back to his office. Personal problems or not, there was no place on the most expensive flight line in the world for someone not giving one hundred percent. Taking a rag from a pocket and a bottle of cleaning solution from a cart, Sergeant Mobley carefully removed any perspiration from the jet that Sergeant Bonner may have left. Glaring at her, he walked back to the other side of the jet where the ordinance people were loading one of two thousand-pound JDAM bombs into the internal weapon store.

As soon as he was out of sight, Sergeant Bonner mumbled, "Is that a fact, little man? A little sweat can screw up this thing? If that's the case, we really paid too much for it." Out of sheer defiance, Sergeant Bonner slapped her hand on the surface of the jet on the starboard air intake, just forward of where Sergeant Mobley had just cleaned the surface of the jet, leaving a clearly visible handprint in sweat.

Thomas and Major Chang walked out of the Life Support area and headed for the flight line. As they approached their respective jets, they saw that the ordinance crews were making final checks to the bombs the jets would carry aloft. Loaded inside each of the two internal weapons bays on both jets was a thousand pound JDAM or Joint Directed Attack Munition. The weapons were standard thousand-pound iron bombs fitted with a tail kit that was the latest-generation of guidance equipment. The computerized guidance system not only uploaded the targeting information from the aircraft's on-board computers once the jet was powered up, but also was directed by any one of the constellation of twenty-four GPS satellites orbiting the earth. Earlier laser-guided bombs required the pilot to keep an invisible infrared laser painting the target until impact, thus necessitating the plane to fly toward the target even after the weapon was released. It exposed pilots to a larger possibility of anti-aircraft measures. With the JDAM, the pilot simply had to reach a point within the kinetic range of the bomb, release it, and could rely on the programming and the satellite guidance to bring the weapon to the target. Putting two tons of high explosive right on top of the most wanted terrorist in Iran was precisely what both majors were tasked with that night.

Both pilots walked around their respective aircraft, checking the surfaces and panels for anything that looked out of place. The F-22 Raptor was the most technologically advanced fighter/attack aircraft in the history of the world. The computing power within its radar and targeting systems was a quantum leap beyond earlier generations of aircraft computer systems and the equivalent computing power of two Cray supercomputers. Once airborne, both pilots would require a minimum of radio chatter because of a flight data link that would allow Major Walsh and Major Chang to know exactly what the other pilot was doing by simply looking at one of the six LCD displays in their cockpits.

After strapping into the restraints in their jets, the two pilots had relatively few tasks to complete to make their fifth-generation fighter aircraft go from several tons of inert titanium, composites, and fuel to the most lethal aircraft ever devised by man.

Thomas flipped a battery switch on the console to the 'on' position. Once the indicator light showed it on, he toggled another switch to his auxiliary power unit to 'start'. That done, he moved the throttles on the left side of his cockpit to 'idle' and within two seconds the right Pratt & Whitney F119-PW-100 engine began spinning to life. Shortly after, the left engine rumbled to life. Within thirty seconds, both engines were fully on-line. Thirty seconds after that, all of the computerized systems were initialized. After checking every system's readiness on the six computer screens in front of him, flipping through various presentations of information by simply toggling switches on his flight control stick—a process the pilots referred to as 'playing the piccolo'—the jet was ready to be taken airborne. The vibration of engine start-up always gave Thomas a rush of adrenaline in anticipation of taking flight. Both pilots tested all of the flight surfaces by articulating them up and down, and left and right, including the pair of triangular flaps that sat above and below the exhaust ports at the back of the plane. The flaps made the jet the most maneuverable plane in the history of combat aircraft, enabling a flight capability unique to the F-22 known as 'thrust vectoring', meaning that the pilot could actually control the angle at which all seventy thousand pounds of thrust from the engines left the aircraft.

Both pilots received a sharp salute from their crew chiefs.

Thomas keyed his radio and broadcast, "Incirlik Ground Control, Dealer One-Nine, taxi."

Major Chang followed suit, broadcasting, "Ground Control, Dealer Two-One, taxi."

From the tower, both pilots heard, "Dealer One-Nine, Dealer Two-One, taxi runway two-five left, altimeter two-one-seven. Cleared for departure."

The sleek jets rolled out of their hangar onto the tarmac, toward the taxiway. Two minutes later, both jets lined up on the runway and both pilots simultaneously pushed the throttles forward to full military power, released the brakes, and shot down the runway. Two thirty foot long tails of superheated gasses erupted from the tails of their planes as they roared down the runway. From directly behind, the thrust vector panels made the exhaust ports look like a glowing pair of demonic eyes.

Thomas, call-sign Dealer One-Nine, performed a quick radio check with his wingman and the two jets slipped through the atmosphere above the cloud cover and up to thirty thousand feet in two minutes. For the next two hours, the jets streaked through the night sky. Avoiding the hostile air defenses of Syria to the south, the two hour flight was completely uneventful. After slowing for twenty minutes to allow each jet to take on fuel from a KC-135 tanker aircraft, the two jets accelerated again to their cruising speed and continued at nearly twelve hundred miles per hour across the dark, Turkish sky toward Iran.

As Thomas looked at the navigation screen, he heard not a single peep from the electronic warning system as they crossed into Iranian air space. It had been as boring a flight as possible for someone at the controls of the most advanced jet in the history of the world but his adrenaline began to pump as they entered enemy airspace.

Thomas was ultimately thankful for the amazing technology that the world knew as stealth. Nowhere on his aircraft was a single structure containing a ninety-degree angle. Ninety degree angles were almost perfect for returning a radar signal back to its source. Additionally, within the construction of the air surfaces, were numerous highly-classified composite materials specifically designed to absorb radar energy. At best, what the scientists called a 'radar cross-section' of the F-22 was no larger than a small bird. It was, for all intents and purposes, invisible to the ground. Invisible, that was, unless something was wrong with the jet. The two pilots had covered the thousand miles to the target in such a short time because the highly efficient engines gave the F-22 a capability known as 'supercruise', meaning it could sustain supersonic flight of nearly fifteen hundred miles per hour without using afterburner. Ultra-fast and ultra-invisible were a powerful combination.

The target area was twenty miles out when Thomas confirmed the bomb inside his starboard weapon store was locked onto the specific building they intended to obliterate. Thomas could see in the screen showing Major Chang's systems that Chang had, without any radio communication necessary, done the same. Once the target was locked into the 'shoot list' of the computer, the only thing left to do was fly the plane to the release point and release the weapon. The computer displayed a red triangle on the building and Thomas's thumb hovered over the weapon release button on the stick. Once the segmented red triangle outline became a solid red triangle in the LCD, indicating he had reached the appropriate release point, Walsh depressed the button. Underneath the jet, a panel covering the internal weapon bay snapped open and the bomb was pneumatically ejected from the internal weapon store. The entire process took fewer than two seconds before the exterior panel snapped back into place and the weapon began its guided fall to earth. Major Chang released his weapon at almost exactly the same instant. The two precision-guided weapons silently streaked through the dark Iranian sky toward a small house five miles ahead.

"Enjoy your seventy-two virgins, my friend," mumbled Thomas. Thinking back to a conversation in the officer's club at

Incirlik, Thomas shook his head at a remark his wing man had once made when the topic of martyrdom had come up.

"I can't really grasp why these whack jobs are all trying to get themselves killed to be rewarded with seventy-two virgins. I mean seventy-two teary, awkward experiences doesn't seem like that much of a bonus to me."

It wasn't a thought that would have ever crossed Thomas's mind but in war, he noticed that humor turned pretty irreverent. For a moment, he thought back to the night he and Grace had consummated their marriage and it had been anything but tearful or awkward.

I can't wait to see my angel again, he thought.

Four miles below, an Iranian SA-10 mobile missile launcher had been training its radar on the sky. One of the last remaining missiliers left in the Iranian Army had been watching a faint but curious radar return for the past three minutes on the screen inside the vehicle. The missile system was manned by a grizzled, experienced veteran named Omar Silfani who had served in the same job since he was a young man during the Iran-Iraq war but on increasingly capable anti-air systems Iran had acquired over the three decades of his career. On his screen, Omar watched as a faint signature had begun to show on his radar scopes a few minutes before. Based on the size of the return signature, he wouldn't have believed it to be an enemy aircraft but its rate of speed and altitude convinced him that it wasn't anything with feathers. Picking up his radio transmitter, he immediately contacted the regional commander of the anti-aircraft forces-what was left of them after six weeks of American precision bombing-and told his superior of his suspicion.

"It is faint but constant. I suspect it might be one of the stealth aircraft the Americans are so proud of. I don't know why I'm picking it up but that is my report."

The regional commander, sitting in the command and control vehicle twenty miles to the north, considered the implications of launching one of the few anti-air assets the Iranian military had left, including the possibility of it being destroyed as soon as it launched, and decided to take a chance.

Sergeant Christy Bonner couldn't have known that the

microscopically-thin layer of oils from her hand back at Incirlik was going to be one of the most expensive acts of defiance in the history of the United States military. The layer of water and oils from her hand had frozen into minute crystals that were returning radar energy back to the missile launcher's radar. Thomas was totally unaware of how dangerous a situation he was in. As he began to apply right pressure to the stick to turn the jet, the Integrated Caution/Advisory/Warning, or ICAW system began to tell him, in a startlingly calm female voice, that he was being tracked by radar.

"Warning, radar lock. Warning ,radar lock."

"How the hell is that possible? Oh, man, this is bad!" he exclaimed into his microphone.

"Fist, somehow you're spiked! I'm going to get a visual on your panel," transmitted Chang. With the slightest touch of the stick, Chang maneuvered below to see if Thomas's external panel somehow malfunctioned. If it was still open, his jet would have as large a radar signature as a commercial jetliner.

Thomas' heart sprinted into overdrive as the ICAW declared, "Missile launch detected. Missile launch detected."

Chang saw on his screen, rather than heard the warning. He was just about to say that Walsh's weapons bay panel was in the correct closed position when the launch warning flashed on his screen. Immediately Chang's training took over and he slammed his stick to the right, distancing himself from Thomas' jet. In the span of a second, Chang went from happiness that Walsh's jet wasn't seriously malfunctioning and putting them both in jeopardy to anger that he was forced to take evasive maneuvers away from his wingman and best friend. It was the worst feeling Chang had ever experienced as a military pilot: having to effectively abandon his wingman. The maneuver went against every molecule in Chang's body but was absolutely necessary. Major Chang had no idea how the most stealthy jet in the history of the world was being tracked, Chang didn't know, but if they both were in close trail formation and Thomas' jet got struck, the missile detonation stood a reasonable chance of taking out both aircraft simultaneously.

Thomas' head instinctively snapped back around toward the

tail of the jet, desperately scanning for visual confirmation of the launches. Looking back over his right shoulder, he could clearly see the glowing engines of two missiles rising up from the earth and beginning to turn toward his direction.

"How the hell are they tracking me?" screamed Thomas into his mask as he slammed the throttles of his two engines forward to the firewalls. The jet streaked forward with the feeling of a race car jumping from the start line.

Looking back, he couldn't visually acquire the missiles anymore but unfortunately it wasn't because he had outrun them even at the nearly sixteen-hundred miles per hour his jet was moving at. From his aspect, they were streaking directly for his jet and the tongues of flame from their motors were obscured from his view by the bodies of the missiles themselves.

Just as he turned his attention back toward his instruments, an impact not unlike being rear-ended in a car accident tossed Thomas's body against his restraints and then back into his seat again. Even without looking, he could tell his jet was on fire and not just by the rapidly increasing temperature in the cockpit. The glow from behind him, visible in his peripheral vision confirmed his worst fear. His jet had been fatally struck but he couldn't wrap his mind around exactly how any missile system could have acquired a radar lock on him. The missile had detonated a mere three feet from his starboard engine, instantly ripping the multi-ton power plant from the airframe and rupturing the internal fuel tanks, sending a flaming spray of fuel out three hundred yards behind the jet as it hurtled through the sky.

"I'm hit, I'm hit!" he broadcast, his voice laden with anger and fear.

Thomas's jet had been flown from final testing and assembly at the Marietta, Georgia Lockheed facility in March of 2006 and had been one of the first jets the 27th Fighter Squadron had received to replace their three-decade-old F-15 Eagles. In the following two years, the jet that was known on the Lockheed books as Ship 28, and to the United States Air Force as Aircraft Number 27-1458, had logged over a thousand hours of flight time. During every war game, training exercise, and twenty-three combat missions flown in that jet, not a single ground or air radar had ever successfully tracked the stealth jet well enough to develop a firing solution.

It was unheard of.

Suddenly, at twenty thousand RPMs, and at a velocity of nearly five hundred miles an hour, the turbofan blade of the port engine, knocked off balance by the devastating impact of the missile, sheared off, explosively slamming through the internal area of combustion and through a fuel line. The JP-5 fuel sprayed all over the interior engine housing and was instantly ignited by the existing flames.

The ICAW had plenty to say then.

"Warning: engine fire. Warning: engine number one shutdown. Warning: engine fire, engine number two shutdown."

Over his radio, Thomas heard, "Fist, you're on fire. You've got to go! Get out! Get out now!"

Thomas craned his neck and saw most of the right side of his jet engulfed in flames. Unfortunately, so did several men sitting around a campfire on the ground. The plane looked like a comet streaking across the Iranian sky.

Thomas took one last look back at the screen that displayed the intended target and at that second, two streaks of darkness converged with the building. Where a small house had stood one moment, a mushroom cloud of flame, debris, and dust existed the next.

"Fist, get out! Eject! Eject! Get out of there!! It's not going to get you back, man!" screamed Major Chang over the radio. From his position above and three hundred yards behind Thomas' aircraft, he could see the plane was beginning to pitch upward, completely out of balance with the missing engine and about to enter a flat spin.

"How the hell did that happen?" yelled Major Chang. To the AWACS command and control aircraft that was orbiting one hundred and fifty miles to the east, over Turkey, Thomas broadcast, "Eyeball this is Dealer One-Nine. Punching out." Taking a deep breath to steel him against the ejection, he reached for the yellow and black striped ejection handles on either side of his seat and yanked them upward. Immediately, he was pounded by tornado-force winds as the polycarbonate canopy was blown off the aircraft by small explosives. A fraction of a second later, the rocket motors of the ACES II ejection seat ignited and suddenly Thomas was at twenty thousand feet with no aircraft around him. The force of the ejection was so violent that he lost consciousness for almost ten seconds. When he came to, he had separated from the seat and the parachute canopy was fluttering above him although he couldn't see it in the dark night sky. Looking around to orient himself, he saw a large fireball corkscrewing through the air down below a few miles ahead of him and knew it was the remnants of his plane.

The eight men were huddled around a campfire, all with long beards as was expected of adult Muslim men. Although in the middle of Iran, only one was Iranian by birth. As Asad abu Bakr, the man responsible for insuring the security of the important men meeting inside, was about to order another patrol around the grounds of the small farm house, it suddenly felt like he was picked up by an invisible hand and tossed through the air like a doll. Momentarily deafened by the blast, he never heard the explosion because the overpressure wave from two thousand-pound bombs detonating a quarter mile away reached him before the sound wave. Lying with the wind knocked out of him, Asad struggled for breath as rocks and pebbles, some quite painfully, pelted him as they fell back to earth. "What in the name of Allah....?" he began to say although he couldn't hear his own voice. Coughing and turning over onto his back Asad gingerly checked his limbs and all seemed to be functioning. Looking back toward where the farm house stood only seconds before, he saw only a gaping hole in the ground surrounded by fragments of burning wood and dirt falling back to earth. He could smell the acrid fumes left from the detonation of the explosive inside the thousand-pound bomb. A veteran of many engagements while a member of the Iranian special forces, known as the *Quds* Force, during the Iran-Iraq war, the smell instantly told Asad what had happened.

Staggering to his feet, Asad began to see three of his men also rising from the ground. Walking back to the position that had been partially shielded from the blast by a small dip in the terrain where they had built their campfire, Asad saw one man that hadn't been so lucky. The man's skull was crushed inward from a softball-sized stone propelled from the blast.

Looking down the dirt road that led to the farm, Asad was grateful to see that the two trucks he and his men had ridden to the meeting in were still intact. He offered a quick a prayer of thanks to Allah that he and his men had been spared the treachery inflicted by the infidel and that they wouldn't be stranded fifty kilometers from the nearest village with no transportation and minimal water. Just then, one of his men began to excitedly point skyward. Asad's hearing was returning and he began to hear the man's words more clearly.

"Look, Asad! There is something falling from the sky!"

The moon was almost full and with the illumination, it was easy to see a contrail leading up from the ground. He knew it must be from a missile that struck the plane that was now a fireball plummeting to earth a few miles off. Suddenly an impulse struck Asad and he sprinted as quickly as his sore left side would allow to one of the trucks, pulling a set of night vision goggles from a backpack. Scanning the skies frantically for a few moments, a smile erupted across his face when he found what he had hoped for.

"Allah akbar!" he joyously yelled and then turned to his men and screamed, "Pick up your rifles and get in the trucks now!"

When Thomas was only a thousand feet from the ground, he saw two pairs of headlights snaking across the ground below him. Using the parachute handles, he tried to steer the parachute canopy to create as much space as possible between himself and where it looked like the vehicles were headed. Unfortunately, a prevailing wind from the west thwarted his efforts, continuing to bring him back closer to the vehicles.

Thomas hit the ground and rolled immediately to absorb the shock. Even though he had landed on rocky terrain, he only sustained a few minor impacts on rocks from the landing. His adrenaline glands were dumping so much of the chemical into his bloodstream that he could have broken a limb and not felt it. The vehicles he had seen from the air were only a half-mile off and appeared to be heading directly toward him. *How can they be closing in on me so fast?* thought Thomas as he quickly slipped out of his parachute harness, got his bearings, and began to run toward a ridgeline that appeared to offer some cover.

Sitting in the front passenger seat of the Toyota pickup, with eight armed men riding in the back, Asad had watched the pilot float to earth through night vision glasses. He knew the man he intended to show hell on earth to must be just over the next ridge.

One hundred and thirty miles above Earth, another eye was watching the drama unfold. A KH-12 satellite, operated by the National Reconnaissance Office, focused its looked down upon the mountainous foothill area of northwestern Iran. In an otherworldly infrared view, the satellite captured and transmitted to the NRO Headquarters in Chantilly, Virginia, a view of a deadly cat-and-mouse game that was just beginning.

**Thirteen Miles East of Arak, Iran
Latitude 34.08N Longitude 49.6E
0647 Hours Local Time
Monday, December 16th, 2011**

Chapter Forty

The sun was coming up and the barren terrain was almost completely useless for finding a place to hide. It couldn't be a worse situation. When he had hit the ground, Thomas had quickly shed his parachute harness, allowing the telltale, billowing object to blow away from him. As he had approached the ground, he had seen the two trucks speeding across the terrain, directly for him, no more than a half-mile off. Any possibility of burying the chute was long gone by the time he had landed.

Frantically grabbing everything he could from the survival kit, Thomas worked hastily because the group of men he knew were looking for him had been only a few hundred yards off, just over the ridge. He could hear the engines of their vehicles growing louder until both vehicles had stopped. As Thomas turned to run, his pursuers were so close that he had heard one man screaming what must be orders to the others. Thomas scrambled as fast as he could over another ridge and then south through a little valley. The cover from the terrain had allowed him to evade direct line-of-sight for his pursuers by the skin of his teeth. He could hear their angry shouts and the fight-or-flight reflex in him gave Thomas a burst of energy that helped him run like an Olympic sprinter even with the twenty pounds of extra communication and survival gear strapped to him.

For the past thirty minutes, as the sun came up over the Zagros Mountains to the west, he had dodged their attempts to find him. There were eight of them, each armed with an AK-47. They had fanned out in groups of twos when their trucks had come to a stop, one hundred yards from his position.

The house on which Thomas and Major Chang had been tasked to drop their weapons was located in one of the last strongholds of the insurgent resistance in Iran. There were no US ground forces staged anywhere within five hundred kilometers and he knew a rescue mission would take some time to put an operational plan together.

The sandy soil and sparse shrubbery provided little in the way of cover and the hilly terrain was virtually impossible to travel over quickly. Finding a crevasse in the ground, Thomas laid himself prone, praying to God that the group of men looking for him would miraculously overlook his hiding spot. Drawing his nine-millimeter Glock from his shoulder holster, he cradled the gun in his trembling hands and watched as a team of two searchers, a hundred yards away, looked like they were going to bypass his position and continue eastward. He could see two more teams moving off in other directions that were not an immediate threat. Suddenly the two men stopped in their tracks and looked directly at his position and his hopes of being bypassed were completely dashed. One man, talking with the other for a brief moment, turned and started heading directly for the crevasse. Their decision to move toward Thomas' hiding place was logical. There wasn't another decent piece of cover anywhere within hundreds of yards.

"Of course he is in that hole, you idiot. Where else could he be!" yelled the first man to the second in Pashto, their native language.

The two men began to jog directly toward him.

"God help me," muttered Thomas.

He knew his pistol was not an even match against the two assault weapons carried by the men approaching his position. He was caught with nowhere to run. As soon as he fired a shot, or did anything to cause his pursuers to open fire, the entire group of men would be on him in seconds. With only eighteen rounds in the high-capacity magazine of his pistol, against eight men armed with rifles, he would be done for. His only hope was the possibility that he would be able to quietly take both men out and then move on.

Thomas fingered the grip of his pistol. The men were by now only fifty yards away from the three-foot deep crevasse. A desperate idea struck. He slipped his shoulder holster off and quickly buried it in the soft sand so as to not tip the two men off that he was armed. Only if absolutely necessary would he try to draw the firearm. Lying back down, he heard the men approach. The footfalls of the men grew louder and louder in the crunchy soil. Suddenly, the first man looked over the ridge and saw him.

"You! American! You come out now!" he barked in heavily-accented English.

"I can't. I'm hurt!" said Thomas, pointing to his leg and adding some writhing in pain to emphasize the act.

The first man seemed to consult the second and Thomas continued the ruse, moaning and clutching his leg.

It worked.

Both men stepped down into the ditch and began to grab him underneath his shoulders. He intentionally made it as difficult as possible for them. Although they were both fairly well built, Thomas was nearly two hundred pounds of lean muscle. When they had wrestled him to his feet, one man turned to cough from the exertion. He knew it was his only chance.

The possum act disappeared in a fraction of a second as Thomas raised his knee to hip height and slammed the edge of his foot into the side of the knee of the man on his right like a jackhammer. As he felt the man's knee snap inward from the devastating blow, he grabbed the barrel of the second man's AK-47 and wrenched it away from pointing at him. The first man fell to the ground, completely stunned by the destruction of his knee. His rifle skittered along the ground away from him. The second, who immediately began to tighten his hand on the wooden pistol grip of his rifle, received a powerful reverse punch to the throat.

In all of the years of training in traditional Japanese karate, Thomas had never actually injured a training partner or other student. He had, however, developed the ability to deliver tremendous force from the ground, up through his highly-trained core muscles, and out through his hands and feet by striking a punching post called a *makiwara*.

Neither of Asad's men was prepared for the shocking force of his blows. As his fist made impact with the second man's throat, he could feel the structures on the man's throat collapse, making a sickening popping sound as the cartilage snapped. The man immediately let go of his rifle and clutched at his throat, making gurgling, choking noises. As the lack of oxygen began to overtake him, the second man fell to his knees. The blow eliminated the problem of that man calling out. It did not, however, eliminate the first man's ability to scream a torrent of obscenities, which he did. The rifle the first man had lost control of lay precariously close to the writhing, furious man's grasp. Screaming, he was inching closer to his rifle and Thomas needed to finish him off or he would reach his rifle in seconds. Still holding the second man's AK-47 by the barrel, Thomas flipped it butt-end toward the choking man and, using both arms for stability, shifted in and slammed the butt of the weapon directly into the bridge of the man's nose. That man dropped unconscious to the ground and a stream of blood from the blow began to flow from his face like a water spigot had been opened.

Turning his attention to the first man who was only inches from his rifle, Thomas shifted across the short distance between them, again brought his knee up, and delivered a lethal blow with his heel to the base of the man's neck. The crunching sound was clearly audible.

Adrenaline pumped through Thomas's body as if coursing through a fire hose. Looking at the two men, one definitely dead as his head lay at an impossible angle to his shoulders and the second quickly turning blue and dying while unconscious, Thomas's tunnel vision began to subside. His immediate sense of victory was instantly crushed. Only two hundred yards away, the other two teams of men that had been much further off were running toward his position. They must have heard the screams of the first man before he could silence him. As he dove back into the ditch, the ground around Thomas erupted in little geysers of dirt as the men opened fire. The staccato sound of automatic fire and the high-pitched whine of a few rounds ricocheting off the rocks echoed around the little mountain foothill valley.

Thomas landed in the small depression the first two men had originally found him in, his heart beating furiously. Terrified of taking a bullet to the arm, he knew he needed more than the single thirty-round magazine in the rifle he had taken from the dead man to have a fighting chance. Sticking his arm above the depression, Thomas desperately grabbed for the carry strap of the AK-47 from the dead man with the broken neck. Finding it with his fingers after an agonizing three seconds of exposing his arm, he snatched it and dragged it to him. Without sticking his head above the ridge three feet above him, he opened fire with the rifle, spraying without actually aiming at the advancing men. It was only meant to stop their advance for a moment until he could gather the ammunition from the two men he had killed and prepare for an assault.

Finding the strap of the harness the man closest to the ditch had slung several AK magazines on, Thomas pulled the hundred and fifty pound man into the ditch with no problem whatsoever. His natural strength was augmented by the adrenaline screaming through his body. He was grateful for the ammunition and counted six magazines on the harness. Putting a fully-loaded magazine into the AK, Thomas took comfort that he now had enough firepower to keep the attackers at bay, hopefully until the cavalry arrived.

Suddenly, as Thomas was about to pop up and try to spot his attackers, it felt like his right leg was simultaneously hit with a baseball bat and stabbed with a red-hot iron. The sound of the shot reached his ears just as he dropped the AK-47 and clutched at his thigh.

The placement of the shot had been intentional.

Asad abu Bakr had lain with the Russian-made *Dragunov* sniper rifle nearly a half-mile off. The man he was searching with had begun to ask if he saw the American when Asad raised his hand in a gesture to silence his partner. It was all he needed to do to illicit immediate compliance. Every man that worked with Asad knew he had a short temper and tremendous violent streak.

With their leader Mohammed Abd al Rashid reduced to bone and flesh fragments in a smoldering hole in the ground, everyone knew Asad wasn't to be trifled with that morning. When the sound of screams from the east reached his ears through the still morning air, Asad and his searching partner had been on the opposite side of the little ridge from where the man they were hunting was hidden. Using the scope from his position that was elevated above where the American had tried to hide, he smiled when he saw that he had a clear shot at the pilot. At first, he had placed the crosshair on the American's head, but just as he began to apply pressure to the trigger, an idea occurred to him.

Praise be to Allah for this glorious opportunity to serve you, he silently prayed.

Moving the crosshair down to the American's thigh, he took a deep breath, exhaled, and then slowly pressed the trigger toward the back of the rifle. In the scope, he clearly saw the round impact the American's leg. Asad picked up his radio and transmitted, "I've hit the American in the leg. Do nothing else to injure him. I will tell you when to advance on his position. I don't care how long we have to wait. Hold your positions."

The other men transmitted acknowledgement of Asad's orders and began a waiting game. Asad watched through the scope as the American pulled a tourniquet from a small bag and applied it to his leg. From the pool of blood on the ground underneath the leg, visible as the pilot lifted it to apply the tourniquet, Asad was pretty certain he had hit the femoral artery.

"It won't be long now," Asad mumbled to the man beside him.

In the ditch, Thomas began to panic. As he tied the tourniquet around his leg, and twisted the dowel rod to tighten it, he knew he was in serious trouble.

Oh, my God...! Where did that shot come from?!? screamed his mind as he desperately scanned the surrounding area while the excruciating pain in his leg began to burn intensely. Immediately, he figured it had to be a position behind him as he was protected by the small walls of the ditch to the front of his position. He could feel his strength leaving his body from the shock and blood loss. His last act, before falling unconscious, was to drag the dead body of the man whose throat he'd crushed alongside him to offer at least some protection from another bullet.

Fifteen minutes later, looking through the scope atop his rifle, Asad happily noted the American looked unconscious. He radioed to the remaining eight men.

"The American appears unconscious. Advance on his position and check if he is still alive. If so, absolutely no one is to harm him."

Slowly the six men advanced. Asad watched as one man cautiously poked the American with the barrel of his rifle. Suddenly, all six men jumped on the American and tied his hands with rope. The infidel was his to do with as Asad believed Allah would have him do. Asad's plans for the American pilot were quite unfortunate for the American but Asad was determined to make something good from the morning's tragic loss of a true warrior against the infidel and decadent west.

Looking off to the east through the scope, the wreckage of the American's plane was just visible. Asad picked up his radio again and said, "Carry the pilot to the trucks and wait for me." He watched as four men picked up the American and began to carry his limp body the quarter-mile back to their two parked trucks.

Five minutes later, Asad and his searching partner reached the trucks. He walked around to the bed where the American lay. From the cab of the truck, he retrieved a canteen and climbed into the bed. Pouring the liquid into the mouth of the American made him cough but didn't fully wake him. Asad slapped the man hard until the American opened his eyes.

"It is good. You are not dead."

"Who are...?"

"Shhhh...save your energy, brave warrior. You still have much to do," said Asad.

He hopped out of the truck and into the cab. From a bag in the back seat, he removed a small camcorder and smiled. With a quick bark of orders, the driver of that truck and the second began to snake their way along the low hills and in thirty minutes, made their way to the site of the F-22 wreckage. Asad smiled broadly and clapped his hands as he saw that a large section of the tail was still visible with the markings. It lay flat on the ground next to the largely charred remains of the rest of the jet. A quick order to four men resulted in their dragging the section of the vertical stabilizer and wrestling it upright against the bed of the truck. It was a surreal sight with the grey piece of military jet against the beat-up Toyota truck. The cost of that aircraft component was equal to nearly fifty of the wheeled vehicle but for what Asad had in mind, the tail was worth its weight in platinum.

"This will be a day the infidel dogs will never forget," hissed Asad to one of his men as he motioned toward the semi-conscious American still in the bed of the truck. Four men quickly dragged Thomas out of the bed and he hit the ground hard.

Noticing his tourniquet had come loose and blood was flowing from his leg again, Thomas tried to reach for the rod to tighten it, despite the rope bounding his hands.

Asad, noticing the attempt, walked up to Thomas and, with a look of pure hatred, said, "Do not bother. It does not matter now."

With that, four men dragged Thomas in front of the propped-up vertical stabilizer section. Through his blurry vision, he saw one man walk in front of him with what looked like a video camera. The reality of what was happening hit him like a bomb and he began to scream and fight against his restraints. He tried to stand but received a sharp kick in the ribs that doubled him over. Having lost nearly half the blood in his body, he was just too weak to resist. The man, now wearing a black baklava and with his back toward Thomas, reading something from a piece of paper, was the same that had spoken a little English to him moments earlier. As the man turned around and drew a large knife from a sheath, Major Walsh screamed, "God help me!" As the knife was thrust into his neck, he just screamed.

He screamed until he couldn't.

Suddenly, everything was calm and warm. Thomas felt no pain and didn't remember the pain. He began to watch a movie of men doing inexplicable things to a man whose face he couldn't see. Suddenly, he realized that he was watching men do these odd things to the body where he used to live. As he watched them, he could see little tendrils of warm light continually try to reach the men, but there was a darkness that had the appearance of strangling vines around their souls that kept deflecting it. A wisdom that seemed like a long-forgotten friend reminded Thomas that the little fragments of light that were unsuccessfully attempting to reach the hearts of the men were prayers. The prayers were from those still on their journey in the place he just left and also from those of the place he was going to. Thomas realized he was watching his lost brothers from above. To his left and right, he saw two men smiling at him. The knowledge that he had just been through a trial with the two souls flanking him came immediately. As if a clever practical joke had been revealed, he broke into laughter with the two fellow travelers. Behind him was an indescribably brilliant light and without looking, he knew it was home. The light that flowed over and through him had a warm feeling and texture to it that was the most comforting sensation his soul had felt in what seemed a long, long time. Before going toward the Light, he looked once more at the men still traveling the difficult path of the place he just left and prayed, *I wish these souls could feel Your Love again soon.*

**VelEx Corporate Campus
Hartsfield Atlanta Airport
Atlanta, Georgia
3:56 P.M. Eastern Time
Wednesday, December 18th, 2011**

Chapter Forty-One

Low clouds hung like a grey blanket over the Georgia skies above the VelEx headquarters two miles from Hartsfield Atlanta Airport. There had been snow flurries the evening before and an approaching storm front made the outlook for real winter weather a distinct possibility. Sitting at his desk, Chris looked out his window considering the possible effect it might have on flight operations throughout the east coast if the meteorology team was correct. With a small sigh, he looked back at his computer screen but not before glancing at one of the several photographs situated on a credenza behind his desk. His son, Thomas, posing on the ladder that led to the cockpit of his F-22 Raptor was an image that always brought a smile to his face.

In the next building over, sat the office housing VelEx's telephone exchange.

"Velocity Express. How may I direct your call?" Donna Reeves, one of two full-time operators answered the call in the exact same cheerful tone she answered all the calls.

"Good morning. My name is General Michael Parks and I'm calling from Dobbins Air Reserve Base. Please connect me with the office of Chris Walsh."

"One moment, sir."

The phone rang through, and on the second ring, Chris' executive assistant, Michaeline Matteson, answered, "Chris Walsh's Office. How may I help you?"

"Ma'am, my name is General Michael Parks. I've just touched down at Dobbins Air Force Base. Is Mr. Walsh scheduled to be in his office this afternoon?"

Immediately knowing a call from an Air Force general wasn't the normal course of business for her boss, Michaeline assumed her well-practiced role of protecting him.

"I'm not prepared to discuss Mr. Walsh's itinerary, General. Is there something I can do for you?"

"May I ask whom I'm speaking with?"

Michaeline identified herself and repeated her offer.

"Ms. Matteson, I flew in from Washington D.C. to discuss a matter personally with Mr. Walsh. I need to speak with him as soon as possible. If you'd like, I'll give you my office's phone number at the Pentagon so you can call to verify who exactly I am."

"General, I'd be happy to take that number," she said. As she said it, a wave of fear passed over her. There wasn't a space on the credenza behind her boss' desk that wasn't filled with photographs of his son Major Thomas Walsh, in, on, or around some variety of aircraft. She was well aware of her boss' son flying over the skies of Iran in the most recent conflict to erupt in the Middle East, Operation Desert Spear. Over her twelve years as Mr. Walsh's executive assistant, she had heard countless flying stories of his own and those related to him by his son. Even Michaeline had learned to differentiate between numerous military fighter jets, and could tell the difference between the F-16 his son used to fly and the new F-22, he was now flying. An unscheduled visit from a general officer elicited in her a gripping fear. She said a silent prayer for the well-being of the handsome young man she'd met twice when he had visited the corporate offices.

"General, is there something that Mr. Walsh should be concerned about?"

"Ms. Matteson, would you please make it possible for Mr.

Walsh to see us in exactly one hour?"

She made one more attempt to learn what she absolutely didn't want to know by asking, "What do you want me to tell him the purpose of your visit is, General?"

There was a three second pause. Her heart sank.

"I don't, Ms. Matteson."

She sat silently for a moment. He didn't have to tell her. She knew by his tone and inflection that the general was bringing horrible news. Michaeline looked at the clock and for some reason, her mind registered the time as 3:52 p.m.

"Ms. Matteson?"

"I'll make sure he's here, General."

Michaeline hung up the phone and sat motionless, looking at the clock and watching the second hand tick. Her mind began to run through all the possible implications of the phone call that had just ended and she kept coming back to the same conclusion. Picking up the phone, she made a decision to call another office.

"Office of Jack Lee," answered Jeanette Scheuerman, Michaeline's counterpart in the next office.

"Jeanette, it's me, Michaeline. Is Jack in?"

"Yeah, what's up?"

"I'm coming over. I need to see him now. Is he alone?"

"What's the matter?"

"I'm not sure yet. I need to talk to him."

"Yeah, he's in his office. He's just finishing up a meeting with Ms. Price."

"I'll be right there."

Michaeline dialed into Chris' office and said, "I've got to step away to the ladies room for a minute, sir."

"No problem. I'm wrapping up some things that need to be done before I go home tonight and wouldn't want any calls right now anyway."

"Sir, how long do you think you'll be in the office today?"

"At least another couple of hours but if you need to go, I'll be fine."

She heard the words and her heart broke at the strong suspicion that it wasn't true. With a supreme effort, she kept her composure and said, "Thank you, sir, but I was just wondering if there was anything I could do to help out."

"You're the best, but I've got this stuff pretty much nailed down. Thanks anyway."

Michaeline felt an inch tall intentionally misleading her boss. She walked out of the double glass doors with the etched glass bearing the VelEx Logo and Chris' nameplate affixed. Taking a left, she walked twenty feet to the other senior executive's office and pushed on the door marked, "Jack Lee."

"Go right in," said Jeanette. As Michaeline walked past her desk, Jeanette lightly grabbed her sleeve.

"What's up, Michaeline? I've never seen you ask to see Jack alone before?"

"I don't know yet. I'll talk to you about it later."

Just then Jack's door opened as Jeanette was about to press for more information.

"Michaeline, come on in. Please."

Without another word, Michaeline walked directly into his office. He could tell by her expression that something was terribly wrong. Jack had never seen a look of such discomfort on his partner's normally ultra-composed executive assistant. After closing the door to his office, Jack went around to his desk and sat down. Michaeline continued to stand.

"Please, Michaeline, sit down. What's going on?" Hearing the quiver in her voice as she began to talk, Jack knew something was beyond just wrong.

"I'd…rather stand, sir. I don't know how to say this any other way than to tell you. I figured this might be better coming from you than me."

She related the call and what was said by the general. As she said it, Jack's own face lost a few shades of color. As a former military officer, Jack knew there wasn't any pleasant reason for a general officer to show up at their office, previously unscheduled. The company had not been participating in anything cooked up by the spies in Langley for several years. If they wanted something from VelEx again, the approach would be much more discreet than an Air Force general marching in the front door to their headquarters. He knew as well as she did that it had to be Thomas.

"You were right to come to me first Michaeline. Let's wait until the general arrives. I'll meet him in the lobby and talk with him first. I'm going to make a few phone calls to see what I can find out before the general gets here."

Michaeline excused herself and returned to her desk in Chris' office down the hall.

Jack sat and went over the possible scenarios that would bring a general to the VelEx headquarters requesting to see Chris without an appointment. It was impossible to know exactly what the military officer wanted. Based on prior experience doing government contract work, there was always plenty of notice when the government wanted something from VelEx. Jack had a an awful suspicion in his heart about why the general was coming but really wished he could know for sure. An idea occurred to him. He searched his contacts in his computer for a number of an old client who, under the circumstances, might be the one person who could shed some real light on the reason for the general's visit. Jack picked up the phone and dialed a phone number in the 703 area code.

The phone rang twice and an operator, not identifying her location, simply asked, "How may I direct your call?"

"Extension 33071, please."

"The name of the party you are trying to reach?"

He told her and was put through without another word.

The phone rang again twice before a gruff male voice answered, "Avernus."

"Gus, it's me, Jack Lee at Velocity Express."

There was a slight pause on the other end that sat in a seventh-floor office at the CIA headquarters in Langley, Virginia.

"What can I do for you, Jack?"

"Look Gus, I know it's been a long time. I also respect that you are limited by what you can do for me but I am hoping you can check on something. I wouldn't even bother if it wasn't incredibly important to me. Chris' secretary just got a call from a General Parks who is apparently on his way to our offices. Can you pull any strings to check on Chris' son. His name is Major Thomas Walsh. He's with the 27th Fighter Squadron, First Fighter Wing. They are operating out of Incirlik Airbase right now. I know this might be classified stuff but I'd like to know if it's at all possible to find out if anything has happened."

"Give me a direct number to reach you at. I'll see what I can do."

Jack provided the CIA officer his direct line to his desk and hung up. Fifteen minutes later, the phone rang again.

"Jack, I'm so sorry to tell you this, but I called a colleague in the Air Force intelligence offices at DIA. Major Walsh's plane was struck by a surface-to-air missile. How the Iranians pulled that off is beyond me. Apparently Chris' son was an F-22 driver, right? Well, a counterpart at DIA emailed me a copy of the radio transmissions from his cockpit to an AWACS plane flying command-and-control for the mission. It looks like somehow the Iranians managed to spot his jet on radar. There were launch warnings on the recording but, again, from what I know as a layman about the F-22, I'm not sure how that was possible. Anyhow, he did apparently bail out. I also heard transmissions from his wing man flying combat air patrol over Thomas as he reported two trucks approaching from the west to the position he last saw Thomas' parachute canopy on the ground."

Jack asked if Thomas had a chance to find cover and the deputy director of the CIA continued, "There was an asset overhead tasked for bomb damage assessment but when the jet went down, it was re-tasked to give local forces some eyes on Thomas. The imagery from it showed Thomas being carried to a truck by a small group of men. It would have been better if they had been regular Iranian Army but we're pretty sure they weren't. The area Thomas was attacking is a known stronghold of *Al Qaeda* insurgents. I will tell you that by looking at the images, it appears that Thomas put up a tremendous fight. It looks like he might have taken out a couple of guys before being captured because I could make out the guys that grabbed Thomas dragging some other bodies into the truck they took him away in. That's all I'm really able to tell you right now, Jack."

"Thank you, Gus."

"I'm sorry, Jack."

Gus and Jack placed their respective phones in their cradles. The spy, sitting in his office, looked out his window at the expanse of leafless trees that surrounded the Langley campus. There was more than just satellite imagery from that morning's events making its way through the intelligence community. The videotape that had been tossed over the embassy wall in Turkey, and was beginning to show up on some of the more nefarious jihadist websites, would quickly become public domain information, but Gus didn't have the heart to tell Jack.

Before standing to go to the lobby to meet the general, Jack sat silently saying prayers for Thomas. He called Erika's office at the hospital and got her voicemail so he dialed her cell phone. On the third ring, she picked up.

"Hey, babe, what's going on? Is everything alright?" she asked as she juggled some patient files and her laptop while she walked toward the physician's dining room.

Jack never called her cell phone during work hours unless it was important.

"Honey, I need you to sit down."

Erika stopped mid-stride as she was about to enter the dining room. With her heart racing, she fell down into a chair in the hallway and knew by his tone it was serious.

"I'm sitting. What happened?"

"It appears Thomas' plane went down in Iran. He apparently bailed out but I spoke with a friend in the government that said there was surveillance video of Thomas being taken away in a truck."

"Oh, my God! How is Chris taking it? Does Keely know yet?"

"Neither of them knows about it yet. I'm going down to the lobby to meet a general they've sent from Washington to tell Chris."

"Do you want me to go over to see Keely?"

"Let me talk with the general first and hear what he has to say. I'll call you back when I know more."

"You said Thomas was taken away in a truck? That means he's alive though, right?"

"Apparently so. I've got to go now honey. I'll call you when I know more."

Jack listened to the voice of his wife and, in that moment, was never more grateful that he could talk with her.

"I...Oh, my God."

"I know. I've got to go. I'll call you back as soon as I know anything."

There was silence between them for a few moments until Jack said, "I love you so much, sweetheart."

"I love you too."

Jack hung up the phone, stood, and went to the wet bar in his office, poured a tall glass of ice water, and emptied it in five huge gulps. He instinctively knew there was more to the story than what Gus shared with him. If Thomas was just a prisoner, why were they sending a general to inform his best friend? As he walked out into the foyer of his office suite, Jeanette looked at him. She knew by the expression on Jack's face that something very serious was happening.

"Is everything alright, Mr. Lee?"

"Yes, Jeanette. Thanks. I'll be out of the office for the rest of the day."

She could tell by Jack's tone that he was withholding something but also had the good sense not to pry. Jeanette knew her boss to be one of the most principled men she'd ever met and if Jack wasn't telling her something, he undoubtedly had good reason.

Jack rode the glass elevator to the lobby, wondering what would have brought down the most advanced jet in the world. As he exited the elevator on the lobby floor, he saw the general's staff car pulling into the circular drive. When it came to a stop, his heart sank as he saw a four-star general exit the vehicle along with a major who wore crosses on his lapels.

A military chaplain was the harbinger of the worst possible news.

Immediately a wave of despair, fear, and sadness racked Jack as he walked to the front door, noting that several VelEx employees in the lobby at the time had also noticed the unusual appearance of the military officers and the president of the company heading to the door to meet them.

The security officer at the sign-in desk looked at Jack and Jack said, "They're with me, Mike."

"Yes, sir, Mr. Lee."

The two officers entered the lobby. Jack walked up and quietly said, "General, Major, I'm Jack Lee."

"Yes, Mr. Lee. We know who you are. We need to see Mr. Walsh."

"I'll take you to his office."

"I think we need to see him alone for right now if that's alright with you," said the chaplain.

Jack looked at the chaplain and said, "Father, I already know about Thomas. When you tell Chris about his son, I'm going to be there. I'm his best friend and it is not open for debate."

The general looked at the chaplain major with a look of surprise, wondering how Jack could already know about the incident.

"Very well, Mr. Lee. Let's go."

The three men went to the lobby elevator bank and silently rode the elevator back to the top floor. Walking into Chris' office suite, Jack asked, "Is he still in?"

"Yes, Mr. Lee. He's..." she tried to talk but began to choke her words out at the sight of the chaplain with the general.

"It's alright, Michaeline. Why don't you head home for the day?"

She stood without a word and walked out of the office, tears streaming down her cheeks as she walked with her head down toward the door.

Knocking on the door, Jack said, "Chris, it's me, Jack. I need to talk with you."

Chris opened the door to his office, first smiling then, seeing the two military officers behind him, his face instantly blanched. A pulse of shock flew through his body as Chris tried to mentally deny the only reason the general and chaplain would be in the foyer of his office suite, unannounced, with Jack. As soon as he could, Chris blurted, "What's happened?"

"Let's go inside your office Mr. Walsh. Please." said the chaplain.

"Chris, please sit down," said Jack. "They'll get him back." The chaplain and general shot each other a look that Chris noticed but Jack didn't see. It appeared that Jack didn't really have the full picture yet. The general looked directly at Chris and said, "Mr. Walsh, I am here at the request of the Secretary of Defense..."

Chris held up his hand and growled, "General, skip it. What happened...?"

"I'm sorry Mr. Walsh. Your son's aircraft was struck by a missile during a mission over Iran. He ejected safely..."

"Then you guys are working up a recue plan to send Special Forces units to go extract him-PJs, SEALs, Delta, right?"

"I'm sorry, Mr. Walsh. We were drawing up plans for a mission to rescue him but this morning a video was tossed over the wall at the embassy in Turkey and is now being aired on *Al Jezzera.*"

"Video? What the hell kind of video?"

"Mr. Walsh, there is no easy way to say..."

"Then just get on with it. Just say it!" screamed Chris, his face already twisted in pain.

"I'm so sorry, Mr. Walsh. The people that captured him read a statement and then executed him."

Chris stared at both men. It took several seconds for the words the general had just spoken to be processed by his brain. He shook his head and said, "I can't believe it. I want to see it for myself! You've got to be wrong! Let me see the video!"

"Mr. Walsh, I cannot prevent you from looking for it. The same video was posted on a particular Islamic terrorist group website and several others have posted it now but I cannot recommend in any stronger terms that you don't ever want to see it. Our people have confirmed it was your son," said the general.

"They posted a video of them shooting my boy on the internet!?!"

The chaplain looked at the general who nodded.

"I'm sorry, Mr. Walsh. They beheaded him."

Chris sprung to his feet and let out a wraith-like scream, grabbed the edge of his desk and, with an incredible burst of strength born of his white-hot rage, threw his desk over onto its side. Jack jumped up to try to grab him but Chris easily pushed Jack away. The general and chaplain tried to help grab Chris to restrain him before he hurt himself as Chris began to furiously kick and stomp his overturned desk. Finally Jack and both military men tackled Chris at the same time, wrestling him to a couch.

"Mr. Walsh! Please, calm down! I understand your pain but this isn't helping anybody!" yelled the chaplain.

"They cut my baby boy's head off. They sawed his…..head… OFF!" screamed Chris as he fought against the restraint of the three men and again screamed, "I'm going to kill every last one of them!"

"I'm so sorry, Mr. Walsh," repeated the chaplain over and over.

Chris fell to the ground, in a fetal position, and began to wail. His inconsolable crying was so deep, his stomach muscles cramped. After a few more moments of struggling against the three men holding him, the wave of unbridled rage subsided and Chris finally lay on the floor sobbing inconsolably.

"Gentlemen, I'll take care of him from here," said Jack quietly. He sat holding Chris in his arms as his best friend simply rocked back-and-forth like a child and wept.

"I'm so sorry. I'm so sorry, Chris. I'm here for you," said Jack as he began to quietly weep.

**Arlington National Cemetery
Arlington, Virginia
2:31 P.M. Eastern Time
Friday, December 20th, 2011**

Chapter Forty-Two

Set back a respectful distance from the site of the service, the television cameras from two dozen news agencies fed live pictures into the homes of millions of viewers. In the front row sat Chris and Keely together. Next to them sat Jack, Erika, and Grace. The rows behind the two families were filled with friends, politicians, and numerous high-ranking military officers.

Staged in a secure lot nearby, being guarded by numerous serious armed men and women were two black limousines, several black Chevy Suburbans, mini-vans, and nearly thirty Metro DC police vehicles of every description.

President Sid Devane took the podium, first glancing at Chris and Keely Walsh, and then, for another few seconds, directly into Grace's eyes.

The president began, "Major Thomas Francis Walsh paid the ultimate price for defending the free world from those who seek only to oppress and enslave others. There are no words that will comfort those closest to him." He paused, looking directly at Grace. "Only time will make the wound of his sudden loss lessen. Before his aircraft went down, Major Walsh and his wingman successfully achieved the highly critical goal of eliminating the senior *Al Qaeda* commander in Iran. That act of military precision and heroism will undoubtedly save countless lives."

From a spot just outside the military cemetery, one of dozens of reporters was delivering the message echoed by most of the news agencies. The woman, wearing a black designer suit, spoke directly into the camera pointed at her.

"The president hasn't personally attended many military funerals but due to his long-time friendship with Major Walsh's father, VelEx CEO Chris Walsh, a White House spokesperson told CNN that the president insisted on attending the service."

At the conclusion of the eulogy, an honor guard delivered the twenty-one gun salute. Grace, not unfamiliar with gunfire as a FBI special agent and world-class shooter, still flinched at each of the three volleys. Colonel Dan Daly walked with precise military bearing over to Grace and handed her the tri-folded American flag and uttered the somber words, "On behalf of the president of the United States, the secretary of the Air Force, and a grateful nation."

She looked up at the colonel and then down at the folded flag. She suddenly noticed, for the first time since the day her world imploded, the diamond ring Thomas had given her, as her hand wrapped around the triangular pile of fabric. She hadn't thought about the ring until just then but in that instant, the impact of that reality slammed into her heart as she realized the man that gave it to her was never coming back. Waves of grief began to overwhelm her. Suddenly, without any thought of the thousands of people both in attendance and watching the service on television, Grace slumped over in her chair and was racked with emotional grief, her body shaking as the tsunami of heartache overtook her. As she raised her hands to her face, the flag toppled off her lap onto the ground. Quickly, Colonel Daly picked the flag up and handed it to Jack. With a slight nod to the colonel in thanks for rectifying what some may have considered disrespect to the flag even in light of the tragedy, Jack tucked the flag under his arm.

Jack and Erika, flanking Grace on either side, wrapped their arms around their inconsolable daughter. Over a minute later, when she could manage to, Grace sat up and dried her eyes with a handkerchief provided by her mother. Listening to the colonel who had given her the flag minutes earlier, and who was then at the podium and talking about her lost love in glowing terms, Grace tried to imagine the whole day was just not happening. As a defense mechanism of denial, she clutched the little locket she had worn for so many years since that magical day Thomas had flown her down to Florida for the weekend with their families. In that moment, surrounded by some of the most recognizable faces in the world paying their respects to the man she loved with all her heart, the flight in the Cessna with Thomas at the controls seemed like a dream. It was like it never really happened.

But she knew it had.

And he was gone.

Shoving her hand in her pocket, she clutched his pair of aviator's wings so tightly that the folding pin on the back came loose and punctured the palm of her hand but her emotional pain was so great in that moment that she didn't notice. They were the very same wings she had given him in that little plane's cockpit; the ones she pinned on him at commencement from the Academy ten years earlier.

The little inscription was still there: "...And touched the face of God. Love, forever, Grace."

Suddenly, a break in the clouds sent a moment of warm, sunlight across Arlington National Cemetery. Everyone looked skyward at the unexpected brilliance of the light that pierced what had been a gray and dreary day. Just as quickly as it appeared, the clouds filled in again and the gloom of the day returned. In that instant, Grace felt a bit of her despair lift. Although still in tremendous emotional pain, the thought burst into her consciousness about her neighbor, Karen Pollard, whose husband Eddie had gone off to war four decades earlier and also never returned from piloting his jet into enemy skies.

Twice, Karen had knocked on her door since the news broke about Thomas. Grace hadn't felt up to any visitors and didn't answer either time, knowing her neighbor only wanted to offer kind words or some measure of comfort, but Grace just didn't want to talk. Now she had more in common with Karen than she ever imagined she would. Certainly Grace always knew Thomas' job was inherently dangerous but she just never entertained the idea that it would happen to him. She knew enough about aircraft from listening to him to know he flew the one jet that was virtually untouchable. She just never thought it would happen to him.

The awful morning when her closest friend and mentor at headquarters, Special Agent John Durkin, had personally walked to her cubicle and asked her to come to his office, she had known something was very wrong. She couldn't begin to figure out where she might have made some sort of procedural error in her current work and her personal conduct was beyond reproach. Her supervisor had always summoned her to his office with a phone call in the past.

When Grace had entered the office and saw an Air Force lieutenant general standing with FBI Director Gordon Calley, both men with somber expressions, she knew it was Thomas before anyone opened their mouths.

"Mrs. Lee, the Secretary of the Air Force has asked me to express his deep regret...," was all the General managed to say before she collapsed to her knees, gasping for breath. Then she screamed, "*NO..no..no...no...nooooo!*"

After Grace's initial collapse, and with tears in his own eyes, her boss told her the worst news. He didn't want her to hear about it elsewhere. There were websites, some monitored by working groups within FBI headquarters, where those fascinated with brutality could download the gruesome execution of the man she loved. Both Special Agent Durkin and Director Calley assured her that the Bureau would use all of its resources abroad to try to glean any evidence to the identity of the murderers in the video first released on the *Al Jazeera* television network.

It brought her no consolation whatsoever.

As Grace collected a few items from her desk to leave to attend to her affairs, her phone rang at her desk. She recognized the number on the caller ID otherwise she wouldn't have answered. She picked it up and heard her mother Erika sobbing uncontrollably on the other end. Someone at the hospital had thoughtlessly mentioned Thomas' name, the video, and the website within earshot of Dr. Lee after hearing about it in the physician's workroom on CNN. It was nothing less than brutal to discover the news about the video that way. Erika had been so distraught that another physician put her on a table and administered a sedative.

Director Calley and Special Agent Durkin escorted Grace down to the parking garage where Director Calley's car and driver sat waiting to bring her home that day.

"I'm so sorry, Grace," was all Special Agent Durkin had been able to say as he closed the door to the director's car.

Sitting amongst an amalgamation of leaders and influential people from all three branches of government on that somber and chilly December day, Grace looked around and then silently said a prayer. Suddenly, the inspiration came that she had to go talk with Karen when she got home. She thought she could actually hear a small voice tell her that Karen needed her help as much as she needed Karen's. Grace suddenly realized that Karen still harbored such anger against the people who killed her husband four decades earlier and something about that seemed so sad.

God, how do I get rid of this hatred? she prayed in response to the dialogue going on inside her consciousness.

The answer she heard came from what she would later look back on and know came from God speaking directly to her soul: *Pray for the people who killed Thomas,* was the answer she heard.

Grace looked around at the people surrounding her, some of the most powerful people on the planet, and again she heard those words so clearly that it seemed someone was standing next to her, whispering in her ear.

If you hate them, you become like them…and the darkness wins.

**Willie's Wings and Barbeque
Shawboro, North Carolina
5:32 P.M. Eastern Time
Sunday, December 22nd, 2011**

Chapter Forty-Three

It had been a seven hour drive from Atlanta. For the first time in decades, Chris intentionally skipped Mass on a Sunday. He was so full of anger at God that he had absolutely no interest in going anywhere near a church. Periodically, during the long drive, Chris had raged alone in his Tahoe, screaming venomous things at a God he believed had abandoned his son and let evil reign supreme.

Chris sat nursing a Diet Coke in a corner booth. The rebel stripes on the flag hanging from the ceiling above him were the only bright splash of color amid the subdued earth tones of the wooden benches and tables. It was a country bar posing as a restaurant, complete with a heavy-set bartender sporting a whiskey company tee-shirt and baby-blue Carolina Tarheels hat, as well as a waitress straight out of a casting call for *The Dukes of Hazard*.

Chris had seen a gleaming red Chevy Camaro with the vanity plate that read, '2cute4u,' sitting among the well-used assortment of Chevy and Ford pickup trucks. He had no doubt that the owner of that car was standing over him with an expectant look.

"Ya' sure you don't want nothing more than a Diet Coke, mister?" asked the blonde waitress who was clearly at the top of the attractiveness scale in rural Shawboro, North Carolina.

Briefly looking up at the girl, Chris simply shook his head and went back to reading his newspaper. Not having given much thought to it, he didn't realize that sitting in Willie's reading a newspaper marked him for an outsider even more than the expensive leather jacket, corduroy pants, and loafers he wore.

"Suit yourself. Just holler if ya' change your mind."

As she walked off toward the bar, Chris looked at the girl and noticed the perfect figure she possessed and his mind began to formulate a type of internal commentary about the waitress that he hadn't made about a woman other than Keely in decades.

Ok, I'm trying to get in enough trouble already, he thought as he dragged his eyes off the woman and fixed his gaze on the door, waiting for his appointment to show.

Had it not been for a conversation with his chief pilot three days earlier, Chris would have had no reason to be in the bar.

Mick Clemons, with over three thousand hours at the controls of various VelEx aircraft over the past twenty years, had spent fifteen years flying for the Army's 160th Special Operations Air Regiment, inserting highly-trained soldiers and intelligence paramilitary officers into some of the nastiest conflicts in history before coming on board with VelEx. Mick had been one of the men tapped by the spies in Langley to help out with the operation to covertly arm the *Mujahedeen* back in the eighties. It was in the aftermath of the Russian-Afghan war that a multitude of fundamentalist extremist schools known to breed terrorism had been founded. It was in that environment of extremism and hatred toward the West that the men who had executed Chris' son had received their training and inculcation to their culture of murder and intolerance. Mick knew well the sort of people his boss wanted to exact revenge on and knew if he were to have any chance whatsoever, Chris would need to retain the services of some of the best operators in the world. Fortunately for Chris, Mick knew such men.

"I know a guy that can help. I'll talk to him if you want, Mr. Walsh, but are you sure you want to go down this road?" Mick had asked when they talked privately in Chris' office at the VelEx complex.

"I'm sure," was all Mick needed to hear to set in motion a call to a guy he knew to be world-class in the skills Mr. Walsh was looking for. The following day, Mick had asked if Chris was willing to offer a thousand dollar fee just for a meeting. When he had said yes, Mick handed him a small piece of paper with the address of the country bar he sat in.

The first few chords of *Days Go By,* by Keith Urban began blaring from the juke box as the man Chris had been waiting for walked in. Chris didn't know exactly what Major Steve Duffy would look like, but he instantly recognized the athletically-built man with the shoulder-length hair and goatee that stood in contrast to his military bearing scanning the room like a guy surveying a combat zone. Identifying Chris at the table alone, Steve walked straight up to the booth and sat down without any handshake or formalities.

"Mr. Walsh, what can I do for you?" asked Steve with a startlingly flat, emotionless tone and a deep, resonating voice.

Chris considered for a moment to offer him the thousand dollars he had been promised just for showing up and cancel the conversation altogether but the little voice inside him began its almost sub-consciousness whispering.

This guy can get them, he heard.

After a few seconds, Chris looked around, wearing the expression of a man who knew he was doing something he would never want as front-page news.

"I understand you have nearly twenty years' experience as a Special Forces operator. My offer is simple. You know who I am and you know what happened to my son. I will offer you and up to ten other men a million dollars each to locate, extract, and bring to me the men in the video. That is what I'm looking for. I need a team that can make that happen."

"Mr. Walsh, do you appreciate the complexities of the sort of operation you are talking about? We are fully capable of executing snatch-and-grabs but you are talking about a team of guys that are legally noncombatants infiltrating a hot combat zone, working to get our own intelligence on the identity and location of the men who killed your boy, and then extracting them out of the country without anybody ever knowing we were there."

"That about sums it up."

The former Delta Force operator sat quietly for a few moments until he said, "I've got the guys that can make this happen, but we'll need access to aircraft."

"I own a fleet of more than a thousand, with more than twenty types, Major Duffy."

The Special Forces veteran, who was currently making his highly-developed military skills available through Blackriver Security as a contractor, considered for a moment the fact that the man across from him had addressed him by his actual rank. If Chris Walsh had access to any information about him, it meant he was highly connected. Throughout his time in the Special Operations Group-Detachment Delta, otherwise referred to by the general public as 'Delta Force', even his rank had been classified. His very existence on the payroll of the United States Army had been handled by accountants in a special office. He just didn't exist according to the regular, main-force Army.

"So, Major Duffy, I can provide the wings. In addition, I have some friends at the FAA and in the government that can smooth out formalities like customs inspections and flight plan clearances. You just go and find the guys, throw them on a plane by any means necessary, but alive, and get back to a destination I specify without attracting any undue attention to yourself, and I'll make sure the path is smoothly paved."

The steely-eyed soldier sized up the guy across from him for a few moments and said, "It will take an advance of ten percent to set things in motion, Mr. Walsh."

Chris pulled an envelope from his pocket marked National Bank of Barbados and handed it to Major Duffy. Opening it carefully underneath the table, the major removed a single-page letter. Reading its contents in half the time it would take the average person, he looked up at Chris. Pulling a brand-new Apple iPhone from his pocket, Chris opened up the internet browser function of the phone.

"I've got a guy at AT&T who acquired this phone as a prototype. The SIM card and IMEI numbers don't exist anywhere. It's an untraceable phone," said Chris referring to the small temporary data chip in all modern cell phones and the

International Mobile Equipment Identification number. The phone was untraceable in so far as ownership of any kind and had been activated on the network using a fake name as an expensive favor.

Major Duffy brought up the online website to access the account detailed in the letter. In three minutes, he saw that he had access to an account with exactly one million dollars in it.

"That looks like we have a deal. Any further contact between us will be through Yahoo Messenger. Give me three weeks to put things together and work up a plan and I'll instant message you. Do you have a Yahoo account, Mr. Walsh?"

"No. I'll set one up tonight."

"Good. My screen name will be Pegasus911 and yours will be?"

Chris thought for a moment and said, "Icarus747."

"Good. I'll come online for exactly five minutes at eight p.m. each night. If you don't hear from me by five after eight, you will know I have nothing to report. I'll let you know what is going on and when we have the packages you're asking for. Also, I don't want to use an airstrip in the U.S. when we come back. I'd prefer one in the Caribbean."

Chris smiled and said, "I agree. That's why I'm having one built right now on a little private island I purchased last year. Once you have the guys, I'll give you the coordinates."

"Fair enough, Mr. Walsh. There is still one thing to consider. Since Iran has been a battle zone since early this year, the guys you want may already be dead. If we go over there and find out to a certainty that they have already taken a magic carpet ride to Allah, I want half of the agreed price for me and my team."

"Agreed, if you bring me their corpses no matter what condition they are in."

Major Duffy's eyebrow lifted and asked, "With all due respect, Mr. Walsh, but what would you want to do with them?"

"That's my business, Major."

Major Duffy looked across the table into the eyes of his new employer. Over his two decades of doing very dirty work in some of the most godforsaken places, he had come across some nightmarishly scary individuals. The tone of voice he heard from

402

Chris Walsh was one of a completely disassociated sociopath—a tone he was familiar with. It was chilling even to the ex-Special Forces soldier who had seen just about every variety of human coldness over twenty-five years. Major Duffy had no illusions that what he was being hired to do was nothing short of delivering some men to what would undoubtedly be an excruciating death if the billionaire across from him could actually get his hands on them. Still, it had been a fellow military officer videotaped being beheaded. Had it been his own son that had suffered Major Thomas Walsh's fate, there was nothing he would have done differently.

"Three weeks from tonight, look for me online at exactly the time we've agreed on and I'll brief you on my preparations," said Major Duffy as he slid out of the booth. Chris looked the man up and down once, noting the triathlete physique and numerous scars he could see on his exposed arms as Major Duffy walked away.

If anybody can bring the killers to me, this guy can, thought Chris.

Sitting in a battered and dented Ford F-150 pickup truck across from his boss' Chevy Tahoe, Greg Ruskin, let out a sigh as he first saw Major Duffy exit the barbecue and, like any seasoned war expert, check his surroundings before proceeding to his muddy, black Toyota FJ Cruiser. Greg could tell by the accumulated mud on the tires, wheel wells, and body of the truck, that the serious-looking customer who hopped into the truck actually used it off-road as opposed to the hordes of urban warriors back in Atlanta who owned one and took it to the nearest high-dollar vehicle detailer when it got the slightest bit of dirt on it. Greg hid in plain sight as Major Duffy drove by, pretending to take a pull off a pint of Jack Daniels that had been in the glove compartment. It was a convenient prop that made the experienced surveillance expert appear to be just a local yokel partaking of some hair of the dog before a night of serious drinking at the bar. Even so, Major Duffy gave Greg a serious look as he drove by.

Pretending not to notice, and not making any eye contact, Greg waited until the Toyota was twenty yards past before turning his head and instantly memorizing the license plate.

As the Toyota pulled onto the two-lane road that ran in front of Willie's, Greg called a former colleague at his home in northern Virginia. After two rings, the phone was answered in the terse, 'talk to me' manner of a guy with a serious job.

"Anderson here."

"Dick, it's Greg. I need some help."

"Hey, Greg! How are things in the cushy public sector?"

Greg smiled, thinking back to the days when he was a mentor to the most naturally-talented investigator he had ever seen during his time as an instructor at the FBI Academy. Having played a major part, behind the scenes, in championing Special Agent Dick Anderson's rise to the director of counterintelligence position, there was a strong professional bond between the two agents of two successive generations.

"Things are still cushy. Hey, can you do me a favor? I need you to dig a little on a guy."

"What do you know?"

Greg gave the description of the man in the Toyota and the license plate. Just then, Chris exited the barbecue place, completely oblivious to his director of security sitting fifty yards away in the pickup.

Keely, concerned for Chris' well-being, had called Greg at home that morning and asked him to keep an eye on her husband. She said he claimed to be going to see an unnamed friend in North Carolina and, with all effective lies, there had been some shred of truth to it. She had said Chris was evasive about exactly whom it was he was going to see and she couldn't remember anyone they knew in North Carolina who her husband would go to see at the drop of a hat.

"Sure, Mrs. Walsh. I'll be happy to keep an eye on him," he had told her that morning. After picking up Chris' SUV as it left their subdivision, he had employed his expert surveillance skills to tail his boss two states and five hundred miles to the little country bar where Greg currently sat, watching a potential legal train wreck develop for his boss.

"Gimme' five and I'll call you back."

Exactly five minutes and twenty-two seconds later, Greg's cell phone rang.

"What in the world are you into there, pal?" asked Special Agent Anderson

"Interesting character?" asked Ruskin, knowing the answer.

"Interesting doesn't begin to cover it. After I checked the name the car was registered to, I cross-referenced it with all operational identities with all current employees and contractors with our friends at Langley. This guy is buried so deep under special access clearances that I was surprised that I could get access to any of it. Your guy has been right in the thick of just about every serious covert military operation over the past twenty years. Think of every special operations tough guy you've ever known, put them all together, and they still wouldn't add up to Duffy's resume. The dude is ex-Delta and now CIA Special Activities Division. This guy defines the real deal. So what's the story, professor?"

Greg sighed and said, "Nothing right now. I'm just checking out somebody for a friend. Kind of a pre-employment thing." He felt awful having to lie to a trusted and respected colleague but knew if he raised any alarms in Dick's head, it would kick over a hornet's nest of trouble before he could try to avert the impending disaster for Chris. Continuing the disinformation ploy, Greg said, "There's nothing evil cooking with this guy. I'm just doing a bit of verifying in case I care to hire him for some security work."

Anderson sat quietly on the other end of the phone for a few moments and said, "Alright, professor, I'll take your word for it," not meaning it, and using the term of endearment he still used for his most significant mentor throughout his career. Anderson couldn't guess exactly why a man who was nothing less than a legend in the FBI was using back-channels to get info on such a fascinating character as one Major Steve Duffy but if Greg didn't want to share, he wasn't going to pry.

"Thanks Dick. Really, if I thought there was anything untoward about this, I'd share. Speaking of sharing, I've still got that place in Tennessee. We'll have to get together and do a little bass fishing," said Greg as he considered how to handle the delicate situation. He had a loyalty to his current employer but also a higher responsibility to his conscience. Greg had no question about why his boss was at the nondescript hole-in-the-wall fifteen miles from the Blackriver Security training facility, meeting with the sort of man Major Steve Duffy was.

His boss was trying to buy payback.

Sitting for a while and thinking about the situation, the brilliant mind that had made him the preeminent spy-catcher in the FBI over twenty years came up with a possible solution. It was going to be difficult and painful for the one person from whom he knew he needed to enlist help if he was going to be able to keep Chris from prison time.

Dialing a private number stored in his Blackberry, Greg was surprised when she answered. It had been a horrible few weeks for Grace. As calmly as he could manage, he laid out the situation and his suggested action. Greg was impressed with the coolness and professionalism with which she wrote down the details, especially as they related directly to the man she had lost. They ended their conversation and Grace began making arrangements for a day trip to Atlanta.

Greg started his truck again and began the long drive back to Atlanta, thinking about what he had just witnessed. In the years that Greg had know Chris, there had never been anything he had ever seen that would make Greg think he was capable of hiring mercenaries for payback. Still, the thought nagged at him that if it had been his son killed in the way Chris' had been, and had he the resources Chris did, Greg wasn't entirely sure that he wouldn't do the exact same thing.

Chris arrived back at home at nearly four a.m. Keely woke from the couch in the front room at the sound of the door opening.

"Thank God! Honey, could you have at least called me?"

"I told you I was going to see a friend in North Carolina. Somebody that could help me deal with the pain."

"Chris, I've been your wife for over thirty years. What have you done that you won't tell me about?"

"Nothing. I didn't do anything."

She knew he was lying

"I'm exhausted, honey. We'll talk tomorrow."

The following day, Chris sat in his home office, a large tumbler of scotch in his hand. Seeing him in that state for the third time that week, and still without a good explanation of his whereabouts the prior day, Keely began to admonish him.

"You know sitting in here and drinking all afternoon won't make the pain go away."

He looked up at her and was about to unleash an unpleasant retort when the phone rang. Keely glared at him while it continued to ring and finally picked it up. Chris watched as her facial expression turned to surprise. By what was said, he could tell she was talking to the security guard at the gate to the community.

"Sure, please send her in. Thanks Charley."

Keely placed the phone back in the cradle and said, "It's Grace. She's here."

"Did she tell you she was coming?" he asked suspiciously, thinking that Keely might just have set up the visit without telling him. Something inside him set off mental alarm bells. He couldn't figure out how, but he just intuitively knew Grace showing up was somehow related.

"No, I haven't spoken with her for a week. Let me go meet her," she said and left the room.

Two minutes later, Chris could hear Keely greet Grace at the door. Her initial tone of welcoming quickly changed and the volume of their conversation lowered. He could hear occasional words in hushed tones downstairs but couldn't make out what was being said. Just as his curiosity was getting the best of him, and he stood to go see what the two women were discussing, Grace appeared in the doorway of his office.

"Mr. Walsh…Chris, we need to talk," she said flatly. It wasn't a tone he had ever heard her use with him. Noting immediately that she wore her shield on her left hip and her service weapon on her right, a chill traveled through him. She had never come to their home without a prior phone call before. He instantly knew the truth about the purpose of her visit.

He could tell by her expression.

He knew that she knew.

"I'm here to tell you that I understand your motive but I…" she began but had to choke off a wave of emotion that was interfering with the serious FBI agent persona she was trying to present.

"Grace, you don't understand...," he began to plead but she held up her finger and glared, her eyes boring into him.

When she regained her composure, she continued, "If you go through with your plans for Major Duffy, I'm not going to be in a position to protect you. Also, if you don't put a stop to it right now, I'm duty-bound to escalate your actions to the attention of my superiors. If it gets beyond you and me, right here in this office, right now, there will be absolutely *nothing* I can do to protect you."

Chris sat, looking at the woman before him, thinking back to when she had been a little girl in their home during much happier times. His mind flashed back to all of the times she and his dead son had spent studying and watching movies during high school in their home. Looking at the armed, grown woman in his doorway whom he had watched grow up, Chris couldn't believe it had come to this: his widowed daughter-in-law threatening him with the entire legal might of the FBI if he didn't cancel his very expensive plans to exact revenge.

How did they know so quickly?

Grace's expression softened at the sight of her father-in-law, a man she had known her entire life, struggling with what she had just told him. She felt sickened at the prospect but was absolutely serious. Once Greg had told her about Chris' meeting with the Special Forces mercenary in North Carolina, she would be required to report Greg's suspicions to her superiors or face charges herself if the plan went one more step forward.

"Chris...I loved him more than life itself. Don't you see that if you go through with this, you aren't any different than the people that did it to him?"

In a wave of fury, Chris blurted out, "You may have been *sleeping* with him, but he was my *son!*"

The words hurt worse than a slap across the face. Grace physically recoiled as if she had actually been struck. Angered at such a callous and thoughtless remark, she subconsciously placed her hand on the grip of her Glock pistol in a position she had used to intimidate people before. In a voice Chris was totally unfamiliar with, Grace hissed, "Look, genius. You have one option that doesn't leave you trading in your closet full of Zegna suits and Ferragamo loafers for three orange jumpsuits and a pair of rubber shower flip-flops. Walk away from this plan right this second or spend the rest of your life in a federal prison. Nobody gets to play God in this situation, including you. Incidentally, Mr. Walsh, did you stop to consider that the people you are trying to employ aren't the types who take backing out of business dealings with a whole lot of humor? Do whatever you need to end this agreement right now. Just walk away. Break all contact with these people and you'll be fine. I'm not threatening you. I'm giving you fair warning."

With that, Grace turned on her heel and walked out of the room.

Chris' plan was totally shattered and he knew to a certainty that she would follow through with her threat of going to her superiors. It wouldn't take an accounting genius, of which the Bureau had many, to dig through his financial transactions to find the money in the offshore bank. As Chris' plan self-destructed before his eyes, a wave of blinding rage shot through him like a bolt of lightning. Screaming a torrent of vulgar profanity after his daughter-in-law, he hurled the remainder of the scotch in its antique cut-glass tumbler at the wall. Hearing the glass shatter, Keely bolted into the room and looked at the shards of glass on the floor and embedded in the drywall and the liquor trickling down the surface. In an effort to try to comfort her husband, she slowly walked toward him and tried putting her arms around him.

Shrugging off her embrace he coldly said, "I just want to be alone right now."

"But..."

"Please, just leave me alone right now."

That evening, sitting in front of his computer, Chris mumbled a string of curses as he effectively donated one million dollars by typing into the dialogue window on Yahoo Messenger.

"Things have changed. Enjoy the donation. Put it to good use. Keep it all. No strings attached. Icarus747."

**Walsh Residence
1055 Tullamore Place
Alpharetta, Georgia
6:37 P.M. Eastern Time
Tuesday, December 24th, 2011**

Chapter Forty-Four

Christmas carolers could be heard two houses over, singing *O Come all Ye Faithful* as Chris sat with a tall glass of scotch in his office. Oppressive darkness permeated the house; darkness made all the more so in contrast to the brightness of joy being experienced by the rest of the world. He watched through his window as the group of neighbors, many of whom he knew well, finished their performance and then continued on to the house across the street. Prompted by the door to that house opening, they began a performance of *O, Holy Night*. He could clearly see Bryan and Debbie Macon in the doorway smile broadly. Even while watching Mrs. Macon smile, he found it difficult to remember why people smiled. The level of grief and anger over the tragedies he was faced with had thrust him into a depression where the entire world felt like it was on the other side of an impenetrable bubble.

Another big swallow from the glass. It did absolutely nothing to quell the pain. It didn't even shut off the sound that would periodically pierce his consciousness: the screams. The inhuman cries his boy made during his last seconds. Chris knew he would have given up everything in his life if he could only have prevented what happened to Thomas.

If I hadn't made him love airplanes, he thought. His world felt so dark and painful. The phone rang in his office, not quite bringing him out of the mental morass of pain he was in.

"Chris, it's me, Father McNamara. I don't normally call parishioners if they don't call me first but just wanted to say that if you want to talk, I'm here. I don't care what time either. God bless."

"What's your point, Father?" mumbled Chris as he rose from his chair on unsteady legs, left his office, and headed to the bedroom. When he opened the door, he found Keely kneeling on the side of the bed. Her rosary lay atop the crumpled duvet. He could see several spots on the comforter where her tears had fallen, leaving an area by her head speckled with moist spots.

"Honey?"

She said nothing, continuing to pray.

"Hey, Keely?"

She continued to ignore him. The liquor and self-pity he felt resulted in a childish outburst that, even as he said it, he regretted.

"Praying for him isn't going to do him one bit of good at this stage of the game!"

Keely turned around with a facial expression, the likes of which Chris had never seen. It was a look of absolute horror and contempt at his words.

"I'm not praying for just Thomas, you selfish fool. I know it would never occur to you that I'm praying for the poor lost souls that murdered him!" she screamed.

Her voice was so forceful that he jumped, as if her words were an object hitting him. When he regained as much composure as the three tall glasses of liquor he had consumed that evening would allow, he compounded his untenable position by yelling back, "What insanity would ever possess you to pray for *them*? They murdered our baby boy!"

"Because it was the only thing that kept *me* from going insane or killing myself when another group of terrorists killed my mother."

Chris stood there absolutely motionless, shocked into an inability to speak the instant retort his mind had authored.

411

The words registered, but he had to replay them in his mind to convince himself that he had actually heard them.

"What do you mean *terrorists* killed your mother? You told me your mother died in an accident on the street!"

"Yes. She did. In fact, to be specific, since you are such a stickler for details, she died in several places on the street. My mother, along with six other innocent people, including two other mothers and their children, were the victims of the O'Shaunessey boys' lack of bomb-making prowess. They probably thought they knew everything they needed to-not unlike another man I'm pretty familiar with these days."

"Forgive me honey for coming across as a bit dense but what in the world are you talking about? I would think that this little story might have come up sometime during our three-decade marriage."

Keely glared at him a moment longer, sighed, and began.

"The O'Shaunessey brothers were building a car bomb out of a beer keg in their little apartment and apparently they weren't the expert bomb makers they fancied themselves."

Chris took in what she said. Her tone was one he'd never heard in her voice over their thirty-four years together. Even through the numbing effects of the alcohol, he intellectually knew that she was sharing a memory that was for her remarkably difficult. She wouldn't have kept it from him for three decades unless it was. Though knowing he should feel empathy for his wife's lifelong pain, Chris just couldn't move past his self-absorbed grief and anger. Instead of being snapped out of his self-pity by the revelation, he began to feel overwhelming rage toward Keely. In a flash, his mind sold him on the self-centered idea that if she had really loved him, she would have trusted him with the truth about what had happened to her mother right before she came to the U.S. In an instant, her lack of trust for him exploded in his mind, creating the indictment, prosecution, and sentencing of Keely for his perception that she had committed the grievous crime of withholding information he was clearly entitled to. Even as the emotion began to overtake his ability to think straight, he could almost hear a small voice in his head whisper *This is stupid. You have no reason to be angry at her. It was her business.*

The anger became unbridled.

"And you've kept that bit of information to yourself for the past thirty-four years we've been married?"

Without stopping, Keely continued.

"Baby, I'm so sorry but please, just listen. My mother was returning from the market and happened to be walking directly in front of their building the moment they blew themselves, her, and six other people to bloody bits on the street. It wasn't a bit of information I really ever wanted to talk about again, but since it bears relevance to your amazingly short-sighted question, I decided to tell you now."

"And what does praying for those monsters that killed our boy have to do with that?"

"I'll tell you precisely what praying for them has to do with it. At the time, I was so consumed for hatred for the O'Shaunessey brothers and anyone else involved with the IRA that I was nearly suicidal. I absolutely couldn't get past my anger and my hatred made my life not worth living. The problem with my anger for them is that, little-by-little, it was killing *me*. I stayed in my room, only leaving the house when absolutely necessary until one day, about six weeks after her death, my father brought our priest, Father Kinney, home and he gave me a way to get rid of the hatred that was destroying me."

"Oh, and would you care to pass on that precious bit of information since we seem to be in an information-sharing mood tonight?" he asked in a hideous tone of smugness. Even as he said the words, he could hear how ridiculous he sounded. Something about his rage and anger, coupled with the alcohol, completely eliminated his ability to moderate what he was saying to the woman he loved so dearly. He felt like some sort of demonic possession had taken control of him and all of his rage was being directed at the one person he would never intend to subject to it. He felt powerless. It was like he was a slave to his emotions, no matter how irrational they were.

Keely looked at him with a pained expression and simply said, "Pray for them."

Again without any ability to govern his mouth, he spat the

words, "And how's that working out for you?"

She stood and tried to move close to him. She didn't feel anger toward her husband, only sadness for the pain he had to be feeling. In that moment, trying to reach him, it slightly alleviated Keely's own overwhelming grief.

Chris felt so isolated within his own skin as she moved across the room toward him. He knew she was the one person on earth who most deeply and unconditionally loved him and was trying to reach out to him even through her own tremendous pain.

He actually took a step back as she approached.

She took another step and tried to put her arms around him, but he backed away again.

"Please, don't run from me. Just listen," she pleaded as he continued to retreat from her embrace.

Finally with his back against the bedroom wall he put his hands up and, with a cold rage to his tone, said, "Look honey, you can pray for them all you want. The only thing I'm praying for them is that they all receive a slow death. In fact, I was willing to pay any price to make that happen until you stuck *your* nose into *my* affairs. Incidentally, I'll be asking for Greg Ruskin's resignation tomorrow."

She stood looking at him, not recognizing the man she married.

As he glared at her for a moment longer, she finally snapped.

"You think you are the only one hurting about this? Do you think I've just been sitting in here all day tending to my knitting? He was my son too! So you want to know how it's working out for me, you selfish jerk? Well I can't say I've forgiven them yet, but I'm just a hair less burdened by the hatred in my heart. You know the kind. The same sort of hatred residing in the hearts of those men when they killed Thomas! So *that's* how it's working out for me, you selfish idiot!"

The phone rang again. Neither of them moved to answer it. When the machine picked up, it was Jack.

"Hey guys, it's us. We just wanted to say that if you need anything, you can call us any time, day or night. Bye."

Chris felt an overwhelming desire to run right then. He needed to get out of the house immediately. He turned and went downstairs to the kitchen, snatching a set of keys to the Mercedes 500SL that sat in the garage. As soon as he started the engine, Keely flew out the door to the garage, a look of terror on her face.

"What are you doing!?! You've been drinking all afternoon. Are you trying to kill yourself?!?"

"I'm fine. I just need to be alone for a while!"

"Chris, for God's sake, please get out of that car right now!"

He pressed the garage door control and the door began to roll up.

"If you drive anywhere, I swear I'll call the police! I'd rather have you in jail than killing yourself. If you leave me, I'll never forgive you!"

Chris put the car in reverse and backed out. He could see her pull her cell phone from her pocket and begin to dial. In the two seconds she pressed buttons, he knew she had just dialed 911. She just glared at him as tears fell down her cheeks.

He could hear her scream one more time, over the sound of the engine, "Chris!"

In the rear-view, he could see the carolers turn to look at him. Everyone in the neighborhood knew who the Walshes were and it was impossible to escape the pitying stares.

The incident had incensed people across the country but in the wars that had occurred since September 11th, 2001, Thomas hadn't been the first American to suffer the horrible fate that had befallen him. He had been the first military officer, though.

Pulling onto Old Alabama Road, Chris headed east toward the interstate. The only sound was the car's powerful engine and the air blowing through the vents. It was too quiet. He needed noise to silence the sounds in his mind. He flipped on the radio and through the expensive sound system heard, "Classic rock all the time. I'm Laura Davis with you on this Christmas Eve and hope you are spending it with loved ones. Now, a little James Taylor. Here's *Fire and Rain.*"

The words pierced his heart.

The melancholy opening guitar chords of the song he knew well from his younger days began and tears filled his eyes.

The song told a story of someone gone the singer always thought he'd see again.

The waves of grief began to rack his body. His rational mind told him to pull over as his vision began to blur. Something in the darkest part of him didn't care what happened.

The road rose and fell around blind curves.

His son's words reverberated in his mind. He could clearly hear the last conversation he ever had with Thomas.

We're doing good work here, Dad. I have to go. Love ya', were the last words Thomas ever said to him, two weeks before Thomas' jet fell from the sky.

When the song verse created images of flying machines in pieces on the ground, Chris lost his failing battle at controlling his grief and began to sob uncontrollably. In that single darkest point in Chris' life, he felt like he was sinking in a dark, inescapable pit of quicksand.

An Alpharetta police cruiser passed his Mercedes, headed the opposite way. The shift supervisor, Lieutenant Steve Garono, was just about to head back to the station to finish up his shift, and head home to his family when he received the call from dispatch about a report of a drunk driver—the person reporting being the subject's wife. As he passed the police cruiser, Chris' car had been straddling the median, drifting over as he only barely controlled the powerful vehicle. He missed broadsiding the police car by less than a foot. Garono stomped on the breaks, bringing his cruiser to a screeching stop, smoke billowing from his tires. Startled by the near-miss, Lieutenant Garono snatched his handset and radioed dispatch that he had found the just-reported Mercedes, and immediately took off in pursuit of the driver.

Man, it's Christmas freaking Eve and now this? thought Lieutenant Garono.

Chris never even saw the blue lights in his mirror.

As he came around the next bend to the left in the road, it was covered by an accumulation of water and he took it too fast. His car, hitting the slick patch, fishtailed and the right rear wheel flew into the soft dirt of the shoulder. The forward momentum of the car completely flipped it twice in the air before it came back to earth. It slid, spinning on its roof, nearly fifty more feet before coming to rest on a grassy area between the road and an entryway to a subdivision.

"Roll ambulance. Suspect's car is signal-fifty!" broadcast Lieutenant Garono, slowing his patrol vehicle.

The last thing Chris saw was the spider webbing of the windshield as the car impacted the ground and the airbag exploding into his face.

"Mr. Walsh, can you hear me?"

Hearing a voice he didn't recognize, and smelling the antiseptic smell, Chris knew he was in the hospital. He could hear the heart monitor and other sounds that his mind categorized as medical in an effort to make sense of where he was. He heard Keely ask, "How bad is it?"

"Remarkably, he's only got minor injuries."

"Oh, thank God,"

That's not fair, he thought.

Just then, a nurse injected some medication into the line in his arm and Chris floated back into unconsciousness.

Four hours later the sun coming in his hospital room woke him. A man with a white coat stood above him. Chris noted the name embroidered on the coat as Levinsohn. Chris sat quietly as the physician introduced himself.

"Mr. Walsh, I'm Dr. Levinsohn. How are you feeling this morning?"

Chris looked at the man and said, "A little pain, but I'm fine. Where is my wife?"

"Well, she's outside but I need to talk to you for a minute. Your injuries were relatively minor and you are lucky to be alive."

"So when can I get out of here?"

"Well, first I need to tell you that some people from the media caught wind of your accident and they're camped out in the waiting room. We've just moved them out of the hospital but I just wanted to warn you so you have the opportunity to slip out another entrance if you'd care to avoid all of that mess."

"So I'll leave by a back entrance or something?"

"Yes. That would probably be quite sensible. Actually, though, there's something else I need to talk to you about aside from that."

"What else?"

"Mr. Walsh, I'm not from the trauma unit. I'm from the oncology center. When you were brought in last night, we saw a few things on some CT imagery and, as a result, we found some indicators that called for further testing. We discovered through a battery of tests that you have a fairly advanced case of lymphoma. It is a particularly aggressive type and there is a mass in your brain that is going to start affecting your neural functions shortly if it hasn't started already. I'm very sorry."

"Are you kidding me? You mean I've got cancer?"

"I'm sorry Mr. Walsh. I can recommend chemotherapy but the reality of the situation is that it will only give you perhaps another six months."

Chris sat motionless, staring at the doctor.

"Would you like me to be here when you tell your wife? She's waiting outside to see you."

Chris looked at the doctor and couldn't speak for a moment. Something inside him felt like it shattered. A rage that was so dark and furious flashed through him and in that moment he renounced God entirely. His mind raged at God. Without opening his mouth, he screamed to a God he didn't want anything to do with anymore, *Fine, God! You killed my boy and now me? I've got no use for You anymore! I renounce You right here and now and I'm going to show you exactly what I think of this life and the miserable people you put here that did this to my boy!*

Regaining his ability to talk, Chris asked, "Does my wife know yet?"

"I was just about to speak with her."

"Hold it, Doctor. I don't want you to breathe a word of this to her."

"But Mr. Walsh...," began the physician when Chris pointed his finger and hissed, "Let me make this perfectly clear, Doctor. If you say anything to my wife about this, I don't care what the cost is but I'll sue you out of existence. I suspect you make a nice living doing what you do. If you don't want to have a legal nightmare on your hands, I suggest you forget we ever had this conversation."

"But Mr. Walsh..."

"Do I sound like a man who is leaving this topic open for discussion, Doctor? I'm deadly serious. If Keely hears one word about this, I'll use every resource at my disposal to end your career."

The doctor, though sympathetic toward Chris' plight, knowing full well about the tragedy that had befallen his unruly patient's son, and now the devastating prognosis, still didn't appreciate being threatened. In as cordial a tone as the doctor could manage, he said, "Fine, Mr. Walsh. Incidentally, once you are discharged, the police have a little matter to clear up with you about the particular blood alcohol level you were brought in with last night. You can call my office for any questions about the lymphoma if you care to." Placing his business card on the table next to Chris' bed, Doctor Levinsohn turned and left the room.

Chris sat motionless for a moment, trying to wrap his mind around what the doctor had just told him. Having known a few people who had suffered through the final stages of cancer, he decided that it was an experience he would skip.

An idea formed.

It came from the darkest place within him. If he was going to leave life shortly, it would be on his terms and he would have company. A lot of company.

"One more flight," he whispered to himself.

419

**Retirement Dinner for Chris Walsh
Ritz-Carlton Hotel Buckhead
Atlanta, Georgia
4:58 P.M. Eastern Time
Friday, January 9th, 2012**

Chapter Forty-Five

Chris and Jack sat in plush chairs near the window in the living room of their hotel suite. It was the finest room on the concierge level of the upscale hotel the company-wide function was being held at.

When Chris and Jack had approached the front desk earlier that afternoon, the hotel general manager, Amedeo Scognamiglio, had been waiting for them and extended his hand.

"Mr. Walsh, I'm so sorry for your loss. It is a small gesture but please allow me the honor of upgrading you and your party to the presidential suite. My son is an Army Ranger."

Chris could only nod in appreciation as Jack had taken the key and thanked the man.

In the adjoining bedroom, Erika and Keely made final preparations to their appearances before the four would head down to the main ballroom.

Noticing the weary look on Chris' face and the numerous yawns he was stifling, Jack was concerned for his friend's ability to make the trans-continental flight they had scheduled the following evening.

"Look, Chris, we don't have to make the flight if you really don't feel up to it. Nobody will hold it against you."

Chris looked at his oldest friend and, although he felt a knot in his stomach from the deceitful statement he was about to make, said, "I appreciate your concern but I'm just fine. You know flying my last flight as CEO to Saudi Arabia will send a powerful message and be good for company image."

Two weeks earlier, Chris had suddenly declared one morning, without any dramatic effect, that he was stepping down as CEO. Jack had hugged his friend and told him he would do whatever he could to make the transition easier. In the two weeks since, Chris had seemingly regained a measure of the enthusiasm that had been destroyed by Thomas' death. His melancholy was certainly understandable given his loss of his son in such a public and horrifying way and the subsequent ugliness of the publicity from his car wreck. It was almost a miraculous transformation to see Chris back to some semblance of his former self.

"I think it would be good to show the world that I don't hold any grudges. What could demonstrate that better than making my last flight as a pilot for VelEx to the city nearest the most holy of Islamic places?"

It was an Academy Award-winning performance.

"It's a great idea, Chris," Jack had agreed. They would announce the farewell flight that night in front of the nearly two thousand employees who had been invited to the farewell dinner.

Thirty minutes later Jack stood at a podium in front of the entire ballroom packed with full tables and dozens more loyal VelEx employees standing in the back of the room.

"It has been my distinct honor to have founded and grown, with the help of so many of you wonderful people, Velocity Express into the global success it has become. One person, obviously, has been there from the very beginning. Chris Walsh, my aircraft commander, teacher, business partner for over thirty years, and the closest friend I've ever had. Together, we've changed the world of cargo transportation forever," said Jack. Looking directly at Chris, who sat at the front table with Keely, Jack smiled. Chris returned the best imitation of a smile he could manufacture. No one could imagine what was going on in his head at the moment. If they could, his thoughts would have utterly terrified them.

Looking down from the podium, Jack continued, "Everyone in this room has felt the tremendous pain from your recent tragedy. If any one of us could take that pain away from you, we would but it's not possible. Your..." Jack was momentarily choked with emotion but he took a deep breath, regained his composure, and continued, "Your remarkable son, Thomas, was a hero in every sense of the word. He was someone I knew his entire life and for whom I have as much love and respect as I do you. He made the ultimate sacrifice so that we could live with a little less danger in the world."

Large tears spilt down Keely's cheeks. Others were similarly moved. Chris, however, sat stoically, showing no emotion. He could feel the stares of others at nearby tables. Thinking, *I should be crying but I can't,* he just looked up at his friend at the podium and continued to stare.

"We're all here tonight to celebrate your thirty-six years helping build VelEx into what it is today but really, we're all here tonight to let you know you have a family that loves you dearly. Every single one of us here cares for you and Keely just like family."

With that, everyone lept from their chairs and gave a standing ovation. The applause from the two thousand plus assembled VelEx employees was awe-inspiring. It brought a smile to Keely's face. Chris realized that he hadn't seen her smile like that since Thomas' death. He wished he could feel the warmth in his heart that he knew he had experienced countless times throughout his life. It felt, however, like the warm part of him, capable of love and kindness, was somehow blocked. It felt as though his heart was completely encased in ice.

Chris stood, walked to the podium, and adjusted the microphone.

"I really cannot say too much other than thank you all."

Looking at the faces in the crowd, a majority of whom he knew by name, they seemed to be hanging on his words. He could tell they were expecting him to say something more. He just couldn't. With a nod, he stepped away from the podium.

Everyone again gave a huge wave of applause.

Final Delivery / Will Dempsey

422

Jack returned to the microphone and readjusted it.

"Ladies and gentlemen, my VelEx family, I want to tell you that Chris and I are going to share our last flight together as captain and co-pilot, at the controls of our newest Boeing 747-800 tomorrow night. We will be flying the aircraft we've named 'Spirit of Freedom' from Atlanta to Jeddah in Saudi Arabia to deliver a new type of medical imaging machine to an anxiously-awaiting hospital there. It was Chris' idea to make his last flight to that part of the world to send the message that we are not a people who hold grudges."

That statement inspired another wave of applause. Jack finished his address and returned to his seat a few minutes later. For the next hour, Chris endured a constant stream of VelEx employees offering words of encouragement, consolation, and appreciation to the four at the table. The party wound down near eleven p.m. and as Chris and Keely stood at the elevator bank they watched the last of the attendees retrieve their valet parking stubs and presented them to the uniformed valet staff under the portico.

"It was a great party," said Erika.

Keely turned to Jack and said, "Thank you for what you said. I know it went without saying, but it meant the world to us, right Chris?"

Chris continued to watch his director of operations for Europe as the valet pulled his Mercedes up to the valet stand.

"Chris?"

"Oh, yeah, Jack. Thanks for that."

"You guys must be exhausted. Get some sleep and I'll pick you up at your house at eight tomorrow night," said Jack.

Chris looked at his friend and simply nodded.

The following evening, Jack arrived at the gate to his community at precisely eight p.m. Fifteen minutes later, they were southbound on Interstate 85, heading to the VelEx facility at Hartsfield Atlanta Airport when a sticker on the rear windshield of a Dodge Durango in front of them caught Chris' attention. It was a weathered American flag sticker with stripes that had faded from red and blue to orange and baby blue. He remembered a time in the fall of 2001 when almost every vehicle in America, including his own, had proudly displayed flags and bumper stickers that proclaimed such sentiments as, "We will never forget." The inner voice he heard cynically mused that the people of Saudi Arabia might be affixing green and white flags to the bumpers of their vehicles in the coming weeks.

After being immediately waved through the guard gate at the VelEx facility, Jack parked and they walked into the Flight Operations Center and were met by dozens of people who offered words of encouragement and handshakes. Assuming the warmest expression he could, Chris dutifully said a few words of thanks as he made his way through the crowd. Jack checked with the on-duty cargo manager and was pleased to know that all cargo had been loaded and their Boeing 747 would be ready for immediate push back from the hangar once he and Chris were aboard.

"Let's get this show on the road," said Chris as they walked out to a VelEx van that sat waiting to drive them out to the hangar.

The scene inside the flight operations building repeated itself when Chris and Jack stepped from the van. Well over a hundred VelEx grounds crewmembers stood in front of the gleaming, five-story-tall 747 in its hangar, and gave a huge round of applause. Again, Chris shook hands and mumbled words of thanks with a passable act of warmth and enthusiasm. He really wished they would all go back to doing what they had been doing.

After completing a cursory walk-around, Chris and Jack walked up the stairs and into the cargo hold of the jet. Chris looked back at the crates affixed with their attendant warnings and markings indicating that sensitive medical equipment was contained within the large crates.

Such a waste...but worth it, he thought as he mounted the ladder that led up to the flight deck.

**Flight Deck of VelEx 747-800
Call Sign: VelEx Two-Nine-Zero Heavy
Fifty Miles East of Barajas International Airport
4:19 P.M. Local Time
Saturday, January 10th, 2012**

Chapter Forty-Six

The giant cargo jet sliced through the skies over the rolling hills of Spain, breaking through a cloudbank. The skyline of Madrid ahead came into view.

"Madrid Control, this is VelEx Two-Nine-Zero Heavy with you at eleven thousand," transmitted Jack.

"Roger VelEx Two-Nine-Zero Heavy, we have you at the outer marker. You are cleared to runway two-seven left. Call level at four," responded the air traffic controller in accented English, the international language of aviation.

"Roger Madrid Control."

Chris sat staring out the cockpit window, trying to conceal the rage seething within him that was growing in intensity during the long flight. His anger was a borne not just from hatred for the people he held responsible for Thomas' death but also the discomfort he was experiencing from the internal battle he was fighting over the duplicity involved in the plan he was setting in motion. Never in a million years would he have predicted that he would intentionally deceive his best friend in the world. Chris also knew, after it was done, his actions would be heartbreaking but his time was limited anyway.

Jack continued through the descent checklist but Chris barely annunciated his responses to the items. Sensing his friend was not mentally present, which was more than a little unsettling as Chris was pilot in command of a half-million pound, four-engine cargo jet. Jack nudged Chris' arm and said, "You know, it might be a long time before you feel like talking about it but you know I'm always here."

Something about Jack's kindness infuriated Chris. He was trying to detach himself from his connections to others in preparation for what he intended to do over the next eight hours and Jack's attempt to reach out to him just made it all the more difficult.

Chris had successfully kept a lid on verbalizing his anger up to then.

"I appreciate it Jack, I really do, but the *only* topic of discussion that would be of *any* interest to me to talk about right now is how I might remove every single fourth-world, jihad-waging subhuman from the face of the earth in the most excruciatingly painful way possible! You want to talk? How about that? You know what I want to talk about? I want to talk about Mecca littered with the charred, unrecognizable remains of a half-million devout believers in Allah. *That's* what *I* want to talk about right now. How about *you?*"

Shocked by the outburst, Jack quietly responded, "Chris, I can't believe you actually mean that. I've known you for forty years. You've been my closest friend and I know you. I just want to help you here and if anybody has a right to care about how you are doing, I do. Nobody can feel your pain for you, but let me ask you to try something."

"What?" snapped Chris with a caustic tone.

"Think about the worst one or two things you've ever done."

After pausing for a second, he continued, "They show up pretty easily, don't they?

They don't even begin to compare to what I'm planning, he thought but he just nodded, not wanting to start talking for fear of loosing his nerve to carry out his plan.

"Well, I'm pretty sure I know you well enough to safely say you believe in God right?"

Chris paused, calculating his answer. After a few moments, he said, "Yeah, you know I do, but that doesn't mean I'm not furious at Him right now."

"Good, that shows you aren't completely lost. It would be impossible for you to be furious at a God you didn't believe in."

Chris hated hearing the reality of that. It was difficult to argue with truth.

"But let me get back to my point. If you had been walking, in those moments, hand-in-hand with that God of infinite love and forgiveness, the God of forever, do you think you could have done those things?"

Chris paused for several moments before answering.

"I hear you but it's different."

"How?"

Chris' temper flared and he barked, "I didn't saw Jesus' head off! So they can all fry in hell for eternity! And, I thank you for your little attempt to cheer me up. I really do appreciate it, buddy, but let it go."

"So you want mercy for you and justice for everybody else, huh?"

"I'm going to strongly suggest you just let this topic of discussion go for right now, pal."

Having heard enough, Jack snapped back, "Hey, man, that's *totally* unnecessary. I *get* that you are in pain. We *all* get it. Spewing hatred at me like that is not only unappreciated but unacceptable. I love you man, but if you can't get it in check right now, I'm assuming command of the aircraft and will formally file a report declaring you unfit for duty the second we land. Do you really want to force me to do that?"

Chris knew Jack wouldn't hesitate to declare him unfit for flying to the local aviation authorities. In the modern world of electronic communication, his license could be revoked and the local authorities notified to prevent him from getting back on the plane in a matter of minutes if Jack made good on his threat.

Seeing instantly how his outburst had jeopardized his plan, Chris immediately took a placating and penitent tone. He said, "I'm so sorry, Jack. You're right. I'm just dealing with it all as best I can right now, which isn't all that well. I know that.

Seriously, I apologize. I've got it together."
"No problem. I understand."

After the nine-hour leg from Atlanta to Madrid, Chris and Jack took a courtesy shuttle to the hotel from the airport without saying much. There was no animosity in Jack's heart toward his best friend. There was only deep concern. Once inside the hotel lounge, and after Chris ordered a soft drink and Jack ordered an unsweetened iced tea, Chris finally spoke his first full sentence since the outburst.

"Thanks for accepting my apology."

"Of course, pal. I'm just happy I could come along."

Jack was comforted by the apparent level of composure his friend displayed at the table when only an hour before, Chris had been nothing short of a raging lunatic. In his mind, Jack wrote his best friend's outburst as completely understandable, if not painful to watch, for a man dealing with such grief.

Chris took another sip of his soft drink and said, "You have to admit, the people at Boeing put this bird together nicely. She flies like a dream. So if I could have told you forty years ago in that little bar at Clark Airbase what we would put together and would be sitting here, right now, would you have possibly believed it?"

Jack looked up from the menu he had been looking over, smiled, and said, "Of course I could have. The God I serve makes anything possible. Let's not forget His role in all of this. You know what came together couldn't have possibly been just our doing, right?"

Sitting in the hotel bar, Chris' anger welled up inside at the mention of God again but he managed to affect a semblance of peace. Smiling as convincingly as he could he said, "Hey, I'm really sorry about what happened up there. I was just venting. I've got it under control now."

"I understand completely. We've been really concerned for you for a while. How's the grief counseling going?"

"It's going. It's still awful but I'm beginning to get sleep again."

"I'm so thrilled to hear that. You are constantly in our prayers. You know that, right?"

"Yeah, Jack. I know."

As Chris looked at Jack, the small voice of his conscience whispered words to encourage him to forget the whole thing. Just then, the darkest side of him thought of Thomas' last moments on earth and the pain sparked from that memory immediately pushed the impulse to abort the whole idea into oblivion.

Fingering the little plastic baggie in his pants pocket, Chris looked at Jack's iced tea. Chris' heart began to pound with guilt over the imminent subterfuge. He needed a few moments alone with Jack's drink. Taking a deep breath and speaking the first manipulative words of intentional deception he'd ever spoken to Jack, Chris said, "Hey, I've got to make a phone call. I promised to call Keely before it gets too late. Would you mind checking the status of the aircraft and I'll meet you back here in about five minutes?"

"Will do."

Seeing Jack take his iPhone from his pocket, and realizing the phone ruse wasn't effective for separating Jack from his drink, Chris quickly came up with another ploy. "You might just want to use the phone next to the bar. I found out that the international roaming charges on our cell phones are pretty outrageous from accounting. It's something we'll have to address with the AT&T people when we get back home."

Jack looked at his phone and then Chris for a second. Then, with a little shrug, he said, "Sure, boss. You're still watching the company dime right up to the end, huh. Our earnings before taxes last year were a little over thirteen billion dollars and a few extra bucks to make a call would keep you awake tonight, wouldn't it?"

Chris grinned as authentically as he could and replied, "Hey pal, a wise golf pro friend of mine once said, 'Millionaires don't pick up pennies; multimillionaires do.'"

"I bet you are going to enjoy your time on the golf course starting next week."

"Yeah. Roger that. I'll go make my call; you go make yours."

Both men stood and headed for a bank of telephones at the back of the lounge. Chris' heart really began to beat in overdrive as he listened to Jack dialing the VelEx flight operations office located at Barajas International. He knew the success of his plan hinged on whether or not the next few seconds went exactly as he needed.

Ten seconds later, Chris hung up the phone, walked up to Jack and mouthed the words, "Missed her," as Jack spoke with the flight operations manager.

Jack shook his head in empathy for his friend and whispered, "They're checking the fueling status right now. I'll be there in a second."

Now! thought Chris as he nodded and quickly made his way back to his table. Sitting in Jack's chair, he removed the plastic baggie from his pocket. He noticed a young couple two tables away. They were the only people who could possibly see what he was about to do. Totally engrossed in each other, they were gazing lovingly into each other's eyes. Chris hesitated for a brief second, noting the joy they seemed to have in each other's company and a movie of himself and Keely at the little Greek restaurant the night he asked her to marry him zipped, on fast forward, through his mind. It was another moment of hesitation before he dumped the white powder from the baggie into Jack's drink and quickly stirred it to dissolve the fifty milligrams of rohypnol, commonly referred to as a 'date rape drug', into the drink. The fact that the beverage was cold made it slightly more difficult to dissolve the powder.

Looking up at Jack, who was hanging up the phone, Chris saw the powder was only barely dissolved as his friend began to make his way back to the table. He was about to get up and move to his side of the table when he decided to stay exactly where he was and stir the drink, trying to create a look of absentminded daydreaming on his face.

"You stealing my drink there, Captain?"

"Oh," said Chris, feigning absentmindedness. He glanced down at the iced tea which had, thankfully, stopped swirling in the glass without any visible evidence of the drug.

Chris shook his head for effect, stood, and went back to his side of the table.

"Must be a bit jetlagged there," he said.

"You want to call it a night?" asked Jack.

Oh, no, thought Chris. If Jack didn't stay and finish the tea, the entire plan would shatter.

"No, actually there are some things I want to talk with you about," said Chris, desperately trying to come up with some topic to keep Jack at the table.

"What's on your mind?"

"Well, what do *you* think about the people who murdered Thomas?"

Jack looked hard into Chris' eyes and he began to have a very uncomfortable feeling. Perhaps it was Chris' tone in asking the question, First the outburst in the cockpit, then back to this topic. Jack considered for a moment calling the flight operations director back in Atlanta and declaring Chris unfit to captain the aircraft for the remainder of the flight but hoped the conversation he was about to have wouldn't give him cause to.

Jack took a deep breath, said a little prayer to ask God to give him the right words to help his friend, and said, "Chris, there's no denying what happened to Thomas was horrible. Nobody deserves what happened to him-even the people who did it." Even as Jack said it, he thought, *If he goes ballistic again, I'm calling Atlanta.*

"I'm trying to forgive them, pal. I'm really trying. Got any suggestions?"

Thank You, God. "Yeah, I do. Let me go back to what we were talking about when we turned final approach. Remember I asked you what the worst thing you've ever done was?"

Seeing a look on Chris' face that was a mixture of pain and shame, Jack said, "Didn't take long, did it?"

"I've made my peace with myself and God over it."

"I don't even want to know what it was. All I'm asking is that if you had been walking hand-in-hand with the God of infinite love and the God of forever that I know you believe in, do you think you could have been capable of doing it?"

We'll see, thought Chris. The question, once again, stirred the tiny voice inside of him that said, *This is a totally insane idea. Stop this abomination right now.*

"So just move on with my life as if those monsters didn't saw my baby's..." The tears blossomed in his eyes and spilt over onto his cheeks before he was halfway through the sentence.

"Chris, nobody can feel your pain for you and I'm sorry for that. I know it's a long road for you and Keely. I honestly hoped this last flight would do you a world of good but perhaps we should call Atlanta and get someone else to sit in the left seat on the last leg."

Composing himself quickly, Chris noted that Jack had taken a few sips of the iced tea and said, "Jack, I'm fine. Finish your drink up and we'll get out of here. I just need a bit of rest."

"Alright, but you didn't let me offer you a suggestion about how to really begin to heal from this."

"I'm listening," said Chris as his friend took another sip of the tea.

Please let this help, prayed Jack

Please let this work, thought Chris as he was intent on keeping Jack talking until he finished the whole drink. The drug in the glass was supposed to render Jack incoherent in a very short time. The substance not only dissolved any cognitive skills but acted as an amnesiac. Jack would remember nothing about the evening and even what he was doing in Spain for several hours.

"Chris, I know this is going to sound absolutely insane but have you tried praying for them?"

You too, huh pal? he thought as he opened his mouth and said, "You must be joking. The only praying for them I've been doing is that God is merciful on their souls."

Jack quietly answered, "He will be."

"Well, a lot of good that does Thomas, or Keely, or me, or the rest of the world that has to live in fear of these third-century backwards creatures bringing hell on earth into their lives because we're the infidel."

As he sat, defending his hatred, Chris noticed that Jack's eyes began to lose their focus and he slumped slightly into his chair.

"Just pray for the…, just pray…um…I mean just praaaay..."

It was startling how quickly the drug took effect and Jack's normally purposeful expression melted from his face.

"Jack, are you alright?" asked Chris.

Knowing the drug was taking effect, and feeling like an absolute fraud in asking his best friend if the drug he slipped into his drink was affecting him, Chris knew he had reached the point of no return.

"You have to…"

Jack suddenly slumped forward. The bartender took notice of Jack when his head hit the table. Chris tried to make it across the table to grab him before his head hit, but he was just a hair late. The glass of tea dumped over, a deluge of cold, tainted ice, water, and lemon slices spread on the surface.

"Dios, mio! Nececita un doctor?" asked the Bartender.

Jose Maria Sanchez knew the man at table twelve wasn't drunk because he hadn't served him anything more than the ice tea that lay spilt on the table. Bartenders the world over could always be counted on to pay attention to the patrons and Jose Maria was no exception.

"No, he'll be fine. I just need to get him to our room. Can you help me get him up?"

Jose Maria came around the bar and helped Chris lift Jack to his feet.

"This man, he need a doctor. He is no breathing!" said Jose Maria with a tone of panic. When he said it, Chris momentarily panicked and put his ear to Jack's mouth. The breathing had become faint but still there.

Thank G…

The sentiment in his mind trailed off. Realizing that drugging his friend might have lethal consequences, Chris quickly considered the situation and said, "Yes, go call an ambulance. Right now!"

Jose Maria dashed for the bar phone as Chris continued to check Jack's pulse which was very slow but steady, and his breathing that had become faint. Chris did his best to keep the waves of panic in check.

Ten minutes later, three paramedics arrived and one, who spoke flawless English, asked Chris a series of medical questions about Jack's background and what Chris might know of allergies, food ingested, and other possible relevant medical history as the other two prepared Jack for transportation on the gurney. As they rolled Jack through the lobby, one medic said, "You may ride with us if you care to."

A crowd of hotel guests stood watching the drama.

"What hospital are you taking him to?"

Hospital de Madrid. It is fifteen kilometers from here. Ten minutes for us, twenty for you if you know the city."

"I will meet you there in thirty minutes. I must call his family and our company."

"Very good. Ask the concierge for directions. It is very simple."

Chris watched as they wheeled his friend out the door, in a near-coma state because of his actions. Again, a wave of panic shot through him as he thought, *If Jack dies, I won't be able to live with myself.*

Immediately, the ridiculousness of the thought struck him.

Another thought came. *If we both die, and if everything you've ever said about God is true, then we'll be seeing each other again soon anyway. Probably on two sides of the fence, though.*

It was a perversely comforting thought.

Walking out of the front door to the bellstand, and watching the ambulance pull away without a second of hesitation, Chris listened to the foreign *hee-haw* sound of the siren. He approached the bell captain, standing at the valet stand watching the same spectacle, and asked for a taxi ride back to the airport. The young man with dark features and jet-black wavy hair whistled loudly the world over, and a taxi zipped up to the curb from the line of taxis assembled a respectful distance away from the portico. Ten seconds later, the taxi pulled onto *Calle de Galleon,* taking Chris on the short drive back to the airport. As Chris sat in the cab, the reality of what he was setting into motion hit him. Details of everyday life began to come into razor-sharp focus. From the back seat, without even having to strain his eyes to read the small script on the taxi license, he could see the taxi driver's name was Ernesto Gallegos.

So, this is what my last taxi ride feels like, thought Chris as he began to go over the details of what he needed to accomplish for the next step of his plan.

**VelEx Flight Planning Room
Cargo Terminal-Barajas International Airport
Madrid, Spain
6:45 P.M. Local Time
Saturday, January 10th, 2012**

Chapter Forty-Seven

"Yeah, Darryl, that's right. Who is the first officer on the next inbound flight? I need another co-pilot for the next leg. Jack must have eaten something at dinner because he barely made it to his hotel room before losing his lunch." Speaking on the company phone to Darryl Hoff, the director of VelEx flight operations, Chris already knew another inbound flight was due to arrive from Atlanta within the next twenty minutes. While still in the planning stage of his last flight, he had checked the schedule to ensure he'd have another pilot to utilize in the completion of his plan before ever leaving Atlanta with Jack. He had planned their late-night departure from Atlanta specifically to give him a three-hour window between his touchdown and the already scheduled inbound flight. Just enough time to offload Jack and get back to the airport.

"I've got a crew that should be on the ground in fifteen minutes. They are on final approach now but if you don't mind me asking, given the, uh...circumstances, Mr. Walsh, wouldn't you prefer to have another crew fly your second leg for you?"

"Not at all, Darryl, I've decided we'll fuel my aircraft and get the next leg knocked out today. I just want to get this over with and get back to the States but I *am* going to finish this flight. I want you to pull the captain of that aircraft off his next scheduled flight and extend his duty-day for another six hours."

"Well, Mr. Walsh, the captain of that aircraft is a guy named Arnold. I'll take care of shuffling pilots to accommodate you, sir, but are you sure you want to get underway right away?"

"Yes, Darryl. I know it's what Jack would want me to do. Would you get the flight plan filed and get me a start-up clearance for thirty minutes from now? I'll also need you to contact the Saudi authorities and get an earlier landing clearance at Jeddah. Just explain the situation to them and they'll understand."

"You got it, Mr. Walsh. I'll call you back in fifteen minutes when I have everything arranged."

Sitting in the director's chair of the VelEx Flight Operations Center In Atlanta, Darryl Hoff began taking steps to contact the captain of an inbound aircraft nearing the outer marker of Madrid International Airport that his day was going to get a lot longer than he expected. Using his computer, he electronically filed a new flight plan for the CEO from Madrid to King Abdul Azziz International Airport in the coastal Saudi Arabian city of Jeddah. Another ten minutes of phone calls resulted in Darryl speaking directly to an authority at the Saudi Arabian airport. He was assured that advancing the time of VelEx Two-Nine-Zero's arrival was not a problem. Darryl did a quick mental calculation about the departure from Madrid only two hours after arriving. There was nothing unusual about the request, other than the exceptionally long day, but if Mr. Walsh wanted to punish himself like that, it was his prerogative. The request from the outgoing CEO and co-founder of the company pushed, but didn't quite break, the boundaries of the sixteen-hour duty day limit mandated by the FAA, provided he got underway in the next thirty minutes.

Briefly, Darryl thought about Jack's ailment. He'd once gotten a bug when vacationing with his family in Cancun and knew how being sick in a foreign country was a special kind of hell. On a console in his office, he connected directly to a satellite uplink to the company radio channel to establish communication with the inbound 747 due to touch down any minute.

"VelEx One-Four-Four-Seven, this is Flight Operations, please respond."

A moment later he received the reply, "Go ahead Flight Ops."

"Captain Arnold, our CEO is waiting for you in the crew lounge when you arrive. Please report to him immediately. You will be serving as co-pilot for his final leg to King Abdul Azziz and depart within the hour. Acknowledge, over."

Slowly blowing air out, Cecil keyed the microphone and responded, "Roger, Flight Ops, out."

Inside the cockpit of the 747-400, both pilots looked at each other. Captain Arnold asked his co-pilot, also a twenty-plus-year veteran of VelEx, "Susan, does he really mean I'm going on to Saudi Arabia with the old man?"

First Officer Susan Sedmak, without looking up from performing her tasks as they made their final turn to line up with the runway, answered, "You're not exactly a spring chicken anymore yourself, Cecil."

Cecil loved Madrid and was looking forward to dinner in one of his favorite restaurants during crew rest, but apparently fate had other plans for him.

"You sure you don't want to help out and work just a bit longer today? I hear there's some great shopping, and beaches in Jeddah?"

"Nice try, Captain. Remember, don't try to impress the old man with your flying prowess. He's not signing the checks anymore after tomorrow."

With a screech and smoke from a thin layer of vaporized rubber, the wheels of the landing gear made contact with the runway and VelEx One-Four-Four-Seven began its taxi into the cargo terminal where Chris sat waiting.

"Cecil, thanks for accommodating me. I know this is an unusual request but I just want to get to Saudi Arabia and back to take Jack home. I called the hospital and they said it was food poisoning, but he'll be cleared to be discharged by tomorrow."

"Thank God for that."

Chris instantly felt a visceral reaction to that phrase. It was something he had said and had heard countless times throughout his life, but when the pilot he was using to implement his plan said it, he paused for a moment.

Chris had taken an extreme risk drugging Jack with the narcotic. He wasn't a physician but knew that people could die instantly and unexpectedly from exposure to drugs. He very well could have killed his friend an hour earlier and also weighed the reality that he might do the same to the man standing in front of him in the next few minutes.

Is this really worth it? he began to wonder.

Without any conscious effort, the sound of Thomas' last screams burst into his mind and the internal rage came back. Again, the self-righteous tone his internal voice had adopted over the past few weeks urged him onward with the plan by saying, *God, You stay out of this. It's none of Your business anymore. If it was, I wouldn't be here.*

While waiting for Captain Arnold to join him in the crew lounge, Chris had called the hospital to check on Jack just after hanging up with Darryl in Atlanta. When he spoke to the doctor, he was told that Jack was awake and responding to questions but that the authorities were enroute to talk with him.

"Authorities? What do they want to speak with him for?"

"Mr. Walsh, we take the possession and use of narcotics very seriously in Spain. We take it particularly seriously when it involves those entrusted to fly large aircraft."

He had hung up after that exchange thankful that Jack was going to survive the narcotics, but angry at himself for not foreseeing the possible legal consequences for his best friend. The voice of rationalization calmed his fears for his friend by telling him that Jack had limitless resources to fight any legal inquiry about the drugs in his system.

"Old habits are hard to break," he angrily muttered, just as Captain Arnold walked into the room.

His plan, as he had conceived it, was to ditch Jack in a local hospital and then get aboard his jet and take off alone. The only challenge to the second half was the necessity of a co-pilot to come aboard with him. Without the second pilot coming aboard, the airport authorities would quickly figure out there was only him in the cockpit and deny him takeoff clearance. His next fifteen minutes would be the most difficult of the entire scheme.

"The flight plan is filed already and the aircraft is fueled. We have start-up clearance in twenty minutes," said Chris.

"I'll just refill my coffee thermos, use the restroom, and be ready to go, Mr. Walsh"

"Please, call me Chris. We've met before at a few meetings, haven't we?"

"Yes, Mr...ah, Chris. I was at your retirement dinner last week as well. You know, it's a real honor to help out on your last official flight. Something I'll be telling my grandkids about."

Chris smiled without feeling any joy and thought, *You cannot possibly imagine how true that it.*

As he walked toward the door to the walkway leading to the jet ramp, Chris' pulse quickened even though he had no reason to be worried about being challenged. The uniformed VelEx security guard had a pleasant, expectant look on his face as Chris and Cecil approached. It wasn't everyday that the founder and CEO of the company paid a visit to a particular facility and certainly not everyday when that man was making his own, historic, farewell flight.

Everyone from the janitors that kept the appearance of the local VelEx on-site offices immaculate, to the fuel and maintenance crew, up through the local hub manager and staff all knew Chris Walsh was still the big boss for at least another twenty-four hours. Not one of them would even consider challenging his unusually quick departure after only arriving in Madrid two hours earlier. Chris' increased pulse rate wasn't due to a real fear of his intentions being discovered, but rather a result of anticipating what he was going to have to accomplish in the next few minutes without being detected. It was going to take tremendous effort and nerves of steel for his plan to not be discovered and shatter like a piece of crystal falling to the ground.

In his right hand Chris carried his pilot's briefcase. Inside were the requisite manuals and documents any pilot would carry aboard his aircraft, but in a pocket inside was a small, metallic case containing a vial filled with a clear liquid and a hypodermic needle and syringe. The substance inside the vial had required some effort to discreetly acquire but with enough money, it seemed anything was accessible.

Chris' phone began to vibrate in his pocket just as they reached the security desk. Pulling the device from his slacks, he saw it was Keely calling. It was one p.m. back in Atlanta and she would have just come from Dr. Hudson's office after another counseling session.

He almost answered.

Rejecting the call, he stuck it back in his pocket and reflected briefly on the grief therapist and the two sessions he had attended with Keely. During the first session, a week after his accident and diagnosis, Chris had sat quietly, thinking about how useful it was that Keely was getting used to grief therapy. He was going to be gone soon too, regardless of whether the cancer got him or if he was able to successfully carry out his revenge. There was a very uncomfortable moment in the office that day when the weight of the secret he was carrying saddened him beyond any level he had thought possible. The pain of not being able to bring himself to tell Keely the truth about his condition and the emotional weight of his anger felt crushing. For a sum total of twenty minutes of the first session, he tried to participate but just as he stood on the precipice of opening his mouth about his terrifying plan and the pain he was in, a dark, unloving part of him would put up a defensive shield. She, being a counselor with over two decades of experience in her field, saw through the act and had told him in each session, in a variety of ways, that if he didn't let go of his anger, it would destroy him. She couldn't have imagined how right she was. It was going to destroy him and, he thought, enough other people that Thomas would be properly avenged and the voices in his head would stop. At least he wouldn't have to endure the indignity of having his diapers changed as he wasted away in some room, attached to tubes and wires.

The letter explaining why Chris chose to leave this life in the way he had chosen would reach Keely in four days. He had instructed his assistant, Michaeline, to mail it on Monday and she had never failed him before. He did remember her expression when she noticed the address was his home.

"It's a surprise," was all he had needed to say to keep Michaeline from inquiring further.

"Have a good flight, gentlemen," said the security guard as Chris and Cecil showed their I.D. cards. Chris half expected him to ask him to open his pilot's briefcase, as if he could read his mind and could see his intention on his face.

"Thanks. We will," replied Chris as he stifled the urge to exhale with relief.

The two pilots entered the jet ramp and, before boarding the plane, stepped through a door on the right and out into the cool, Madrid air. Taking the stairs attached to the ramp that led down to the tarmac, the two pilots walked around the mammoth jet, doing a cursory pre-flight check of the plane. It was critical to his plan that Chris be seen with Captain Arnold doing the check.

Every maintenance person and aircraft fueler on duty that night had decided to come out to pay respects to the outgoing VelEx leader. Usually a crew of ten people would be preparing and loading a cargo 747 but there were at least twenty people on the tarmac, each coming to shake Chris' hand. Something in his head said that the gesture, as each person smiled and clasped his hand, should be making him feel good but it just felt like he couldn't connect on any level with the dozens of people coming to express their well wishes and respect for him. It was like they were two-dimensional cardboard cutouts moving around him and what they were saying was really meant for a different Chris Walsh. These were people he had probably never met, but all of them knew exactly who he was. They just smiled and shook his head and said, "Good luck, sir," or, "Have a great flight, sir."

He just pasted a smile on his face each time, shook their hands, and nodded.

As the two pilots reached the forward crew door to the jet, Cecil stopped, turned and said, "You know, Mr. Walsh, it goes without saying but as one of the most senior pilots working for you, I just want to say that everybody that flies for you has a debt of gratitude that we'll never be able to repay."

Chris knew that Captain Arnold was just echoing a sentiment that he had been hearing since the retirement dinner the prior week. He tried to let the words reach him each time, but it just felt like there was something blocking him. It felt like there was a thick sheet of ice around his heart that kept everybody away. He'd even had a dream about it with that exact imagery the night before.

Chris thought he knew how to melt the ice.

It was going to take a lot of heat.

"Thanks, Cecil. So, let's get this show on the road."

The two men boarded the jet, took their seats in the jumbo jet, and began the lengthy process of setting the knobs, dials, and computer systems to bring the four huge engines to life and other systems of the plane on-line. As they neared the completion of the start-up checklist, Chris said, "Can you finish up? That darn coffee is really insisting on a bathroom break before we get underway."

"Sure. I've got it from here."

Chris unbuckled himself, stood, and headed aft, quickly grabbing his briefcase. His pulse quickened in anticipation of his next move. Heading into the crew bathroom, he laid his briefcase on the small, metallic sink, opened it, and removed the small case holding the hypodermic needle. With a trembling hand, he managed to insert the needle into the small vial of liquid and extracted five cubic centiliters of the drug, just as the man he'd purchased it from had directed.

When he tried to place the drug back into the case, the vial slipped from his hand and fell to the floor, skittering behind the commode. For a moment, he tried to reach it but then realized it was completely unnecessary. Looking at the syringe, he saw he had already loaded it with enough of the drug for his purpose. Looking at the clear liquid in the syringe, he thought back to what the man who had sold him the drug had told him.

"If he's a normal-sized guy, that dosage will put him out right away and keep him out for at least a few hours. Just don't get creative with the dosage. Some people might go into cardiac arrest if you exceed it. You said you just want the guy out cold for a few hours, not dead, right?"

Just out cold. Not dead. Yeah, right, Chris thought.

Palming the instrument with the needle facing downward and

his thumb on the plunger in the manner an experienced knife fighter would hold a blade, Chris took a deep breath, pushed the door to the lavatory open, and slipped out into the small passageway back to the cockpit. Only four steps later, he was directly behind Cecil who was just about to start the number one engine.

Chris hesitated for a half second, looking at the spot in the neck the former doctor who sold Chris the narcotic said to aim for. Sensing that Chris was hovering over him rather than retaking his seat made Cecil begin to turn his head. Chris reached around to the area just above Cecil's right shoulder, driving the instrument up to the plastic into his neck.

"What the he...," yelled Cecil but the words were muffled as Chris threw his forearm around Cecil's neck, placing him in a choke-hold and pinning him to his seat, using every ounce of his strength. Cecil tried to unbuckle his harness but Chris' muscles, fueled by the adrenaline screaming through his own body, gave him a burst of super-human strength to restrain his co-pilot. For the next five seconds Chris' heart pumped blood furiously through his body and a wave of panic overtook him when Cecil continued to fight. Chris began to think he had injected the drug in the wrong place or that the man that sold it to him had given him a useless dose when, much to his relief, he felt Cecil begin to go limp. Had the drug been ineffective, Chris' entire plan would have been destroyed. It would be nearly impossible to explain his actions if a still-conscious Cecil was able to fight back and call for an armed intervention from authorities.

Chris un-harnessed Cecil from his seat and, with tremendous effort, pulled him out and began dragging him aft. Once he dragged Cecil beyond the door to the crew latrine, he reentered the lavatory and retrieved three pairs of flex-cuffs and small, folded length of duct tape from his briefcase that still lay on the floor and shoved them in his pockets. He was going to have to lower or drag Cecil to the lower cargo deck into the bottom of the aircraft and if he bound the man's hands right then, he risked seriously injuring Cecil's shoulder joints as he did so.

Five paces behind the flight deck, a hatch gave access to a metallic stairway to the cargo levels below. Unfastening the hatch, Chris opened it and lowered Cecil to the deck. It was a remarkable effort from Chris to manhandle the nearly hundred and seventy pound Cecil down the stairs without dropping him.

He almost made it.

Just two steps from the bottom, Chris' grip on Cecil's wrist slipped, sending the limp body crashing to the metallic floor of the upper cargo deck. To his dismay, he saw a nasty gash open over Cecil's right eye that began to bleed profusely. "Sorry, Cecil!" he grunted as he began dragging him toward the front of the cargo area in the nose of the aircraft. His muscles began to burn like they were on fire. Chris wasn't the devoted runner and workout fanatic Jack was, and began to regret it right then.

Halfway up to the front of the aircraft, leaning against one of the LD-1, or standardized loading device containers, Chris had to stop dragging Cecil. He spent nearly thirty vital seconds regaining his strength and almost began to panic. Knowing if he didn't finish up with Cecil quickly, return to the cockpit, and make his call to the tower, his twenty-minute start-up clearance window would expire and bring some serious questions from authorities. There was also the risk that an alert person in the control tower with a pair of field glasses might just notice there were no pilots in the cockpit of a jet that was within its start-up clearance time. The surge of fear-fueled adrenaline again shot Chris into motion. Thirty seconds later, Chris had Cecil's body in front of the LD-1 container he wanted. That particular container had a cloth side access panel that Chris unfastened and began clearing the packages out of. When he had emptied the space he needed, he reached into his pocket, retrieving the flex cuffs and duct tape. Quickly binding Cecil's wrists, ankles, and then binding them together with another set of the super-strong plastic restraining devices, Chris covered Cecil's mouth with the duct tape. Even if he regained consciousness, it would be nearly impossible for anyone to hear him or for him to extricate himself from underneath the packages Chris began to conceal him under.

Another minute later, Chris had re-packed the various boxes into the LD-1, completely obscuring Cecil from view. His entire shirt was drenched in sweat from the exertion and stress. As soon as Chris velcroed the cloth flap on the container back into place, he made his way along the small ledge outside the containers back to the ladder and up two levels to the flight deck. Retaking his seat, he surveyed the surrounding area, half expecting a swarm of cars with flashing blue lights to converge on the jet any second. Everything looked completely in place as Chris took a deep breath, keyed the radio to contact the tower, and continued his deception.

"Tower this is VelEx Two-Nine-Zero Heavy requesting extension on start up clearance. My final load and balance computer check shows us overweight by roughly five thousand pounds. I'm going to have to offload some containers."

His heart pounded in his chest over the several seconds it took for the tower to reply.

"Roger VelEx Two-Nine-Zero Heavy. Your start-up clearance has been extended another three-zero minutes."

Chris exhaled and changed the radio frequency to contact the local operations office.

"I'm going to raise the nose and I need your guys to remove the forward most two LD-1s. The balance computer shows us overweight by about five thousand."

"You got it Mr. Walsh," replied the on-duty supervisor. It was an unusual request as loads were always pre-calculated before departure. He made a mental note to check out the paperwork on this flight but not before immediately complying with the CEO's orders.

Ten minutes later, the two LD-1s that Chris ordered off his aircraft were on a flatbed truck and being driven back to the package sorting and loading area. As Chris engaged the controls to lower the nose section of the jet and prepare for departure, the thought that what he intended to do was a waste of time annoyingly popped into his consciousness. He even began to calculate the legal costs and possible penalties if he quit right then and had to face the consequences for what he did to Captain Arnold.

You've come this far and owe it to Thomas, was the voice he heard in his head.

From his briefcase, he removed a small DVD player and popped its screen up. Before leaving Atlanta, he knew he'd have moments of waning conviction so he had burned the video of Thomas' execution onto a DVD and brought it along. Starting the video, Chris couldn't bring himself to actually watch the vicious killing and fixed his eyes on a point across the airport, but he didn't miss hearing one second of the primal screams from his boy's last moments alive.

Breathing heavily, Chris took several seconds to compose himself before contacting the tower. After receiving clearance to push back from the cargo terminal, he began his roll out to the taxiway.

"There's no turning back now," said Chris to an empty flight deck.

Yes, you can, heard Chris. The words sounded like they were spoken directly in his ear. He whipped his head around toward the back of the flight deck, terrified that someone had managed to get aboard. Realizing it was only voices in his head, he screamed, "Shut it. Shut your mouth! If it wasn't for You and the demon-spawn You put on this godforsaken planet, I wouldn't be doing this!"

Chris lined up on the runway and shoved the throttles forward and released the brakes, shaking with rage and his heart pounding. The sound of blood pumping in his ears nearly drowned out the sound of the jet engines. Forty seconds later, Madrid dropped away from him as the huge jet lifted into the sky. With over four thousand hours at the controls of aircraft in his flight logs, according to his plan he only had five left.

Hospital de Madrid
Plaza del Conde del Valle
Room 219
10:07 P.M. Local Time
Saturday, January 10th, 2012

Chapter Forty-Eight

"*Señor* Lee, how are you feeling?" asked the man with the dark mustache and white lab coat standing at the foot of the bed. Jack's vision cleared as he awoke. He looked at the man and realized he was in a hospital but had no idea why.

"Where's Chris?"

The doctor looked at his patient and asked, "Em...Mr. Lee, you came to the hospital alone in the ambulance. There has been no one inquiring about you at the desk as of yet. Who is this Chris?"

Jack sat speechless for a second. His mind began to try to piece back together some of the events leading him to end up in the hospital, grasping at wisps of memories that couldn't form into any clear picture. The last remnants of the drug we being processed out of his body but most of his cognitive skills were coming back on-line. Still, he couldn't come up with a single explanation for why he was in the bed with a doctor standing in front of him. Jack was certain the doctor must be misinformed about Chris. If he had wound up in the hospital then Chris would undoubtedly be sitting in some lobby, waiting for word. Jack assumed it must be a language barrier. With his resources for explaining his situation exhausted, he finally asked, "Doctor, what am I doing in the hospital?"

"Mr. Lee, I am required by law to report any incident where a commercial pilot comes to the hospital under the influence of controlled substances. You were admitted after an overdose of barbiturates. Do you have a substance abuse problem, Mr. Lee?"

This guy's really got the wrong patient, thought Jack. Reviewing, as best he could, the events prior to his trip in the ambulance, which were beginning to come back into focus, he remembered Chris' tirade, the short trip to the hotel, then the lounge.

"Doctor, I have never taken any drugs whatsoever. You must have the wrong patient information. Would you please check your records and while you do that, I need to make a phone call."

Mr. Lee, regrettably, I do not have the wrong records. You were brought in after an overdose of barbiturates…rohypnol to be precise. Feel free to make any telephone calls you need to but I still must report this to your Federal Aviation Administration and to our police and government aviation officials."

What is this man talking about? thought Jack in speechless amazement.

The doctor left the room and Jack picked up the phone. The line immediately rang to an operator at the hospital.

"Si, bueno noche."

"Do you speak English?"

"Un momentito, por favor."

A moment later, he was transferred to another operator. Looking at his watch, Jack realized it had been over four hours since his last conscious memory.

"I need to make a phone call to the United States."

"Ah, regrettably our records show that the hospital hasn't established any form of insurance or method of payment for your treatment. I apologize but..."

Jack, for the first time in years, came completely unglued.

"Lady, I am president of a multi-billion dollar corporation in the United States. Perhaps you've heard of the little package company Velocity Express?!? You probably receive half the supplies for this entire hospital on our trucks so if you'd be so kind, I have to make an important phone call right now!"

The line went dead.

Jack looked down at the intravenous line in his arm and figured there couldn't be anything being run into his vein absolutely crucial to his survival. Carefully, he removed the needle from his arm, feeling slightly nauseous. Jack was brave but had a total squeamishness regarding blood. That was particularly true when the blood was his.

Looking down at his chest, he removed the heart rate sensors. Almost immediately, a large male nurse came running into the room.

"You must not do that."

Jack stood, and said, "I want my personal property right now. You are not a law enforcement officer and have no legal right to detain me. I cannot tell you how unfortunate it will be for you and this hospital if you don't bring me my wallet and cell phone immediately."

The nurse sized up the patient for a moment and, with only an hour left on his shift, he didn't feel like starting an incident that would require hours of paperwork. He nodded, left the room and returned with the doctor in a few moments.

"Mr. Lee, it is impossible to discharge you until the authorities have a chance to ask you about the narcotics you were under the influence of," said Doctor Ghersi.

"Fine, then get my wallet and fix the payment situation with the hospital accounting office. I have an American Express in my wallet that should take care of anything you need until you can verify insurance."

"Mr. Lee, the bill for this treatment may, regrettably, come to many thousands of Euros. It is not..."

"Look pal, it's an American Express Centurion Card. There is no limit. You'll also find my insurance card in it that covers overseas medical treatment. Not that it is any of your business, but I'd recommend you go to the nearest computer and look up the senior management of Velocity Express. You'll see my pretty face staring back at you under the profile of the president of the corporation. Are you familiar with the Forbes 500? It's down toward the bottom but you'll find my name under the category 'billionaire', chief, so I suggest you get me my wallet and we can end this ridiculous discussion."

The doctor nodded to the nurse. He quickly exited the room and returned a few moments later with a sealed plastic bag with Jack's personal effects inside. Removing the phone and powering it up, Jack listened as the line clicked and connected internationally back to the United States.

The phone in the Flight Operations Center rang directly at the director's console. "Hoff here," answered the man responsible for all aircraft operations worldwide.

"Darryl, Jack Lee here."

"Mr. Lee? How are you feeling?"

How are you feeling? thought Jack. *How long have I been here?* "What are you talking about Darryl? I'm calling you from a hospital in Madrid. There's been some kind of major screw up and these people say I was brought in here unconscious, overdosed on rohypnol."

There was absolute silence on the other end of the phone.

"Darryl?"

"Uh, Mr. Lee, are you sure?"

"Do I sound like I'm making this up to jerk your chain, Darryl? I'm standing here in this hospital room with this Doctor Ghersi and a nurse looking at me."

"Uh...Mr. Lee, I got a call from Mr. Walsh saying you had food poisoning and he wanted me to pull the captain off the next inbound flight to complete the next leg. He personally requested I file a flight plan to KAIA in Jeddah for immediate departure. He said he was sure finishing the flight was what you'd want him to do and he'd pick you up on the return through Madrid tomorrow."

"So he actually took off?"

"Affirmative, sir. We show them as being over the Mediterranean, just about to cross the Suez Canal and head over the Red Sea right now.

Jack sat perfectly motionless for what felt like an eternity but was actually ten seconds, his heart pounding and a cold wave of fear feeling like a pair of hands around his throat. The horror of what he suspected Chris was attempting became shockingly clear.

The effect was paralyzing until he gulped a huge breath like he was drowning, snapped out of it and exclaimed, "God help us!"

"Mr. Lee, what's wrong? What do you need from me?"

"Right now, get on the internet and get me the phone number for the United Stated Embassy here in Madrid. I want the number to the desk of the ambassador and the military attaché."

Darryl quickly navigated through the U.S. State Department website to the Madrid Embassy and provided Jack the number.

"What do you want me to do on this end, Mr. Lee?"

"Nothing. I'll call back if I need something. I might be wrong and don't want to cause Chris any embarrassment, but I think something horrible is going to happen. Don't you say a word of this to anyone right yet. I don't want to start a panic."

"Right, Mr. Lee," said Darryl as he began to panic.

The doctor and nurse stood looking at Jack. Having observed his patient's face quickly lose its color, the doctor said, "Mr. Lee, we have to get you back into bed."

"Doctor, please step away from me right now. I need you to leave the room."

"But..."

Jack took out his black American Express Centurion card and handed it to the doctor.

"Now, go and deal with your accounting people."

The two medical professionals left the room. Jack quickly dialed the main switchboard of the U.S. Embassy.

"Thank you for calling the United States Embassy Madrid. For English, press one, for Spanish, press two."

Jack navigated the automated system until, growing frustrated with it, simply pressed zero. The phone seemed to ring endlessly in the quick double ring style common to European phones. As he was about to hang up and try something else, a voice said, "United States Embassy Madrid, how may I help you?"

"My name is Jack Lee. I'm President of Velocity Express. I'm currently in a hospital up the road from you. I need to speak directly with the Ambassador or the Military Attaché. This is a matter of national security for the United States. I have a strong reason to believe the pilot of an airborne Velocity Express aircraft may have intentions to crash it into Mecca."

The tone in the operator's voice instantly told Jack that there was to be no major urgency assigned to a random phone call in the middle of the night with such an outrageous claim.

"Mr. Lee, if you'd be kind enough to provide me your phone number and where exactly you are hospitalized, I will be happy to have someone from the Ambassador's staff call you during business hours tomorrow."

"Listen pal, I know it sounds ridiculous but I need to speak with the Ambassador right now. I swear that if you don't do this, and I'm right about the captain of the cargo 747 I co-piloted into Barajas International today, you will go down in history as the guy at the embassy that could have stopped an act of terrorism that will make September 11th look like a minor inconvenience by comparison. I'm not some kook, pal. I'm the president of Velocity Express-perhaps you've heard of us? I'll give you the direct line to my director of flight operations in Atlanta if you want to confirm my identity."

With no more urgency to his voice than he originally had, the duty officer at the embassy answered, "Sir, like I said, I'm happy to take your phone number and…"

Frustrated beyond words, Jack slammed the phone into its cradle and a cold wave of fear cascaded down his spine as he realized there was precious little time to do anything. If Chris was already over the Suez Canal, he only had about an hour and a half more flight time to reach Mecca if that was his intention. His heart racing, Jack called Darryl back and asked him to Google directions from the hospital to the Embassy.

"Sir, it's slightly less than two miles from your location," said Darryl as Jack jotted the directions down on the back of a sheet of paper from his chart.

"Good. Now I don't know how this is going to turn out, but thank you Darryl. Stay by your phone in case I need you."

"Roger that, sir."

Hanging up, Jack realized he had to leave the hospital very quietly or he suspected that hospital security would try to stop him. Jack peeked his head out the door to his room and was grateful that nobody was in the hallway. He quietly left his room, walking briskly down the hall with his wallet and cell phone clutched in his hand. Thankfully, the nurse's station was located at the opposite end of the wing and he didn't need to pass it to reach the elevator. As he stepped into the elevator, he heard a loud yell reverberate from the direction of his room. He could easily see the doctor glaring and pointing at him from the door of his empty room. He could hear heavy running footsteps as the doors began to close. As the elevator began to descend, he heard furious pounding on the doors. Knowing it would only be a matter of seconds before the doctor alerted whatever security apparatus was at the hospital, Jack pushed the button for the next floor and exited the elevator, walking directly toward the end of that floor's hallway, praying to God there would be a stairwell he could take.

Finding a door with a pictogram of stairs, Jack ducked into the stairwell and took two steps at a time, arriving at the ground floor in a matter of seconds. Seeing no security at the front of the hospital, he bolted for the door. Just as he reached the main entrance, he heard a yell from the elevators. Two security guards came bounding toward him.

Out on the street, Jack took off in a direction he hoped would lead him to the embassy. Still in his hospital gown, Jack realized that getting a taxi would be almost impossible and there was none to be seen. The security men made a valiant effort to catch up but were absolutely no match for the man that regularly finished in the top two hundred runners in the Peachtree Road Race every year.

When he was sure he wasn't being followed, Jack ducked into a darkened alley to consult the directions he had written. Seeing *Calle de Serrano* up ahead, Jack said a prayer of thanks that he had chosen the right direction upon exiting the hospital. Darryl had given him the address of Seventy-Five *Calle de Serrano* for the embassy. He was about to start off for the embassy again but realized that showing up at the gate, late at night, in a hospital gown and sporting a wristband would only get him a quick arrest and ride in a police car, not in front of the Ambassador.

God, what do I do here?

An idea struck him. Scrolling through his contact list on his phone, Jack found the home number for someone that might have enough juice to get through to the ambassador at this late hour.

The phone rang four times and then went into voice mail. "You've reached the personal cell phone for Congressman Paul Miller."

"For crying out loud!"

Jack dialed again, desperately hoping that whatever Congressman Miller was doing just then, a second call from the same number would get his attention. Again the voice of Congressman Miller's administrative assistant prompted him to leave a message. On the third try, when Jack had all but given up hope, he heard a familiar voice. In that moment, it was the most beautiful sounding voice Jack had ever heard.

"Paul Miller."

"Congressman, thank God! It's Jack Lee. I need you to listen very carefully," exclaimed Jack.

Explaining everything from Chris' tirade on approach to Madrid, to waking up in the hospital, and the conversation with the flight operations director in Atlanta, Jack painted the picture to the Congressman in as rational-sounding a tone as possible.

"Paul, I'm hiding in an alleyway in Madrid in a hospital gown. I need you to get hold of somebody that can get through to the ambassador here right now. They'll throw me in jail if I show up at the gate looking like this with this sort of story!"

Just then, a police car cruised past Jack. His heart rate exploded and a wave of adrenaline washed over him. Another prayer of thanks as the car continued down *Avineda de América*.

"Jack, how sure are you about this?"

"Paul, I'm *not* sure, but you should have heard him. Chris said he couldn't wait until Mecca was reduced to a smoldering pile of rubble. Sitting in the bar later, he seemed in control and said he had been just venting but now I end up overdosed on drugs in the hospital and he's continued on to Jeddah without me? I'm sure he drugged me to get rid of me and if he wanted to get me off the plane, I can only believe he's got something awful planned. Seriously Paul, you have to admit it looks really bad."

"Alright, Jack. You hunker down somewhere and give me twenty minutes. I'm going to make some serious calls right now. I'll call you back on this number."

"Right."

Jack sat in the darkened alley of a foreign city. The feeling was beyond surreal. If he were right, he was one of three people in the world who knew of an imminent act of terrorism that would be so awful as to put his best friend in the world in a class of loathed monsters reserved for people with names like Hitler, Hussein, and bin Laden.

Please, please, God, let me be wrong about this, prayed Jack as he looked up and watched the navigation lights of a jumbo jet pass overhead through the clear night sky.

Thirteen minutes later, Jack jumped as his phone rang.

"Jack, get your tail to the Embassy. I got a hold of the assistant secretary of state who called the ambassador directly. They'll let you in at the gate and Ambassador Ceejay Wilson is on her way to the embassy right now along with the defense attaché. They'll listen to your story and if it's deemed credible, every Blackberry in the beltway will be going off in short order. Everybody will get called into work. I mean everyone. It's up to you now."

"Thanks Paul. Say some prayers because before this night is over, I'm going to need them."

"Will do. Call me back if you need anything else. I'm not going to bed anymore."

Jack ended the call and took off running toward the embassy. Stepping on a sharp pebble a few hundred yard from the embassy, he yelped in pain. Several people Jack jogged by gawked at what had every appearance of an insane escapee from a hospital, his bare bottom all too visible in the back of the hospital gown.

Turning left on *Calle de Serrano,* Jack was never more grateful to see the United Stated flag illuminated on its flagpole at the embassy up ahead. As he was less than twenty yards from the gate, a police car came to a screeching stop, pulling directly onto the curb ahead of him, trying to cut Jack off. From the car emerged a portly member of the Madrid police force.

"Alto, ahora mismo!" screamed the policeman, holding his baton menacingly.

Jack vaulted over the small space between the corner of the police car and the bricks of the building to his right.

Marine Lance Corporal Freeland's eyes went wide from within the guard booth when Jack slammed his wallet with his Georgia driver's license against the bullet-resistant glass.

"I'm a U.S. Citizen! I'm the guy the ambassador called about!" screamed Jack.

The guard depressed a button to open the gate just as the Madrid policeman reached Jack. Easily outweighing the paunchy cop by thirty pounds, Jack turned and flung the cop off of him when the officer tried to grab Jack around the shoulders and pull him from the guard shack. Quickly assessing the unfolding situation, another Marine quickly came from the shack and, in machine-gun Spanish, told the police officer that Jack was now on sovereign territory of the United States of America.

The police officer began to yell back in equally rapid Spanish, but the Marine turned to Jack and said, "Go with this Marine inside. We've been expecting you."

Another two Marines appeared at the gate, both looking like they had just stepped off a recruiting poster.

"Mr. Lee, please follow me."

Jack turned one last time to see the Marine and the police officer exchanging what were obviously colorful words in Spanish. The Marine brought his M-16 rifle to port arms as perfectly intimidating punctuation. The matter of Mr. Lee was no longer open for discussion.

Jack followed the Marines inside and into an elevator. As the three men rode silently, the words 'deemed credible' kept reverberating in his mind.

A groggy Ambassador Ceejay Wilson walked into her office ten minutes later. Five minutes after that, a naval commander serving as the defense attaché at the embassy sat with coffee, listening to the events as Jack related them.

"You really think your boss intends to do something crazy with the plane?" asked Commander Mason.

"Well, if you check the original flight plan filed, we weren't supposed to depart until 0900 tomorrow morning."

"Yeah, but what makes you think he wants to fly his plane into Mecca, Mr. Lee?" continued Commander Mason, looking at a laptop he brought from his office. On the screen was a classified file on Mr. Christopher Walsh that he had requested from an FBI database. There had been three speeding tickets over twenty-two years and nothing else remotely criminal. There was absolutely nothing in the dossier that gave any indication of previous erratic behavior or instability from the man. According to all information available to the commander which, as an intelligence officer of the United States government, was quite extensive, Chris Walsh appeared to be a typical billionaire businessman.

Looking at the skeptical expressions on both the face of the ambassador and the military attaché, Jack felt a wave of desperation come over him.

They weren't buying his suspicions.

"Look, somehow I was drugged, my best friend has taken off to Saudi Arabia without me, which I can't believe he would do knowing his closest friend was in the hospital in a foreign country, and before touching down earlier tonight, Chris was ranting and raving about how he would like to incinerate Mecca. I know that's all circumstantial but if you guys don't do something to at least try to intercept his aircraft, I know in my heart something horrible is going to happen."

"Mr. Lee...," began Ambassador Wilson in a tone a mother would use to placate a child having a tantrum.

"Excuse me, Madam Ambassador. I appreciate the late hour and the fact that both of you want to be one hundred percent sure before creating a potentially embarrassing or dangerous incident but I'm telling you, I know something terrible is going to happen."

"Jack, we'd love to be able to help but...," said Commander Mason when Jack interrupted and said, "I know I don't have any proof but all the narcotics and him leaving me here aside, you do have to consider what happened to his son. It occurs to me that if my daughter were killed the way his son, Major Thomas Walsh was, it might...," Jack paused, looked at the ambassador and attaché with an expression of desperation, and nearly choked on the words, "drive me over the edge."

Commander Mason knew everything Jack was saying made sense but without any more evidence to assess his claim a credible threat, the naval officer just couldn't justify escalating the situation to military involvement.

"Mr. Lee, I'm so sorry. I admit it does look suspicious but I just don't have enough here to escalate this. You realize you are talking about committing United States military assets to intercept a civilian aircraft in international airspace and that's not a small deal, Mr. Lee. Additionally, we're not just talking about an everyday commercial pilot. We're talking about a billionaire like yourself and a guy with lots of friends in high places. I'm just an embassy guy, but I do know a little more about VelEx's contributions to the United States than you might think, Mr. Lee. If we get this wrong, heads will roll. I'm sorry, but I just don't have enough here to escalate this. I really am sorry."

Jack looked at both the Ambassador and commander and just hung his head. He just sat quietly, on the verge of tears, staring blankly at the ornate rug on the floor and beginning to pray.

VelEx Cargo Sorting Facility-Madrid
Barajas International Airport
Madrid, Spain
10:52 P.M. Local Time
Saturday, January 10th, 2012

Chapter Forty-Nine

Aranxca Calderon rubbed her eyes and glanced over at the clock. It had been a long day and she really didn't feel like doing one more iota of work while waiting for the graveyard crew to take over at eleven p.m. Grateful that several of the night shift crew had already arrived and were preparing to take over officially in eight minutes, Aranxca stretched her aching back.

Leaning against one of the LD-1 containers that had been offloaded from the 6:45 p.m. departure of VelEx flight Two-Nine-Zero, she fingered the packet of cigarettes in her pocket. She could almost taste the smoke going into her lungs. The trek a half-mile away to the nearest point where smoking was permitted made cigarette breaks rare. She usually was so busy through her shift that she just toughed out the nicotine cravings until after work. The pay made her sacrifice worthwhile.

Just as she was about to head for the computer terminal she clocked out on, she heard the sound of some boxes shifting within the container she was leaning against. Shaking her head, she suspected the load device hadn't been properly packed by one of the crews. It wasn't uncommon for some of the standards of loading to be slightly 'modified' by the crews. Each load device had a plan for maximizing the useable space inside and packing procedures were carefully designed. No shipping company wanted to have wasted space inside aircraft that were costing, on average, nearly seven thousand dollars an hour in operating costs each time it moved.

For a moment, Arancxa almost reached over to open the Velcro-sealed flap and inspect the load, but it was quitting time. She made a mental note to add the observation into the computerized pass-on log for the next shift to deal with. A minute later, she was just signing her last form for the night when she heard another rustling of packages but the sound's duration was much longer than would have been if there were just a few packages settling.

What in the world?

Pulling the Velcro-attached blue canvas flap aside with a sharp jerk sideways, Aranxca let out a yelp of fear and shock when she saw a man in a pilot's uniform glaring at her, trying to scream through a gag that had been duct taped onto his mouth.

First screaming at the top of her lungs and then, gaining a tiny bit of composure, Arancxa yelled, "Cesar! Cesar! Get over here right now and call the Civil Guard! There's a guy—a pilot—in here!"

The terrified screams of the normally soft-spoken Arancxa immediately got the attention of her supervisor, Cesar Mederas, from across the hangar. He was in the middle of the shift change transition with the incoming supervisor of the graveyard shift when Arancxa's blood-curdling shriek turned the heads of every VelEx ground crewmember within a hundred yards.

"What is that woman screaming about?" joked one of the other VelEx employees.

"She must have broken a nail," from another man. The men surrounding him broke into laughter.

Cesar jogged over to the container. When he looked inside, his stomach felt like it completely flipped as he saw Captain Cecil Arnold struggling and kicking furiously. Immediately he began to toss packages out of the load device and said, "Sir, just stay still! We'll get some help and get you out of there."

Cecil stopped thrashing around but the air passed forcefully in and out of his nostrils from the exertion.

Cesar knew the man tied up in the box was the beginning of an extremely long night for him. "Every one of you people, nobody goes anywhere!" he screamed to his crew.

"Aw, boss, we're done for the day. Whatever it is, I'm sure you can handle it," called back one of his more free-spirited crew.

"You walk out that door, you'll collect your last paycheck tomorrow!" roared Cesar as he reached for a phone next to one of the sorting tables. That got the attention of the employees heading toward the door. They all immediately halted and began looking at each other. Somebody was in serious trouble.

Picking up the phone, Cesar dialed the Madrid Civil Guard dispatcher and within two minutes, a wail of sirens began to rise to a deafening level. Blue flashing lights began to illuminate the windows of the building as a fleet of police and ambulances descended on the sorting facility. Within seconds, the building was filled with dozens of uniformed Civil Guard officers, security officials, and a team of paramedics. In a few minutes, they had freed Cecil from his bindings and loaded onto a gurney.

"Call my flight operations center in Atlanta! That crazy psychopath drugged me!" screamed Cecil.

Senior Inspector Guerra of the Civil Guard dialed the number of VelEx Flight Operations. It was nearly five p.m. back in Atlanta when Darryl Hoff's assistant buzzed his phone.

"Mr. Hoff, there is a man identifying himself as the senior inspector of the Civil Guard at Barajas International asking for you."

"Put him through," said Darryl. Not surprised at all by the call, Darryl's heart sunk. Just before the line connected, Darryl prayed, *God, let Chris be alright. Please let Jack be wrong.*

"Mr. Hoff, I'm Senior Inspector Guerra with the airport police here at Barajas International Airport," said the voice in perfect, slightly-accented English.

"How can I help you, Inspector?"

"We have just found a captain of your company tied up in one of your company's loading devices. It was actually removed from the cargo hold of your flight Two-Nine-Zero. He claims he was drugged by the pilot and, he claims, was stuck in the loading device and offloaded."

"God help us all! I'll have to call you back, Inspector. I think something really bad is about to happen!"

"But I...."

Darryl hung up and sat with his heart pounding for a minute, trying to figure out what he should do.

He reached for his phone.

Jack Lee sat in the Ambassador's office wearing a U.S. Navy sweatshirt and sweatpants that Commander Mason had retrieved from his office so he could have more dignity than the flimsy hospital gown had afforded him.

"Look, I know you guys aren't buying this but what if I pay for the fuel used by any jets you send to intercept him? You know I'm good for it."

Commander Mason shot the Ambassador a glance as his eyebrows raised a fraction of an inch.

Just then, Jack's phone began to vibrate on the table. Seeing the call was coming from flight operations, he snatched it up.

"God in heaven," said Jack almost silently. There was no doubt in his heart anymore, much as he desperately wanted to be wrong. His best friend was on a suicide mission. The shock of the news about Captain Arnold's discovery in the loading device almost caused him to vomit. The wave of fear was overpowering.

"Commander Mason, it's my flight operations director. You need to speak with him," said Jack as he handed the phone to the naval officer. Jack's hand was shaking.

After what seemed like an eternity, as Darryl related to Commander Mason the news about Captain Arnold's incapacitation and discovery in the cargo container, the commander handed the phone back to Jack and stood straight up.

"New information, Commander?" asked Ambassador Wilson.

"Unfortunately, I now have something to work with. I have to send a flash priority message to the Pentagon," the attaché said as he walked briskly out of the room.

The White House
Washington D.C.
4:36 P.M. Eastern Time
Saturday, January 10th, 2012

Chapter Fifty

White House Chief of Staff Sean Frost sat at his desk working on a few changes to President Sid Devane's itinerary for the next day. From his credenza, the STU-III phone began to warble in its distinctive ring. From the electronic caller ID, Sean could see that it was the duty officer at the State Department's Counterterrorism Division.

"Frost here," he answered in a tone of slight annoyance, which wasn't uncommon for him. The monumental task of being the executive in charge of just about every functional area of the White House often taxed his patience.

"Mr. Frost, Undersecretary of State McLean just arranged for an emergency meeting with an American citizen at the embassy in Madrid. The man claims to have knowledge of a plot of an American pilot on a suicide mission into Mecca. Allegedly this American pilot is at the controls of a cargo Boeing 747 and airborne over the Mediterranean at this time. Ambassador Wilson and the defense attaché at the embassy are en route to meet with him."

Sean considered the information for a moment and then asked, "How did this guy in Madrid get a hold of someone at the State Department with enough clout to roust the ambassador out of bed at…," he said as he looked at his watch and did the math, "at ten p.m. local time?"

"Sir, it was actually Congressman Miller from Georgia who contacted the undersecretary at home. Apparently the American citizen is Jack Lee of…"

"VelEx," said Sean, cutting off the diplomatic officer on the other end of the line. After thinking for a moment, Sean asked, "But why does the good Mr. Lee think there is some nefarious plot going on?"

"Sir, he claims to have been drugged, awoke in a hospital, and the aircraft he and the other VelEx co-founder, Chris Walsh, piloted into Madrid has already departed without him and has a flight plan filed to Jeddah twelve hours ahead of their original arrival time."

Just then, his executive secretary, Elizabeth Barrett, walked in unannounced with his tuxedo that he would be wearing to the reception for the Irish prime minister.

"Has anyone actually contacted the people at VelEx to confirm any of this?"

After a momentary pause, the man on the phone down the road in Foggy Bottom offered, with no real enthusiasm, "I'm not certain, sir." The watch officer immediately realized that something fairly obvious had been overlooked in escalating the event with only one man making fantastic accusations and that man had just woken up in a hospital. Even to him, it sounded a bit thin.

With a of a tone of admonishment, Sean continued, "So essentially the good congressman has taken it at face value when one of his constituents wakes up on drugs in a foreign hospital and claims to be the only one that knows about an impending *American* terrorist attack? Also, if this is so solid, why hasn't the Pentagon contacted us?"

"Sir, at this point, we only have the suspicion of one man to go on. Mr. Lee is a rather connected person to set these wheels in motion so quickly but it is just his suspicion at this point. The ambassador and defense attaché should be arriving at the embassy momentarily."

"Call the Situation Room if this develops into something we

need to act on." said Sean. He hung up the phone without any further pleasantries.

"Everything ok?" asked Elizabeth, noting the fact that her boss had been talking in serious tones on the secure telephone unit, which was almost always the harbinger of serious events occurring in the world.

He looked at her and decided to downplay the conversation so at to not start any rumor mills grinding in the West Wing.

"It was just a call from State about something in the Middle East. It's always something about the Middle East when State calls these days."

She nodded and left the office. Sean knew FAA rules and safeguards would make it impossible for someone to get clearance to pilot a jumbo jet alone. An ex-Navy pilot, Sean was confident that the authorities on the ground wouldn't grant take-off clearance to just one guy in the flight deck of a multi-engine aircraft. FAA rules prohibited it. As Sean began to change into the tuxedo for the reception, he looked out his window toward the procession of limousines arriving through the gate, each being thoroughly inspected by officers of the Uniformed Division of the U.S. Secret Service.

"The guy must have had a bump on the head or something," muttered Sean as he began slipping the little onyx studs into place on the shirt.

Forty-two minutes later, as Sean held a glass of champagne from which he had not yet even taken a sip, talking with the prime minister of Ireland about a possible distant crossing of their family lineage, he saw the presidential military aide, Colonel Karl Rappaport enter the room and head directly for the president. The tall, broad-shouldered African-American colonel walked directly up to the president and tapped him on the shoulder.

"Excuse me just a moment, Mr. Prime Minister," said Sean. Seeing the look on the face of the military officer, and knowing that the only reason he would be present at the official function would be to summon the president to the Situation Room, Sean wondered what could be going on. The phone call from the State Department earlier didn't even register as a possible cause. It had been such an unlikely scenario.

Sean walked up just in time to see Colonel Rappaport discreetly whisper in the president's ear. He knew what the military aide would be saying: "Mr. President, you are needed."

President Devane was savvy about many things including how to leave an official White House function under escort from a military officer without creating any panic. Smiling at the people enjoying meeting him, he simply said, "I have to go attend to something for just a moment. I'll be back shortly." Turning to see Sean where he instinctively knew his closest advisor would be, the president said, "Sean, with me, please."

"Wonder if anything is wrong," said one of the partygoers to another.

"It's probably nothing. He didn't look too concerned."

"Sean, you mean to tell me that State called an hour ago about this and you didn't tell me immediately?" asked President Devane incredulously as they walked through the suite of offices toward the stairs leading down to the Situation Room.

"Mr. President, we only had the suspicion of a guy that just left the hospital after being told he had been brought in overdosed on barbiturates. Not what I assessed as a credible threat at the time."

Colonel Rappaport cleared his throat and said, "Mr. President, we've just been contacted directly by Admiral McMillan at DIA. The defense attaché at the embassy just confirmed with local authorities that the replacement co-pilot for the next leg of Mr. Walsh's flight was found tied up in an offloaded cargo container at Barajas International. Apparently Mr. Walsh has successfully fooled the airport authorities into giving him takeoff clearance with only himself at the controls of a Boeing 747. Also, he apparently moved his departure time from Madrid up twelve hours. We've confirmed with VelEx that both he and Mr. Lee were not scheduled to depart tonight and Mr. Walsh himself ordered a new flight plan filed."

As they reached the stairwell that led down to the Situation Room below the West Wing, President Devane asked, "What makes you think this guy is on a suicide mission?"

"According to Mr. Lee, Mr. Walsh had been making some statements to that effect. He claims Mr. Walsh said that, 'he couldn't wait to see Mecca reduced to a smoldering pile of rubble.'"

Stopping at the bottom of the stairs, the president turned abruptly to face his chief of staff and said, "Sean, we know Chris Walsh. I mean we've had dinner with the guy. I've had him to my home in Virginia. How does a guy go from upstanding member of society and a brilliant businessman to the American reincarnation of Mohammed Atta?"

"I wasn't sold on the story either. It's why I didn't advise you of it when State called earlier."

Colonel Rappaport, in the ultra-professional tone he used when addressing the commander-in-chief, continued, "Mr. President, we realize that there is no way to gauge Mr. Walsh's intentions at this point but there are a few other things you should know. We contacted the FBI to see if they have anything to support this possibility and apparently he has been put on their watch list. According to them, Walsh allegedly contracted some Blackriver Security guys a few weeks ago. He allegedly wanted to hire some ex-Special Forces operators to go into Iran and try to extract the guys in the video with his son."

"Oh...that's right...his son," said the president. It hadn't hit him until just then but the man they were talking about, along with millions of others around the world, had been exposed to an unspeakably gruesome videotape of his son being beheaded.

"So why didn't DOJ go after him if he was trying to buy revenge like that?"

"Apparently he called the whole thing off before it was really put in motion. It was discussed but under the circumstances, the AG decided not to pursue the matter...given the circumstances."

As they reached the entrance to the Situation Room, a Marine opened the door. Seeing as many military officers and National Security Council staff in the room as were present the first night of military action in Iran, he knew the military was taking the threat seriously. Everyone stood to attention as she entered.

"I want your best assessment, Admiral Micillo," said the president to the Chairman of the Joint Chiefs of staff.

Turning from a computer screen that depicted the flight path of VelEx Two-Nine-Zero, as it was making its way across the easternmost tip of the Mediterranean, he said, "It's going to be a long night, Mr. President."

"We have a squadron of F-22s at Incirlik that can intercept, right?" asked the president.

"Affirmative, Mr. President."

"I want that jet intercepted now. Flash message to the unit commander and base CG."

"Yes Mr. President," answered Admiral Micillo as his aide began typing out the message and simultaneously accessing the direct contact uplink to the base.

Major Fred Bauerlein rapped forcefully on the door jamb surrounding the bedroom door of General Jeb Helton, base commander of Incirlik Airbase. The major didn't wait for the general to fully wake before stepping into the room.

"What is it, Major?" grumbled the general as he reached for the light switch on the nightstand lamp.

"Sir, we have a flash message from the White House Situation Room. Grabbing his radio from his web belt, he transmitted to the duty officer at the communications center to put the call through to the general's residence.

The phone on the nightstand began ringing almost instantly.

General Helton snatched up the phone.

"Helton."

"General Helton, this is President Devane. We have a situation Admiral Micillo is going to brief you on right now that requires immediate asset deployment for airborne interdiction of a commercial 747 cargo jet."

General Helton shot straight out of bed and was reaching for his boots even before sharply answering, "Understood, Mr. President."

**Flight Deck of VelEx Boeing 747-800
Call Sign: VelEx Two-Nine-Zero Heavy
12:32 A.M. Local Time
Sunday, January 11th, 2012**

Chapter Fifty-One

The repeated radio hails from two different control centers over the past hour, plus the foot-long strip of telex messages emitted from the console next to the throttles, gave Chris an uneasy feeling. Chris had been a professional aviator for the better part of forty years. The increased frequency of communication attempts weren't a coincidence. People on the ground knew something wasn't right. He just hoped they didn't know the magnitude of how wrong things were going to get. Chris ran his hands through his slightly greasy hair and rubbed his eyes. Thirty thousand feet above the Red Sea and one hundred and twenty nautical miles northwest of Mecca, Chris needed to take a bathroom break. It had been four hours since he lifted off from Barajas International Airport back in Madrid and he was about to begin his descent into Jeddah.

"VelEx Two-Nine-Zero Heavy, this is Incirlik Control. Please respond. I repeat, Velocity Express Two-Nine-Zero Heavy please respond. Your flight operations center in Atlanta has made several attempts to reach you on telex and requests identity of first officer on your aircraft."

"For crying out loud!" exclaimed Chris. He knew at that moment that either the airport authorities had discovered his handiwork with Captain Arnold and that he had taken off without a first officer or perhaps Jack may have woken up, or both. Either way, it was irrelevant. The autopilot would keep his jumbo jet on the heading at his current altitude while he ignored the radio transmissions. As long as he didn't say anything, it would look like he was continuing on to King Abdul Azziz International Airport to drop his load. What could they really do to him? Even if they sent some fighter jockeys to sniff around, they would have no authority to intercept him in international airspace. It would only be when he executed his planned touch-and-go landing, slammed his throttles forward, and screamed skyward toward Mecca that the authorities might sound the alarm, but by then it would be too late. He knew that at full power, it would only take six minutes to reach twenty thousand feet and complete his dive into the holiest place in the entire Muslim world. Mecca was a mere forty-five miles southeast of where the airport sat in Jeddah. At that point, the Royal Saudi Air Force had zero chance to scramble quickly enough to stop him, even with the fighters based at nearby Taif Airbase that lay between Jeddah and Mecca.

Chris had done his homework and knew the average response time fighter jet pilots could be airborne and vectoring onto a target when they received an alert. Additionally, he was confident that the Saudis wouldn't immediately realize it was a deliberate attack, just as it took the United States precious time to realize what was happening on September 11th.

His plan was simple: At the very moment he would normally hit the thrust reversers on landing, Chris would hit the takeoff/go around function, climb out with the throttles firewalled to the stops, and streak skyward. All he would have left to do, six minutes later, would be to line up on Mecca, push the yoke all the way forward to nose the aircraft over, and plummet directly into the middle of the most hallowed place in all of Islam. While planning his revenge, Chris had considered how the jet that hit the Pentagon came in at a flat angle. He had other plans for Mecca. The black building at the center of Mecca, the *Kabbah,* would be his aiming point. Chris, in his delusional rage, had calculated that a sharp angle of attack would create the most damage and highest body count possible. He was hoping for a quarter million.

470

As he washed his hands in the crew latrine, Chris reflected that if a military control tower was inquiring about his first officer, he hoped it was because Jack had woken up from the narcotic and not just authorities piecing evidence together. If Jack had awakened back in Spain and discovered the Spirit of Freedom had left without him, he must have screamed like a banshee to the authorities. It was less likely that Captain Arnold had regained consciousness and extricated himself from the cargo container but that was also possible. Regardless of what was generating the increasing frequency and urgency of the attempts to hail him, Chris knew it was no coincidence that the authorities were asking about his first officer. He realized it was probably the first time in modern aviation that a person had intentionally flown a Boeing 747 solo. It must have been Jack waking up.

Attaboy, killer, he thought.

The likely discovery that he was alone on the flight deck was a minor complication. How Jack had alerted anyone and involved the military so quickly was unexpected but not surprising given his resourcefulness. As Chris exited the lavatory, he had a brief moment where, the inevitable consequences to Jack, should his mission of destruction succeed, played into his mind. There would be numerous investigations by the authorities to determine exactly what Jack had known and when he knew it, but they had both been through that sort of game before. Having been the co-founder of one of the most recognizable companies in the world planet, Chris couldn't count the number of times he and Jack had sat through hearings at the Department of Transportation, Department of Commerce, Federal Aviation Administration, as well as in Congressional inquiries that were conducted by people with tough questions and even tougher agendas. Jack had always handled those situations with masterful aplomb and Chris was sure he would handle the tough times to come with equal ability.

The anger consuming Chris changed the channel in his head once again to the thought of the Saudis having to empanel their own turban-wearing January Eleventh Commission. The voice in his head dripped with a tone of smug superiority.

As Chris was re-taking his seat in the cockpit, the sense that something wasn't right hit him a microsecond before his cognitive

471

powers locked onto the anomaly in his awareness. He was conscious of movement in the corner of his eye the instant before he looked.

Something out of the window flashed where there should have been nothing but blackness.

He knew what it was.

A wave of fear washed over his entire body as he saw, one hundred meters off his port and starboard cockpit windows, a pair of F-22 Raptors flying alongside him. For a second, he hoped he was having a hallucination brought on by the stress of Thomas' death. It was too much to hope that the planes he saw flying close formation with his jet could be his son visiting him from beyond the great divide and having brought a fellow specter for good measure to make the visitation all the more impactful. Suddenly, the aircraft on the right side of the plane dropped back out of sight.

Just play it cool, he thought as the fear cascaded down from his brain into the depths of his stomach. *They have no legal authority to do anything to me out here.*

The presence of the hundred-and-forty-million-dollar pieces of military avionic technology shadowing his aircraft instantly destroyed any hope that the authorities wouldn't have a clue until it would be too late. If they had scrambled fighter jets to intercept him, they must suspect his intent.

Over his radio, he heard a voice with the distinctly cool fighter jet pilot cadence hail him over the radio, "Velocity Two-Nine-Zero Heavy, this is flight lead in the Air Force F-22 off your port wing" As he said it, the pilot dipped his wing and then leveled out. Continuing, Major Mike Chang said, "Be advised there is a second aircraft, now in your six o'clock firing position."

Chris knew the game was over unless he was able to talk his way out of the situation. It was the avionic equivalent of being pulled over by the state police.

The pilot off his port wing continued, "Pilot, we've been ordered to ensure your safe passage back to Incirlik Airbase. We've also been advised that you took on ninety-eight thousand pounds of fuel and have plenty of gas to divert. You are instructed to enter a left turn to a heading of three-five-zero degrees and follow us back to base. "

Man, those things are stealthy. Uncle Sam really got his money's worth, thought Chris. There had not been a single indication of them on his radar. The ultra-sleek jets had just slipped up on him like avionic ninjas.

Knowing there was no escape from the most advanced fighter jets in the history of the world in the lumbering 747-800, Chris keyed his microphone and replied, "Air Force flight lead, I've just resolved a communications problem with my aircraft. Is there an emergency? I haven't received any communications over the teletype and I have time-sensitive load of medical cargo needed in Saudi Arabia, including two transplant organs." He didn't have high hopes for the ruse but perhaps it might just give him enough time. According to his flight computer, his position was approaching one hundred and ten mile point to Jeddah. At his current speed of Mach .8, he would reach his destination in a little over twenty minutes.

"VelEx captain, we are ordered by National Command Authority to escort you back to Incirlik Airbase without further delay. Please enter a left turn to heading three-five-zero degrees." Chris knew they were deadly serious. By National Command Authority, the pilot meant the president of the United States. If his flight had made it all the way up the chain of command into the Oval Office, then he knew his intentions must be known or at least strongly suspected.

"Air Force flight, I have to repeat my last. I have medical transplant cargo aboard that will not wait. There is no possible way for me to deviate from my flight plan. It will cost lives if I do. I'm former Air Force and know you have no legal authority to intercept civilian aircraft in international airspace," said Chris as authoritatively as possible. Sweat beads began to form on his upper lip and brow.

"VelEx Captain, you are just outside of one hundred miles from crossing into Saudi Airspace We are fully authorized to shoot you out of the sky if you cross the hundred mile threshold and we *will* execute that order. This is the last time I will instruct you to enter a left turn to a heading of three-five-zero degrees," commanded Major Mike Chang.

473

Chris found it astounding how cool the fighter pilot sounded threatening to kill him. The only touch of emphasis the fighter pilot had used was on the word "will" as if the pilot was confident it was all the convincing he would need.

Two stories below ground level, in the White House Situation Room, President Devane sat with the assembled military, intelligence, and diplomatic professionals, looking at a large computer display on the wall indicating the position of the jumbo jet. Admiral Micillo stood alongside Secretary of Defense Mace. Secretary of State Thomas Mantz entered the room just as Secretary Mace said, "Mr. President, I have to urge you in the strongest possible terms that if he crosses the hundred mile threshold, you have to authorize the fighters to do what we know is necessary."

Secretary of State Mantz looked at the screen while a Marine lieutenant colonel on the National Security Council staff quickly briefed him. As the military officer explained the suspected intent of Chris Walsh, the eyes of the chief diplomat of the United States went wide in horror. It didn't require a doctorate in foreign relations from Georgetown, which Secretary Mantz had, to understand the global ramifications if the suspicions were true and Mecca was reduced to a smoldering ruin. Although Chris' ability to effect that horrible possibility had been averted, the damage done to the United States' standing with Islamic countries would be irreparably damaged if the situation wasn't handled perfectly.

President Devane stood, looking at the screen and the red blip designated "290." Five minutes earlier, he and his assembled cabinet level staff watched as two other blips converged on Chris' aircraft from behind, their velocity relative to the jumbo jet making it appear as if the 747 was barely moving at all. As president, he needed no briefing from the assembled military officers as to the significance of the radar blip indicating VelEx Two-Nine-Zero's position. His time as National Security Advisor and then Secretary of State theoretically prepared him for working through almost any conceivable threat against the United States. There was, without a question, nobody better than him to understand the ramifications if, as a nation state, the United States itself, international leader in the 'Global War on Terror', entered into the black hole of terrorism.

Once, while serving as the former president's national security advisor, he had visited Little Creek Naval Amphibious Base—home to the East Coast Navy SEAL Teams—to familiarize himself with the capabilities of the world-renown commandos. An old command master chief had told him something he never forgot. As they had observed a four-man element of commandos practice close quarter battle techniques using live fire in a kill house, the hardened warrior with steel green eyes had said to him, "In war, a man's brain turns to water and runs out his ears no matter how long he's practiced for it." What the seasoned special warfare veteran was saying in his own way was that combat decisions must be instinctive. At that moment, President Devane knew the United States had a new and wholly unforeseen military combat action taking place over the Red Sea. It was the most pivotal engagement in the last thousand years and, unless resolved quickly, would lead to a global war not between nation-states but between the entire populations of the Christian and Muslim worlds. It was too high a price to pay and he knew what the answer must be if Chris didn't immediately comply with the fighter jets. President Devane knew the decision to shoot Chris Walsh out of the sky would be painful but not nearly as painful as the consequences if he didn't. All of the United States credibility as a nation would be shattered in the same way that the hate-addicted militant Islamic factions sponsoring terrorism became the devil incarnate to the civilized world on September 11th, 2001.

The president knew what had to be done but wanted to try one more option before he gave the order.

"Admiral, patch me to Incirlik's tower so I can transmit on the Guard channel. Make it happen in the next three minutes," said the president. Immediately Admiral Micillo picked up a secure line and spoke with General David Wilkinson, head of the White House Communications Agency, the military unit responsible for all technical details pertaining to the president's communications to military units throughout the world. Two minutes later the phone rang through to the Situation Room. The Admiral picked up the phone, barked, "Micillo," and listened for exactly three seconds before saying, "Mr. President, we have a secure link to Incirlik Airbase and they are prepared to broadcast you directly on the Guard frequency."

Secretary of State Mantz, a holder of a multi-engine pilot's license, and familiar with aviation protocols, was shocked at what he knew the president was about to attempt. As the president took a seat at the communication console, the secretary exclaimed, "Mr. President, as soon as you begin broadcasting on the Guard channel, everyone in an aircraft cockpit in the eastern hemisphere will know what is happening. Keeping a lid on this will be impossible from that point and there will be tremendous damage to our relationship with the Saudis if we don't notify them first of our suspicions about Chris Walsh's intentions."

"Tom, if we alert them before we exhaust all efforts to dissuade Mr. Walsh ourselves, the Saudis will launch their own intercept F-5s from Taif Airbase with authorization to go weapons free. As you can see on the screen, there are already two F-22s intercepting Mr. Walsh's aircraft, one in a firing position. If we simply tell the Saudis what we suspect, they will launch their jets with orders to shoot. When that happens, are we supposed to order our fighters to protect a United States citizen, albeit a suspected mentally-deranged one, in international air space, as we would have the legal responsibility to do? Additionally, Mr. Secretary, do we want to risk an aerial engagement between our jets and the Saudis when it seems highly likely that I'm going to have to task our pilots to shoot Mr. Walsh out of the sky any moment?"

Secretary Mantz began to respond and President Devane cut him off with an upturned hand, saying, "Tom, I always value your opinion but I can't address diplomacy issues now. Unfortunately I have to order combat action. I summoned you here to advise me on how to proceed with the Saudis *after* this is resolved, which will be in less than five minutes one way or the other. The bottom line is that if anyone has to down Mr. Walsh's aircraft, it absolutely *has* to be us. I'm sure you see the reasons for that."

"Mr. President, the secure link to Incirlik tower is established and ready to transmit," said the secretary of defense.

"And we've confirmed transmission to the telex inside the

aircraft?" asked the president, referring to the numerous attempts to send text messages to Chris Walsh via satellite uplink to the jet that would print out from a panel between the pilot and co-pilot's seat, looking much like a cash register tape.

"The technical guys say they have confirmation that the jet received the message signals," replied Secretary Mace.

"Then keeping this quiet just expired as an option," said the president as he took the offered communication headset from a Marine lieutenant colonel and keyed the transmit button. "Velocity Two-Nine-Zero Heavy, Velocity Two-Nine-Zero Heavy, this is the president of the United States. Captain Walsh, do you recognize my voice?"

Major Chang's eyes went wide behind the mirrored shield on his helmet at the sound of the President of the United States directly addressing a pilot across the Guard channel. Switching to a secure frequency and transmitting back to the communications officer at Incirlik Airbase, he keyed his microphone and said, "Incirlik Control, this is Jackpot Six-Five. Can you confirm that is POTUS transmitting on Guard?"

The reply came immediately.

"Jackpot Six-Five, you have positive confirmation that the transmission is authentic. We are in direct communication with National Command Authority to broadcast on Guard."

Keying his wingman, Captain Ivy, the major transmitted across the secure channel, "Jackpot Six-Six, we may be ordered to go weapons free and engage any second."

Captain Ivy, having also heard the unprecedented direct transmission by the president of the United States, choked out, "Roger," into his own microphone, his heart rate highly elevated and adrenaline beginning to course through his body as the reality of the situation hit him.

"Chris, this is President Devane. I say again, this is President Devane. Please comply with the jets flying with you. I do not wish to order them to destroy you but if you do not immediately comply, I will be forced to," pleaded the president with great effort to keep his voice even despite the feeling of desperation. He didn't know when he had woken up that morning that he would be thrust into the middle of a pivotal point in human history, but that possibility was always part of the unofficial job description for the leader of the free world.

Secretary of Defense Mace, watching the screen, said, "Mr. President, he's not turning. We now show four aircraft taking off from Taif Airbase. It's logical to assume the Saudis have heard your broadcast and pieced things together by now."

The President looked at the large screen on the wall and, indeed, two pairs of aircraft lifted off within ten seconds of each other and were streaking across the Arabian Peninsula on an intercept course with the blip designated VelEx Two-Nine-Zero.

Come on, Chris, for the love of God, please don't make me do this, prayed the president as he brought his finger to the transmit key of the radio for one last try.

**Cockpit of F-22 Raptor
Call Sign: Jackpot Six-Five
12:43 A.M. Local Time
Sunday, January 11th, 2012**

Chapter Fifty-Two

We're really going to have to splash this guy! thought Major Chang. Suddenly, the piece of information that had been nagging at him detonated in his consciousness.
Oh, my God!
The first name of the cargo pilot the president just said locked Major Chang's mind onto the awful reality. A chill shot through him like an electrical shock and he felt a wave of nausea.
The President just called the pilot Chris...Chris Walsh!
Everything fell into place with horrifying clarity.
Until President Devane had said the first and last name, the only identification the two pilots had for the 747 was its call sign, Velocity Two-Nine-Zero Heavy. Now the face, barely visible to the Air Force pilot's exceptional eyes from one hundred meters off the Jumbo Jet's cockpit, became recognizable.
He knew this man.
Major Chang had met his deceased wingman's father his first day at the Air Force Academy fifteen years earlier, had spent time in his home on two occasions, had eaten meals with this man, and even had a picture of himself, his former wingman, and the man he was about to be tasked to shoot down on his wall at home. It was a photo taken on the morning of his commencement back at

the Academy. Keying his microphone again to a secure radio frequency Major Chang transmitted, "Mark, I just realized who is piloting this bird. It's Thomas' freaking father."

A thousand meters behind the jumbo jet in a textbook firing position, Captain Ivy thought, *You've got to be kidding me!* The horrible death that a fellow pilot and comrade had met at the hands of the terrorists in Iran was known to virtually everyone in the western world. That the man piloting the jet a thousand meters ahead was that man's father was a scenario Captain Ivy wouldn't have been able to predict in a million years. Captain Ivy's flight leader had even flown the very mission with Major Walsh that had taken his life. Captain Ivy knew how close Major Chang had been to the son of the man piloting the jumbo jet. Although Captain Ivy didn't know Thomas nearly as well as Major Chang, he had graduated from the Academy in the same class with their fallen comrade. The knowledge instantly made Captain Ivy hate the mission he was tasked with and something inside of him absolutely raged at the prospect of being in no position to refuse orders if he were ordered to shoot the huge jet down.

General Helton stood with Colonel Dan Daly, the air wing commander, monitoring the intercept mission. Both men simultaneously realized exactly who was at the controls of the jumbo jet. Instantly furious over the situation, Colonel Daly risked a charge of insubordination by exclaiming, "All due respect, General, but why didn't we get the identity of the jumbo pilot when the order to scramble jets came through? I most certainly would not have put Major Chang in that position," growled Colonel Daly.

"Colonel, I didn't get that information either. I completely agree with you but we can't change that right now. We have orders to carry out," replied General Helton.

Also realizing the magnitude of the coincidence, Colonel Daly's operations officer, Major Greg Houchins, let out a long exhale, realizing that they had inadvertently sent the best friend of Thomas Walsh to most likely shoot his father out of the sky.

"Do you think Major Chang will have any problem executing

the shoot order if he has to?" asked General Helton.

Colonel Daly thought for a moment, turned to the base commander and, meeting the general's eyes, coldly said, "No, sir, he won't."

Both men turned back to the airman sitting at the console and listened as President Devane continued his appeals on the Guard channel. From the communications console, both military officers heard their commander-in-chief transmit, "Chris, please don't make me order your destruction. You know you aren't going to make it. If you don't immediately comply with the fighters along side you, I'll have no choice but to directly order them to fire on you."

"He's not going to turn. The poor idiot is playing a version of suicide by cop," said Captain Ivy as he locked his firing radar onto the jumbo jet. Pressing a button on a console on the left side of the array of instrument panels, Captain Ivy identified the jet as the only target in the computer's shoot list. A red triangle instantaneously formed on the heads up display just below the clear canopy. The red triangle indicated the weapons system already had the target locked and had a perfect firing solution. The only thing left make Velocity Two-Nine-Zero immediately burst into a disintegrating fireball, plummeting from the sky, was for Captain Ivy to apply two pounds of pressure to a trigger on the stick between his legs, moving the switch five millimeters. Once done, the AIM-9C Sparrow missile would be ejected from the internal weapon store on the port side of the aircraft and less than an eighth of a second later, its motor would ignite and send the rocket forward at nearly twenty-five hundred miles per hour. It would cover the distance between the two aircraft in less than two seconds and, upon impacting the jumbo jet, its twenty pound warhead would detonate, sending explosive force and pieces of shrapnel through the airframe of the jumbo. The plane would almost certainly lose its entire tail section and careen to the earth.

Glancing at another screen, Major Chang saw four inbound aircraft from Taif Airbase. He knew it was no coincidence they were headed on a direct intercept course with the 747 and his position.

"We have four bogeys inbound. Radar confirms F-5s. Twelve hundred knots closure rate," broadcast Captain Ivy.

"This is going to cost me my job but I've got to try something!" yelled Major Chang inside his oxygen mask. Adjusting the channel again so that he would be transmitting to the 747 ahead, Major Chang mumbled the words, "Please, God," before depressing the switch and began.

"Mr. Walsh, I can't believe this myself, but you know who I am. This is Mike…Major Chang. I've been in your home, I know your family. I was your son's wing man the day he punched out of his jet. I flew combat air patrol overhead and watched them take him away in the truck. Please don't do this. In twenty seconds, we are going to fire on you and there is no way Thomas would want you to die like this."

In his ear, Major Chang heard the voice of Colonel Daly scream, "Major Chang, you are to cease transmitting to the 747 immediately! That is a direct order!"

Knowing his next words could end up in a court martial and prison time, Major Chang keyed the microphone one more time, compelled beyond his fear of dire consequences, to give one more effort.

"Mr. Walsh, your son loved you more than anyone in the world. He talked about you like you were a god to him. What you're doing is not brave. It is not making a statement. It's just plain stupid. Please, hear me when I tell you that if you make us shoot you down, it's nothing short of a useless suicide. Don't make us do this!"

The major's words began to reach Chris despite all his efforts to block them out. He knew this kid in the fighter jet but if he wasn't going to get his revenge, he didn't have any desire to die of cancer in some godforsaken federal prison infirmary. Chris tried to choke back the emotions. His whole body began to tremble under the weight of the words from Major Chang.

Effectively ending his own career with the final transmission, "This is just wrong, sir!" Chang eased the throttle off a bit, deployed the air brake on the top of his jet, and pulled the stick to the left, falling back into a firing position with Captain Ivy's F-22. In his radio, from Incirlik, Chang heard a tone of voice that was clearly the death knell of his military aviation career.

"Major Chang, you are interfering with a direct communication by National Command Authority! You are hereby ordered to prosecute your mission and return to base. You are to taxi to the ramp and remain in your aircraft," commanded Colonel Daly.

"I tried," said Major Chang.

"We have hundred-mile threshold in ten seconds," transmitted Captain Ivy, who remained intensely focused on the imminent release of his Sparrow missile.

In the Situation Room below the White House, President Devane transmitted the most awful order he'd been required to give since assuming the presidency. With the most presidential tone he could manage while ordering the execution of a friend, President Devane broadcast, "Jackpot Six-Five and Jackpot Six-Six, this is National Command Authority. You have authorization to go weapons free and take the target out."

Turning to the assembled military officers, diplomats, and intelligence community professionals in the room, he looked at each of their faces, searching each one for something he couldn't verbalize. Giving that order wasn't their job. He sat behind the desk in the Oval Office, not them.

The decision was his alone.

"It had to be done Mr. President," said Secretary Mace.

"I know it did."

Inside the 747 cockpit, Chris heard Major Chang's last words, "This is just wrong, sir!" but oddly he heard them in Thomas's voice. Suddenly a deluge of memories of his boy began to flash through his head. He watched in vivid detail vignettes of Thomas' life: The day Thomas got to sit in the fighter jet at the air show and his little model planes gliding through the air in their back yard. Chris began to feel as if he was floating but he found the sensation strangely comforting. More flashbulbs of Thomas' life continued to pop through his mind's eye: The night he and his fifteen year-old Thomas had left the house in his school suit to pick up little Grace Lee for the spring dance, the morning his teenage son had run into the kitchen with his private pilot's license hanging out of the envelope from the Federal Aviation Administration just before leaving for the Air Force Academy. Chris could see, as clearly as if Thomas was standing in front of him, the look of pride and joy on Thomas' face when, after retrieving his hat from the snowstorm of hats on the parade ground, he said to him, "I made it, Dad!" The last memory that flashed across his mind was Thomas' words when they had talked the night of September 11th, 2001. When he told his dad about arriving on station well after Flight Seventy-Seven had impacted the Pentagon, and the feeling of helplessness, and the emotion in the voice of his beautiful little boy who had grown to a brilliant fighter pilot, had painfully uttered the words, "This is just wrong, sir!"

All of those thoughts and memories were somehow complete in his consciousness while each one only lasting a fraction of a second. It was the proverbial life flashing before his eyes, but it was Thomas' life he was watching.

Suddenly, a vision of what he had intended to do flashed before his eyes as clearly as if they were wide open and watching a high-definition screen. He could see, all at once, the shattered lives and misery his insane plan of revenge would inflict if he had been successful. In that instant, Chris could see how far his own hatred had taken him from the path of humanity.

Something from the depths of Chris' soul screamed, *God forgive me!* The words weren't annunciated, but they resonated from somewhere so deep within his being that they sounded louder than any words he could have yelled.

Then it happened.

Closing his eyes to brace himself for his imminent destruction, he felt an indescribably bright light illuminate the cockpit through his shut eyelids. He was sure he was experiencing the disintegration of the aircraft because the entire cockpit was bathed in a brilliant golden light. Suddenly, it felt like a tremendous weight on Chris' chest flew off of him faster than the velocity of the jet he was in. Somehow he knew the oppressive force that had been weighing on him was his own hatred. If someone was able to see Chris' face that moment, they would have seen a smile the likes of which hadn't been on his face since his childhood. Huge tears streamed down his cheeks, not from grief or anger, but from joy. In that instant, it felt like what he was always told heaven would be like. Chris saw himself in a cockpit that looked not like that of the jumbo jet in which he sat, but the cockpit of the T-38 Talon he had flown forty-five years earlier, floating above the atmosphere and looking down at the beautiful blue ball below. Unlike the time in the small jet, the cockpit air being completely still, Chris felt a warm wind blowing through the aircraft and, it seemed, through him. In that moment, the cognitive part of his brain could only identify the sensation as a current of infinite love. All of the dials and displays of the jet were backlit by the same brilliant white light he had seen at the beginning of the experience and he heard a voice that said as clearly as if it was spoken directly into his ear, *Not yet, my child. You still have work to do.*

The brilliant illumination around him and the sensation of unlimited love flowing through and around him lasted for what seemed another minute but while in the middle of the experience, Chris had the sensation that time didn't exist wherever he was.

Just as if waking from a dream, which Chris somehow intuitively knew it wasn't, the light faded and he found himself sitting in the cockpit of the jumbo jet again. Again, he heard Thomas' voice, as clearly as if his son was sitting next to him, yell, *Turn her now!*

Instantly, Chris stomped his foot onto the left pedal and simultaneously slammed the yoke fully to the left. The fly-by-wire computerized system, which normally produced a slight delay between the time the pilot applied inputs into the controls and when the jet responded, performed an inexplicable miracle. Had the engineers at Boeing reviewed the flight systems data from that moment in flight, they would have found no human explanation for the plane's absolutely instantaneous response to Chris' inputs. It just wasn't possible. But it happened. It was a miracle that was physically, scientifically, and in engineering terms, absolutely impossible but the miracle gave him an extra half-second.

The half-second saved Chris' life.

Captain Ivy's brain sent the impulse to the muscles in his forearm and hand poised on the trigger the exact instant Chris put the jumbo jet into a hard left bank. The fighter pilot's finger was depressing the trigger on the stick the moment he saw her turn. Had Captain Ivy's finger traveled another one millimeter, the electrical connection from the trigger to the computer that fired the missile would have been completed. In a reflex reaction that was physiologically impossible for the brain to process in such an infinitesimally short time, Captain Ivy's index finger felt like it flew off the stick as if pulled by some outside force. That very instant, his radio received Major Chang's screaming voice, "Hold fire! Hold fire! He's turning!"

Captain Ivy looked down at his hand, having never experienced a sensation of being controlled from without. One instant, he had every intention of firing his missile and destroying the jet up ahead, the next, he sat with his hand resting on the stick, his fingers nowhere near the trigger. Something about the bizarre experience made the pilot smile.

"Thank God!" responded Captain Ivy into his radio.

Suddenly a warning tone went off in both F-22 cockpits, alerting both pilots that the Royal Saudi Air Force F-5s, still slightly over thirty nautical miles from the three jets, were attempting to get missile lock on the jumbo jet.

"Royal Saudi Air Force flight, this is Major Mike Chang, United States Air Force. What are your intentions? You are attempting to engage a civilian United States 747 in international airspace. We are a two-ship element of F-22s flying escort on said aircraft. You will immediately cease attempts to engage it or we will be forced to engage you. Please acknowledge."

All three aircraft had entered into a sharp left banking turn, coming around to a heading toward Incirlik Airbase in Turkey. Almost immediately, the warning tone inside the fighter jets' cockpits ceased and Major Chang could see the four-ship flight of Saudi F-5s begin to turn back toward Taif Airbase.

The President of the United States removed the headset, let out a sigh of relief, suppressed a momentary wave of nausea, and turned to Secretary of State Mantz.

"Well, Tom, I think you people at Foggy Bottom better put some coffee on. I suspect you are going to be a bit busy tonight. This is going to take a pretty good bit of State Department savvy to calm the Saudis down over the events that just took place. I think I need to make a phone call to King Fahd right away."

The chairman of the joint chiefs, Admiral Micillo, turned to Secretary of Defense Mace and said, "What if the guy in Madrid had woken up an hour later?" What if the other pilot hadn't been found yet?"

Secretary Mace suddenly lost a few shades of color as he exhaled, shook his head and said, "I don't want to think about it."

"But we really, really should."

**Walsh Residence
1055 Tullamore Place
Alpharetta, Georgia
5:53 P.M. Eastern Time
Thursday, April 9th, 2012**

Epilogue

The medical monitors surrounding him wouldn't be of use for much longer. Chris lay on his bed with a facial expression of complete contentedness. Father McNamara concluded last rites as Keely sat holding his hand, gently caressing it. Intermittent pangs of grief sent waves of emotion, momentarily taking her breath away but she would look over at Father McNamara each time and there was something so comforting about the pastor's presence. His kind expression helped her regain her serenity each time she met his eyes. It was like she was being infused with the comfort of God's love although the priest said nothing. Jack, Erika, and Grace stood with her. The feeling in the room was that utterly unique experience of knowing someone amongst them would be departing into eternity any moment. The small black box affixed to Chris' ankle was going to be totally unnecessary within a few moments but after returning to the United States three months earlier, he had felt blessed beyond description to receive the terms of his house arrest.

His last ever flight at the controls of an aircraft was nothing short of attempted mass murder. He knew it, the attorney general knew it, and the highest levels of the military, legislators, and even the president knew it. All of that aside, Chris knew in the core of his being that, whatever God was, His magnificence was so far beyond the mere reasoning ability of man. He smiled at his wife and felt a glow inside from the joy of what was about to be set in motion. He had the opportunity and means to make amends on a global scale. Father McNamara assured him that by doing so, the priest was convinced they were on the verge of something miraculous occurring.

What was giving Chris ultimate comfort and joy in his last moments was reflecting on how the God he knew was using the worst thing he had ever attempted to do to potentially create so much good. This truth had proved to him, beyond any possible argument that he would ever accept, that there was a God. What was to be put in motion upon his passing was going to hopefully help the world in ways beyond his ability to foresee. He had received the inspiration one night after a visit from Father McNamara during which they had talked, at length, about what Chris had attempted and how he could repair the damage his actions had caused.

Immediately upon engine shut-down at Incirlik Airbase in Turkey, Chris had been taken into custody as quietly as possible by heavily-armed military police and FBI agents and whisked into a waiting FBI Gulfstream G-V. He had been kept in a secure room at Johns Hopkins Medical Center for a few weeks while officials from various branches of the Department of Justice had lengthy discussions about how to proceed with prosecuting the crime without creating worldwide panic and blowback consequences of a wave of retaliatory terrorist attacks. The original plan was to try to keep the incident classified but due to the broadcast on the guard channel, there had been too many pilots who had heard the shocking exchange between the president of the United States and Chris during his last flight. As with any newsworthy event that big, the network and cable news programs—sometimes referred to as the "intelligence services for the masses"— began a relentless push to get details. Eventually enough people told what they knew for the story to become international news. For a few very long weeks in January, Chris

Walsh was viewed by the global community as everything from a deranged sociopath to a national hero who attempted to do what many said they would, given the same circumstances. In a private discussion between President Devane and Attorney General Vick Barnes, it was decided that, due to his verifiable terminal illness, Chris Walsh would be allowed to spend the remainder of his very limited days under house arrest. The doctors at Johns Hopkins determined that the lymphoma had metastasized and was simultaneously attacking his liver and kidneys and it was doing its catastrophic damage quickly.

Many people throughout the world screamed for Chris' head on the proverbial stake but the president had decided there wouldn't even be a trial. There were some officials in powerful positions throughout the government who knew Velocity Express had gone above and beyond in service to the United States and a very select handful within the corridors of power that knew everything.

By the terms of his plea agreement, Chris was to never come within one mile of any aircraft again, to adhere perfectly to the terms of the house arrest, and to pay a seven-figure fine for his lapse of judgment. All of these conditions had been adhered to thoroughly.

Through a friend close to the president, Chris had made a personal request for leniency toward Major Chang regarding any discipline resulting from his communication during the incident. The following day, the secretary of the Air Force contacted General Helton at Incirlik Airbase, where Major Chang had been flying a desk for the past two months. The secretary ordered Major Chang's flight status immediately reinstated, the investigation into Major Chang's conduct regarding the incident halted immediately, and the secretary informed the base commander that Major Chang would be receiving the Air Force Distinguished Service Medal and promoted to Lieutenant Colonel Chang by order of the president.

Keely stood next to Chris, holding his hand. He smiled at his wife and then motioned to Jack to come closer. Jack walked over and stood on the other side of Keely but Chris motioned for Jack to lean in closer.

"Thank you for helping with the arrangements," whispered Chris to Jack and looking over to Keely, he said, "I love you so."

Choking back tears, Jack asked, "Will we always be friends?"

Looking at his oldest friend, Chris smiled widely and in the raspy voice he could manage, he answered, "Friends and prayer partners...forever." Jack inhaled as huge tears spilled down his cheeks, glistening with reflected light from the medical monitor screen. As Jack began to step back to give Keely space to share what were obviously Chris' last few moments, Chris unexpectedly reached up and grabbed his wrist. Again he motioned for Jack to lean in. Inches from Chris' lips, Jack heard Chris whisper his last words.

"When I see Him, I'll whisper your name in His ear."

Father McNamara knew the time was near and excused himself from the room to give them their privacy. He went down to the kitchen to wait and then would offer what comfort he could once Chris was gone.

The heart monitor emitted a slowly decreasing pace of electronic beeps as Chris began to slip away. Keely could feel his fingers, which had been intertwined in hers, relax. His eyes still looked at her the same way they did in the little airport bar thirty-six years earlier. Jack, Erika, Grace, and Keely looked at each other and knew it was time. They held hands around the bed, reciting the Lord's Prayer with tears in their eyes. At the end of the prayer, Keely took her dying husband's hand in hers. A moment later, Chris ever so slightly squeezed Keely's hand once more. Her face was the last vision he had of this world as he left. The world began to fade away comfortably. As he finally let go, Chris could feel a warm, golden light begin to completely envelop him. The brief sense of loss of leaving Keely was immediately supplanted by a wave of joy with an intensity that felt familiar but that had been gone for so long. It was familiar to him, but how?

Thomas then appeared from the wall of light, smiling. A tidal wave of happiness erupted from Chris' soul. Suddenly, on the curtain of light, images of the men who had sent Thomas to this place before Chris appeared.

Can they come too? was the prayer Chris begged from his

heart.

Hatred couldn't exist where he was.

That is how you come home, answered His voice. *It is the only lesson you need from where I sent you. Love is the only lesson. Welcome home, my child.*

Father, can You forgive me for what I tried to do? prayed Chris as he entered the Realm.

It was all part of My plan. Watch what I do with it.

Chris went toward the light in utter rapture. As he turned back one last time to look at the world he was leaving, his spirit eyes could clearly see what was going on everywhere on earth and what was transpiring in the lives of the souls still on their journey there. He was able to understand in totality what was going in the journey of the six billion souls still in the world he had just moved on from. The ability seemed familiar to him and he knew he was headed for his true home. The last thing he saw before being entirely embraced by the Light was something that brought his spirit indescribable and absolute joy. He saw a little building in the desert and a small glimmer of Light where there had been none before.

Jack walked over to the heart monitor to silence the electronic whine assaulting their ears just as the doctor had discreetly shown him how a few days earlier. Grace hugged Keely for very long minutes as she sobbed quietly. Just as Jack was about to try to put his hand on Keely's shoulder to add to the actions of comforting love already being given by Grace, Keely looked up from Grace's shoulder. Her face suddenly broke into an unexpected smile that momentarily shocked Jack until he realized what had caused it. Grace, whose belly had really begun to show two months ago, had been pressed up against the unborn infant's future grandmother when he had kicked.

Both women had felt it.

"He's going to be just like...," said Grace before emotion choked her words. Keely held her daughter-in-law tightly for a few more moments and then excused herself and headed downstairs into Chris' office. Picking up the phone she dialed a number she knew by heart and the call was immediately answered

on the first ring. It was a short conversation.
"All the arrangements have been made, Mrs. Walsh."
"Thank you, Homer."
Keely hung up the phone with the family attorney, Homer Holland, and with a seemingly out-of-place, yet radiant look on her face, she went toward the kitchen to talk with Father McNamara.

Three days later, which happened to fall on Easter Sunday, fifty-eight million dollars worth of two-page newspaper buys were published in every major newspaper in the world. The content printed on the page had been personally crafted by Chris with the help of Father McNamara five weeks earlier. What was printed on the page was met with such worldwide astonishment that it became a news story in itself and virtually every paper of note would eventually translate it into every language on the planet.

When Chris had tasked his personal attorney with the daunting assignment of having his staff contact and arrange his last media release ever, it seemed like it would be an impossible project. Miraculously, publication editors the world over, once having read what Chris wanted printed were, without exception, completely agreeable to both the content and the timing of its release. Besides, Chris authorized paying whatever the periodicals demanded for the pages. He had his attorney handle it, rather than the extensive VelEx marketing department because he didn't want it to appear to be a sales pitch of any kind. The difference between these extremely expensive full-page media buys was that the pages that Chris had purchased weren't an advertisement of any kind.

The pages were a global apology.

The second and third page of nearly four thousand newspapers worldwide read:

An open letter of apology from Chris Walsh to the entire Muslim world:

I am Chris Walsh, admitted terrorist and attempted mass murderer. I am also, at this very moment, facing judgment from what some call God, others Allah, others Yahweh, and a multitude of other names. By whatever name you refer to Him, or whether you don't believe at all, is your personal affair.

When you read this, I will be dead. The reason I'm offering this apology to you is that my actions of January 11th of this year, although not resulting in any actual physical deaths, have undoubtedly caused deep spiritual harm to millions. You may be furious with what I tried to do and have every right to feel that way. I fully admit and utterly regret that I attempted to single-handedly perpetrate an act of terrorism on thousands of innocent Muslims who were simply expressing their faith in God. I had completely lost, through my own rage and insane desire for revenge, my connection to the God I know. There are not words sufficient to express my sorrow for what I tried to do. What I can tell you is that while I was in the cockpit of that aircraft, I personally experienced the presence of the universe's Loving Creator. I'm not asking you to believe that. I, however, know that fact more definitively than anything I ever knew in my life. Until that moment, I was incapacitated by a spiritual illness. My anger over events in my life deluded me to not only think that I was right to do what I attempted, but that

God would approve. I, in fact, attempted to play His part, deciding what my insanity told me was right to do to others. I couldn't see past my own anger to the simple fact that doing what I attempted would make me just as spiritually sick and lost as the poor, angry souls that killed my son.

In that cockpit, just before two U.S. Air Force jets were about to destroy me, I had an experience that I hope with all my heart was foreshadowing of what I'm experiencing now. In that moment, I saw clearly that I was totally addicted to the illusion of power my rage gave me. I can assure you that the experience I cannot describe any better than being completely immersed in His presence—what appeared to me as a golden light—wasn't a psychotic break from reality. I will never know why the God I know chose that moment to reveal His irrefutable presence to me but He did. At that moment, I realized the only truth I know for certain is that He exists, regardless of what name you call Him, and I was attempting to harm His children.

If you are angry with what I tried to do, I beg your forgiveness and I beg that you don't let the very same anger that drove me to attempt the insane and indefensible action I did destroy any more lives. As you read this, I hope both you and He have forgiven me for what I tried to do. I beg your forgiveness and prayers for my soul, but more importantly, I beg you to try to pray and send love toward those in the world living in the darkness of hatred. I no longer live in that desolate place and, with my whole heart and soul, wish those that took my son's life make it to heaven.

Remorsefully,

Chris Walsh

As newspapers made their way to the streets from thousands of presses across the world, the sun began to rise over six billion people that Easter morning. People the world over were utterly astounded as they read the words.

Yousef al Jalani sat in his sparsely furnished room within the *Madrasah* in central Yemen. In two days time, he was to start his journey halfway across the world to the town in northern Mexico and then into the United States to meet up with his brethren already there. He had been shown by the experts how to create the explosives. There were assurances that there would be contacts in the United States who would help him obtain the chemicals and the cyanide. It wouldn't take much explosive to create the lethal cloud inside the shopping mall situated in a wealthy section of the city where the demon infidel lived. On his computer screen was a schematic diagram of the Phipps Plaza shopping mall near the home of the late Chris Walsh.

Yousef's operational plan called for him and several other teams of men to enter shopping centers on December 24th of that year throughout the country and teach the infidels a lesson about worshiping false gods and material goods. He had been given the honor of executing his attack in the home of the man his Imam called the most unworthy human since the president from Texas that had started the war on their brethren in Iraq and Afghanistan.

Clicking on the *Al Jazeera* website, Yousef came across the letter as a part of a minor story about the despised American. Somehow, he felt compelled to read the letter, if only to know better the mind of the enemy that had made his upcoming mission a necessity.

As Yousef began to read the translation of the letter, with his eyes moving from right to left across the page, his mind instantly began to become engaged with the words. Something about the words seemed to ring with fidelity although Yousef tried to push the feeling away. Still, he couldn't argue with the feeling in his heart as he read. Although totally obedient to the teachings, a small, quiet voice deep within him had always whispered that the teachings of the Imam at the school about the *fatwa* and *jihad* always seemed a little one-sided. Suggesting another way of thinking at the strict religious school would be, at best, dangerous and quite possibly lethal. During his education and training, Yousef had observed any sort of dissention being dealt with by extraordinarily harsh methods. Although he had been totally obedient to his teachers, Yousef sometimes had a hard time wrapping his mind around how the bloodshed being perpetrated by his organization around the world was really accomplishing anything constructive.

    Sitting at his desk, he scrolled through the pages of the online *Al Jazeera* website reading the letter several times. His heart began to beat quickly as his realized the truth in the words of the hated American billionaire who had attempted to destroy the most sacred mosque in *Makkah*. Although his head tried to dismiss the letter outright, it couldn't deny the truth his soul immediately recognized. Regardless of the disclaimer from his Imam that morning that the letter was simply another ploy of the infidel who had been caught in the act, the words of the letter deeply moved him. Just then, he heard a yelping, pleading cry from outside his window. Two men were beating another classmate with long poles. Yousef had felt the sting of the poles himself on two occasions for being late to prayer and for failing to recite the hundred and tenth *Sura* correctly.

    It was in that moment that the decision Yousef had been wrestling with for years was finally made.

    As night fell on the cluster of buildings, Yousef went to the door to his room and peered around the corners of his door both ways to see if anyone would possibly discover what he was about to do; an act that would bring almost certain execution by beheading if caught. Yousef steeled himself with a small prayer to Allah and went to the small chest containing the few personal effects he was allowed to keep. Stuffing his possessions into his backpack, he quietly made his way to the door of the building. Once past the final building on the western side of the compound,

Yousef ran faster than he ever had before. As he made it over the first ridge a few hundred yards from the school, grateful there had been no fusillade of bullets ripping into him or shouts of alarm that would mean certain death, Yousef glanced back at the cluster of small buildings that had been his home for the past two years. As he did so, he felt a sensation of joy and warmth from within. Yousef wondered why he felt such peace considering he had fifty miles of unforgiving desert to traverse before reaching the nearest town but somehow the feeling made sense and Yousef was schooled in the ways of the desert. Looking up, he noticed a particularly bright star in the brilliant tapestry of the universe above him and thought, *I've always wanted to see Australia.*

Acknowledgements

I must thank my parents, Bill and Eileen Dempsey, who came up with the only useful (and often utilized) punishment for me during my highly...precocious years. As a child, I marched (or stomped at times) to the beat of my own drum. When my parents had had enough of my incessant drumming and when (not *if*) I was grounded, my father would drop me at the Northbrook, Illinois Public Library before work, politely ask the librarian to make sure I didn't wander off, and pick me up nine hours later when he was finished with work. Grounding at the library was what hooked me on books. The most important gift I must thank you for, besides the loving home you provided, (sometimes under very challenging circumstances) is my upbringing in the Church that made it possible for me to come back from my self-imposed hiatus. I love you both dearly.

I wouldn't be here to write this story without the selfless act of love performed by my biological mother, Nancy Walsh, in August of 1971. I've really enjoyed getting to know you over the past few years. You made a terribly difficult decision that gave me a gift I'll never be able to repay. There are no words adequate to thank you for giving me life. I love you.

Without my cherished friend Scott Lee who, through your stories, took me inside the cockpit of the C-141 and T-38 Talon, this story couldn't exist. The opening chapters of this book are mostly composites of your own experiences woven into the framework of the story I wanted to craft. I aspire to develop into the sort of principled, selfless, and kind individual you are. I want to see flight level five-three-two (and above) for myself.

Deepest gratitude to the late Keith Lewis for being one of a handful of men that inspired me to return to the Church of my childhood. The Catholic Church and all of mankind lost a true treasure when Keith went home on November 15th, 2007. I must offer sincerest thanks to Dom and Terri Micillo, Tom and Jill Morgahan, and Dave Sloan for their friendship and encouragement of my return to fully embracing my faith. The journey back to my Church, largely inspired by my parents and these six individuals, helped shaped the model for one of the characters in this book, Jack Lee. Throughout the story, that character tries to adhere to the way of living exhibited by these people I know and love.

Captain Josh "CATA" Arki, 55th Fighter Squadron, was immensely helpful in fleshing out details about the U.S. Air Force Academy experience and a modern combat jet pilot's life. You are truly a real-life Major Thomas Walsh and the sort of person that I admire immensely. Thanks for all your time and your wedding was awesome. Cornflakes couldn't have married a more honorable man.

Captain Tim Gross of AirTran Airlines who looked over the civilian aviation elements of this story and made invaluable suggestions. You are a great pilot and an even better friend. Thanks for the tour of your "office." Perhaps I'll have my own someday.

This book wouldn't have made any sense without the fantastic editing by Katie Devane of Jacksonville, Florida and Kelly Bateson of Colorado Springs, Colorado. Thank you both for your hard work and friendship.

I offer sincerest thanks to Per Andersen for technical assistance and for your friendship. You and Jen (*squirrel!...*) are treasured friends.

I am grateful to Tom Dempsey, Deb Helton, Emily Giffin, Dianne Price, Deborah Bovaird, Dennis Young, Brad Schinstock, Scott Kucharchuk, Jean and Karl R., Tony Oliver, Jane Cole, Honey Shackelford, Linda Tarkenton, Kelley Ibuki, Veronica Cicilian, Sally Corbett, and my colleagues in the Fine Jewelry department at Saks Fifth Avenue Atlanta for graciously taking the time to read the chapters as they were born and giving feedback. Your words of encouragement motivated me at times when I didn't feel like this story had a purpose. There are so many more people who offered me encouragement or inspiration during the creation of this work that I couldn't possibly list here but you know who you are and thank you all so much.

Sincerest thanks to my friend, Joan Gutermuth, for introducing me to the joys of the Adoration Chapel. Many of the ideas for this book came to me while spending time there. I wish you and Ellie much joy and love.

Finally, but most importantly, my deepest gratitude is, and always will be, to God. My personal belief is that there are no "coincidences" that I've known the afore-mentioned people. My relationship with a God I'll never understand, but see amazing evidence of on a daily basis, is a direct result of my relationships with the people around me and my woefully lacking, yet unceasing attempts to be the best version of one of His kids that I can be.

Will Dempsey
Smyrna, Georgia
December 2010

Will Dempsey is a fourth-generation jeweler at a luxury department store in Atlanta. He graduated from New Mexico State University in 1998 with a degree in business. He is a parishioner at the Cathedral of Christ the King and a member of the Knights of Columbus, Council 660. He enjoys golf, traditional Japanese karate, and participation in the Reader to Patient Program at Children's Healthcare of Atlanta in his free time. He aspires to be a pilot. He lives in Smyrna, Georgia.

For additional copies of this novel, please email me directly at
willdempsey71@gmail.com
Feel free to find me on facebook.com as well

I would be grateful for any feedback about Final Delivery.

God bless.

Made in the USA
Charleston, SC
15 January 2011